Award-winning author Anthony Masters knows how 'to hook his reader from the first page' *Books for Keeps*.

Anthony has written extensively for young adults and is renowned for tackling serious issues through gripping stories. He also writes for adults, both fiction and non-fiction. For the Orchard Black Apple list he has written the *Ghosthunter* series, the *Dark Diaries* series and four novels: *Spinner, Wicked, The Drop* and *Day of the Dead*, which was shortlisted for the Angus Award. He lives in Sussex with his wife and has three children.

Anthony Masters also runs *Book Explosions*, children's adventure workshops that inspire adrenalin and confidence in children, so that they can do their own creative writing.

Also by Anthony Masters

Dark Diaries

DEAD RINGER
FIRE STARTER
DEATH DAY
SHOCK WAVES

DAY OF THE DEAD
WICKED
THE DROP

Ghosthunters

DANCING WITH THE DEAD
DARK TOWER
DEADLY GAMES

Predator

HUNTED
DEATHTRAP
KILLER INSTINCT

shark attack

ANTHONY MASTERS

ORCHARD BOOKS

ORCHARD BOOKS
96 Leonard Street, London EC2A 4XD
Orchard Books Australia
32/45-51 Huntley Street, Alexandria, NSW 2015
ISBN 1 84121 906 1
First published in Great Britain in 2003
A paperback original
Text © Anthony Masters 2003
The right of Anthony Masters to be identified as the author
of this work has been asserted by him in accordance with
the Copyright, Designs and Patents Act, 1988.
A CIP catalogue record for this book is available from
the British Library.
3 5 7 9 10 8 6 4 2
Printed in Great Britain

Contents

For Sarah Dudman

The Great White

"There's a Great White," said Manuel Gonzales. "He's a killer – and I should know." He fingered the shark-tooth necklace round his neck. "I caught one of those devils a couple of years ago and made myself this."

Jack and Carrie watched the fin of the shark travelling through the water behind *Mexican Eagle*, a motor cruiser designed for tourists and owned by Manuel and his brother Juan.

"How big is he?" asked Jack.

"About six metres long," said Manuel. "You can

always recognise the Great White by his torpedo-shaped body and white bony teeth. Then there's that quivering snout with the nostrils trying to scent food."

Jack had never heard him speak such good English. Then he realised he must have mugged it up so that he could shock the tourists.

"Did you really catch a Great White yourself, or are you just making it up?" demanded Jack suspiciously.

Manuel laughed uneasily. "Of course I did," he said and looked away.

Jack couldn't work out whether Manuel was a fake or not.

"Once he smells blood, he's on target," Manuel chuckled, his wide, dark tanned face wreathed in a grin.

"You're just winding us up," said Carrie, Jack's younger sister.

"No, my little one – I'm not winding you up. The Great White's only got two objectives – feeding and breeding. What you can see at the moment is the top fin, slicing through the water like a submarine with its periscope up. Watch – I'll give him a few fish scraps – then you might believe what I'm telling you."

"What else do they eat – besides human beings?" asked Jack.

"The Great White hunts seals and sea lions, dolphins or swordfish. They even eat smaller sharks, but right here they go for elephant seals. Humans are a treat. A rare treat." Manuel grinned again. "But humans are only at risk if they're splashing about, or maybe if they've cut themselves on a rock and there's blood in the water."

Manuel was short and powerfully built. He was in his early thirties and the muscles in his arms stood out like whipcords as he picked up a heavy pail and threw the scraps overboard.

"Watch out for unexpected visitors – one of the sharks could jump right out of the water on to our boat!"

"Thanks for telling us," said Jack drily.

"What's in that pail?" asked Carrie, wrinkling up her nose.

"It's called chum."

"Sounds like dog food."

Manuel gave Carrie a puzzled look. "I'm talking about a mixture of blood and rotting fish."

"Yuk!" was all that Carrie could reply and Jack suddenly felt queasy and hoped he wasn't going to be violently sick. Fortunately the feeling soon disappeared.

"Did you know these sharks are descended from monsters?" asked Manuel with increasing enjoyment. Now Jack was sure he was setting out to wind them all up.

"What kind of monsters?" he asked, watching the chum floating on the surface.

"Prehistoric. The Latin name for the Great White is *Carcharodon Megalodon*." Manuel sounded as if he was reading from his well-worn script again. "That translates as megatooth shark which, I think, is entirely appropriate. Did you know that Carcharodon teeth have been brought up from the ocean floor?"

"No," said Jack.

"And did you know they measure five inches in length and that fossilised teeth of the same size have been found in rocks?"

"No," said Jack again.

Manuel paused for effect and then said, "Watch out for the Great Whites. They're also known as white death."

"Nice one." This time Jack shivered.

Suddenly a huge blunt head with a wide gash of a mouth and a staring black eye on either side of a huge snout burst out of the water. The Great White's teeth were triangular and chunky looking, but Jack was sure they were also razor sharp and there seemed to be dozens of them. As it began to feed on the chum, the shark's eyes rolled back in their sockets, revealing the white surface of its eyeballs. Jack gazed at the thing in horror. Manuel's build-up had been tame beside the grim reality of the shark itself.

But slowly his shock subsided. Jack knew he was well out of its reach, that he was watching it from the deck of *Mexican Eagle*, almost as if he was watching a film. He was safe, protected, in his own world. The shark inhabited another – an ocean that was cruel, mysterious and relatively unexplored. They had no connection with each other. But, all the same, he was relieved when the terrible head disappeared back under the surface with a mouthful of bait.

"Wow," said Dave. "He *was* a big fella."

Manuel grinned, delighted that his sales talk had so convincingly sprung to life.

Jack winced, wishing his stepfather wouldn't be so

embarrassing. He was always saying something uncool.

Jack gazed down at the surface again and saw that the shark must have dived, for there was no trace of him, not even his dorsal fin.

The Simmonds were on holiday in California and had chartered *Mexican Eagle* with another family for a whale-watching trip on the Pacific Ocean. Already Dave Simmonds had got them all laughing uneasily with his corny jokes. He was beginning to get on Jack's nerves and Carrie felt the same.

Their own father had died when Jack was six and Carrie was four. Although he was now twelve and Carrie was ten, the hurt of losing their real father was still just as strong. Dave always seemed to be showing off and trying to get them to love him. But Jack was certain they never would.

Mum had married Dave a few months ago. Both Jack and Carrie knew how lonely she'd been, but if only she'd married someone else!

Dave was showing off even now, trying to impress the Charltons who were also British, and had two young children.

"What's the stomach capacity of a shark?" Dave

asked Manuel. "I bet it's vast." He stood there in his Bermuda shorts, khaki shirt, white socks and sandals, fat and pale-skinned, with carroty hair, his arm round Mum's shoulders as if he owned her. She was willowy and slim and he almost had to stand on tiptoe.

Jack felt hot with embarrassment, sure that Manuel must think his stepfather was a complete fool. But Manuel smiled blandly. He had a business to run and Dave was a customer.

"You're right, Senor," he said. "The Great White's stomach is enormous. Much bigger than mine." Manuel slapped his paunch and laughed heartily. So did Dave. "Do you know what they found in the stomach of a Great White that was caught off Ensenada?" Again, Manuel paused for effect.

"Tell us," said Dave, squeezing Mum's waist, the sweat shining on his pale freckled face that wouldn't tan.

"Well," said Manuel, pleased he had an audience that not only included the Simmonds, but the Charltons as well. "In his stomach was a goat, a turtle, a tom-cat, a smaller shark, three anoraks and a car number plate."

They all roared with laughter and Dave had to say,

"Anything else? How about a deckchair? Or an American breakfast?"

There was more laughter and Manuel's grin widened with a look of contentment. Jack didn't believe a word he said. Manuel seemed like an overgrown kid, in love with his life, mixing truth and lies together so often that he didn't know the difference. But he was good company all the same and Jack liked him. Manuel's brother Juan was different, much more withdrawn, and Jack had noticed what he thought was a look of contempt appear on Juan's face when Dave was cracking yet another corny joke.

When Jack glanced down again at the surface of the ocean, he could see a tail fin zigzagging through the water behind them. For a moment he shivered again, no longer feeling protected. Suppose he fell overboard and that huge head reared up at him with its razor sharp teeth? Then Jack reminded himself that they were all safe on *Mexican Eagle* with Manuel's stories and Dave's jokes. Nowhere could be safer than that.

"What about the whales?" asked Mr Charlton. "Weren't we meant to be whale watching?"

Manuel's grin spread, but Jack noticed Juan giving his brother a warning glance. Have they been conning us over the whales, wondered Jack, noticing that Dave looked concerned too, as if he had suddenly realised he might not be getting his money's worth.

"Whales are further on," said Manuel easily. "Up the coast a little. Now who wants a beer?"

While the adults jostled for refreshment, Jack gazed out at the coastline which was strange and desolate, with gaunt high cliffs and few signs of civilisation. Earlier, through Manuel's binoculars, Jack and Carrie had seen the skeletal remains of whales on the empty beaches.

Then he saw a dark shadow on the water, and when he looked up, he realised clouds were suddenly hurtling across the sky. Some of them were black.

Juan was gazing up at them too. "Bad weather coming," he said. "We turn back." His English was not as good as Manuel's.

"What about the whales?"

"Bad storm. We go home to Ensenada."

Carrie was up at the small bar, drinking lemonade, and Dave was laughing loudly with Mr Charlton.

No one had heard about the change in plans yet, but Jack was sure Dave would be furious. He'd been delighted at an opportunity to impress his new family with a whale-watching trip. When Mum had told him that Dave's first wife had walked out on him and he had been very lonely – just as she had – Jack had felt sorry for his new stepfather. But somehow Dave always managed to spoil things with his frantic desire to please them all, and it was hard not to feel irritated.

Juan was whispering to Manuel now, as they gazed up at the clouds. Then Manuel reluctantly went over to the bar and cleared his throat uneasily. "Very sorry," he said.

"What's up?" asked Dave cheerfully. "Don't worry about the whales. I'm sure we'll spot some after lunch. When I've had a few beers I'll spot anything – even the Loch Ness monster."

"Who?" Manuel looked at him in bewilderment.

"What are you sorry about?" asked Mum suspiciously.

"We go home."

"What?" said Dave, the grin fading from his fleshy face. "What did you say?"

"We go home."

"Why?"

"Bad weather coming." Manuel waved a hand at the fast travelling black clouds.

Dave was looking up at them as if they didn't really exist. "Come on," he said. "I paid for this."

"We go back," Juan said bleakly.

"Is there compensation?"

"What?"

"Do we get our money back?"

Juan looked at Manuel who went smoothly into action. "We can't compensate for the weather. Storms are unpredictable."

"How long have we got?"

"Long?" Manuel, who normally spoke such good English, was taking refuge in not being able to understand.

"Before the storm."

"A few hours – maybe."

"Then let's carry on." Dave was no longer grinning. He means business, thought Jack. "I don't mind a bit of bumpy weather. I want to see a whale or two."

"Maybe we give you another hour." Manuel was

compromising now.

"Are you sure?" asked Mum.

"I'll make it worth your while," said Dave with a wink at Manuel.

Manuel looked at Juan and shrugged. "Maybe we see some whales."

"I get sick if the sea's rough," said Carrie.

"I've got some pills," said Dave. "Real little miracle workers. I often feel a bit queasy bouncing up and down. How about everyone taking one?" He pulled out a box and offered the pills round like sweets. "They're not on prescription. Just a good branded product over the counter."

But no one took up his offer. Not even Carrie.

"Carry on," said Dave. "Carry on up the Khyber." He laughed again.

Manuel shrugged.

Juan frowned.

The clouds got blacker.

The Storm

As *Mexican Eagle* motored on, Jack felt a strange kind of stillness that was somehow disturbing. The surface of the ocean looked dark and sluggish, as if made of treacle, and the dark clouds were denser. Manuel handed out sandwiches and more beer as the heat became intense.

Jack returned to the stern, followed by Carrie. They both felt uneasy. Jack was tall for his age and strongly built, with short blond hair. Carrie was small, with dark hair and an oval face that tanned fast.

"I don't like this calm," she said.

"The calm before the storm." Jack was equally uncomfortable. "I didn't realise it would be like this."

"Like what?"

"Such a weird colour. I can't see any sign of a fin though, can you?"

Jack and Carrie scanned the empty surface and felt reassured.

"I didn't like that shark following us." Carrie shuddered.

Jack stared out at the treacly ocean and noticed there was some dark green weed bobbing up and down on the surface. He felt repelled by the stuff.

Looking up at the sky again, Jack was amazed how rapidly the clouds had met in a dark canopy above them, tinged with purple.

"We should have turned back earlier," he said. Jack felt he could hardly breathe. If only there was a breeze. The hot and sticky atmosphere seemed to wrap around him like warm, damp cotton wool.

"It's Dave's fault," said Carrie.

"It's *always* Dave's fault," replied Jack. "Do you think Mum will ever get fed up with him? I am."

"So am I," said Carrie. "But it's not *really* his fault, is it? We can't blame him for everything."

"Why not?" Jack suddenly felt ruthless about Dave.

"He's spent a lot of money bringing us out here. We got to go to Disneyland for two whole days, and there's been masses of other stuff. He just wants us to like him." She sounded doubtful.

"You can't buy people," snapped Jack. "And that's what he's trying to do."

Carrie sighed. "I know what you mean. If he makes one more stupid joke I'll go mad."

Jack nodded and swung round to see that Dave was arguing with Manuel and their voices were raised.

"We have to go home, Senor."

"I want my money back then."

"I'm afraid we cannot help. We are not responsible for the weather – but we *are* responsible for your safety."

There was a low rumbling of thunder and suddenly a flash of lightning lit up the darkening sky.

Jack and Carrie joined the group of adults. Mr and Mrs Charlton were looking scared and their two young children, Amy and Robert, had started to cry. Jack sighed. Why hadn't Dave listened to Manuel? Why hadn't he agreed to return to Ensenada half an hour ago?

More thunder rumbled.

"Dave," said Jack. "We should go back to Ensenada right away." He spoke crisply, full of a new authority, realising that their situation was getting out of control. Manuel, and even Juan, were too deferential, while the other adults seemed to be looking for a leadership that didn't exist. A sense of reality was needed. Jack thought about the shark. That was reality all right.

Dave gave Jack a strange, hurt look, obviously feeling he had humiliated him in public. "What's a bit of rough weather?" he blustered.

But Mum intervened. "I'm sorry, Dave, but I think Jack's right and, anyway, Senor Gonzales is in charge. He's the captain."

Dave gave a mock salute. "Aye, aye, sir. Is that a parrot on your right shoulder?"

"A parrot?" Manuel gazed at Dave as if he really had gone crazy. "What would I want with a parrot?"

"What indeed?" Mr Charlton glowered at Dave and then turned to Manuel. "Can we go back?"

"Of course," said Juan, speaking on his brother's

behalf. "We should have gone before." He turned to Dave angrily. "You held us up."

"And I'm afraid there is no question of anyone getting their money back." Manuel was clearly no longer trying to please. "The weather is an act of God."

The first breath of wind came about ten minutes later as *Mexican Eagle* was chugging back to port at the fastest rate of knots she could manage.

At first the breeze was refreshing, but as the force strengthened, Jack's anxiety rose. He glanced at Carrie and knew she was feeling the same, while Amy and Robert were crying again.

"It's OK," said Manuel. "We'll get home. Would you all like to go below?"

"No chance," said Dave. "I'd feel trapped."

"Rain may come," warned Juan, shouting from the wheelhouse. "We have no more oilskins."

"Then you should have," bellowed Dave.

Jack caught his mother's eye. She smiled brightly, but he knew she was scared. Well, so was he. Jack didn't want to go below, not if the sea was going to get rough. He couldn't imagine a worse trap.

*

The wind built up fast and so did the waves.

"We'll be OK," said Jack, trying to reassure his sister.

But Carrie was far from reassured. "Why should we be OK?" She was always a realist and didn't like false encouragement. For a dreadful moment Jack realised he was behaving like Dave and the thought made him feel ashamed.

As if to underline his mistake, Dave stretched and yawned and said, "Don't worry, folks. We're in safe hands."

The Charltons glanced at Juan in the wheelhouse and Manuel on deck, looking up at the sky thoughtfully. Neither of them seemed reassuring.

"*A life on the ocean wave*," Dave began to sing.

"Shut up!" said Mum.

Jack felt a thrill of what should have been pleasure, but was really apprehension. This was the first time he had heard his mother telling Dave off and a dim memory of his father came into his mind. He had always regarded Dad as the one man who would keep him safe. But Dad hadn't been able to protect himself from the cancer that had overwhelmed him.

The wind had now become so fierce that the waves were white horses and spray was drifting over *Mexican Eagle's* prow as she cleaved through the lashing sea. The wind whistled and howled around the wheelhouse and Mum said to Dave, "We shouldn't have delayed them."

"I was only trying to get—"

"Your money's worth. Yes, I know," said Mum bitterly. "But did you forget the value of our lives?"

The *Eagle* Goes Down

Soon conditions became much worse as *Mexican Eagle* was tossed about, plunging into the trough of a wave and then riding the next, her bows streaming with water.

Jack felt sick. Carrie was looking pale and the Charlton children were *being* sick, not neatly over the bow, but messily on to the deck. Manuel produced some small towels and kept telling everyone not to worry – which made Jack worry even more.

Thunder was growling all around them and streaks of lightning bathed the boat in a yellow light. Soon the waves seemed mountainous, the wind had risen to gale force and *Mexican Eagle* was taking on a lot of water. They were all wearing life jackets, but Jack was sure his was too big and might come off if he had to jump into the sea. The fact that it didn't fit hadn't mattered at all when he'd put it on in the safety of the harbour sunshine. Now it could be a matter of life or death. He tried to tighten the straps, but couldn't manage to shift them at all.

Manuel spotted his sudden panic as he clung on to the rail and came over to him, putting a strong arm round his waist to keep him steady and tightening his straps at the same time.

"Are you OK?" he asked, yelling above the screaming wind.

"Yes," Jack bellowed back untruthfully. "How far is it to Ensenada?"

"We'll be there in an hour. Maybe less." Manuel hesitated. "Maybe a little more." He suddenly seemed indecisive again. Could he be frightened too, wondered Jack. But when he looked up into his leathery face, he saw no sign of fear. In fact he couldn't see any sign of emotion at all.

"You must come below," said Manuel. "The wind and the waves are getting strong."

"No way," said Jack. "I wouldn't feel safe." He walked over to stand by Carrie.

"You could be swept overboard." Manuel went over to Dave and appealed to him. Juan had just spoken to the Charltons and, surprisingly, they were heading obediently for the cabin.

"Maybe we should," said Carrie shivering. "I'm getting soaked."

Just then Dave came over and yelled, "We're all going below – and there's no choice."

Jack looked appealingly at his mother, who shook her head and shouted, "Dave's right. You *must* come below."

Dave isn't right, Jack thought rebelliously. He didn't *ever* want Dave to be right. Anyway, it was Manuel who had given the orders.

"OK," he said. "But what happens if we capsize?"

Dave laughed and clapped Jack hard on the back. "Avast there, me hearties. There'll be no mutiny on my ship."

"It isn't your ship," yelled Jack, but Dave already had

a hand on his arm, almost dragging him towards the companionway ladder, followed by Mum and Carrie.

Jack had the feeling he had been thrown into a dungeon beneath the sea.

"The storm's stopping soon," Manuel called down to them. "No one's to worry. Everything will be all right."

Jack had to disagree.

They sat in the main cabin around a table that was bolted to the floor – Jack, Carrie, Mum and Dave and Mr and Mrs Charlton with Amy and Robert on their knees.

There was a small galley which was full of stores and cooking equipment, while in the cabin there were piles of boxes, books and magazines. The space was very small and felt extremely claustrophobic, as *Mexican Eagle* lurched about erratically in the storm.

Even Dave seemed subdued and no one spoke, staring down at the table which was scarred with cigarette burns and rings made by hot mugs.

Only Amy and Robert seemed happy, snuggled cosily

in their parents' arms.

As *Mexican Eagle* wallowed in the troughs and then broke through the waves themselves, objects began to fall from shelves and slide around the floor. Jack only just managed to dodge a large box file and Carrie got hit on the head by a navigation chart.

"I wonder how long this is going to last," said Mum, expressing all their thoughts, but none of their fears.

As Jack had suspected, conditions were much worse down here than up on deck. He felt completely trapped, and with each roll of the boat he could see his rising fear reflected in the others' eyes. But Amy and Robert had drifted off to sleep and he envied them their faith that their parents could protect them from anything.

Jack wished he had the same kind of trust, but he didn't. He was too old for that, and so was Carrie.

He looked down at his watch. Manuel had said they'd be back in port in about an hour, and they had only been in the cabin for about ten minutes. He felt panic-stricken at the thought of staying here for much longer, unable to see what was happening and trying to cope with the continuously falling objects that ended up rolling and rattling around the floor.

Jack could feel Carrie shivering beside him, and he put an arm round her shoulder. "Manuel and Juan are probably used to storms like this. They know what they're doing."

"But we don't," said Carrie, continuing to shiver.

Just then Dave struggled to his feet, lurched towards the door of the toilet and just got inside before he was violently sick. He made a great deal of noise, competing with the screaming of the wind and the crashing of the waves.

Suddenly the boat seemed to spin round at a crazy angle and Jack had the terrible feeling that they *were* going to capsize. Somehow *Mexican Eagle* righted herself, but almost immediately was sent into the awful spinning motion again. Jack could hear something breaking on deck as she rolled sideways, recovering once again, but with the ominous sound of grinding metal.

Jack knew he couldn't bear to stay down here any longer. Amy and Robert had woken up and their parents were now trying unsuccessfully to comfort them.

Then Dave came stumbling out of the toilet, looking grey and ill, tripping over something on the floor and banging his head hard against the table.

"Are you all right?" gasped Mrs Charlton.

Dave was half kneeling on the floor, hands gripping the edge of the table.

Mum got to her feet, reached out for his arm and pulled Dave down next to her. There were tears in her eyes.

Then *Mexican Eagle* pitched forward, there was an appalling roaring sound, and for a terrifying moment Jack thought they must be buried in a wave. Somehow she righted herself once more.

Jack got up. "We'd be safer on deck," he yelled at them all.

"We'd be swept off," said Mrs Charlton. "Sit down."

"We'll be trapped," he shouted at her. "We're in real danger."

"Jack's right," said Carrie. "We can't stay down here."

"Well, you can't go up on deck either," shouted Dave. "So do as you're told." He put his head in his hands while *Mexican Eagle* burrowed and rolled, shook and wallowed and rode high for a moment on a wave, before burying her nose once again in a trough. Then she shuddered, the grinding sound came again and Manuel threw open the cabin door.

"You come out. You come out now!"

There was blood running down his face and one eye was puffy and partly closed.

"You bet," said Jack, but the others weren't so keen until water began to pour down the steps and into the cabin.

"What are we going to do?" Mum shouted at Manuel.

"Abandon ship," he replied calmly as he fingered his shark-tooth necklace.

Mexican Eagle gave another lurch and began to list badly as more water poured into the cabin.

Manuel clambered down and stood at the bottom of the steps and pushed them all up and out on to the lurching deck.

Jack was appalled at the scene of devastation. The wheelhouse had disappeared and so had all the aerials and radar, and *Mexican Eagle* was listing badly.

Then he saw the two dinghies which seemed ludicrously small.

"OK," yelled Manuel above the noise of the storm. "The Charlton family go with Juan – and the Simmonds family, you come with me. You get in now. The ship – she is going down."

"How do we get the dinghies afloat?" yelled Dave.

"You leave that to me."

"Wait a moment – I've left my camera down below," Dave said.

"You leave," bellowed Manuel.

"But—"

"Shut your mouth and get in the dinghy!" Manuel's usual courtesy had deserted him. "She'll float clear."

Juan meanwhile was giving similar instructions to the Charltons. Jack could hardly believe what was happening. This will be something to tell my friends at school, he thought. If we survive!

Throughout the trip down the Mexican coast Jack had not only felt protected, but also in an environment that barely seemed real. But now reality had torn apart the protection and they were facing a terrifying tumult of wind and water. And sharks. He tried not to think about them. But the brutal reality of the danger they were all in kept pounding in his mind.

"Get in the dinghy!" shouted Manuel.

Mum and Dave obeyed him instantly.

This is all down to Dave, thought Jack. Manuel tried to please him – and now look what's happened.

Jack and Carrie clambered into the dinghy too, and they all crouched in the small damp space, waiting for Manuel to join them.

"We're in the eye," said Manuel, still standing on the deck. "The eye of the storm. That means it's going to be a little calmer for a while."

He was right, for although the waves were still lashing the deck, they were not so high and the wind had lessened. Jack felt a glorious sense of relief and, looking round, he saw that both the dinghies were equipped with oars. But there was no sign of an outboard motor.

"Don't we have any power?" he yelled.

"What power?" asked Manuel.

"An outboard motor?"

"We do not have any outboard."

Suddenly *Mexican Eagle* shuddered and tilted further until she was almost at water level. Manuel scrambled into the dinghy a few seconds before it began to float away from its stricken mother ship and grabbed the oars just in time.

Jack glanced back and could just make out Juan and the Charltons in the other dinghy, enveloped in a white mist of spray.

Manuel pulled strongly and they bobbed up and down until a wave slammed them back against the sloping deck.

"Push off!" he yelled at Jack, who was with Carrie in the stern, while Mum and Dave were in the bow. Manuel was in the middle of the dinghy, clutching the oars and trying to push them off the deck of the stricken *Mexican Eagle*.

At last, with a combination of pushing and pulling with the oars, Jack and Manuel managed to get the dinghy clear.

Then Manuel began to row frantically and Jack could just make out Juan doing the same until they were out on the waves under the black and purple sky, where one minute they were perched on the crests and the next they were tumbling down into the troughs. This frantic motion had been bad enough on board *Mexican Eagle*, but it was much worse in such a tiny craft.

"There she goes." Manuel's voice broke and tears streamed down his face as *Mexican Eagle* suddenly rolled over, completely capsizing, showing a rusty keel for a few moments and then disappearing from sight. "She was all we had," he wept.

"What about the insurance?" yelled Dave, but Manuel didn't reply, still pulling strongly on the oars, putting more distance between them and the sunken ship than Jack had thought possible in such a short space of time.

"Now what?" asked Mum.

"We go home."

"In this?" Dave demanded. "Did you make a Mayday call?"

"Of course." Manuel didn't meet his eyes, concentrating on the oars.

"Is rescue on its way?" asked Mum.

Jack could no longer see the other dinghy that was

being rowed by Juan. Maybe they were lost in the trough of one of the waves that were beginning to build up again as they came out of the eye of the storm.

"The radio – the radio got bad." Manuel's English was rapidly deserting him in his battle to keep the dinghy going.

"What do you mean?" She was horrified.

"We tried Mayday. Maybe someone heard. But in the storm the radio broke."

"So no one knows we're in trouble?" Dave yelled at him. "I'm going to take you to court for this. I've never known such crass irresponsibility!"

Jack tried to block Dave out. He scanned the water, but he couldn't see the other dinghy at all now. His eyes returned to Manuel and the shark-tooth necklace.

And then it began to rain.

Overboard

The wind had once again reached gale force and the little dinghy seemed all too vulnerable as she began to take on board a good deal of water.

Pointing to a couple of scoops floating near them, Manuel bellowed, "Take turns to bale. You bale fast."

Grabbing the scoops, Jack and Dave began to bale vigorously, but the job was incredibly difficult, as far more water came in over the bows than the amount they managed to bale out.

"You work harder!" bellowed Manuel. The rain had

lessened, creating a thick haze in the air that gradually became fog.

"We *are* working hard," shouted Dave indignantly. "It's the waves breaking over us that's the problem."

Manuel said something in Spanish and Jack guessed that it was something unpleasant about Dave.

They continued to bale until Jack's arm ached so much that he was in real pain, and from the sight of Dave's screwed-up face he had to be feeling the same.

But with the coming of the fog, the sea quietened and there was no more rumbling thunder or flashes of lightning.

"Women take over!" yelled Manuel.

Mum and Carrie started to bale, and to Jack's surprise were much more effective than he and Dave had been. They seemed to have more energy and rhythm, working as a team.

Slowly the big waves turned into rollers and the dinghy lurched about, making little progress, despite strenuous efforts by Manuel with the oars. Then the rollers flattened out a little and became a heavy swell, with the fog slowly beginning to clear.

Carrie and Mum continued baling until Manuel, the sweat pouring off him, asked Dave and Jack to take over once again. Hurriedly glancing down at his watch, Jack saw that the time was just after three in the afternoon.

The grinding hard work seemed to be paying off and there was now less water in the dinghy.

"How far are we from Ensenada?" gasped Dave.

Manuel shrugged. "A long way."

Jack glanced around him in the clearing fog and could see no sign of the other dinghy.

"Where's Juan?"

Again Manuel shrugged. He looked totally exhausted and his rowing was beginning to get sluggish.

"Let me take over," said Dave.

At first Manuel refused, but after a while Jack could see he badly needed a rest.

"Come on." Dave was impatient. "Don't you think I'm capable of rowing?"

Eventually Manuel gave in. "We have to be careful while we pass each other," he warned Dave. "We'll both stand up and then we'll change positions. The dinghy is too much loaded already so make a mistake and one of us will go overboard."

"OK." Dave looked anxious and Jack actually felt sorry for him. He was obviously incredibly nervous about standing up and making the little craft even more unstable.

The sky was rapidly clearing and there were already patches of blue, while the sea was becoming calmer, the swell decreasing.

"I still can't see the other dinghy," said Jack.

Manuel said nothing, but he looked worried. Then he said again, "*Mexican Eagle* was all we had." Manuel paused, and Jack felt there was something deeply moving about his loss, particularly as he hadn't tried to blame Dave, who was responsible for them not returning to Ensenada. But then, thought Jack, Manuel should never have given in to him in the first place. He had made a fatal mistake by compromising.

"We change over now," said Manuel.

"Right," said Dave, struggling clumsily to his feet.

"You go slowly," warned Manuel.

For the first few moments the changeover went smoothly as Dave and Manuel edged past each other carefully. Then the dinghy jerked wildly and the two men collided, momentarily clinging on to each other and then falling.

Dave pitched into Jack's lap while Manuel fell overboard with a wild cry, disappearing under the surface and then coming up spluttering.

"Get him in!" yelled Jack at no one in particular. Then, a sudden movement caught his eye. He looked beyond Manuel floundering in the water and saw what could only be a fin cleaving a path of white foam directly towards him.

"Shark!" yelled Jack.

Manuel looked over his shoulder and then began to swim to the dinghy, clinging to the bows and struggling to lever himself in again. Jack and Carrie frantically tried to grab him as the dinghy heaved up and down, becoming increasingly unstable in the heavy swell.

"Get in!" shouted Carrie.

But that was the problem. Manuel was heavy, and although Jack and Carrie both held on to him, they didn't have the strength to pull Manuel up over the bow.

"Hurry up!" yelled Jack.

Now the fin was circling the dinghy.

"No worries," gasped Manuel. "I have this charmed life. He's not going to get me. I can promise you that." Jack gazed at the shark-tooth necklace around Manuel's neck and hoped he was right.

Imbued with Manuel's confidence, Carrie and Jack began to edge him up over the bows of the dinghy.

"You'll never get him up on your own," said Dave. "Keep the boat stable and I'll help you."

"No!" yelled Manuel. "Don't move. You'll have everyone in."

Suddenly the fin disappeared.

"The shark's gone," said Jack.

"Where is he?" gasped Manuel.

"I've told you. The shark's gone."

"He's diving." Manuel pulled at the bows of the dinghy desperately, his eyes wide, pupils dilated with fear. "For God's sake help me. You've got to help me."

"We can't just sit here." Mum began to struggle up but the boat rocked wildly and Dave pulled her back.

"We'll get you out somehow." Jack was now under one of Manuel's shoulders and Carrie the other. But he was still a dead weight.

"Hurry!" bellowed Manuel. "You've got to hurry."
Then he began to scream.

Death in the Water

Manuel was being pulled back into the water by something that was incredibly strong, something that none of them could see, and his screams were appalling to hear.

"We've got you," shouted Carrie.

Manuel's face was contorted in agony and Jack saw the water was turning crimson.

Jack and Carrie desperately tried to hang on to Manuel, but he suddenly wrenched his arms free so abruptly that they were both forced to let him go.

Still screaming, Manuel was dragged under the surface while Jack and Carrie looked down in horror at the spreading crimson stain on the water.

"What's happening?" shrilled Dave.

"The shark's got him," replied Jack flatly. He couldn't believe what had happened, couldn't believe his own eyes. The shark he had seen earlier had been an enormous shock – but a shock that belonged to the movies. Now, without even seeing Manuel's attacker, he had witnessed him being dragged down into the depths.

Carrie began to sob, but Jack had mercifully gone numb. A couple of hours ago they'd been riding out a storm, with the sharks in the depths of the ocean, safely away from them, wild creatures they would only see in a zoo or a marine park or from the deck of *Mexican Eagle*. But now the barrier between them had been removed. They were no longer protected.

Suddenly, without warning, Manuel's head resurfaced, his mouth open in a silent scream, the shark still somewhere in the depths, jaws fastened around him.

Blood bubbled out from Manuel's mouth. He still

made no sound, but his eyes were wide open and pleading. For a dreadful moment Jack met those eyes and in them saw the full horror of what was happening.

Then Manuel was dragged down again and didn't resurface.

Suddenly Jack saw more fins cleaving the surface, moving in fast, and his numbness disappeared. He counted three of them and shouted, "There's a load more of them coming. They could wreck the dinghy."

Then the fins vanished as the sharks dived.

Now Jack felt so cold that it was as if his blood had turned to ice.

Meanwhile, Dave began to shout out Manuel's name, and Mum clung to him in disbelief.

Jack grabbed Carrie's arm and tried to pull her to the other side of the dinghy, away from the crimson stain which was still spreading on the swell. He had never seen anyone die before.

There was no chance for Manuel now. Then Jack saw something bob up to the surface, floating towards the dinghy, carried by the current.

It was a shoe. One of Manuel's trainers. Inside was part of his foot.

Jack began to vomit over the side of the dinghy, pushing his sister away with one hand with such force that she fell on to her back and struggled to sit up.

"I saw the shoe," she said.

Jack raised his head, the sweat standing out on his forehead, his hair soaked. "You didn't see," he began. "You didn't see—" But Jack couldn't finish his sentence, however much he tried.

"I did see," said Carrie, sounding much older. "I did see what was inside his shoe."

"Don't talk about it," Jack bawled at her.

"I need to talk. His foot was in there."

"My God," said Dave over and over again, so many times that Jack thought he would never stop. "My God. My God. My—"

Mum grabbed his hand and said, "Just try to be quiet. Be really quiet."

There was still no sign of the sharks, but Jack was sure they were feeding on Manuel somewhere under the dinghy. Did they realise they could have other victims? Did they know that if they attacked the dinghy with their deadly strong jaws they would have a feast? Was it only the smell of blood that gave them direction? Wasn't it the vibrations from the boat as well?

"You're right, Mum. We *have* to be quiet," whispered Jack, turning round to the family and putting a shaking finger to his lips. "We mustn't make a noise or they'll hear us."

Again and again Jack saw a picture in his mind's eye of the sharks sinking their razor sharp teeth into Manuel's leg. He began to vomit overboard again. Just as he found he couldn't throw up any more, he saw the sharks' fins, circling the dinghy again. He began to count. Three sharks. All ready to savage them.

The crimson stain still spread, but began to darken. Suddenly the sun came out and Jack felt a shaft of warmth on his skin, but no way could the warmth drive away the ice cold fear.

Then another shoe floated to the surface. The trainer bumped against the dinghy as if needing to be picked up. Mercifully the other shoe had drifted away. Then, to Jack's relief, the second trainer began to drift after its companion.

That was all that was left of Manuel.

He might never have existed.

"Jack," whispered Mum. "My dear Jack."

But he didn't move or even incline his head towards her, for the fins had stopped circling them and for a dreadful moment he thought they were coming in for the kill.

But instead they began to move off in different directions.

"They're leaving," he yelled, forgetting to be quiet. "The sharks are going!" For the first time he turned round to look at Carrie and Dave and Mum. They all bore the same expression on their terrified faces – complete and utter disbelief.

The dinghy drifted, oars shipped, the crimson stain gone. Above them was a blue sky with a few white clouds and the surface of the sea was relatively calm.

A current had taken them and the dinghy was moving, lethargically rocking up and down.

Jack had no idea whether they were moving in the right direction. No one spoke. Carrie gave an occasional half smothered sob. Dave gazed ahead, staring but not seeing, and Mum was doing the same. The shock had been immense and they were still in its grip.

"We should row," said Mum eventually, her voice husky and shaking.

"No map. Not even a compass. We don't have the faintest idea what direction to take." Dave was negative and indecisive.

Carrie gave another smothered sob, while Jack said, "Manuel was rowing that way."

"Which way?" asked Dave.

But when challenged, Jack couldn't say. "We're drifting," he said.

"That's obvious." Dave was scornful.

Again there was a silence.

"What are we going to do?" asked Mum hopelessly.

"Maybe we'll be seen." Jack tried to be reassuring.

Dave looked round him. "Who by?"

"When *Mexican Eagle* fails to dock at Ensenada, they'll organise a rescue boat, or a plane or a helicopter." Jack knew he sounded horribly vague.

"I'd better row," said Dave with sudden decision, standing up and making the dinghy rock wildly.

"Be careful," yelled Carrie. "You'll capsize us."

Eventually Dave sat down and grabbed the oars.

Jack watched him, feeling almost hypnotised. Dave didn't seem to be very good at handling the oars, but maybe that was because he was trembling so much. Several times the oars missed the water completely and then went in too deep, making the dinghy lurch alarmingly.

"We should wait for Manuel," said Carrie, looking behind her. The trainers were still bobbing about, but they were little specks now.

Jack looked at Carrie in concern. Had the shock of Manuel's death been too great for her? Was this her way of trying to block what happened? He felt a wave of panic. He always relied on Carrie to keep her cool. Jack didn't think he'd be able to cope if she cracked up.

Surprisingly, Dave seemed to be making some erratic progress, but Jack had no idea if they were heading in the right direction. They would be very lucky if they were, he thought, and then wondered again about the chances of rescue. *Surely* someone would do something when *Mexican Eagle* failed to return. What time would she have berthed? Jack looked at his watch and saw that it was just past four in the afternoon.

"We should wait for Manuel," said Carrie again.

This time Mum replied. "There's no need, darling. He won't be coming back to us."

Carrie looked at her mother incredulously, as if she couldn't possibly accept what she had just said.

Jack, however, had not only accepted the horror of what had happened, but was feeling increasingly desperate about the possibility of another attack.

Meanwhile Dave rowed on, gradually getting used to the rhythm; he had stopped trembling now that he had something positive to do.

There was still quite a lot of water in the dinghy, mainly due to Dave's initial flailing movements with the oars, so Jack began to bale and soon Carrie joined him. She was silent and didn't refer to Manuel, but Jack knew that his sister was someone who usually held back her feelings, while he always expressed them. Mum had once said, "You're as different as chalk and cheese, you two. With Carrie I never know what's going on inside her head. With you, Jack, why you tell me the lot."

Rather than being pleased, Jack had felt rather exposed. Why couldn't he be more of a mystery, he had thought at the time. He didn't want anyone to read his thoughts so easily and he envied Carrie for not giving herself away.

"Can I have a go at rowing?" asked Jack, trying to take some initiative. "Carrie and I could take an oar each."

Dave shook his head. "No way. I want to make some progress."

"You could be taking us in the wrong direction."

"You're right," Dave observed. "But whichever way we're headed, I need to make some progress."

Jack didn't reply. Dave made him feel like a child – an unwanted child at that. Suddenly he really hated him.

After about another ten minutes, Dave shipped the oars and slumped down. "I'm bushed," he said.

You would be, thought Jack, turning to his mother for support. "Can't I have a go? On my own?"

"Let him try, Dave."

"No way."

"We all ought to be having a go with the oars, and that includes me," snapped Carrie, and Jack felt relieved. At least Carrie was back to her normal self.

"Is there any water in this dinghy?" asked Jack.

"Only sea water," said Mum. "I've checked her out

and she doesn't have any supplies. No food and water and no flares."

Up until now, Jack hadn't even bothered to think about provisions. He had been too horrified by Manuel's death to think of anything else. But now he realised how parched he was, and the more he thought about water the more he desperately needed a drink. If only they had managed to store some of the rain. But how?

"Let me row," Jack persisted, and Dave finally gave in.

"All right." He was grudging. "But don't splash half the ocean into the dinghy."

"I'm not likely to do that – not after all the work Mum, Carrie and I put in!"

Jack got to his feet and crossed over to where Dave was sitting. This was how Manuel had fallen in, making a changeover. Panicking, Jack came to a shaky halt. But he managed to balance the dinghy and it was only when Dave joined Mum in the prow that the little craft began to rock.

Dave sat down hurriedly and Jack began to row, smoothly and strongly, determined his stepfather should recognise that he was able to take on the task and be successful. In fact, he had always been athletic, and although he'd never done much rowing Jack soon got the hang of the rhythm.

For as long as he could remember, school work had presented Jack with far more problems than sport. He had always found reading and writing quite difficult. One of the teachers had recently told Mum he was slightly dyslexic and Dave had seized on this as yet another opportunity to show off. "You need some extra lessons after school, Jack," he had said. "I'll pay someone."

In fact, Dave had never followed this up. He's a man of words, not a man of action, thought Jack, trying to step up the speed of his rowing and then suddenly losing his balance and sprawling in the dinghy, letting go of one of the oars but keeping a grip on the other.

The oar he had lost immediately began to drift out of reach.

"You idiot!" yelled Dave. He turned to Jack's mum. "I told you it wasn't a job for kids."

But Jack had already scrambled to his feet and was leaning over the bow, trying desperately to reach the drifting oar. He felt terrible. The oars were the most precious things they had. Without one of them they'd just drift.

"Watch it!" yelled Dave, as Jack leant out as far as he could.

"Jack!" shouted Mum.

"I'll hold your ankles," said Carrie. "Then you can lean out more." She got up and grabbed him while Jack leant out even further. There are *no* sharks now, Jack kept telling himself. He just managed to clutch the end of the oar, almost losing it again, but at the last minute just getting a grip. The dinghy again rocked wildly as Carrie pulled Jack back to safety.

"Thanks, Carrie," he gasped. "I'll carry on rowing."

"You won't!" Dave warned him.

But Jack coolly moved back into position and began to row strongly.

No one said anything.

He continued to row.

Dave was looking away and Mum was gazing out at the horizon.

What kind of chance *did* they stand, Jack thought suddenly. Wouldn't it have been more sensible to have stayed around the place where *Mexican Eagle* sank? Surely that was where Air-Sea Rescue might be looking for them? But Jack had no more idea of where *Eagle* had sunk than in which direction Ensenada lay. He continued to row, feeling depressed, putting a lot of effort in, but aware that he could be taking entirely the wrong direction.

How big was the Pacific? Were there shipping lanes? Islands? He realised he was in total ignorance. And what about Juan's dinghy? Where had he got to?

Gradually, the late evening sun slid down towards the sea and there was a glorious sunset which Jack knew they would all have admired if they'd been sitting on a beach. But out here, the dying of the light was seriously threatening.

"There *was* no Mayday call," said Dave suddenly.

"We'd have berthed by now," said Mum in attempted reassurance. "So they'll soon be sending out a search party."

But Dave was not so easily convinced. "Who knows if any particular time was given? I reckon Manual and Juan were running a cowboy outfit."

"Rubbish!" said Mum.

"They were great." Carrie backed her up. "They tried to look after us."

"Look after us?" Dave's voice was incredulous. "They made no attempt to outrun the storm and this dinghy hasn't got any supplies – not even water. I'm parched."

Jack's own throat felt as dry as dust and he kept imagining glasses of cold lemonade.

"We're all thirsty," said Carrie.

"Wait a minute," said Mum, searching under the seat. "There *is* something here after all." But she only pulled out some plastic sheeting and a bucket.

Dave swore but Jack was more hopeful. "If it rains again we could put the bucket out and we'd get some water." This time he saw in his mind's eye a cold jug of lemonade, brimful with ice, and he tried to banish the image.

"Don't be so stupid," said Dave, his voice rising. "Where are the flares? Where are the life jackets?"

"We're *wearing* life jackets." Jack was pulling away at the oars, his arm muscles beginning to hurt. But he didn't want to let himself down in front of Dave.

His stepfather wasn't listening and his voice rose again. "What are they doing about rescuing us? Don't they care?"

"Of course they care," said Mum, turning to Jack. "Let me have a go on the oars now. You've done your stint."

But Dave was the last person Jack wanted to sit next to. "Let me have another five minutes. I've really got into the swing of it."

"You almost lost that oar," said Dave angrily. "You could have cost us our lives."

"Why don't you stop whining?" rapped out Jack, feeling a blister coming up on his right palm which hurt badly. "Just shut up and let me get on with the rowing." As he spoke, Jack realised he'd overstepped the mark this time.

"Don't you speak to me like that," Dave roared, and Jack knew his stepfather was losing control.

Suddenly he was frightened. If Dave *did* lose control, he could capsize them. Turning back, Jack caught Carrie's eye and realised she was thinking the same thing.

"I said – don't speak to me like that!"

Jack didn't reply, and Mum said, "Leave it, Dave. We've got enough trouble without all this."

"Without all what?" snarled Dave. "I'm not taking

any lip from that little boy of yours."

"Shut up!" said Jack, beginning to lose his temper. "Just shut up."

Dave got to his feet and the dinghy began to rock wildly. "I'll sort you out." His voice was shrill and Jack almost laughed, but just stopped himself in time.

"Sit down, Dave," said Mum.

"No."

"You've got to sit down." The dinghy was still rocking and more water was already slopping aboard.

"*Please* sit down," said Carrie. "Jack didn't mean to wind you up."

"Wind me up?" Dave was cruelly mimicking her voice and Jack felt a surge of hatred at his shallow stupidity. Dad would never have behaved this way. But then Jack realised he could hardly remember what Dad looked like, let alone how he behaved.

"Look," said Jack. "Mum's right. We're in enough trouble. Don't let's make it worse. I'm sorry, I was – rude."

But Dave had completely lost control and his voice, already high, had risen to a screech. "Trouble? I'll give you trouble! You're worthless – that's what you are.

Absolutely worthless."

Jack forced himself to keep silent. Now he knew how much Dave loathed him. Well – that was no problem. He felt absolutely the same about his stepfather.

"I'll fix you!" Dave screeched, wobbling towards Jack, fists clenched, the dinghy rocking even more and threatening to capsize as even more water came aboard.

"Dave! You've *got* to stop this." Mum wrapped her hands round Dave's pink knees. "You must sit down."

There was a long pause. Then Dave sat down.

Adrift

Suddenly, Dave seemed to take a grip on himself. "Sorry about that, Jack."

"It's OK."

"Can't have us chaps falling out – not with a couple of damsels in distress."

Jack grinned at Carrie, who gave him a cautious smile. She had obviously been equally scared when Dave had started to crack. If that was the way he was going to be after only a few hours, what was he going to be like over a longer period?

Suddenly Jack was even more afraid, not just of his

unstable stepfather, but of the other insurmountable problems that surrounded them. They had no food or water and although there weren't any sharks around right now, Jack knew they were out there.

"We've got to have a plan," said Jack.

"Dead right," agreed Dave. Jack thought his stepfather had chosen an unfortunate turn of phrase.

Carrie grinned, this time more sardonically, and once again Jack knew she was thinking much the same.

"We should keep someone on the lookout," said Dave. "That means we must draw up a watch rota for the night. If we all go to sleep we stand a good chance of missing out on any rescue attempt." He seemed to be very much back in control now.

"Good thinking," said Jack, giving unwilling praise. "I'll take first watch – I could try some fishing."

"What with?" asked Mum.

Jack looked down at his denim shorts to see a loose thread which he began to unravel and then, bending down, ripped the thread off with his teeth. As he did it, he knew it was an act of sheer desperation.

"You won't get anywhere with that. What about bait?" There was a sneer in Dave's voice.

Jack said nothing, and his mother came to his aid. "At least he's trying," she said.

"Very trying," said Dave with a mirthless laugh.

Jack looked away, suddenly close to tears, feeling humiliated and stupid.

"I'll take the first watch," said Dave. "Then I'll wake your mother. You kids need your beauty sleep."

"I don't," said Jack.

"Neither do I." Carrie was impatient.

"But that's the way it's going to be," said Dave firmly.

For once Jack decided not to argue. His mouth was so dry, suddenly all he wanted to do was to shut his eyes against the image of the lemonade jug full of clinking ice.

Slowly, he shipped the oars. "You thinking of doing any rowing during the night, Dave?" he mumbled as he stumbled over to Carrie and sat down beside her.

"Not while I'm on watch. We're drifting in some kind of current so let's see where that takes us."

Jack curled himself up in a cramped position on the bottom of the dinghy, lying uncomfortably against

Carrie. For a long while he stared up at the night sky and the shimmering stars, feeling incredibly small, as if he didn't matter at all, as if his life could be thrown away and no one would notice.

Shifting uneasily, trying to get more comfortable, Jack's thoughts returned to Manuel's terrible death and the crimson stain that had so slowly disappeared from the surface of the sea. Glancing round, he saw his mother lying behind Dave, who was sitting on the seat and, despite what he had said, rowing slowly and steadily. Suddenly, Dave seemed a reassuring figure. So why *did* he dislike him so much? Well, he was loud and corny and insensitive, always throwing his weight about. But wasn't that an act designed to impress them, to become their leader, to *be* their dad? After all, as Carrie had said, the holiday of a lifetime that had just turned into a disaster must have cost him hundreds of pounds – more like thousands – and Dave had surely spent the money to win family approval, to be accepted.

Dave worked as a chef in a small hotel near where they lived in south London, and Jack was sure he didn't earn a large salary. So he'd saved and made sacrifices for them. And now they were bobbing about in a dinghy on a shark-infested sea.

Jack began to doze and the steady splash of the oars made him fall asleep, despite his cramped position. But then he began to dream. He was swimming desperately and there was no sign of land. The day was clear and the sea was calm, lapping on his shoulders. He was treading water, looking around him, waiting and watching for a fin to appear on the grey-green surface.

Suddenly he saw them. Three fins cutting through the water, heading towards them unerringly.

Then Jack saw that one of his fingers was bleeding, the blood running down his hand into the sea, an incredible amount for such a small cut. He tried to swim away from the crimson stain, but his finger continued to bleed and however hard he swam the crimson continued to spread around him. Jack looked back and saw the surface of the sea was entirely crimson now. Then the three fins appeared, cleaving towards him, with only one purpose. The sharks had scented blood – an ocean of blood.

Now the sharks were almost on him and he had stopped trying to escape and was floating on his back.

They surfaced, jaws open, revealing the razor sharp teeth that made them such efficient killing machines. Jack woke screaming to find that Dave had grabbed his wrist and was holding on to him, trying to be comforting.

Jack wrenched his hand away from Dave's grip and in the moonlight saw the look of hurt in his eyes.

"Bad dream?" whispered Dave.

Jack nodded.

"Your mum and Carrie are still asleep. They didn't hear you, so if we keep quiet, only speak in whispers, they won't wake up."

The night was warm and the full moon lit the gentle swell that rocked the dinghy like a cradle. Jack suddenly felt the need to talk to someone – even if that someone was Dave. The dream had been so bad that he couldn't keep his fears to himself any longer.

"Will the sharks get us too?"

Dave shook his head. "No."

"Why not?"

"Because there's no reason. They only get to be killers when there's blood around." Dave spoke with a fatherly confidence, but Jack could see the flaw.

"They attacked Manuel."

"He was splashing about. Of course he had to – to get back to the boat. It was terribly bad luck." Dave made Manuel's death seem trivial. But Jack still needed to talk, to hear an adult, even Dave, saying everything was going to be all right.

"Seen any ships?" asked Jack hopefully.

"No – but *Mexican Eagle* will have been reported missing by now. They'll come looking."

"Who?"

"The local equivalent of Air-Sea Rescue. A chopper maybe, and boats as well."

Dave again sounded confident and Jack began to feel better. Were they really going to be all right? His throat felt dry and dusty, so dry that he could hardly force the words out. Jack gazed at the swell. Ironically, they were surrounded by water, but it was salty, undrinkable, and the need to drink overcame him to such an extent that slaking his thirst was all he could think about.

Water, water, everywhere, Nor any drop to drink. 'The Rime of the Ancient Mariner' filled Jack's mind.

"I'm so thirsty," he said.

"So am I," said Dave, and he gave Jack a rueful smile.

"Will there be more rain?"

"I don't know."

Jack was annoyed with himself. Why was he behaving like a child, permanently craving reassurance? But at least Dave hadn't lied to him about the rain and Jack's respect for his stepfather went up a notch or two.

"I'll make sure the bucket's in position." Dave gave a croaky laugh, and Jack realised his throat was as dry as his own. There was a strange comfort in that, sharing hardship with a man he had always disliked.

"So we're shipwrecked together." Dave's normally irritating hearty manner was reduced to a whisper.

Jack was silent, not knowing how to reply, waiting for his stepfather to make himself clearer.

Eventually he did. "I want us to get on, Jack."

"Mmm."

"I know it's hard and I haven't handled it right."

Jack shrugged.

"I'm a clumsy oaf."

"No—" Jack wanted to help him out, but didn't know how. He began to torture himself with a new image – an enormous bottle of mineral water, fresh from the fridge. He *had* to stop thinking about it and try to listen to what Dave was saying. Jack felt guilty, knowing that Dave was trying to reach him. "It's not been easy," he muttered.

"Of course it hasn't. You see me as an interloper. I know how much you loved your dad and I'm not trying to replace him."

Jack looked up at Dave in surprise. He still saw the round face, the clumsy body, but this time didn't immediately seek a way of sending him up. Jack realised that he was recognising his stepfather as a person for the first time and he felt moved.

"I just want to be friends, not enemies."

Jack nodded.

"And the same applies to Carrie."

He nodded again.

"I want to get through to you both."

"Yes. I'm sorry."

"There's nothing to be sorry about."

"I didn't mean to be so rotten to you."

"I know why you were. Now – get some more sleep, and I'm sure we'll be picked up soon."

"We could have been going in the wrong direction."

"Whatever the direction, a helicopter would find us in minutes." Dave sounded very sure.

"Then why haven't they?"

"They will. Soon. Very soon." Dave now sounded so ultra-confident that he was very convincing. Fatherly and convincing.

Jack curled up again on the damp floor and suddenly fell fast asleep, as if a curtain had been drawn over his eyes.

Rain

Jack woke to moisture on his face.
Then to his amazement there was a drop of water
on his lips and he was licking the wonderful liquid
down, wanting more, lots more. Could he be
dreaming again?

He looked around him, seeing grey dawn clouds
that were spitting rain. Rain, glorious rain!

Jack struggled to his knees, knocking against Carrie,
making her mumble and cry out in her sleep. But he
didn't think about Carrie. He didn't think about anyone.
The dinghy was damp and he must have slept heavily

through the rain. How had he done that? All he had thought about was water, and now it was everywhere.

Then he saw Dave. He had his head in the bucket. Was he being sick?

Or had he managed to collect some water and was surreptitiously drinking the precious liquid under their noses? All Jack's suspicions about his stepfather returned and what had happened last night was forgotten. But how could Dave have collected so much water? To have even half filled the bucket would have meant a downpour of torrential rain and surely this would have woken them all?

"What are you doing?"

Dave looked up guiltily. His lips were wet.

"I caught some water in the plastic sheeting your mother found. Tipped it into the bucket. I was just taking a look – seeing how much there was to go round." He was very flustered.

"You were drinking."

"Of course I wasn't." But Dave's damp lips gave everything away.

Jack felt a great rage boil up inside him. Dave was back to being Dave. Dave the boaster. Dave the clown.

Dave who had always let him down and was now letting them all down.

Jack looked up at the sky. The grey clouds were easing and the sun was filtering through. He locked his eyes into Dave's and all he could see was guilt.

"I've been working out how the water should be rationed," said Dave, his voice quavering.

"Let me see." Jack got up and the dinghy rocked.

"Careful—"

Now he was standing beside Dave and staring down into the bucket. There was a tiny pool of water in the bottom. But he could also see a wet line where there must have been just a fraction more. Jack gazed at Dave's blubbery lips again.

"I know what you did."

"I simply tested—"

"You drank as much as you could."

"Rubbish. There was hardly anything *to* drink." Dave paused. "Maybe just enough to moisten your lips."

Jack grabbed the handle, but Dave wouldn't give the bucket up.

"You'll spill what's left." Dave made the fatal verbal slip and their eyes met again.

Jack knew that he had definitely helped himself to the tiny pool of water that should have been shared.

Dave released his grip and Jack took the bucket over to his mother who was stirring in her sleep, her head uncomfortably wedged under the seat in the prow.

"Mum."

"What is it?" She struggled to get up, looking round, startled by where she was, temporarily unable to remember what had happened. Then she did and her eyes widened with fear.

"I've got some water."

"No—"

"There's not much. Hardly anything in fact."

His mother gazed down into the bucket.

Jack was about to tell her that Dave had drunk some of what little there was, but something stopped him. What would he have done if he'd been awake? If he'd collected the precious liquid while the others slept? Would he have guzzled it? Of course he wouldn't. But a nagging doubt remained.

"There was some rain in the night. We slept through it."

"Is this all we managed to collect?" His mother

looked around her, as if there'd been some kind of mistake.

"It was just a light shower," said Dave. "I would have woken you, but it was over in a minute."

Jack wished Dave would stop overcompensating. But the doubt still nagged at him. What would he have done? He'd have shared the water. Of course he would.

Mum looked at Dave in bewilderment. "Did you collect this?"

"I know it's not much."

"Why didn't you wake us?"

"I told you – it didn't last long enough and I was busy collecting water. I didn't want – to miss a drop."

Mum nodded, satisfied.

"Carrie," she called. "We've got some water. Not much – but just enough to moisten your lips."

Carrie sat up and a delighted smile spread over her face.

"There isn't much," Mum warned her again. "I suggest we take a sip." She bent her head and took her sip, passing the bucket to Jack. "Be very careful," she said.

Jack took his sip, remembering Dave with his head

in the bucket, drinking as much as he reckoned he could get away with. The taste of the sip of water was wonderful – incredibly wonderful – but he only wanted more.

"Whose turn next?" he asked.

Dave intervened. "I'll go last. Take the bucket to Carrie, but be careful. Don't spill a drop."

"I won't."

He crawled over to Carrie on his hands and knees, making the dinghy rock lazily. She put her head down eagerly while Jack gently tilted the bucket, taking a sip of water, then looking desperate for more. "Will it rain again?" Carrie gasped, gazing up at the sky that was now turning a bright blue, the sun already getting warmer. "How could we have missed it?"

No one replied.

"I'll sacrifice my turn," said Dave.

Jack hesitated. Why didn't he tell them all how Dave had betrayed them. But he couldn't get the words out, for he was still wondering if he would have drunk the water and made the same betrayal. He hoped he wouldn't but Jack couldn't be sure.

"You can't do that," said Mum.

Reluctantly, Jack passed his stepfather the bucket and Dave took his sips, rather self-consciously – or so Jack supposed.

The morning sun was getting brighter and hotter all the time. Gulls began to fly low, seeing if there was anything to eat.

But there was nothing.

Only thirst, and now Jack was being persecuted by the familiar painful images of ice cold water, in ice cold jugs.

Dave had suddenly gone to sleep in the bows, large and red and clumsy looking, snoring away and getting on Jack's nerves.

"Can't you stop him snoring, Mum?"

She shook her head. She was crouched on the seat in the prow, gazing at the ocean.

"Are they looking for us?" asked Carrie.

"I'm sure they are."

"Why don't they find us then?"

"It's a big ocean."

"*That* big?"

"I expect we drifted," Jack said. "Or Dave was

rowing in the wrong direction."

They dozed, throats parched, and woke feeling incredibly hungry, dizzy from the lack of food, to see a haze that was slowly turning to mist rolling up on the horizon.

"Does that mean rain?" Carrie asked.

"I don't know." But Mum sounded hopeful.

Dave woke with a final snorting snore and Jack remembered that he and his stepfather had actually got close to each other last night. But Jack was now sure Dave had drunk their water ration and could never trust him again. So much for closeness, he thought.

Glancing at his watch, Jack saw the time was just after midday and the mist was rapidly turning to fog as the dinghy lazily rocked in the gentle swell. Without any shelter, and above all any progress, they were beginning to feel deeply depressed.

"I'd better start rowing," said Dave.

"Let me." Jack spoke so fiercely that Mum and Carrie looked at him in surprise. "I need to be doing something," he said hurriedly.

"I'm not sure that we *should* be rowing," said Mum. "We don't even know what direction we should take.

We could be putting ourselves out of the search area."

"I agree," said Carrie. "We should wait."

"Dave took us outside the search area," snapped Jack, seeking to blame his stepfather.

"I can assure you we haven't come *that* far," said Dave hesitantly, looking vulnerable.

"So I can row then," said Jack.

"No." Dave was adamant. "There's no point. I agree with your mother and Carrie. We should let her drift."

"But you said—"

Dave shrugged. "Don't let's push our luck."

"You pushed yours, didn't you?" spat out Jack, suddenly cracking up and knowing he was about to embark on a subject he'd regret.

"What do you mean by that?"

"We slept through that shower of rain."

"So?"

"And you had more than your fair share of the tiny amount of water you collected."

There was a long silence while his mother looked angrily at Jack. Carrie stared out to sea. Dave looked hurt. Then he said, "It was only a quick shower – that's why I didn't wake you. All I managed to get was a few drops and that's God's truth."

Jack gave him a look of utter contempt.

"Wait a minute," said Carrie. "At least Dave tried to get us water. You're completely out of order, Jack. Dave wouldn't betray us like that."

"He wouldn't?" sneered Jack.

"You should apologise to Dave," snapped Mum. "How dare you make accusations like that?"

"I saw him with his head in the bucket making slurping noises." Jack knew he sounded childish. "I saw him – you didn't."

"Look, Jack." Dave seemed cool, calm and confident again. "I wouldn't dream of doing something so selfish and so cowardly." His voice shook. "You may think all kinds of bad things about me, but there's a limit."

"You don't have to dream about drinking our water." Jack knew he must sound as if he was whining now. "You took it for real."

"Jack!" shouted Mum.

"You're out of order," yelled Carrie again.

"Don't worry," said Dave. "The situation's obviously getting to Jack. It's getting to all of us, so I understand why your brother isn't thinking straight."

Jack didn't know where to look, sensing that everyone was against him. Mum and Carrie looked ashamed, while Dave had an air of martyrdom.

Suddenly he'd lost out and Jack felt like a naughty, selfish kid. He sat down, trying to get as far away from the others as possible, but in such a tiny space he had no chance of succeeding.

Meanwhile the fog rolled in until they could hardly see a metre ahead of them.

"No one will spot us now." Jack clasped his hands round his knees as if he was pleased the fog had come down.

"Shut up, Jack," said Carrie.

"Don't be so childish," said Mum.

A long silence lengthened and Jack had never felt so humiliated. He'd pay Dave back for this. Somehow.

A Missed Chance

The chattering noise seemed to come out of nowhere and when Jack looked up the sound was directly overhead. "It's a helicopter!" he yelled.

But the fog was too dense to see anything.

"They can't see us." Dave sounded on the edge of hysteria again. "If only we had flares – but that idiot Manuel didn't think of—"

"We'll have to shout." Jack stood up and the dinghy rocked from side to side. "Really shout." He began to bawl at the top of his voice, "HELP US!" over and over again. The others joined in, screaming, shouting, imploring.

"YOU'VE GOT TO HELP US," Jack bawled.

Then the chattering sound began to grow distant and to his horror he realised they'd neither been seen nor heard.

Their chance had gone.

But still the four of them yelled and shouted – praying that the helicopter would return. But apart from the lapping of the calm water and the mewing of a single gull there was no sound at all. The helicopter had gone.

Now the lone seagull sounded mocking as its mewing continued above their heads.

Slowly, very slowly, their shouting subsided.

They looked at each other in grim silence.

Then the dinghy suddenly lurched.

"Something's underneath us," whispered Carrie.

"Maybe we've got ourselves a sea turtle," said Dave. "If we move fast we could have a meal. And there'll be eggs if the turtle's a female..." Dave's voice died away as he realised how ridiculous he must sound.

No one replied.

There was no more bumping and the dinghy stabilised in the calm sea.

Jack looked up at the sky. Ironically, now it was too late, the mist was rolling away and the sun was struggling to break through. Would the helicopter come back?

Then there was a slight nudge and the dinghy rocked again, but only slightly. Turtle? There was a tense silence. Now Jack was waiting for another nudge and he went rigid, cold in the warmth of the sun. His dry mouth seemed, if possible, to get drier. Jack thought again of cold water. Ice cold water in an ice cold jug. If only he could push the thought away, but the vision kept returning, torturing him.

Another nudge, this time slightly harder. Again the dinghy rocked.

Jack glanced across at his mother and she stared back. He watched her fear grow. For the first time he was seeing her as someone vulnerable and afraid. He had always regarded her as Mum – a source of massive, blanketing reassurance. If she said things were going to be all right, then things *were* all right. He remembered the occasions when he'd sat exams, played in a rugby match, gone to France to stay with his penfriend, set off on an adventure holiday, cycled the London to Brighton bike ride, run in a cross-country race – she'd always said it was going to be all right, and sure enough whatever he had undertaken *had* been all right.

He had known, of course, how much Mum had suffered over Dad's death. Hadn't they all? And of course she had never been able to say that was "all right". For everything else though, Mum had been like a lucky charm, a talisman all his life. But Mum had another name; she was a woman called Laura. Laura couldn't make everything all right. Only Mum.

There was another nudge, this time a little weaker and the dinghy hardly rocked at all, but the tension was mounting all the time.

"Are you sure it's a turtle?"

"Pretty sure," said Dave.

"And I'm sure Dave's right," Mum croaked and then looked away. She was not Mum any longer. She was Laura. Nothing was going to be all right.

Jack closed his eyes and vividly remembered the day

his mum had married Dave. He could see the registry office now, with them standing in front of the official. His mum had been wearing a white outfit which seemed to Jack incredibly wrong. She had looked young and vulnerable. Dave's pin-striped suit had a cutaway collar and he was wearing a floral tie. The suit was enormous and had made him look even bigger; Jack had had the impression that his mum had been trapped by a monster with red hair – a kind of evil-looking troll. He had shared his thoughts with Carrie later. At first she had laughed, and then, moments later, cried.

There was another nudge.

Dave laughed, but the sound was more like a bark in the silence. The dinghy rocked as the nudge came again, this time much more sharply. "I'm going to take a look-see," said Dave suddenly.

"You're going into the water?" gasped Carrie.

"Don't be a fool, Dave." Had Laura taken Mum's place for ever, Jack wondered.

He said nothing. Was Dave showing off yet again? Jack suddenly remembered the talk they had had last night when Dave had actually seemed human. They had reached each other, but not for long, and now he hated him as much as ever – maybe a little more after the bucket episode and Jack's humiliation at the hands of the whole family. Let him go overboard. Let him be shark bait.

"I'm just going to take a peek." Dave leant his large, pink, sweaty body over the side of the dinghy and peered into the water. "It's gone cloudy," he said at last.

"Maybe we're on a sandbank," said Jack, risking a comment and waiting to be disagreed with.

Dave had now stretched both his legs and torso across the dinghy. Jack hoped he wouldn't touch him. Being crowded together in the dinghy was beginning to revolt him.

"Be careful, Dave. You don't want to—"

There was another nudge.

"Definitely a turtle," said Dave in a voice of great authority.

"Can you see it?" said Jack eagerly.

"Not exactly *see* it."

"Then what?"

"Hang on. There's something—" Dave leant over

even further and, for a moment, Jack thought he was going to topple in.

The next nudge was even harder and then Dave began to scream.

Holed

"What is it?" gasped Carrie as
Dave hauled himself back inside the dinghy but,
before he could answer, the huge head of the
shark reared up out of the water, the slit mouth
open, the dozens of white teeth bared, eyes
staring. The sheet of spray soaked them all, but it
was the head that terrified Jack, a head that was
huge, much larger than the shark that had killed
Manuel. Then the shark reared up again and Jack
could see cuts and scars on its head, no doubt
caused by battling with its prey.

Dave went on screaming.

Laura and Carrie gazed at the shark in utter horror, but Jack felt curiously numb and stared silently into the menacing, hungry eyes.

Suddenly, the huge bulk vanished back into the ocean with more spray settling over the dinghy and then reared up for the third time, its mouth open again, upper jaw protruding to display its teeth.

The shark seemed to be asserting itself, warning off other predators. But were they its target, wondered Jack. If so, they were done for. They all stared at each other in silent desperation, waiting to see what would happen next.

Then, with incredible relief, he saw the shark turn. A seal had surfaced to their right. The shark leapt out of the water and just missed as the seal dived and weaved. The shark followed, and then leapt again, the huge body soaring over the surface of the sea and this time reaching the seal, biting it deeply.

Jack was horrified.

Dave was whimpering now while Mum and Carrie were completely silent as they watched the carnage, blood spurting from the seal which was thrashing about noisily in the water. The shark veered away and then attacked yet again, launching its torpedo-shaped body at the seal, the water seeming to explode around it. The huge dark fin disappeared under the surface and then came up again as the shark bit once more into the seal which was now floating on the surface, the crimson stain spreading.

As the shark began to feed off the seal Jack turned away, not able to take any more. He felt as if the attack had gone on for hours, although in fact it had been over in seconds.

Then Dave began to scream again.

Jack leant forward and grabbed Dave's wrist. He just *had* to stop his screaming somehow.

"Dave!" yelled Jack, squeezing his wrist as hard as he could. "You've got to stop. Shut up, now – you've got to shut up."

Dave stopped screaming.

"Well done, Jack," muttered Mum.

Jack felt pleased at the praise, but that didn't last long.

Dave was moaning softly now, his eyes were wide

with terror, still watching the shark tearing at the flesh of the seal.

"Are you OK?" said Jack.

Dave didn't reply.

The nudge came again.

The dinghy rocked.

Carrie muttered something and cringed back.

Jack could hear his mother beginning to pray, asking God to help them. Dave was silent, staring ahead.

Jack squeezed his arm despite the fact that he was certain another shark was just below them. "It's going to be all right," he said, unconsciously imitating his mother's familiar reassurance. "It's going to be all right." Then he turned round to see that the first shark had satisfied its appetite. The seal slopped up and down on the swell, blood spreading from the massive wounds. Was that how they were all going to look in a moment?

Jack waited for the next nudge, sweating and trembling all over.

But it didn't come.

No ferocious head rose from the depths.

The dinghy was rocking up and down, and they went on waiting for something to happen, for the attack to begin.

But there was no attack.

Jack didn't know whether the second shark had gone away or not. There was no sign of a fin cutting a path towards them and the nudging of the dinghy had definitely stopped. Why didn't the second shark emerge? Why didn't it start feeding off the seal?

Maybe the second shark wasn't hungry, or maybe it had gone after another victim, hunting beneath the surface. Jack looked again at the half-eaten seal and heard the screaming of gulls as they flew in to take their share of the kill.

Then Mum yelled. "We're leaking!"

Jack saw that water was slowly seeping into the old dinghy and guessed that the rubber was rotten.

"Start baling," he yelled at the others. "Start baling now!"

They all four began to bale with the bucket, emptied of the last of the drinking water, the scoops and failing that, with their hands. But the water kept coming in and their baling couldn't keep pace with the leak.

Eventually they were forced to give up baling, realising the task was hopeless, and they lay exhausted in the dinghy, the oars useless on the deck, as she sank lower and lower in the water.

They all avoided eye contact, not daring to look at each other in case someone gave up and admitted defeat. But what was there to hope for, wondered Jack. Soon they would be swimming for their lives, knowing that last desperate effort wouldn't last for long, for the sharks would soon return – and devour them in minutes.

We're finished, thought Jack. Completely and absolutely finished.

Then he saw his mother put a hand to her eyes and a terrible grief consumed Jack. She was crying and there was nothing he could do. He sat up and tried to reach for her hand, but she suddenly struggled to her knees, staring ahead intently from the prow. She seemed fascinated.

"What is it?" he asked as the water lapped around his ankles.

"Land," she said flatly.

"What do you mean – land?" demanded Dave, staring at Mum as if she'd gone mad. "There can't be—"

"I think there can," she said hesitantly. "I really think there can."

Jack stood up and stared into the distance, seeing a dark mass that at first he thought was cloud. But wasn't it too dense? Suddenly he had the impression that the dark mass was getting smaller. Could they be drifting away from it? His mouth was so dry now that he could hardly speak, but eventually he managed to blurt out, "We need to row."

"Row?" repeated Dave. "I thought we agreed we shouldn't do that. The helicopter could be back soon. We don't want to miss the—"

But Carrie interrupted, gabbling in panic. "It really is land and we've got to get there. We can't just wait for this stupid helicopter. Anyway, the dinghy's half full of water and it won't be long before she sinks. Jack's right. We should go for whatever it is. The sharks could come back any minute."

"We should stay still. Very still," snapped Dave. "The moment I start rowing the shark could hear the oars and come and get us."

"I don't think sharks hear like that," said Carrie. "They feel vibrations."

"What do *you* know about it?" snarled Dave.

"All right." Jack tried to seem calm. "Let's put the decision to the vote."

Dave looked taken aback. "That's crazy," he muttered.

"No it's not," said Carrie. "Putting the decision to the vote is fair."

Dave scowled as Jack turned to his mother and Carrie.

"All those in favour of investigating, raise your hand."

Carrie put up both hands and Mum simply half raised her wrist, gazing at Dave almost pleadingly.

"And who's against?" rapped out Jack.

Dave put up his arm in what seemed like half-hearted defiance.

"Let me row," said Jack, making a statement and not asking a question.

Dave shrugged as Jack retrieved the oars that were floating in the dinghy and began to row with long, painful strokes, while the others baled as hard as they could. Half full of water, the dinghy was a dead weight, but Jack made slow but steady progress, sweat streaming into his eyes, his muscles aching. He kept glancing over his shoulder to see that the land mass was slightly nearer and his hopes soared.

Carrie looked uneasy and Jack wondered if she might have changed sides. Sides? What was he thinking about? They were somewhere in shark-infested waters with a leaking dinghy and distant land that might just be a cloud; to survive they had to work as a team.

Jack was finding rowing the waterlogged dinghy increasingly difficult. His arms hurt so much that he knew there were tears in his eyes and he tried to blink them away, determined not to ask Dave to take over.

"Want me to have a go?" asked Mum.

"I'm OK."

"No you're not," said Dave. "You can't be a hero all the time. Isn't it my turn?" He sounded hesitant, unsure of himself. "You're great, you kids," he said, but for once he didn't sound patronising.

"You'll have to wait," said Mum. "It's my turn."

"Now hold on, Laura—"

"Do shut up, Dave. I'm quite capable of rowing a dinghy, even if it *is* half full of water."

"And so am I," said Carrie indignantly.

Jack nodded, still blinking away the tears of exhaustion, and splashed over to the stern while Mum changed places with him, the dinghy rocking and listing slightly. Jack knew they didn't have much time before she sank but continued to bale as hard as he could.

And suppose the land *was* cloud? That would be too much to bear.

Jack scanned the surface for a sighting of any fins, but all he could see was sunlight glittering and sparkling to such an extent that the dazzle made him screw up his eyes.

Mum rowed strongly and in a slow rhythm, and Jack realised she was making more progress than he had, although the dinghy had now shipped even more water.

He glanced ahead at what he prayed was land. Slowly, a long, low coastline appeared and Jack was sure he could see waves breaking over rocks. He gave a loud cheer and the others joined in. Never had Jack felt so elated.

"Could this be Mexico – or is it an island?" he asked Dave.

"I don't know," was all that Dave could say.

"It's an island," said Carrie. "I'm sure it's an island."

Jack took a careful look, but couldn't be sure for there was still no real indication where the sea ended and the land began.

Now the coast was nearer and Jack was certain that Carrie had been right and they *were* looking at a long island with a rocky foreshore.

"Do you think there's any water there?" he asked desperately.

"There might be," said Dave hopefully.

"I'm sure there's water." Carrie was determined to be optimistic. "Can I help row now, Mum?"

She nodded eagerly, shipping the oars, and as she did so they all noticed that they were now slowly drifting in a current which seemed to be taking them towards the island.

Carrie struggled across the dinghy towards her

mother, but as she reached her, the dinghy rocked so violently Jack thought they were going to capsize at any moment.

Again he nervously scanned the sea but there was still no sign of a fin.

"How far away are we?" Jack asked Dave.

"About half a mile. Come on, keep baling! If we can keep the water level lower, then we've got a better chance of making a landing."

Jack continued to bale and so did Dave, working as hard as they could, the level of the water seeming to remain the same however great their efforts.

When Jack looked up again, the island seemed just as far away. Were they making any progress at all? Had the current changed? Perhaps it wasn't taking them to the island after all.

Head down, Jack started baling again, not daring to look up and be disappointed. At last he could bear it no longer – he looked – and what he saw made him sigh with relief. They *were* getting nearer.

"Great work, Carrie," he said. "We're getting close. Do you want me to take your oar?" Jack asked, seeing how tired she was.

She shook her head. "What are you trying to say, Jack? That you can row faster?"

"I wasn't saying that."

"That's what you were thinking," she insisted, the sweat pouring down her drawn face.

"I only wanted to help," he muttered.

"You only want to put me down – to convince everyone you can do better than me. Well – you can't. I'm going to help land us on that island if it's the very last thing I do."

"Shut up, you two," gasped Mum.

"We haven't got far to go." Dave looked up from his useless baling and Jack saw that the dinghy was much lower in the water than before. In fact the gentle swell was beginning to break over her bows.

He wondered how far they still had to row. Two hundred metres? Three hundred metres? Jack could now see surf breaking over rock. Was there a channel to the shore? For a moment Jack panicked. Surely they were going to be torn to pieces on the rocks? And if the rocks didn't get them, then the sharks would...

"Does that reef run right round the island?" His mother sounded fearful, and to Jack she was Laura again – someone who wanted him to work the miracles for a change.

"There must be a gap somewhere," said Jack with a confidence he didn't feel.

But unexpectedly Dave came to his aid. "Yes, Jack's right. There must be a gap."

Jack looked at his stepfather in surprise. Could they really be allies?

As a result of their mutual encouragement, Carrie and Mum began to row much more strongly, while Jack returned to the baling with greater zeal.

Slowly, agonisingly slowly, they approached the island until they could distinctly see the line of rocks over which the waves were breaking.

Looking up from the endless baling, Jack could see that the rocks were jagged and sharp. If they got washed up on to this reef, he knew they would have very little chance of survival. They would be cut to ribbons. Desperately glancing down the line of fortress-like rocks, Jack thought he could see a gap through which the waves roared and tumbled, ending up in a cloud of spray.

"There's a channel," he shouted at Carrie. "It's the only way through."

Carrie glanced over her shoulder and nodded, trying to make for the gap by pulling even harder on her oar. But the boat was now weighed down with water, and however quickly Jack and Dave baled it was too heavy to steer.

As they approached the reef, the current was stronger and Dave yelled at Carrie, "You've got to pull harder. It's down to you. Ease off, Laura. We're going on to the reef."

"I can't," Carrie shouted back. "I can't turn her." Carrie's eyes were wild with fear and she was grunting with the pain of trying to stop the inevitable.

"Let me row," said Dave. "I'm much stronger than either of you."

He was already on his feet and splashing towards Carrie and Mum to take over the oars and, realising that he was right, they stood up, struggling to keep their balance, and then moved out of the way.

Panting and gasping, but determined, Dave took the oars and with his face screwed up in anxiety, put all the strength he could into turning the dinghy away from the jagged reef towards the gap where the spray rose high into the blue sky. As he rowed, Dave yelled and swore, his red face soaked in sweat, the panic building in his eyes.

Instinctively, Jack shouted, "Go for it, Dave! You can do it!"

Dave nodded as if in appreciation of his unexpected encouragement, and slowly, very slowly and unwillingly, the dinghy began to turn as Jack kept up his shouting, desperate to ensure he supported Dave in his virtually impossible task.

"Go for it, Dave. You can do it! You *are* doing it!" he bellowed, and a painful smile fleetingly crossed his stepfather's face.

Dave's breathing was laboured, grunting and groaning, building up his willpower.

Jack continued to shout and the others joined in, imploring, encouraging, urging him on to greater strengths.

"You *are* doing it," shouted Jack. "You're really making a difference." And he was. Jack and Carrie and their mother returned to their baling duties, trying to lighten the load for Dave, who, with the veins bulging in his forehead, swore and prayed as the waterlogged dinghy eventually turned away from the reef.

Swimming for Shore

Jack now realised there was the added threat of being so low in the water that if a wave broke over them they'd be swamped. But the rollers continued without breaking and Dave rowed as hard as he could, keeping them away from the rocks and the deadly pull of the tide.

Then Jack saw the gap, a boiling patch of sea where the waves crashed through to a sandy beach, rebounding on themselves and sending up even higher clouds of spray.

Even if we capsize, thought Jack, we might be able

to swim through the channel to the beach – or would they be dragged out again by the suction as the waves retreated over the reef?

Now they were approaching the gap and Dave turned the dinghy towards it, trying to steer so she would pass through somewhere in the middle without being thrown against the rocks on either side. Maybe we do have a chance, thought Jack, not bothering to bale any more, and when he looked round he could see that Mum and Carrie had stopped baling too. They were out of control and completely at the mercy of the current. Jack knew their chances of getting through the gap unscathed were slim and they might capsize any moment.

Then, high on a roller, the dinghy began to turn sideways and there was no longer anything that Dave could do to steer her. Decisively, he shipped the oars and the dinghy slowly began to spin round on the gathering crest.

Through the rocks, Jack could see a wide beach of white sand which looked safe and welcoming, but he was more sure than ever they'd have to swim for it. Meanwhile the dinghy was circling faster.

"We'll have to swim for the beach," Jack yelled and the others gazed back at him indecisively. Then the swirling of the dinghy began to speed up until, suddenly and without warning, the next crest got under the hull and they were thrown out into the boiling surf.

As he was pushed and pulled by the waves, Jack struck out in a fast crawl. Heading for the beach and trying desperately to avoid the rocks, he saw that Mum and Carrie were doing the same. They were all strong swimmers and, at home, the three of them regularly went to the swimming pool together, swimming length after length, building up their stamina just for fun and exercise. Now this was really paying off, because there was an undertow from the rebounding waves and Jack knew if they didn't swim hard they'd simply be pulled out to sea again.

Then he had a sudden thought. Where was Dave? He couldn't see him anywhere and remembered that his stepfather had once admitted he was "not much of a swimmer".

Turning, he saw him floundering, doing a feeble breaststroke but doggedly making progress. Treading water, fighting against the strong pull of the tide, Jack saw that Dave, in desperation, was pulling more strongly and was almost level to the incoming and outgoing crests as they clashed together in a frenzied plume of spray.

Jack gazed round him and saw Mum and Carrie had somehow managed to swim through the colliding waves and were now beyond the pull of the tide, each on a crest, being hurled towards the beach.

"Go for it, Dave!" yelled Jack. "You'll get there." But then he realised that his stepfather was being pulled back by the tide, only just managing to cling on to a spar of rock that had been worn smooth by the waves, the surf breaking over him, threatening to make him lose his tenuous grip.

"Stay there!" yelled Jack above the thundering spray. "I'm coming to help you."

Dave shook his head, still grimly clinging on.

Jack swam over to him, fighting against the pull of the tide until he eventually managed to reach his stepfather.

"Make a last effort," Jack shouted.

"I can't. I keep getting swept back."

"It's not far."

They both looked ahead to see Mum and Carrie standing on the white sand, waving at them. Jack was worried they might try to swim out to help Dave. If they tried, he was sure that they'd get swept out to sea again. They'd be too exhausted to battle the waves for a second time.

"Stay where you are!" Jack yelled, but Mum and Carrie just stood there. Jack realised that he'd never make himself heard above the fury of the surf. "Try again," he shouted to Dave. "I'm frightened they'll come in after us. If they do they won't be strong enough to stop being pulled out."

Dave nodded and Jack was relieved to be actually communicating with his stepfather.

"I'll swim beside you. All you need is a bit of extra strength – a bit of extra willpower."

Dave nodded again and was about to let go of the rock, but Jack, who had been glancing over his shoulder at the state of the tide, suddenly saw a single fin cutting through the waves towards them.

*

Dave latched on to Jack's gaze, and gave a little whimper of fear. "It's bad enough already," he gasped.

"Maybe the thing'll go away."

They watched in horrified fascination as the fin began to level with them, the shark easily handling the pressure of the tide. Then the fin disappeared.

"Maybe it's found something to feed on," said Jack uneasily. "If we stay as still as we can, the shark might not see us."

Dave didn't reply, smothering another whimper and then closing his eyes. Something brushed against Jack's legs and he let out a cry of terror.

"I'm going to take a look underwater," he said, his fear bringing on a sudden rush of adrenalin.

"Don't move," Dave pleaded.

But Jack was already underwater, opening his eyes, silently screaming and swallowing water, as he saw a giant black squid uncoiling its tentacles, lazily moving them like fronds.

Although the squid revolted him at such close quarters, Jack stayed where he was, looking for any sign of the shark. But he couldn't see anything, and slowly pulled himself back to the surface, trying to control his spluttering and choking.

Dave's eyes were wide with terror.

"Let me take one last look," Jack yelled at him.

He dived again, opening his eyes in the murky depths. The squid had retreated behind a rocky outcrop with only one tentacle trailing and a number of small grey fish swimming around him. They didn't look big enough for even a baby squid to feed on.

There were some larger fish further away, another squid trailing tentacles, a number of smaller, lizard-like fish with miniature feet perched on a rock and a jellyfish with its membrane parachute. There was still no sign of the shark.

But when Jack bobbed up for the second time he gasped, while Dave stared ahead as the fin circled.

"It's coming," said Dave with a sob in his voice.

"Stay still."

"What do you think I'm doing?"

"Just don't move."

Jack gazed at the fin hypnotically, imagining the monstrous bulk underneath.

Dave closed his eyes as the shark lazily circled towards them, and Jack prayed as he had never prayed before.

"Please, God – don't let it see us. Please, God, let us get to the beach."

He could just make out the figures of Mum and Carrie on the white sand, looking bleached out by the sun, completely motionless, staring out to sea, shading their eyes. They seemed like statues. Time stood still. They were all frozen in the moment.

Trying to pull himself together, Jack's eyes returned to the circling fin. Then, suddenly, the fin wasn't circling any more. The shark was coming straight towards them.

Marooned

We've had it, thought Jack. Maybe the two of them constituted a light meal, or were they just a snack? He almost laughed aloud at the thought of working out what a shark's daily diet was, and then the fear swamped him again like a freezing tide and he began to shake all over, waiting for the first bite, the first agony.

Suddenly, the fin changed direction. Unaccountably, it headed for the open sea, occasionally buried by the surf, but continuing in a straight line, eventually disappearing through the gap.

Petrified, Dave and Jack clung to the rock, waiting for the thing to come back, sure it was playing some kind of game with them. But soon they saw the shark surface near the dinghy which was half underwater, stuck in a cluster of sharp rocks.

"Let's go," said Jack.

"I'm so weak," muttered Dave. "I'll never make the beach."

"You've got to try."

"I'll be dragged out to sea."

"Not if you can just get beyond where the waves meet. You'll be OK. You've got the willpower. Now use it."

"Give me a minute."

"We have to go now, Dave," said Jack desperately. "The shark could come back."

"All right." Dave reluctantly released his grip. "You'll wait for me?"

"I'll swim alongside you," promised Jack, not knowing how possible that might be.

Dave nodded and they both struck out for the beach.

Jack watched Dave as he struggled, wondering

whether he was going to make it. But he seemed to be swimming a little more strongly than before.

Just as they were about to reach the point where the waves rebounded on each other, Jack dived into the tumult and resurfaced, feeling the tide tug at him, but less strongly than he had imagined. Could it be on the turn?

Anxiously glancing round, Jack saw to his surprise that in spite of his clumsy breaststroke Dave was close behind.

"Keep going," yelled Jack, as he knew there was still a considerable undertow, and if they stopped fighting the current they could both still be swept back. Increasing his speed, Jack finally arrived in the shallows and staggered to his feet, seeing Dave only a few metres behind but swimming weakly.

"Come to me," he yelled, but Dave was only dog-paddling now and was gradually being pulled back to where the incoming and outgoing waves clashed. "Come to me, Dave!" Jack bellowed over and over again, and Dave suddenly made a last supreme effort, coming alongside him, staggering to his feet, falling and then struggling up yet again.

Jack grabbed his stepfather's wrist and pulled him towards the steeply shelving beach.

This was the last effort, a joint effort, and although Jack didn't have the strength to drag Dave along with him, the contact seemed to be encouraging, as his stepfather floundered behind him until they both collapsed on the white sand, the tide washing at their ankles in defeat.

Jack lay face down on the hot sand, gasping for breath, unable to believe he was on dry land again, after all they had been through.

He looked up and saw Carrie sitting beside him, hands clasped round her knees, while Jack heard Mum muttering to Dave.

Jack sat up, still breathing heavily, and stared into Carrie's eyes with a combination of wonder and joy. "We made it."

"Thank God," she said.

"I was praying," gasped Jack. "I don't think I've done that since I was a kid."

"So was I," said Carrie.

Jack gazed out to sea. "I just can't believe what's happened."

"You'll have to."

"Let's go and explore," Jack said, with a sudden burst of energy. "We might find some water and even some food."

Carrie looked at him doubtfully.

"Rainwater must collect somewhere," persisted Jack.

"Do you think so?" she asked eagerly.

"I don't know," said Jack, not wanting to take responsibility for her disappointment.

They both got up and walked over to their mother who had an arm round Dave's shoulders, comforting him as he wept openly with relief.

Jack felt a twinge of jealousy.

"We're going to try and find some water," said Carrie.

Mum suddenly looked apprehensive. "Be careful," she sighed and flopped down on the sand beside Dave.

"Let them go," he said. "Maybe they *can* find some water and something to eat."

Mum looked at them both hopefully. "Wouldn't it be wonderful if you could?"

"We'll try," said Jack.

*

The island was small, with a steep hill at the centre. Standing on the top, Jack and Carrie were able to see a lot better.

The reef ran round three sides of the island and they could see the channel which they had only just survived. The tide had soothed the turbulent waves, which were smaller, but still colliding with each other. On the fourth side there was a much longer, less protected sandy beach. The whole island could have been no more than half a mile across.

There were a few palm trees – Jack counted fourteen – and some scrubby bushes in the centre.

"What's that?" asked Carrie, pointing to the far corner of the long sandy beach.

"Looks like a hut," replied Jack eagerly. "And there's something else I can't quite make out."

Carrie screwed up her eyes. "Looks like an upturned hull of a boat and some kind of – tank."

"A tank?" Jack repeated. "If it's a tank—" He paused.

"If it *is* a tank, then there might be—"

"Rainwater," finished Jack.

"Don't build up your hopes," warned Carrie.

"I'm not." But of course he was and they both began to run down towards the beach.

Soon they were both sprinting as hard as they could, exhaustion forgotten, tearing over the rough ground, throats parched, until Carrie tripped and fell, lying spreadeagled on the ground, one of her knees bleeding.

As Jack helped her up, he noticed for the first time that her arms and legs were covered in cuts and bruises and were also badly burned by the sun. But when he looked down at his own body he could see that he was also cut and bruised. Neither of them seemed to have noticed, and Jack realised the damage must have been done as they swam through the rocks. But all this paled into insignificance beside his overriding desire to drink.

In a few minutes Carrie gasped, "It's a hut and an upturned boat – and those *are* tanks. Do you think they've caught any rainwater?" She was croaking again now, her throat was so dry.

"We'll soon see," said Jack shakily, hardly daring to believe in the possibility of slaking his thirst. He could barely remember his last proper drink; it seemed a lifetime away, in another world, another life.

*

There were two tanks just behind the tumbledown hut that was made partly of corrugated iron.

"Do you think anyone's inside that hut?" rasped Carrie.

"Robinson Crusoe and Man Friday?" asked Jack, without thinking. All he wanted to know was if those tanks contained water. But he didn't dare let his hopes dwell on the prospect, because he was suddenly sure he was going to be disappointed. Fresh water was too much of a dream to turn out to be a reality.

Jack burst into a stumbling run and Carrie joined him. They dashed across the arid ground. There were a couple of palm trees that gave some shelter and a light breeze was coming off the sea. The setting was like an advertisement for a tropical paradise – in fact it *was* a tropical paradise, Jack reminded himself. But there was no bar, no hotel, no attentive waiter with a tray full of iced drinks, not even a cold, glistening jug of water.

Then they reached the tanks.

Carrie got there first, standing very still, staring down.

Jack came to a halt, unable to bear the

disappointment that was likely to come. There was no such thing as a tropical paradise. This was an inhospitable island with no water, surrounded by a cruel reef and a shark-infested sea.

Were Carrie's shoulders drooping?

Wasn't that a sigh of bitter disappointment?

Didn't she have that completely beaten look that he had expected?

"Well?" he asked despondently, still not daring to join her, to inspect the empty tanks – or the tanks that only held salt water. But how *could* they hold salt water? They were some distance from the sandy beach.

"They're...full," Carrie said slowly.

Jack's heart leapt, but then he knew he couldn't allow himself the fool's luxury of hope. Sure they were full. Sure they were full of salt water. That was all they could contain. His head spun.

"They're full of *water*," said Carrie.

"Yeah. It's a shame." Crushing disillusion filled him.

"What's a shame?" She turned to him, puzzled.

"You can't drink salt water."

"Of course you can't." She sounded irritable and then suddenly leant over one of the tanks and began to make gulping sounds.

Jack stared at her. Was she mad? Had his sister gone crazy and was now drinking salt water? The stuff could make her really ill.

"Don't!" he shouted.

But Carrie didn't look up, continuing to gulp, making loud, slurping noises.

"Don't be a complete idiot," Jack rasped, his tongue clinging to the roof of his mouth, almost sticking to the back of his throat.

Carrie still didn't look up.

Then she did, her hair wringing wet, dripping droplets of water on to the silver sand. If only it was fresh water, thought Jack. If only he could really slake his thirst.

"Come on," she yelled. "Come *on*, Jack."

"You can't drink salt water," he said stolidly, admonishing her, standing rigidly where he had come to a halt, seemingly riveted to the spot.

"What are you on about?" she yelled.

"I told you – it must be salt water – you're crazy to drink—"

"Why don't you shut up?" She was suddenly

laughing at him.

"What's so funny?"

"It *isn't* salt water," Carrie yelled.

"*What*?"

"This is rainwater and we can drink our fill." Carrie reached out with her hands and scooped up the precious liquid. "Come on, Jack," she grinned. "Don't let's waste a miracle."

A Miracle

Jack raced up to her to find that both tanks were full of water and the contents felt quite cool. The tanks must have been more shaded by the palm trees than he had imagined.

The water looked incredibly, magically refreshing. He couldn't believe what he was staring at and his throat was so dry he could hardly speak as he watched Carrie laughing at him, plunging her hands in again and again and shouting in pure, delighted, amazed exultation. Jack gave a huge cry of delight and dipped his hands into the tank.

*

Jack opened his mouth and drank. The water had a slightly brackish taste, but there was no salt. Jack shut his eyes to the rest of the world and drank and drank and drank.

It was only when his stomach was aching that he looked at Carrie, who was staring up at the burning sun.

"This is fantastic," she said, with a satisfied grin.

"I never thought we stood a chance of finding fresh water," said Jack. "We should get back to Mum and Dave and tell them. We can't leave them to fry out there."

"You're right," said Carrie. "We're being incredibly selfish. Can't we find a container or something to take some water back to them?"

"Let's look in that hut."

Jack suddenly realised the significance of the primitive little building. Maybe the island was visited regularly? If so, they stood a better chance of rescue. He turned towards it, but as they passed the upturned boat, he paused. Although he felt exhausted, he was also filled with a most amazing elation. They'd survived the wreck, survived the sharks, survived their thirst — was there more good luck in store for them?

There wasn't.

The boat had a hole in her hull and there was no sign of any oars, but lying beside her was a mast.

"I wonder if there's any rigging in the hut," he said. "Maybe some sails."

"What about the hole?"

"We might be able to fix it." He stared out to sea. The afternoon was still clear and the sun beat down, but there was nothing on the horizon and nothing in the sky.

Jack suddenly felt dizzy again. They hadn't eaten for forty-eight hours. Starvation was something they might not survive, thought Jack gloomily.

They approached the hut cautiously. The ramshackle building had partly collapsed and the roof was sagging. But the door was still in place.

Jack pulled the door open and saw a tail. The tail was quivering. Then he saw there were two tails.

Jack gave a yelp of panic as two rodent-like creatures rushed past him, scampering over the sand and then disappearing from sight down a hole.

"Rats!" he cried in disgust.

"No, they're not." Carrie laughed. "They're ground squirrels. Don't you remember seeing them in Ensenada?"

"How did they get out here?" Jack demanded.

"Maybe on a ship. Maybe they breed here. So we won't starve." It was as if Carrie had been reading his mind earlier.

"Eat ground squirrels?" Jack was revolted.

"We can't be choosy," she replied as they went inside. "They'd be OK, roasted over a fire."

"Would they?" Jack felt another surge of panic. They were actually stranded on a desert island. He could hardly believe it. Jack was reminded of a radio programme where a supposed castaway was asked to name eight pieces of music they'd like to take to a desert island, along with one luxury. His luxury would be a large and juicy hamburger, that had absolutely nothing to do with roasted ground squirrel.

The irony of his situation struck him. Once or twice he had imagined himself on a desert island and had spent some time choosing music in his imagination.

Now he was in a position to do it for real it seemed completely pointless. Jack looked round the hut.

There was rigging and a couple of sails as well as what looked like a daggerboard, a rudder and a pair of oars. But Carrie, ever practical, was foraging in a cupboard, and suddenly gave a whoop of joy.

"Tins!" she said. "*And* an opener. We can have a feast."

"What is there?" asked Jack.

"Beans. Soup. Salsa. Tuna. All sorts of fruits. There's quite a pile. The labels are all in Spanish. Maybe this hut's some kind of stop-over point for fishermen."

"There's something on that bench," said Jack. They looked at it carefully and saw it was a rough chart which showed the mainland coast in relation to the island. "I can't work this out," said Jack.

"Maybe Dave will," suggested Carrie and Jack shrugged.

"He's a saint," said Carrie.

"Dave?" Jack looked at her in amazement.

"No, you idiot. Whoever took the time and trouble to stock up the island *and* draw a chart." Then Carrie paused. "I wonder if people have got wrecked before."

"Let's get back to Mum and Dave."

"I'll try to find some kind of container." But although she thoroughly checked the hut she couldn't find anything that would do.

"OK, we'll bring them back here," said Jack impatiently.

"Wait a minute," said Carrie. "Couldn't this be useful?" She grabbed a battered looking compass from one of the shelves.

"If we ever manage to make that boat float," said Jack pessimistically.

He hurried out of the hut and then paused by the dinghy. The hole was large, but there didn't seem to be any other damage. *Maybe* they could fix it. Then he caught sight of the name of the dinghy, upside down on her upturned hull.

Hope.

They both gazed at the name in silence.

"I think we could make some repairs," said Jack with a return of his usual optimism.

"I don't fancy going back to sea," Carrie blurted out. "Won't they look for us here?"

Jack shrugged.

As they hurried back to the beach, Carrie said, "How do you feel about Dave now?"

"I'm not sure." He paused and thought, his mind feeling as refreshed as his throat. "In a way I felt closer to him while we were hanging on to the rock. But now—"

"He was quite brave – in the shipwreck. OK, so he made a lot of noise, but we were just as scared."

"But we didn't make any noise."

Carrie laughed. "He's a noisy man."

"He's pathetic," said Jack.

"I just think he tries too hard, that's all."

"I don't want him round Mum."

"So it's that bad?" She sounded slightly disappointed.

"I thought you felt the same. Or have you changed your mind?" Jack was accusing.

"I don't exactly like him." She was hesitant. "But I don't exactly dislike him either."

"What's that meant to mean?" he asked impatiently.

"I think we should give him a chance."

"Of staying in our lives? Of staying in Mum's life?"

Carrie was silent.

"I'm not going along with that," snarled Jack. "Just because we've shared this horrible experience with him. And we're not out of it yet. He's too much of a jerk to know how to repair the dinghy."

"Are you sure about that?"

"And then he'll be panicking about sharks again."

"Who wouldn't?"

"Listen." Jack was suddenly angry despite all their good fortune. "I don't know what you're trying to say, but I don't like it – OK? I don't want him in our family." He paused. "Do you?"

Carrie didn't reply.

"There's water," shouted Jack.

"There's food," yelled Carrie. They were gasping as they ran down the beach to where they'd landed. "*And* a chart and a compass."

Both Dave and Mum scrambled to their feet and stood up, incredulous. Then Dave ran up and embraced Jack and Carrie and Mum did the same.

"Full marks for initiative," bellowed Dave, and Jack immediately felt patronised, as if he had been set a task which had required little imagination and he had managed to get right under strict guidance.

But Mum could only say, "I don't know what we'd do without you." And her hug meant everything.

When Jack and Carrie went on to tell the rest of the story, Dave said, "I'm sure I can fix that boat."

Once again Jack felt resentful. Why did Dave always have to take over?

Twenty minutes later, Jack and Carrie, having shown Mum and Dave the way to the hut and watched them drink ecstatically from the tanks, helped Mum open the tins while Dave gazed down at the dinghy knowledgeably, to Jack's irritation.

But the thought of food completely overrode his jealousy and they all ate chilli con carne, washed down with a fruit salad. Although it was simple food, it felt like it was the best meal of their lives. But once they'd finished they felt starving all over again.

"Can we have some more?" asked Jack.

"No," said Dave. "We need to ration ourselves. After all, we still don't know how long we're going to have to wait before we get picked up."

Jack knew Dave was absolutely right, but resented his stepfather for being so practical. He would have liked to have made the rule himself. As it was, he had been made to look like a greedy and irresponsible child. I've got to stop hating Dave, Jack told himself. To hate was dangerous. They had to be united.

"Not even those pears?" asked Carrie.

"Not even those pears." Dave was stern.

"Let's get on with the boat." Jack was anxious to show real initiative.

"All right, my lad," said Dave, and Jack winced. He looked at his watch and saw that it was late afternoon, just after five. "The girls can do the washing up."

"*What* washing up?" asked Mum, obviously irritated by Dave's chauvinism.

"Well, maybe you could fix up the hut for the night then," Dave droned on in his usual style.

"We're going to sleep in the hut?" Carrie was surprised. "Why can't we just sleep on the sand?"

"We still don't know what's on the island."

"What are you afraid of?" Jack's voice was terse. "A herd of wild buffalo?"

"There could be snakes," said Dave defensively and

Mum backed him up.

"I agree with Dave. I think we should tidy the hut up and then we'll be more comfortable."

A woman's tasks are never done, thought Jack. Why was Dave always so predictable? "I think we should build a fire," he said, trying again to seize the initiative. "If anyone *is* searching for us, then they'll see the flames. We should keep a fire going night and day and I'd like to make that *my* responsibility. Carrie's and mine." Jack hurriedly included her so he wouldn't sound like Dave. But he would have included her anyway, wouldn't he? Jack swore at himself inside. Why did he have this sense of permanent competition with his stepfather that seemed so unstoppable?

"Don't know where you're going to get the wood from," said Dave.

"There's some driftwood further up the beach." Jack deliberately sounded crushing.

"Is there?" Dave went over to the hut. "There's some tools in the hut, so I can make a start on the boat." He sounded more hurt than anything. "And, by the way, if you do find any substantial driftwood, let me have some – and that's a priority. I don't think I'm going to be able to chop down a palm tree." He went over to the hut, while Mum, standing up to follow him in, glanced over her shoulder and caught Jack's eye.

She winked.

Blood in the Water

Jack and Carrie spent the rest of the evening collecting driftwood and making a stack on the beach just below the hut. They managed to build up quite a pile, even finding some flatter pieces of wood that might help Dave with his repair of the dinghy.

But Dave only moaned that the wood was no good and when Carrie found a much larger piece, he was only grudgingly thankful.

Jack, who was exhausted and hungry again, suddenly couldn't take any more and lost his temper.

"Why don't you ever thank anybody?" he rapped out.

Dave, who was silently surveying the dinghy, turned to Jack in what appeared to be surprise. "What are you on about?" he asked.

"You," said Jack bitterly. "You – and the way you are."

"I don't get you."

"You're always patronising, aren't you?" Jack was suddenly shaking with rage and his fists were clenched as his anger and exhaustion turned to hatred. "And you never thank anyone."

"Leave him alone," said Mum, overhearing as she came out of the hut.

"No way," he retorted.

"Jack—" began Carrie.

"Shut up, you. I'm talking to Dave and I'm telling him I don't like his attitude. In fact he's got an attitude problem."

"Have I now?" Dave had turned to Jack, his face red. "Pity you don't think about yourself. Pity you aren't capable of self-criticism."

"I am," said Jack more quietly, his rage becoming a hard lump inside him. "I've told you – you're the one who's got the attitude problem. You're ungrateful, bossy and sexist. What are you?"

"Be quiet!" Dave's arms were hanging by his sides and, like Jack, his fists were clenched.

"You're a coward too," Jack continued.

"I said – be quiet!"

There was a short silence. Jack and Dave were standing within inches of each other.

"Now look, you two—" began Mum.

"There's no point in—" said Carrie, but neither of them managed to finish their sentences.

"You're a coward," repeated Jack. "A coward and a bully and that's all you've ever been. I wish you'd get out of our lives and leave Mum alone." He was bellowing out the words now and didn't care what he said. "I wish you'd been eaten by the sharks. We don't want you." In his vehemence, Jack was spitting, the spittle spraying Dave's chest. He wondered if his stepfather was going to wipe it off, but he didn't seem to have noticed.

"Jack!" yelled Mum. "You've got to stop this."

Carrie was silent.

Jack turned to them both. "He's nothing. This guy

is nothing at all."

There was another silence, this time deeper and longer.

"So I'm shark bait." Dave tried to make a joke. "Well, there's plenty of me, and at least I'd provide a good meal." He paused. "And talking of meals—"

"We'll eat what we like when we like," shouted Jack. "You're not our father."

Dave turned away and looked down at the boat.

Jack's rage ran out of steam and then suddenly evaporated. Dave swung round on him and he was guiltily aware that there were tears in his stepfather's eyes.

"I'm sorry you think so badly of me, Jack. I've just been trying to do the very best for everyone, and it's a pity that I've been—"

"Shut up!" said Carrie.

"*What*?" Dave swung round on her, in distress rather than anger.

Carrie was standing very still, listening intently. Then they all heard the droning sound.

Twilight had crept over the beach and the sun was setting in a blaze of colour, slowly dipping into the sea, making the water gleam in a mysterious, almost menacing way. Then, just before the sun sank below the horizon, they could all now see the light plane, high in the air.

"Help!" yelled Jack, jumping up and down and waving his arms desperately. They had to be seen. Surely the pilot couldn't fail to spot them.

They all began to shout and wave, but the plane suddenly stopped circling and headed off into the sunset.

They continued to shout and wave for a long time after the plane had gone.

"Well," said Dave. "That proves they're looking for us at least."

"It doesn't mean anything of the kind," said Jack. "And if we'd started a fire ages ago they wouldn't have missed us." But he muttered the words, not wanting to provoke any more argument. Somehow he suddenly felt bad. If only Dave had hurled the same kind of abuse back at him. Dave simply looking hurt seemed to put Jack in the wrong.

"Any chance of supper?" ventured Carrie.

"Of course," said Dave. "But I'm not your leader.

Jack's made that clear, and I'm sure—"

"Wait a minute," said Mum. "I don't agree with you, Jack, I'm afraid. I don't agree with you at all."

Jack turned on his mother as if she was a traitor.

"We all need leadership, and you took responsibility for the fire. You can't blame Dave for that."

"Maybe the plane wasn't searching for us in the first place," suggested Carrie.

"Either way," said Jack. "They would have spotted a fire. I didn't do what I said I would." He was at pains to be honest.

"I suggest we vote on decisions in the future," said Dave.

"Surely we don't need to—" Laura looked uneasy and, immediately, Jack felt a stab of fear.

"Don't you have any faith in voting now?" he asked her.

"OK. I give in."

"But no buts," said Dave, sounding more like his irritating old self. "I'll help you get that fire going."

"What about supper?" asked Carrie again.

"We need to vote on how much we should have," said Dave. "Shall I make a list of what we've got?"

Everyone nodded agreement in a rather self-conscious way.

There were two boxes of matches in the hut and they were dry. Carrie lit some smaller fuel they had placed at the centre of the pile of driftwood and soon the fire was blazing away as Dave returned with a list of supplies.

"This is what we've got," he said. "Eleven cans of chilli. Eleven cans of tuna. Six cans of salsa. Four cans of beans. Seven cans of different tinned fruits. Four cans of rice."

"That's it?" asked Jack.

"That's it – so we've got to be careful."

Jack nodded. Suddenly what had appeared to be large stocks now seemed quite inadequate. "What are we going to do?" he asked with a chill of fear, and then realised that after all the fuss he'd made he was suddenly dependent on Dave. He was partly annoyed and partly relieved.

"We've got two options." Dave sounded crisp and efficient now. "We can either stay here and wait for rescue. Or take the boat after I've fixed her up and try to make the mainland with the chart." Dave paused and the silence lengthened. "We'll have to vote."

Jack now felt more than inadequate. There were pros and cons for each of the two options. On the island they were safe, but they might never be rescued; in the boat they were exposed to the weather, the tide and the sharks. But at least they had the chart. They might find their way to the Mexican coast.

Then Dave said surprisingly, "I've had a look at the chart and reckon if we sail due west, we'll reach Ensenada. I dinghy sailed when I was a kid, and later on I did some navigation classes with a view to buying a bigger boat. But I could never afford one."

"But you remember the classes?" Carrie asked hopefully.

"Oh yes," Dave seemed confident. "I can read a chart and handle a compass."

"How long would that take us?" asked Mum.

Dave shrugged. "I can't tell you that."

"I'd vote for staying here," said Mum.

Dave turned to Carrie.

"I'd vote for staying here too," said Carrie. "There's too many sharks out there."

"And you, Jack?"

"I'm all for taking the dinghy. We've got the chart and the compass." But was he really telling the truth, he wondered, or just trying to look brave?

There was a long pause.

"What about your vote?" asked Carrie.

Dave was silent. Then he said, "I think we should stay here for a while at least. I can read the chart, but we can't be sure the compass works. I'm sure that plane was searching for us."

"Some search," said Jack. "They didn't come down low enough."

"The light was against them, and we didn't have the beacon fire we've got now. Let's give it a swing."

Jack sighed with relief. He realised he had just cast his vote to appear more intrepid than Dave. Suddenly he felt ashamed.

Once they had eaten, Jack and Carrie had kept the fire blazing away by continually gathering more driftwood. Now they felt utterly spent and exhausted.

"We'll keep watch," said Dave. "Why not have a two-hour watch each – that'll mean we get some sleep.

Or maybe even a three-hour watch."

"Let's do that," said Jack, yawning. "And whoever's on watch has to hunt for more driftwood and keep the fire going."

"So who would like to start?" asked Mum.

"I will." Jack sounded stoic, but then yawned again.

"You've got to keep awake, you know," Carrie said crossly.

"I will. Who shall I wake up when I've got through my three hours?"

"Me," said Mum. "And then Dave, and Carrie."

"The night will be over by then," said Carrie.

"We might be having a lie-in," joked Dave. "So I wouldn't bet on that." He laughed too brightly, and Jack began to realise how badly he'd hurt him. As a result he felt partly still ashamed and partly still full of bravado.

The night was clear, with a myriad of stars and a bright moon. The ocean was still calm and Jack could hear the dim surge of surf gently breaking on the sand.

Wandering over to the beach he found more driftwood and began to make a large number of journeys to and from the fire, making sure the wood stocks were adequate and the blaze well tended.

On the last trip, he stood by the ocean, gazing out at the dark horizon, thinking about the sharks. He was slowly realising that he should have voted to stay on the island rather than setting out in *Hope* to try and find Ensenada. Jack shivered, once again seeing the crimson tide of Manuel's blood on the surface of the water.

The blood could so easily have been his own.

Were the Great Whites out there now? He imagined them, deadly and purposeful, the killing machines that Manuel had talked about. Then he wondered about Juan and the Charlton family. Had their dinghy foundered? Or were they already back in Ensenada, safely away from the sharks?

Jack returned to the fire and sat down, blinking away sleep, checking his watch to see how much time he had left. Two hours. They seemed like an eternity.

Making sure the fire was still blazing, Jack returned to the shore again and stood in the shallows, letting the surf tumble over his feet, staring out into the middle distance. How was he going to keep himself awake, Jack wondered. Maybe he should have a quick swim which would be refreshing and might even wake him up. Jack paused and then began to wade out until he was up to his knees.

He thought about the sharks. Surely they wouldn't swim into such shallow waters? Of course they wouldn't. Jack continued to wade out until he was up to his waist. Immediately he felt recharged and dived into a small wave, surfacing and diving again.

He felt wide awake now, completely restored by the gloriously cool water. The island was so beautiful at night; it could have been an advert for a luxury holiday.

Jack swam on, conscious only of the refreshing coolness, diving every now and again, his fatigue gone. Then he looked back and saw the island was further away than he had thought. He hadn't realised he'd swum out so far and began to fast-crawl back, feeling the force of the current, realising the tide was going out again and he was being forced to battle against it. How on earth could he have been so foolish?

Jack thought he was just winning, when he put his foot down to test whether he was still out of his depth. He felt something sharp which hurt badly. With a howl of pain, Jack swam on.

Tentatively, he put his foot down again, but didn't come into contact with anything and realised he must have hit an isolated sharp rock, as his foot was hurting badly. He could feel it throbbing, pumping blood into the water.

Blood, Jack thought. Blood in the water. What did that mean? Suddenly all his exhaustion was back and he couldn't think clearly. Blood? Blood in the water?

That would attract a shark. Maybe several sharks. Wouldn't it? Jack wracked his brains to remember what he knew about those human killing machines. What had he learnt at school? What had he seen on TV? What other gory details had Manuel mentioned?

Now he was exhausted and swimming much more slowly, his limbs even more leaden now. Disjointed facts about the deadly danger of the sharks began to filter through his mind. Wasn't a large portion of the shark's brain used for smell? Particularly smelling blood? Although he was still swimming for the shore, surely his movement would be giving him away, attracting those jaws whose teeth could slash him in two? He whimpered slightly and continued to swim, but he was having to push through the swell as if he was swimming through treacle.

Over and over, the same phrase repeated itself in his head. *Blood in the water. Blood in the water.*

Life and Death

Jack was certain he could see a shark's fin moving towards him. He knew he had to get back to the beach, but he couldn't move his arms at all. Panic swept over him as if he was locked into a bad dream.

Get a grip, he told himself, forcing himself to turn and to stop treading water. He began to swim, stiffly and slowly at first and then faster, back into his crawl, aiming for the beach. He was sure the shark would reach him at any moment. Wasn't their sight particularly good in the dark? Or had he got that wrong?

His foot was numb.

He imagined the tearing and rending of flesh and bone.

In his mind, Jack saw the bulbous head with the tiny eyes and the jaw crammed with teeth.

He *had* to get back to the beach, which still seemed a long way as he fought the strong tide. What had he said to Dave before? "You've got the willpower. Now use it." Now it was his turn to search deep inside himself for additional strength.

Somehow he managed to find a second wind, to fight harder, to cleave the water more effectively. And, at last, to his surprise, he found he could put his good foot down on firm sand. But the blood was still pumping out of the other as if he was sending a generous invitation to the Great White.

Pushing through the shallows, Jack felt as if he was moving in slow motion and was sure he could sense a fin cruising behind him, the shark poised to tear at his flesh.

Then Jack was out of the shallows, on the beach and gazing up at the still blazing fire. He ran on, beyond the fire, gasping and crying out, "Someone help me.

Someone's got to help me."

Dave came running out of the hut, a bulbous figure in the pale moonlight, followed by Mum and Carrie.

Jack was shaking as he stood before them with the blood still welling out of his foot.

Mum was first to see the wound. "What's happened?" she asked.

"I went for a swim to keep me awake," he gasped. "And then—"

"You were attacked by a shark?" Her voice was shrill with horror.

"I cut my foot on a rock – and I was afraid the blood would—"

"Attract the Great Whites," said Carrie. "Well, it could have done. You shouldn't have gone swimming alone. That's crazy."

"And irresponsible," added Mum.

"Crazy," repeated Dave. "Absolutely crazy."

Jack wondered whether anyone was going to look at his foot which was hurting badly.

"That's nasty," said Dave. "You'd better – we'd better get the sand off." Without warning he seized Jack in his arms and bore him quickly down to the sea.

"What are you doing?" Jack yelled, struggling.

"Washing your foot. We've got to get all the sand off."

"Let me down!"

"Don't be daft. Did you see any sharks out there?"

"I thought I did," said Jack defensively.

"Either way, you were really stupid to swim without anyone else around."

"There's quite a current," Jack admitted, suddenly needing to be honest.

"Exactly," replied Dave.

He dunked Jack's foot several times in the shallows, pronounced himself satisfied, and then carried him back to his mother. Jack felt like a young and helpless child.

"Let's take a look at that," said Mum, just able to see in the moonlight.

"I think the blood's drying up now." Jack was defensive.

"Not quite," she said. "You've got a nasty cut there, which would normally need stitches. I'm going to use Dave's T-shirt. It's quite dry, but not very clean. Anyway, it's all we've got."

Dave emerged from the hut, already ripping his T-shirt into strips.

"The fisherman should have left us a first-aid kit," he joked. "That was one essential he overlooked."

"He couldn't think of everything," Mum snapped, winding one of the T-shirt strips around Jack's foot, tying the ends together and tightening the improvised bandage as best she could. Then she used another strip as an outside covering.

"Look," said Jack. "There *is* a fin out there." He was certain he could see something in the faint light of the moon.

"I don't see anything," said Mum.

"Nor me," added Dave.

Carrie was gazing out at the ocean. "I'm not sure," she said.

"There *was* a shark out there," insisted Jack. But was there? Wasn't he making it all up to force them to feel sorry for him?

Jack slept dreamlessly and deeply, waking to find a misty sun was up and the time was just after eleven. He staggered to his feet, wincing as the sharp pain shot through his foot and then realising he had overslept so badly that he would look a fool.

Emerging from the hut, he saw Mum and Dave working on the dinghy and Carrie stacking more driftwood by the embers of last night's fire. Someone had drawn a huge SOS on the smooth sand by the shore. What a brilliant idea, he thought, and then wondered whose idea it was. The red dinghy sails were laid out on the sand, and the tins they'd finished had been placed to reflect the sun.

But clouds were coming up and the mist over the ocean was deepening.

"Why didn't someone wake me up?" Jack demanded angrily. "Who did all that stuff?" He stared at the SOS and the sails and the tins.

"Dave," said Mum.

Jack didn't reply. He couldn't stop himself feeling resentful, despite everything Dave had done to help him the previous night.

Carrie looked up from the embers, her face drawn and serious. "Something's happened." Her voice was flat.

"What?"

"We saw this plane, but it flew away."

"Just like that?"

Carrie shrugged.

"You should have lit the fire again." Jack had to find something to criticise. "What time did you see the plane?"

"About half an hour ago." Carrie shrugged again, her face expressionless.

"We did all we could," said Dave, looking up from patching the bottom of the dinghy with a neat row of pieces of overlapping driftwood that he had hammered into place. "But as Carrie said, the plane flew away." Dave seemed depressed and Jack felt a wimp for oversleeping. "How's the foot?" asked Dave.

"OK." Jack kicked at some sand. "You should have woken me."

"You needed all the rest you could get," said his stepfather, returning to the task in hand.

"What can I do?" Jack asked glumly.

"Get yourself some breakfast," said Mum. "We're all allowed some tuna and half a can of fruit. We put out your share on the shelf in the hut."

Jack said nothing, but suddenly ravenous he went back inside and ate his breakfast.

When he'd finished he came out again, went to the tanks, took a long swig of water and looked out to sea.

The mist had shifted and the sun was trying to break through.

Then Jack saw the ship.

At first he couldn't believe his own eyes. She seemed large and wasn't moving. Could she be at anchor? He turned to Carrie and bellowed at her, "There's a ship!"

They all looked up and stared at the distant vessel in amazement. Then Dave began to wave frantically and the others joined him. But as they waved and shouted, Jack realised she was too far away to see them.

"We've got to get out there," said Dave forcefully. "She's only half a mile offshore."

"Is the dinghy seaworthy?"

"Yes, but we'll have to row. We haven't got time to put up the mast and sort out the rigging and fix the sails."

"Let's go," said Jack anxiously.

"All of us?" asked Mum. "That's going to be a real load again." She turned to Dave. "Why don't Carrie and I stay here and get that fire going?" She paused and then continued, "Look, you know I'm making sense. Let's be brutally honest." Her voice shook and Jack could see the tears in her eyes. "If you – if you survive the trip, then Carrie and I will be rescued. If you don't – and please God that won't happen – then it leaves at least two members of our family alive."

"Mum—" Carrie began to protest, but stopped abruptly when she caught her mother's eye.

There was a moment's hesitation. Then Dave said, "I don't think—" He paused, as if he had finally run out of words.

But Jack didn't want to hear any of this. There was a ship. She wasn't moving so she must be at anchor. If she was only half a mile out they could get to her before she moved on. But if they stayed here talking, the ship would sail away.

"Let's go," yelled Jack. "Nothing will happen to us. We've got to try."

"That's right," said Mum. "Carrie and I will be fine here. Now go – before we lose our chance."

Impelled by her urgency, Dave grabbed the nose of the dinghy and began to pull her down the beach towards the sea.

"Get the oars," he yelled. "They're in the hut."

Heart pounding, Jack ran to the hut and came back with the oars, the urgency making him tremble.

"We'll be back soon," Jack said, glancing at his mother and Carrie and knowing how lonely and miserable they would be. He gave them both a quick peck on the cheek and repeated, "Don't worry. We'll be back soon. Very soon."

Neither Mum nor Carrie said anything as Jack raced to the water's edge with the oars and fitted them into the rowlocks. Dave was already in position and grabbed hold of them. Jack then pushed *Hope* into the shallows and scrambled on board, grabbing one of the oars. Looking back he could see Carrie and Mum on the water's edge, their hands half raised in farewell.

Dave and Jack each took an oar, rowing in unison, their strokes fast and somewhat erratic. Nevertheless, the repairs to *Hope* were holding as no water was coming in and Jack felt a rush of confidence. Dave had been very skilful and he should have thanked him. Instead, Jack put all his remaining strength into the rowing.

Slowly the mist came down, obscuring the ship.

Then Dave paused, dragged out the compass and

tried to take a reading.

We're losing time, thought Jack. The ship had seemed so near. Suddenly he was sure they were going to fail.

Hope

"Row harder," yelled Jack to Dave.

"I am."

The mist lightened again and then, within seconds, seemed to thicken as if the elements were playing some kind of demonic game with them.

Dave groaned aloud as the pain in his arm muscles intensified.

Then something nudged the bottom of *Hope*.

"What's that?"

The nudge came again and Jack felt a stab of terror.

Dave stopped rowing. "I've got cramp in my arm,"

he said, determined not to accept or even refer to what might be happening.

"Let me take your oar or we'll go round in circles!" yelled Jack, now very much in command. "Go and sit in the stern. Hurry up. We could lose that ship."

Shipping his oar, Dave scrambled unsteadily to his feet, but the nudge came again, much harder this time. He fell back, making the dinghy rock wildly, and Jack stood up, trying to retrieve the oar that was now threatening to slide into the water.

Then Jack lost his balance and with a wild cry fell overboard. He splashed and yelled and splashed again while Dave leant over the stern of *Hope*, trying to grab him.

"You should have told me you wanted a swim," said Dave, putting out a hand while he tried to keep *Hope* stationary with an oar. But they seemed to have been caught in another current which was pulling the dinghy away from Jack, who was beginning to really panic now, his arms trailing. Then he realised with a sudden shock that he was behaving like a fool; his frantic movements would be bound to attract a shark and if his wound broke open there would be blood in the water...

Dave managed to spin *Hope* round and headed back towards him. He pulled up close, shipped the oars, and stretched out his arm. But as Jack grabbed at Dave's hand, the current pulled again and once more *Hope* drifted away.

"Try and swim to me," Dave yelled.

"What do you think I'm doing?" Jack was a strong swimmer, but the current had caught him and he was making no progress. Dave tried to swing the boat around again, reached out and only just missed Jack's hand. "Try harder!" Dave urged him.

Jack exerted every effort and reached *Hope*'s stern, grabbing at Dave's hand again – and missing. Then, far far away, maybe as much as thirty metres away, Jack saw a dark triangular shape cutting through the waves. Had it heard them? Could it smell them? Was it making for the boat? Jack didn't know, but the surge of terror that ran through him was so great he almost passed out. Then gradually the terror subsided into numbness, almost as if he had accepted his fate.

"Dave!" Jack said quietly. "Can you see what I can see?"

"Yes." Dave was very calm. "Don't worry. Just save some strength to haul yourself over the stern. You've got to get yourself into the boat."

"I can't."

"You've *got* to!"

Somehow Dave had managed to manoeuvre *Hope* against the pull of the current. At last she was more stable and he was able to hold his position.

"Come on, Jack!" Dave was suddenly yelling at him angrily, all his calm gone, and Jack responded, losing his inertia and swimming towards Dave's hand again, trying not to splash, desperately anxious not to draw attention to himself.

But now Jack could see the shark's white fin more clearly. It seemed to be circling them.

"Come *on*!" Dave shouted. "You've got to go faster than that."

"There's a shark!"

"Don't panic." Dave sounded ridiculously in control.

The fin was moving in a straight line, faster now, finally homing in on them, on him.

Jack fought for control, determined to exert every ounce of strength he'd got.

"Grab the stern and I'll haul you over," Dave shouted to him.

"Don't let it get me," Jack spluttered. "Don't let it get me!"

"I won't," shouted Dave. "Come *on*, Jack!"

There was a note of increased urgency in Dave's voice and when Jack turned his head he was horrified to see a fin only a couple of metres away from him.

"*Swim*, Jack!" yelled Dave. "Just give it all you've got."

Jack tried as hard as he could, the fear driving him on. He imagined the deadly jaws, the teeth about to bite into his flesh.

Jack knew from the expression on Dave's face that the shark was very close to him now.

It's going to get me. Blood in the water, he thought. Blood in the water.

With a sudden burst of energy, Jack swam faster while Dave, splashing wildly with the oars, tried to hold the dinghy still.

At last Jack managed to grab the stern, but he was too exhausted to haul himself up. The shark was circling closer, about to come in for the kill. Suddenly

Dave threw himself overboard and using every ounce of strength in his body, he heaved Jack up out of the water. Then, as Dave tried to grab the stern himself, the dinghy rocked out of reach and he slid below the surface.

Frantically Jack grabbed at the oars and began to row back towards him. But still the fin circled, one potential victim replaced by another.

"What are you *doing*?" shouted Jack, as Dave's head surfaced. "What on earth do you think you're doing?" All Jack could feel was utter confusion.

"Try to keep the dinghy steady," Dave bellowed. "I'm coming back on board."

Jack pulled on the oars, fighting against the current which was much stronger than he had imagined. Bringing her round as best he could, to his relief Jack suddenly found that the dinghy was free of the current and he could make a wide sweep back to where Dave was struggling in the water.

Jack rowed as hard as he could, openly praying, saying over and over again, "Please, God, help us. Please God, help us."

Now he was bringing *Hope* alongside his stepfather

and Dave was able to grab the hull. "I'll pull you in," yelled Jack, shipping the oars, standing up and grabbing Dave under his arms. He pulled and pulled again, but Dave was a dead weight.

"You've got to help me!" he shouted and Jack remembered Manuel saying those very words which now seemed a lifetime ago.

"I'm trying to." But his stepfather's heavy body slid back into the water again and Jack fell into the bottom of the dinghy, making her list and take in more water. When he had dragged himself back to his feet, Jack stood in the crazily rocking *Hope*, desperately staring into the swell. But he couldn't see any sign of his stepfather. "Dave!"

"I'm over here!"

Jack grabbed the oars and rowed towards the sound of his voice. Suddenly there was no sign of the shark. Could it *possibly* have given up? But there was no sign of Dave either.

Then Jack saw him in the trough of a wave, swimming slowly towards the prow of the dinghy and cursing as he made progress at last.

"Come on!" Jack shouted, shipping the oars and

leaning over the prow to grab Dave's hand.

Dave was almost in the dinghy when his face contorted with a shrill cry of anguish.

The Rescue

Still clutching Dave's hand, Jack kept pulling, gazing into his stepfather's twisted features as he roared encouragement. But Dave didn't utter another sound and his hand slipped from Jack's grasp.

Then the shark broke the surface and Jack could see the blunt head, the terrible eyes, the open jaws and the razor sharp teeth that were already streaming with blood – Dave's blood. Now Jack could see the wound – a long tear in Dave's side.

"Do something!" Dave suddenly screamed,

grabbing at the prow of the dinghy.

Knowing they could capsize at any moment, Jack grabbed an oar and instinctively hit the shark hard over the head. Then he hit it again. But the blood still poured through his stepfather's slashed flesh, streaming into the sea, turning the water crimson.

Jack hit out again and again, driven on by sheer desperation, but the blows seemed to make no difference. The shark stayed where it was, taking the punishment, seemingly resilient. Jack knew that if he tried to hit it any harder he could fall into the sea, just as Dave had, and then they would both be at the mercy of the thing.

As he hesitated, the shark dived under the dinghy, leaving Dave still hanging on to the prow, his blood a crimson stain on the surface of the water. The mist was denser now and Jack couldn't see more than a few metres ahead. The dinghy was rocking wildly again and Jack tried frantically to stabilise her.

Suddenly Jack heard the deep resonant sound of a klaxon and a large rubber dinghy roared out of the mist. Inside were two men and, as they appeared, Jack saw Dave's eyes glaze with agony.

"You've got to get my dad out," yelled Jack. "He saved me from the shark and it got him instead!"

But the man at the tiller was already turning the dinghy and within seconds they were alongside Dave, and his companion was hauling him up out of the water.

As he did so, Jack could see his stepfather's side was a bloodied mess – and he turned away and was sick.

"We're coming alongside," yelled the man at the tiller. "Get ready to abandon ship."

"My mother and sister are still on the island," shouted Jack.

"We'll get this guy back to our ship first. He's losing too much blood and he won't have long if we don't stop the bleeding."

Slowly but surely their rescuers pulled Dave over the side of the rubber dinghy and then Jack clambered across too, leaving *Hope* adrift in the swell.

There was no sign of the shark as the rubber dinghy turned and began to make for the ship at high speed. Jack watched *Hope* drifting alone and felt a huge lump in his throat. It was over. They were safe.

Dave lay in the bows, apparently unconscious, as

one of the men dragged out a first-aid box and began to pad the wound and tie a thick bandage around Dave's chest.

"We saw you in the mist. We launched the dinghy as fast as we could."

"Is he going to be OK?" asked Jack.

"If we can stop the bleeding."

Jack gazed down at Dave, but despite the padding and bandages the bright red liquid of his blood was slopping about in the bottom of the boat. There seemed to be so much of it.

Dave opened his eyes as the needle of a syringe sank into his arm. 'That'll help with the pain.'

Dave was gazing up at Jack. "I'm sorry," he muttered.

"What for?" asked Jack.

"Messing it all up."

"Don't be an idiot. You saved my life."

"I don't remember." Dave's eyes were beginning to close.

"I do. You never thought of yourself." Jack's voice shook with emotion.

Dave's eyes closed and he didn't seem to be breathing.

"Is he dead?" whispered Jack.

The crewman knelt down and put his ear to Dave's chest, then grabbed his wrist, searching for a pulse. "He's still alive, but it's going to be a close-run thing. He's lost so much blood."

Suddenly, out of the mist loomed the lettering: *Spirit of the South*. The ship looked as if she was some kind of bulk carrier with container units stacked on her decks.

"Stay still," said their rescuer. "We'll be winched up."

An hour later, after Mum and Carrie had been picked up from the island, they all three waited in a cabin near the sickbay, desperate to hear news of Dave.

The medical officer had already confirmed that he had lost so much blood that he might not live.

"He meant to be a good stepfather," Mum wept. "He really did, but he just didn't know how to handle it all. Dave tried to be generous, tried to reach you. But he just tried too hard."

"He doesn't need to try any more," said Jack. "The trying's over. We need him."

The door of the cabin was suddenly pushed open and they all got to their feet, certain they were going to be told that Dave was dead.

Then the medical officer smiled. "He's going to pull through," he said. "He's in one hell of a mess, but we're arranging to transfer him to hospital. We'll let you know when the helicopter's due." He paused. "By the way, a guy called Juan Gonzales and a couple with a young family were picked up yesterday by Santa Cruz."

"They were with us on *Mexican Eagle*," said Carrie.

"Well – they're safe."

"Can we see Dave?" asked Jack.

"Only one at a time."

"Do you want to go in, Mum?" Jack was hesitant.

"Why don't you start, and then Carrie can be next."

"Only a few minutes each," warned the medical officer. "He's very weak."

Jack sat by Dave's bunk and took his hand.

Slowly, Dave opened his eyes.

"Thanks," said Jack.

"I didn't think." A faint smile came over his

stepfather's face. "That's me all over. Either I think too hard and everything goes wrong, or I think too little – and everything goes wrong."

Jack squeezed Dave's hand. "We're all safe now. Because of you."

"Where's Laura?" His voice was weaker now.

"She's coming to see you in a minute."

"Where are we?"

"On a container ship. They sent a rescue boat and now they're getting a helicopter to transfer you to hospital."

Dave closed his eyes. "What about the shark?" he whispered.

"He went hungry," said Jack.

Dave didn't say anything for some time. Then he muttered, "Am I going to die?"

"The medic says you'll get better, but it's going to be slow."

"Is it going to work?" muttered Dave.

"You're going to make it," Jack reassured him.

"I didn't mean that," Dave said awkwardly. "I mean – is our family going to work?"

"Oh, yes," said Jack confidently. "We're going to

work all right." He squeezed his stepfather's hand again.

Jack was standing on the deck, looking towards the stern and the wake of the container ship. Carrie joined him.

"Mum says Dave had a good night," she said.

Jack nodded. He was pleased about that. The morning was fresh and bright and the sun was already beating down on a calm ocean, without the slightest trace of mist or fog.

"What are you staring at?" asked Carrie anxiously, but the sheer size of the vessel and the great distance from the deck to the water calmed her fear. "Can you see – see a fin?"

Jack shook his head. "It's as if it's not real."

"What do you mean?"

"On this ship – it's like looking down at a theme-park ocean. That's how I felt when we were with Manuel, too. But once we were in the dinghy – and then *Hope* – we were really close to the ocean and we knew we were in danger – terrible danger."

"I'll never forget the head of that shark," shuddered

Carrie. "Those little eyes and all those teeth."

"You will forget," said Jack. "Eventually we'll both forget the real horror of it all. But right now I wanted to remind myself."

"I know what you mean," replied Carrie. Together they leant over the rail and gazed down at the grey-green water.

If books could kill...

Read about another electrifying encounter with a dangerous predator... the wolf!

"Masters knows how to pack a story full of fast-moving incidents, sharply drawn characters and emotional turmoil." *Junior Bookshelf*

ANTHONY MASTERS

ISBN   1 84121 904 5   £4.99

Panic

The electrical storm was getting worse and the four-seater Cessna shook, engines roaring against the full blast of the gale. Luke was terrified, certain that they would soon be forced down on to the snow-covered mountains below, a vast expanse of jagged peaks that now seemed horribly near.

Luke had just seen what he thought was an avalanche, as rocks and great banks of snow slid noiselessly down a gully. If the Cessna came down here they wouldn't stand a chance.

The light aircraft shuddered and Luke glanced across at his cousin Finn, who was sitting next to him, avoiding eye contact. Luke was sure he knew the reason why. Finn was determined not to show how afraid he was, and that had been the problem ever since the start of the trip. Finn wouldn't, couldn't show his feelings. He had to be perfect – brave and super-efficient and completely sure he was right. They had already had a couple of days' skiing, staying in a resort hotel, and Finn had been deliberately patronising about Luke's abilities.

"You're not as experienced as I thought," he'd told Luke more than once, sapping his confidence and making him feel clumsy and awkward.

Luke had tried to tolerate Finn's attitude because he knew how much he'd suffered, but it was hard not to feel put down.

Even his own father, Sam Taylor, seemed inferior to Finn's father Brett, who was a brilliant skier as well as an experienced pilot. The two men were brothers, but they couldn't have been more different. Brett, who was in his early forties, had emigrated to North America in his late teens and become a park ranger. Sam was Head of English at a South London comprehensive school.

Now they were all in Canada on a kind of holiday. Sam was in the co-pilot's seat while Brett was flying the plane, but even in this crisis Brett was talking almost casually to the flight controllers at Rock Airport, where he still expected to land, despite the extreme weather conditions.

Luke could just hear Control at Rock responding in what he thought was an alarmingly unhelpful way. "We advise you to divert. Repeat – we advise you to divert."

But Brett was insistent. "I'm low on fuel. I have to come in."

The flight controllers responded immediately, reversing their original decision. Their reply made Luke realise how serious the situation was. "OK. We have you on radar. We'll talk you down. We'll have emergency services standing by. Good luck."

A peak veered up out of the rapidly darkening gloom and Luke was certain they were going to crash. The Cessna was so close to the mountain he could see the snow-covered fir trees.

Brett's plan had always been to fly them to Rock, a

small airport in a broad mountain valley within easy access of the nature reserve where they could enjoy some cross-country skiing. All the gear was stowed in the hold in the tail of the Cessna, although their backpacks were stacked at the rear of the cabin.

Luke began to shake, his mouth dry. They wouldn't get any skiing now. They were going to die instead. Their bodies wouldn't be found and he'd never see Mum and his sister again. And as for— Luke brought himself up short, trying to force the raw panic out of his system. Brett was an experienced pilot, he told himself, and this was just a bad storm. The landing was going to be fine. After all, his own father didn't look particularly worried. Or did he? Luke could see his father's hands were clutching the arms of his seat so hard that his knuckles showed white.

Finn had begun whistling, although the tune was more like a dirge and could barely be heard above the engines and the screaming of the wind outside. The whistling was getting on Luke's nerves, but he said nothing.

Luke wished again that he could make some kind of contact with his cousin. But communication wasn't

Finn's strong point. Luke knew Finn had experienced something so awful last year that Luke couldn't even begin to imagine how he had coped.

Finn's little brother, Karl, had been dragged off a camp site during the night – not a million miles away from here, in fact – by a wolf. At least, that was what everyone had supposed, as, although there had been a trail of blood leading into the forest from Finn and Karl's tent, Karl's body had never been found. But Finn was convinced his brother was alive. This conviction had become an obsession.

"We'll find him one day," Finn had told Luke so many times he'd lost count. "Karl's a resourceful sort of kid. He'd be able to live in the wild."

Luke had nodded feebly, not daring to meet Finn's eyes, but he could feel the force of his obsession, as if Finn was saying over and over again inside his head: *You've got to believe me. You've got to believe me.*

Dad had told Luke that Finn had been through months of counselling yet he still clung fiercely to this impossible dream. The tragedy and its aftermath was the main reason why they had all met, and why they were flying through a storm in a light aircraft that now seemed as fragile as a moth.

To distract himself from the roaring of the Cessna's engines and the buffeting of the gale, Luke tried to focus on his cousin, attempting to work out how he could help him.

Finn was stockily built like his father, but there the similarity ended. Finn was competitive and aggressive, determined to prove himself better than Luke at everything. Not that that was particularly hard, Luke thought. From the moment they'd all met, Luke had felt right out of his depth – threatened by Finn's aggression, and all too conscious of his own skinny frame. Finn seemed much more able than he would ever be, despite the fact that he'd been so traumatised by the appalling death of his younger brother.

Dad had tried to talk to Luke about his cousin before they left London.

'I want you to enjoy the trip, but I'm also hoping you'll help Finn come to grips with his life. You know what happened. But he's got this fantasy that Karl could still be alive.'

'And being brought up by a wolf pack?' Luke had asked curiously, wondering for a moment if that was possible. Just after Karl's disappearance, the press had had a field day, even in the British newspapers. He could remember the headlines now:

```
BOY ABDUCTED BY WOLVES IN CANADA
COULD KARL TAYLOR STILL BE ALIVE?
TRAIL OF BLOOD MAKES HOPES FADE
```

The possibility that Karl might still be alive, or at least, the rumours put about by the hysterical media, had clearly fuelled the grief-stricken Finn's hopes.

PREDATOR

Will Luke outrun the Wolf Pack?

Read the rest of *Hunted*
to find out what happens next!

Can Tom combat Lion Country?

**A pride of lions circles its prey. Tom
can see the killer instinct in their eyes.**
It's one big, adrenalin-fuelled chase. But this
is no pumped-up action movie. There's no "pause"
button, no "rewind". And Tom must hit the
ground running…if he wants to stay alive!

ISBN 1 84121 908 8   £4.99

Got the guts for some Grizzly Action?

A great grizzly zooms into focus. It's the photo opportunity of a lifetime...
if Glen had a camera. And there's another threat to his safety – the forest fire. Will this shoot cost Glen his life? Or can he escape from the deathtrap?

ISBN 1 84121 910 X   £4.99

More Orchard Red Apples

Predator

❏ Hunted	Anthony Masters	1 84121 904 5	£4.99
❏ Deathtrap	Anthony Masters	1 84121 910 X	£4.99
❏ Killer Instinct	Anthony Masters	1 84121 908 8	£4.99

Danger

❏ Aftershock!	Tony Bradman	1 84121 552 X	£3.99
❏ Hurricane!	Tony Bradman	1 84121 588 0	£3.99

Jiggy McCue Stories

❏ The Poltergoose	Michael Lawrence	1 86039 836 7	£4.99
❏ The Killer Underpants	Michael Lawrence	1 84121 713 1	£4.99
❏ The Toilet of Doom	Michael Lawrence	1 84121 752 2	£4.99
❏ Maggot Pie	Michael Lawrence	1 84121 756 5	£4.99
❏ The Fire Within	Chris d'Lacey	1 84121 533 3	£4.99
❏ The Salt Pirates of Skegness	Chris d'Lacey	1 84121 539 2	£4.99

Orchard Red Apples are available from all good bookshops,
or can be ordered direct from the publisher:
Orchard Books, PO BOX 29, Douglas IM99 1BQ
Credit card orders please telephone 01624 836000 or fax 01624 837033
or e-mail: bookshop@enterprise.net for details.

To order please quote title, author and ISBN
and your full name and address.
Cheques and postal orders should be made payable to 'Bookpost plc.'
Postage and packing is FREE within the UK
(overseas customers should add £1.00 per book).

Prices and availability are subject to change

CORKSC EWED

CORKSCREWED

P. THEOPHILUS

Matador
9 Priory Business Park
Kibworth Beauchamp
Leicestershire LE8 0RX, UK
Tel: (+44) 116 279 2299
Fax: (+44) 116 279 2277
Email: books@troubador.co.uk
Web: www.troubador.co.uk/matador

ISBN 978-1783064-724

British Library Cataloguing in Publication Data.
A catalogue record for this book is available from the British Library.

Extracts of lyrics from *What Would I do* and *Ode to Easy* have been used with the
kind permission of songwriter Steve Gardner.

Typeset in Aldine by Troubador Publishing Ltd

Matador is an imprint of Troubador Publishing Ltd

...Friends

Ernest started trumpeting, and cracked his
   manger,
Leonard started roaring, and shivered his
   stall,
James gave the huffle of a snail in danger
   And nobody heard him at all.

                                        A. A. Milne

CAST LIST

N.B. Some characters may play more than one part

Michael Anthony Cunningham (Mack) – *central character*
Anthony Cunningham – *Michael's father*
Lily Cunningham – *Mack's mother*
William Cunningham – *Anthony's brother*
Mr. Cunningham senior – *father of Anthony and William*
Rose – *Lily's sister*

Christine Usherwood – *assistant to Anthony Cunningham*

Toby Pillinant – *Mack's friend*
Martha Pillinant – *Toby's mother*
George Pillinant – *Toby's father*

Stuart – *one of Toby's four friends from university*
Sophia – *one of Toby's four friends from university*
Ursula – *one of Toby's four friends from university*
Rufus Rollinson – *one of Toby's four friends from university*
Oswald Rollinson – *father of Rufus*

Maureen Boswell – *seller of antiques*

Elizabeth Doughty – *deputy manager at Citizen's Advice bureau*

Josie – *manager of counselling service at St. Joseph's*

Sheila – *manager of nursing service at St. Joseph's*
Caroline – *dietitian at St. Joseph's*
Alistair McDowell – *departmental manager at St. Joseph's*
Reginald Blenkinsop – *business manager at St. Joseph's*

Weston Wisbeach – *Secretary of State for Health*

Gerald Martinez – *vice president of American company, Omniwell*

Hugo Lubbock – *American wine merchant*
Arabella – *Hugo's partner*

PREAMBLE

As I grow older a trilogy of memories from my childhood, little understood at the time, re-emerge.

There is the child from down the street – dubbed a liar and snubbed by many – whom I was told I *must be nice to* because they were not lies, merely spoken dreams.

Then came a school friend who wanted to run away (with me as a companion) in search of a lost father.

The third was when I was a teenager, not a child, but is now so distant as to belong more rightly with childhood than with maturity: I was seventeen when a neighbour had a crisis. A young mother bolted, leaving behind three children, aged between two and six. My mother volunteered my services to 'watch' the children whilst the desperate father went to work and concurrently sought permanent childcare. I had only a couple or so weeks free, then I was to take up a post in the Civil Service.

My instructions were to concentrate solely on the children (of whom I had no previous experience and little knowledge). I did nothing but play, read, feed in rotation from eight in the morning until six in the evening, trying to halt their cries for their mother (whom I was told, by their father, was to be dead to them from then on) and to make them smile.

I had some success. We laughed. But was it success? I too then walked away.

When I came home from my first day at work I was asked to go round and say 'hello' to the middle boy, aged four: before lunch he had chosen a place by the fence to wait for me, and would not move from it until I arrived.

His face on that day is the most painful of memories. I cannot begin to describe his expression other than to say that the recollection of it in my dotage begins to make sense of what had gone before, and continues to inform what comes after.

I struggle not to intervene when, on a bus or in a supermarket, I think a child is being treated harshly. Not out and out abuse, of course, but a 'For God's sake just bloody shut up' screech in response to a simple curiosity about the world.

Stories that make the news slots bring a different sort of heartbreak. One which most of us have little power to prevent: And that is the crux.

If only we could write a perfect life and the writing of it create the reality. But that is a ridiculous notion, we are not in a fairy story. Life, both personal and organisational, is lived along a continuum of human interaction; observation at one end, stretching through influence and manipulation to control at the other. We know it and yet it traps us: we cannot manage the diversity of personalities, the complex set of forces and circumstances inhabiting and invading the continuum, in an attempt to achieve the perfect balance for ourselves, without effecting and affecting others.

With that in mind, I offer you *Corkscrewed.*

The story centres around the time when Michael Anthony Cunningham (Mack), in his twenties, comes to learn the value of his corkscrew collection.

It was my purpose to tell the story objectively (to stay

firmly at the observational end of the continuum); to not impose my perceptions on you, my reader. For that reason I do not, in *Corkscrewed*, write that Ursula's hair is a vibrant red – your colour vision may differ from mine. And an image of a 'friend' known only from an Internet site is no more than a prompt for the imagination, of which no two are alike. I have mine, I leave you to yours.

But no story can be told in full and there is an inevitable degree of manipulation in the act of selecting.

And I own that, as I wrote, I was at times influenced by my characters, or sorely provoked by them when they refused to evolve as I had wished. The temptation to either empathize with… or to take a jibe at… before scuttling back to the narrator's end of the continuum, was strong.

There I go, blaming my characters for my failings. I might just as well blame the reader that has a different perspective. Finally we each create our own story. Don't we?

P. Theophilus
2013

1. PRE-COLLECTION

It had happened before.

That time, Mack had been woken up from his sleep by the clapping of doors opening and closing throughout the house. His mother had come upstairs and told him 'There's nothing for you to worry about'.

(She shouldn't have said that: it was a bad spell. Those were words she had used as she had ushered him out of the room the day Grandma had fallen from her chair at the dining table. He had never seen Grandma again.)

The next morning had been especially quiet – *the doors must have tired themselves out,* he thought. But then the next morning, and the next, the same stillness, the same nothingness, the same sadness.

Mack toyed with his yellow plastic spoon. It was an old spoon, past its best, but still Mack's favourite. Mummy told him to get on with eating his cereal. He pushed the chocolatey rings together and when they were soggy enough he tried to form them into mounds. Fingers worked best he found; he discarded the yellow, once much loved, spoon. Mummy didn't notice. He got away with his bad table manners. Daddy wasn't at the breakfast table.

Nor was Daddy at lunch, nor at tea nor supper. Mack didn't eat well. Nothing seemed able to pass the lump, trapped in his chest.

Mrs Martha coaxed Mack to try one of her chocolate cookies. Mack spent all the time he could at Toby's house – that was when Toby's mother, Mrs Martha, wasn't round at Mack's house, talking to his mummy or tidying up. (His mother's friend Martha had become Mrs Martha to him when he and Toby had started school together, just a few weeks before. It was part of learning how to be more polite, now that they were growing up.)

Mack wished Mrs Martha was his mummy. She was clever. She knew things. Mack stayed quiet and tried to shush Toby to listen to the two grown-ups talk. He heard Mrs Martha tell Mummy that she would lose everything if she carried on the way she was going. Mack was amazed! How had Mrs Martha known that Mummy was losing stuff? Mummy hadn't told her. And Mack was certain that he had said nothing about Mummy not being able to find his P.E. shorts, or his first reading book, or the slip of paper to give permission for him to visit the farm with his class. For sure, Mrs Martha must be a white witch or a good fairy. And she could listen with her eyes. Mummy couldn't do that anymore.

All the same, Mack wished he hadn't told Mummy that he liked Mrs Martha best. It made her cry. She cried a lot; and drank a lot. When the bottle was empty she put her arms around him instead; squeezing hard, too hard, and saying over and over 'you're all I've got left: we'll look after each other now'.

He felt very bad about wishing he was playing with Toby and eating Mrs Martha's cookies, and wished he had never made Mummy cry. He tried to make amends by telling Mrs Martha, when she was tidying away a mess, that there was no need to do that because 'we like to live like this'. He had heard

Mummy say it. But maybe he should not have said such a thing after all; it made Mrs Martha's eyes watery. Mack tried to say the right things but seemed to get it wrong. He did a lot of trying and a lot of wishing but he did not make Mummy happy.

Mack liked it better when Daddy started to visit. And then, when Daddy was still there at breakfast time, it was almost like it used to be.

And yet, Mack still liked being at Toby's house more. It was cosy. Playing and eating were messy sorts of activities and Toby's house was a mess. But it was a good, warm, friendly sort of mess.

The mess in his own house was cold and frightening. Magazines and mailings were piled high on the table top where Mack wanted to put his bowl of cereal – though it didn't matter too much because he never felt very hungry when he was at home.

When he was at Toby's and Mrs Martha was making a soup, he would start to feel hungry as soon as he could smell the vegetables being prepared. Toby and he would race each other to reach the raw sticks of carrot Mrs Martha pushed to one side. By the time the bread came out of the oven Mack was ravenous and he thought there would never be enough food to satisfy the hunger. He would eat and eat, until all the spaces inside him were filled. And once he was full, the lingering foody smell seemed to keep him topped up for quite a while.

Mack never wanted to have soup at home. Soup, like all other meals, was a disappointment. It fought to have its own aroma identified above the smell of an over-full waste bin. Any traces of its presence disappeared as soon as it had pushed its way down to his stomach. And it was always a puzzle to Mack as to why there was no clean bowl sitting expectantly in the cupboard. Both at Christmas and at Easter he had been given clean pots (filled with edible goodies, long since gone) but those bowls and mugs must now be somewhere amongst the dirty piles of stuff in the sink, on the draining board, worktops and table.

It had always been so. Poor Mummy had never had anyone to help her. Daddy never did any work in the house, not like other daddies did. Toby's daddy was often working at home – though usually he stayed in his study, he was rarely to be seen in the kitchen. He was rarely to be seen anywhere. But Mack knew he was there because Toby would say 'be quiet. We mustn't disturb Daddy, he's working'.

All the same, Mack was quietly ecstatic to have Daddy back home. The lump in his chest had grown wings and fluttered around whenever he heard Daddy's car coming down the drive.

At times, especially when Mummy was irritable, that "thing" did grow heavy again; so heavy that it dropped down to his stomach and stayed there until he had checked that Daddy's clothes were still in the cupboards upstairs.

The jumble of heavy, empty "things", of fear, excitement, anxiety and relief, was difficult to sort.

Mack was disturbed by the sound of doors clapping.

This time, if Mum came up to see him and started to tell him that there was no need for him to worry, Mack would tell her to shut up. He was old enough now to decide for himself what he would or would not worry about.

But, this time was different: no one came upstairs. Glasses clanked; no one came upstairs. Mack heard the loud voices of strangers; no one came upstairs. He could not work out what was happening. That awful lump started to expand and fill his insides. He could hardly breathe because of it. He got out of bed and checked the cupboards. Dad's clothes were still there. He went downstairs.

Mack didn't pick out either parent's voice from outside the door of the sitting room. A couple of strangers were browsing through books in the dining room as he passed. He came to the kitchen. There, in the kitchen, he saw Mum and Dad, in the arms of one another, smiling. Mack almost screamed with delight. He almost screamed, but didn't; the joyous sound lingered in his throat and mingled with tickles.

'Sorry darling, did we wake you?' Mum asked.

Mack shook his head in reply as he found the words 'I wasn't asleep. I'm not tired'.

'Daddy's got a promotion and so we're having a bit of a celebration', his mum explained.

'Can I stay down for a bit?'

Dad gathered up his giggling son and threw him towards the ceiling. Mack reached up and touched the pointy bits of plaster.

'Aha! You've grown Michael; but you're not big enough yet to join the party I'm afraid. Come on son, I'll take you back up.'

Mack didn't mind in the least that his pleadings to stay downstairs were laughed off. It was part of the game. He snatched a sort of bottle opener in the form of a smiling waiter from off the worktop, before he was to be whisked away from this magically transformed kitchen. (By no stretch of the imagination could it be called tidy but there was a good smell, warm and comforting like his blanket.) Mack's eyes rested on the pictures of party foods on the boxes – smoked salmon blinis, mushroom and Stilton vol-au-vents, mini banofee tarts… His mum read his thoughts.

'Go on then. I'll bring you up a couple of things when they're ready.'

Mack thought that this was the happiest he had ever been in his whole life.

'If you're taking that waiter up with you be careful you don't hurt yourself on the corkscrew bit. It's very sharp' said his mum.

Mack and the waiter made strange bedfellows; Mack reflecting the waiter's cheerful countenance, even in his dreams.

The strangers who were downstairs that evening all remained strangers to Mack for several months. Dad's brother, Uncle William, had been at the party but, apart from him, they were work colleagues and Dad rarely brought home anything to do with work.

It was just after Mack's sixth birthday – so around five months after the promotion – that there was another small gathering of, mostly the same, work colleagues. The extra time Dad spent away from home 'has paid off', as Dad put it. Their bid had been successful; a lucrative contract was now 'in the bag'.

Mack chose to go to his bedroom before the guests arrived. He didn't much like intruders and, although there was no concern in particular that he could pinpoint, there was not the same optimistic air that had followed the promotion. When Mack put this to Dad – as 'why isn't this party as happy as the other one?' – it was explained as 'the principle of diminishing marginal utility'. (The word "explained" has been used loosely. Mr Cunningham merely quoted the phrase and suggested to Mack that it was something he could learn about when he was a bit older.) His dad had a book about it. Dad had books about everything. However, Mack chose one of his own to read that evening. He could do that well now, read by himself.

He had just finished a chapter when, without fully registering the sound to which he responded, he walked over to his bedroom door to greet the footsteps. But they stopped before they reached his room. Mack looked out to witness a woman push open the door to his parents' bedroom and, without moving her feet, peer in.

'Excuse me but visitors aren't allowed upstairs, unless they're sleeping over' Mack called out. He was about to add, for absolute accuracy, 'unless it's Toby come round to play and we're going to build Lego in my room', when the woman excused herself.

'I was looking for the loo. The downstairs one is occupied.'

'Well, you're not allowed to use that one anyway.' (Mack had presumed she was considering using his parents' en suite facility – a proud addition to the house.)

The woman stayed rooted to the spot.

'You must be Michael. Glad to meet you at last. I'm Christine Usherwood, your father's P.A.... that is, his personal assistant. Has he mentioned me?'

(No one but his father called him Michael – Mr Cunningham hated for names to be shortened. Michael Anthony had been *his* choices which, according to Mrs Cunningham, entitled *her* to personalize them. She had teased by first using Mickey, then Tony when addressing or referring to their baby son. Finally, she fashioned "Mack" and stubbornly stuck with it until it was adopted by nearly all but his father.)

'No, never.' Mack said out loud as, concurrently, he thought, 'Why would anyone want to mention you? You're just horrible!'

A bit unnervingly, Christine Usherwood seemed to answer his thought, though, of course, even in thought the question had been rhetorical.

'Typical. He damned well ought to have done by now. If it hadn't been for me we wouldn't have got this bloody contract and if he thinks he can keep on pushing me into the bloody background he's got another think coming. He's not doing that again.'

All the time she spoke, her eyes flicked from Mack to the bedroom, like a clicking camera. Mack informed her, politely, that the downstairs loo was most likely free to use now. But her eyes didn't listen. They were too busy flicking. He did not like Christine Usherwood.

A few weeks later, Mum and Dad had a big argument about Ms Usherwood. It was something to do with Ms Usherwood having texted that she was *'not going to give up this time'*.

Mack was not sure what to do. Should he say something about her rudeness on that earlier evening? He decided against it. After all, he was in the next room to his parents and not supposed to be listening to their argument. Plus, he might get into trouble for not having told Ms Usherwood where the other upstairs lavatory was; the "communal" one, for use by him and visitors.

The argument ended badly. Dad left.

Mack reflected: perhaps he should have sided with Mum

when Dad sided with Christine Usherwood? Not much made any sense: why should that woman have texted to Mum her opinion of Mum's poor choice of decor in their bedroom? And why had that upset Mum so much? Ms Usherwood should have kept her opinion to herself. But, perhaps Dad was right too. Perhaps Ms Usherwood was not a manipulative, controlling bitch – so called by Mum.

Mack wondered and worried about whether he ought to have, or could have done or said something to make Dad want to stay with him and Mum.

Mrs Martha said that in no way was it his fault. He was a treasure and deserved better. Toby said that he was probably naive. Mack did not know what naive meant or whether it was a nice thing to be or not. Toby did not know either.

The waiter corkscrew and Mack became firm friends. Mum told him the waiter's life story: the corkscrew, generally referred to as being in the form of a barman or bartender, had been bought by Mack's grandpa when he was on a holiday with Grandma – it may have been on their honeymoon, his mum thought. The purchase had not been intended as a souvenir, its purpose had been utilitarian, but memories of the Italian wines the corkscrew had enabled them to enjoy had given it a special place in their hearts. Mum almost smiled as she handed the waiter corkscrew back to Mack. (She never smiled fully.)

Mack knew that Grandma would be rejoicing in heaven when, at a local flea market, he found a mate for his waiter. (He would tell Grandpa when he next saw him: he didn't know when that would be – he hadn't seen him for quite a while – but he looked forward to making Grandpa happy and seeing him smile.)

He had been undecided whether to buy, as a companion, a female version of the waiter or a corkscrew figured as a kindly woman in a tall top hat. The lady was in Welsh costume, Mack was told. His mum recited *My sweet Jenny Jones is the pride of Llangollen, My sweet Jenny Jones is the girl I love best*. Mack bought the Welsh lady.

About a month later, there was a table-top sale at his school. Mack searched through several boxes of items on the same stall – or table-top – which his mum described as utter junk. She was wrong. He was rewarded with the find of a small, Scotty dog made out of metal. He thought it a bit strange that it said "Germany" on one of its paws, rather than Scotland. But as soon as he spotted the folded up worm under its body – the woman at the stall told him the screw part was called a worm – he knew he must have it. The dog was the family pet of his waiter and Welsh lady.

Such was the start of Mack's collection of corkscrews.

2. AT THE HOUSE OF CHRISTINE USHERWOOD

Christine Usherwood and Mr Cunningham received two sets of visitors in the house to which Mr Cunningham had fled. (Likely they had more callers but any others are of no concern to us. And Michael's visits are of no significance in this context – he barely stepped over the threshold.)

Christine and Mr Cunningham prepared themselves: expected were William Cunningham (Michael's uncle) and Mr Cunningham senior (Michael's grandfather).

'What do you think they want?... Just to rant at me?' Mr Anthony Cunningham asked Christine.

'To persuade you to go back to your wife, I should think.'

'They may as well not bother coming then because I'm not giving you up.'

'You don't have to give anything up. Not me. Not Michael. Not anything.' Christine reassured him. 'You are entitled to some happiness after all you've had to put up with. And if they care for you at all they'll see that. We'll face them together.'

'I don't know if I can. They'll go on about Michael and how upsetting it all is for him. I can't bear to hear it.'

Christine guided Anthony to a comfortable chair in the diner-kitchen and made coffee as she spoke.

'It will be all right. You know it will be better for Michael – once he gets over this initial upset. We've talked about it. Remember. You can see him as often as you like here. He needs to get away from that drunken environment. He will be safer here. Just give him time to get used to the idea. Don't rush him. Children need to come to things gradually.'

Christine always managed to make Anthony see sense. He was apprehensive still, but a little calmer by the time his brother and father arrived.

The visitors did not rant. They enquired of Anthony how he was, implicitly referring to both his physical and emotional health: the concern was genuine. They declined refreshment but accepted a seat. The journey, though of some distance, had gone smoothly. They had been keen to travel the eighty miles to put their minds at rest regarding Mack's future welfare, and were grateful they had been allowed the opportunity. It was William who expressed those sentiments, on behalf of both the visitors.

Christine listened attentively and shot a look towards Anthony. Anthony was sharp in his response.

'I'm going to support him, of course. If that's what you're worried about!'

There was no evidence, from Anthony's manner, of the warmth usually apparent between members of the Cunningham family.

'It's just that we wondered why you hadn't been to see him, or spoken to him lately. It's been over two weeks now, hasn't it? That's a long time to a little boy who is used to seeing his daddy every day. He's confused and frightened. He needs something from you Anthony' said William.

Christine raised her eyebrows slightly as she looked at Anthony. It was as much as was needed to bring back to his mind the essence of a previous conversation; of Christine's clear thoughts on the situation.

'I'm going to see him in a few days, when he's got over it a bit. At the moment, if I ring the house his mum answers and it's difficult. When Michael hears me, he cries. It's too upsetting.'

It was clear that Anthony relived the experience as he spoke. He was close to tears. William showed no sympathy.

'For you, maybe. But it's even more upsetting for Mack not to see you. He'll be less traumatized if he can rely on seeing you often, very often. And on the days you don't see him at least speak to him. Ring him up and say goodnight or something. Surely that's not too much to ask is it?'

Christine changed position. She moved closer to Anthony's eye line, better placed to give him her silent support.

'I can't. Sometimes we're out at the time Michael goes to bed – and I don't take my mobile with me. It's not fair on Christine: it drives her mad when people keep pestering me. And I can't keep going back every two minutes to see him. He won't get used to my not being there if I do…. This is where I live now. My life is with Christine. She's waited long enough, I can't ask her to wait any longer or I'll lose her' he said.

Such talk angered William and caused Mr Cunningham senior to despair: the latter hid his face in his hands. Again it was Anthony's brother who took up the baton.

'This is ridiculous. For God's sake Anthony, no one is saying go back home to live: that's your decision. All we're saying is do right by your son. Don't let him down, he's done nothing wrong and he's still your responsibility. See him!'

Anthony adopted the same posture as his father, his tears hidden. Christine was obliged to break her silence; lend her vocal support.

'Tell that to his wife. She won't let Michael come here; she's using him to get Anthony to go back. She wants to split us up again. He's the father. He's got his rights.'

William had not gone to that house to speak to that woman! (An onlooker would have seen his lips tighten to stop the transmitted thought escaping; seen the displaced anger in his eyes and trembling cheeks, and might have feared a little for Christine.) But it was her house and William remembered his manners; he drew breath with which to state the obvious – and ignore the ludicrous.

'*Mack's* rights and Anthony's responsibilities are the priorities. Mack is the child, Anthony… both of you are adults. Your relationship is of no concern to me, other than in trying to limit the damage it causes to Mack, the *innocent* child in all this.'

Those were not the words Christine wanted spoken in front of Anthony, he in such a vulnerable state of mind. It was unfair. She retaliated.

'I'm sick to death of being treated as the bad one! I moved house because Anthony said he wanted to be with me: it's costing me childcare (*neither William nor Mr Cunningham senior understand the statement but had no wish to deviate, so let it pass*) and extra rent. And now Anthony's being made to feel so guilty about leaving a drunk in charge of his son, that he's saying he's not sure anymore about coming here. After all I've done for him; all I've given up. You're ruining our lives!'

Christine started to sob and struggled to get out the following words.

'Leave my house. Just get out. Go with them Anthony, if that's what you want.'

The sobs then consumed Christine and prevented any further dialogue.

Anthony said nothing at first. He went towards the door. As he opened it for his father and brother to leave, his words were desperate.

'I can't have anything to do with you until you accept Christine as my partner and welcome her into the family. Goodbye.'

William, choosing to ignore the rebuff, moved to embrace Anthony. Anthony drew back.

No member of the once close Cunningham family was without a heavy heart; not one, not in any of the four houses across which they were now so thinly spread.

It was a few months later before the next visitors of consequence descended on, and entered the house of Christine Usherwood.

Anthony Cunningham needed no preparation for the visit of Martha and George Pillinant: it had been decided (by Christine) that their reason for making the request to speak to Anthony would be ascertained by Christine, in private, and relayed to Anthony afterwards, again in private. Anthony's constitution had become far from robust; the constant pressure, exerted mainly by the Cunninghams, to do this or to do that for Michael's well being, had taken its toll. It was expected, by Christine, that the Pillinants would add to that pressure.

Martha and George Pillinant were surprised and disappointed to discover that Anthony was not at home. George had been clear, when he had telephoned beforehand, that they wished to see Anthony. Neither Pillinant felt kindly toward Christine and, besides that, they had missed seeing Anthony over the previous months and had wanted to take advantage of the opportunity to renew contact, regrettable though the circumstances were.

The Pillinants lived but a few minutes drive away (close to Barkham Avenue, on which number 2, the house on the corner, was that of the deserted mother and son Cunningham). And though their business had a certain level of urgency, the precise timing of the visit did have a degree of flexibility; one or other of them could, and would be happy to return at Anthony's convenience. This position was put to Christine.

However, their protestations that it really was Anthony they needed to see, met with a "tell me, and tell me now or forget it" attitude. Anthony *had* to know the purpose of their visit, so there was no alternative but to tell through the medium that was Christine. George did the telling.

'Mack's mother has been admitted to hospital. We have Mack staying with us – and we are happy with that – but we wanted to speak with Anthony in case he preferred to be with Mack until his mum was back home.'

Christine bought herself a little thinking time with her thanks for the information and offers of refreshment. Martha – anxious to be away before the end of the school day – declined the offer. Christine, equally anxious that there be no return visit, rapidly made and gave a judgement – expressed in such a manner as to infer it was the opinion of the absent Anthony.

'Anthony feared it would come to this. Thank you for taking Michael in, it will be such a relief to his father. Of course, Anthony couldn't return to Barkham Avenue because it would be confusing and unsettling for Michael when his mother came out of hospital and his father left again. And, much as we'd love to have him with us, he couldn't stay here because we think it is too soon for Michael to know about my daughter. But I'll let him know where Michael is. I'm sure he'll be in contact with you to thank you himself. Thanks again.'

Martha was indignant that Christine, by her observation that it had "come to this" seemed to infer that the malady requiring admission to hospital was alcohol related. The Pillinants had been careful to divulge to *that* woman (who generated in them a similar, frustrated anger as noted in her previous visitors) no more information than was absolutely necessary and that most certainly did not include a diagnosis. (Though perhaps Martha's indignation was *less* to do with the fact that the woman had dared to presume such an outcome, and *more* because she had happened to presume correctly.) Added to that insolence was the lack of any remorse for the destruction her selfish, evil actions had wrought. Martha had been friends with Lily Cunningham for quite some years, in fact from before Lily became Mrs Cunningham. They had become friends at a time when Lily was going out with Anthony and she with George. Martha was in no doubt that the persistent, predatory pursuance of Anthony by the Usherwood woman was the cause of Lily's current pitiable state. And had said as much to George many a time.

However, despite the provocation, Martha retained her dignity by stifling her fury and refusing her thoughts a voice.

There was nothing more either Martha or George could do, other than repeat their regrets at not seeing Anthony; to hope he was well and re-affirm that they looked forward to seeing him when he called to see Mack – as they expected he would want to do.

Ms. Usherwood did not concur with that expectation nor make any commitment on behalf of Anthony.

Martha and George left, feeling as they had felt on arrival, disappointed.

3 .CORKSCREW COLLECTION

Mack's collection of corkscrews numbered 471 by the time he had reached the age of fifteen; the time when the rate of collecting had been at its greatest. Not that he then stopped scouting for them entirely, but the pace had slackened, purpose had been diverted.

Not all in his collection could be described as either impressive or collectable. And some, bought in job lots, duplicated types he already had. Nevertheless, amongst his treasures were some rarer examples – an 1880s Greenways beer bottle opener and a brass, butterfly wing nut operated, nineteenth century Farrow & Jackson, to name but two. Several collectable finds pushed the total pound value well into four figures, on a good day close to five.

He had kept meticulous notes over the years, noting down everything the sellers were able to tell him about his buys and the prices he had paid; never higher than low tens and often in single figures.

He read around his subject – increasingly so, as he became interested in the development and mechanics of corkscrews – but for the most part Mack disregarded any increase in monetary value his research might bring. Neither was he swayed by which items fellow collectors covetted. It has to be said that there were times when engineering, and all logical aspects were totally disregarded: he was reluctant to admit to emotional ties, yet Mack's favourite was undeniably Grandpa's waiter.

Later, there was another favoured one (favoured at times, not consistently). It was an unremarkable corkscrew, modelled in the shape of two birds "kissing", bought after the pace of collecting had slowed right, right down; all but stopped.

As with Grandpa's waiter, it was likely the memory of its acquisition that elevated the position of the bird corkscrew within the jangle – or whatever is the collective noun for corkscrews: he had had an interesting chat with the seller, Maureen Boswell.

A woman so seemingly wise and yet, from her appearance, not of a dissimilar age to himself. They had got on easily right from the start. Mack's casual opening gambit (merely a comment on the eclectic items she had for sale – ceramics, kitchen paraphernalia, tools, toys, books – any miscellany imaginable) was all it took to trigger quite a lengthy chat. It somehow would have seemed churlish, given all the attention she had paid him, not to have invited her for a coffee after the fair closed. Maureen had been pleased to accept. Pleased enough to close down earlier than the other sellers – a good deal earlier. Immediately.

Maureen's stall had none of the grandeur of those stands displaying the highest quality, lavishly decorated ceramics; nor the enticement of luxurious jewels and polished precious metals locked away in glistening, glass cabinets. No, her wares reflected the origin of her selling experience: Maureen had accompanied her mother to a car boot sale where, together, they had sold off the lesser items from the redundant household of some relative or friend. The better things had gone to auction. She had become addicted to the thrill and had purposely bought more items to sell, albeit on a small scale.

Mack passed the time of day with Maureen several times

during that and the next year. Their meetings were always at antiques fairs. Nothing specific was ever arranged but the particular fairs they each enjoyed were repeated frequently, at three of the same venues across the country. They knew where to find each other. Or rather, Mack knew where to find Maureen.

Sometimes, Maureen would come across some corkscrew or other and hold on to it for Mack's consideration. He always bought it, out of gratitude for her thoughtfulness, but did not necessarily consider the later offerings as special to the collection as he did his first purchase from her.

After a while he followed Maureen's suggestion to supplement his physical searches with occasional searches on-line, which were much more efficient. The cost in time and fuel for an increasingly higher number of fruitless road journeys had contributed to an unwillingness to hunt for corkscrews; a lessening in enthusiasm, which had temporarily been reversed after meeting Maureen.

Mack was confused by Toby's attitude to her (and, to a lesser extent, corkscrews).

Initially, Toby had seemed to welcome Mack's desire for Maureen's company. He had been with Mack on the day they first met and it was he, in fact, who had been the first to dash across to her stall – attracted by a slide rule of some description. Mack had sauntered after him but as he approached the stall, Toby had moseyed on.

Toby claimed little recollection of Maureen, only of the slide rule (Mack remembered details of both stall display and stall holder), but had been keen to listen to Mack enthuse.

'What did she say to you?' Toby had asked of Mack, repeatedly, at each and every suggestion of a turn in their conversation. Toby must have been as familiar with what had passed between Mack and Maureen on that first day as they themselves.

There had been nothing of a romantic nature in their words. And, before such a relationship had chance to develop Mack had established that none was possible: she had a husband and they had a young daughter, apparently just beginning to toddle. Consequently, the conversations between he and Maureen, though warm and considerate, continued to retain a deliberate level of formality. One which restricted progress to any level of intimacy that might breed suffering.

Toby knew only the content of the first conversation. He never asked about further ones: never knew she was married. He could have no justification for disapproval on that account. What then, prompted his subsequent change in attitude? His reluctance to chat on any subject that referenced her?

It puzzled Mack.

Any subsequent dejection at the futility of his friendship with Maureen was borne privately. And yet, he did wonder whether Toby's repeated encouragement to 'drop the frigging corkscrews' might have been a euphemism to "drop" Maureen and, as such, indicate a degree of perception he had not previously credited to Toby.

By the time Mack came to sell his collection, his affections were stronger elsewhere... but there is more to tell before then: I have rushed on and must take a step back, to a time before adulthood, before Maureen.

4. RETROSPECTIONS

FLUX

For Martha and Lily, Toby and Mack had been the shared experience of motherhood: Toby and Mack had been as brothers. The babies had crawled after each others' toys… in primary school years, each boy had supplied the other with an opponent for intergalactic battles… and when Mack's mother became unwell, Mack was taken in by the Pillinants. This undeniably mitigated the effect on Mack of his mum's hospitalization.

Unfortunately, after two relapses in Lily Cunningham's health, George Pillinant saw a necessity to call for a change of arrangements. Fond as he was of Mack, he had to put his own family first. Martha saw none of the risks to her own health in caring for Mack that were so apparent to her husband. But that, said George, was precisely why he must act in her interest and insist on an alternative solution for Mack's care.

It was all ifs and buts.

Martha tried to make contact with Mack's grandfather, but all attempts were to no avail. Attempts to contact his Uncle William met with a similar fate. These were the only relatives of Anthony known to Martha, and they had become out of reach. It might have been thought that Martha would know more of Lily's family than of Anthony's. But no. Had she thought to ask Lily beforehand – for Lily Cunningham was not very communicative once in the throes of a severe, acute phase of illness – it may have been different.

Social Services (the last resort) never managed to put Mack with a family. He was placed at "Fallowfield Residential Home", a place not regarded by him as a home (though, for that matter, nor would have been any stranger's house). In other circumstances, Fallowfield could have been inviting: a large, impressive, gothic styled house in its own lawned grounds, he could have imagined himself a visiting poor relation of a wealthy aristocratic family. But he didn't. He was afraid. Not of going into the house (he had no fear of ghosts) but of leaving his own home and mother. He clung onto the words spoken by his social worker, 'it's not for long' and chose to anticipate his, and his mother's imminent return to Barkham Avenue.

He spent as many hours in bed as were permitted in those early stays. Snuggled under his covers with the secreted, smiling waiter, Mack would imagine that the voice of the male carer downstairs was that of his father: Dad had heard that Mum was ill again and had come to scoop up his son and take him back home. The dream made all else disappear.

(It was his own home, in Barkham Avenue, that Mack imagined they went back to because he had never seen his father's latest home. It was too far away. That was why his father could no longer get to see him very often: plus, he was very busy with the new company he had formed with his one-time secretary. Mack knew that. It was fact, not part of his imaginings.)

Mack had visited his father fairly frequently between the time of his leaving Barkham Avenue and the subsequent move further afield. He might not have thought on those visits too much – especially when in the care home – but they had been made and ought to be recorded.

If I may remind you, Christine Usherwood's house was but a short distance from the Cunningham household in Barkham Avenue. The distance was short and so too was the duration of each of Michael's weekly visits.

The routine (Christine knew the importance of routine in a child's life) was that Michael be picked up from his own door by his father and taken to Christine Usherwood's door, out of which Christine would then step to join them. Only rarely would Michael go into her house – such as when his father needed to pop in for something he had forgotten – and even then he would go no further than the kitchen, the room into which the outside door opened. The three of them routinely went straight to the café, conveniently next door.

Michael would be returned to Barkham Avenue after either one or two hours. If the weather was fine they would go for a play in a nearby park for an hour or so after the café snack. But in inclement weather the play in the park was omitted and Michael would be taken home, by his father, immediately on leaving the café. (Christine did travel with them once but it was judged, from the expression on the receiving face of Lily Cunningham, that the sight of Christine in the car was objectionable. Christine said she would not accompany them in future, 'if it's going to lead to trouble', and she kept her word.)

Such was the general routine. Excepting that during the months December to February, the weather was sometimes

so inclement as to prevent Michael's father from making the short journey to collect him. In those weeks there was no visit to the café either. No contact other than a text expressing regret at the circumstance.

But, as Christine emphasized in a series of separate texts to Michael's mother, it was not because Anthony didn't want to spend more time with Michael. No, Lily was wrong to suppose such a thing.

Anthony was sensitive to the fact that the presence of her own daughter might stir up feelings of jealousy and resentment in Michael. And, as Anthony's situation had forced her to move away from her own family support, it was not possible to make alternative care arrangements for her daughter in order to accommodate Michael. Oh, the number of times Christine had to repeat these things to Lily!

She tried to reassure Lily that, in time, as Michael adjusted to the changes, all would feel more comfortable. Christine also tried to persuade Lily that if only she would be reasonable and allow her to explain more of her feelings and actions, Lily would not judge her so harshly and **all** could "move on". (Perhaps that would have been so. Perhaps not. We shall never know as Lily remained as intransigent as Christine.)

Much was accepted, not questionned. Not even the horrible time, before bad weather set in, when the routine was otherwise not adhered to: the time Mack's mother had responded to a text from his father and taken Michael herself to the Usherwood door.

The text had been somewhat ambiguous but Lily read with optimism the words *'Not well. If you bring M will make amends for missing his birthday'*. (A plan – formed between Mr and Mrs Cunningham – to arrange something "together" for Mack's seventh birthday had gone awry.) But Lily's optimism in the text was misjudged. There was to be no belated, one occasion togetherness for the sake of their child. It was not Anthony who faced her. It was her humiliator.

The Usherwood woman stepped from her door to take charge of the child...

'Thank you Lily for bringing Michael: Anthony is still indisposed' she said (pronouncing the last word "in deesposed" as she stifled a sneeze).

His mum's startled expression morphing to one of extreme pain was upsetting for Mack. As was the way she sped away without a backward glance. He might have cried but for the shock of it.

'Oh dear, she is in a mood isn't she Michael? Come on, let's us have a cake.'

Michael was not consoled. And the visit got worse.

Christine Usherwood took Michael by the elbow to head towards the café. Mack looked back at her house; he looked at the window, wishing for a sight of his dad.

And, to Mack's surprise, there he was! Standing back from the window a little, he was only just visible. But certainly, there he was, looking out, watching them.

Mack was overjoyed and shouted out.

'Dad *can* come too. He's *not* in Deesposed, he's *back*, he's *here*. Look!' Mack pointed to the figure in the shadow.

As Ms. Usherwood, too, turned towards the window, Anthony Cunningham dropped his head and simultaneously raised a hand to cover one side of his face. (Unnecessary movements; it was too shadowy for the bruising to have been seen in any case.)

Clearly, Christine Usherwood did not share Michael's joy at his father's appearance. She offered no explanation for maintaining the separation of father and son, nor gave Michael any options: she gripped his arm firmly, dragged him away, into the café and pushed him down onto the nearest seat. He struggled and strained to see out of the café window; to catch a further glimpse of his father – actions for which he was reprimanded.

'Sit still can't you? There's nothing for you to see so stop being such a bloody nuisance.'

His behaviour was so troublesome that the treat of a cake was denied. He was being honest not "bloody cheeky" when he said 'it doesn't matter, I'm not hungry'. So, it could be argued that the violent kick he received from under the table – which badly bruised his shin – was deserved even less than was the cake. But Mack conveyed no sense of injustice. He said not a word as his chaperone continued to damn his lack of appreciation of her plight. Couldn't he see how hard she was trying to cope with his visit under such trying circumstances? Apparently not: he answered nothing. He did nothing, other than to keep his feet tucked underneath his chair and fix his eyes on the table top in front of him.

Within a quarter of an hour Christine Usherwood had used Mr Cunningham's phone to text Mrs Cunningham, informing her that, as Anthony was no better, she could collect Michael immediately. To Michael's relief, Mrs Cunningham obliged.

Once safely home, Mack told his mum that he had had a horrible time and, if he wasn't going to be with his dad, he never wanted to go there again. He volunteered no more on the subject and his mother never asked.

Number twenty-seven was in the middle of a row of terraced houses; small, terraced houses. It was not a good omen. According to electoral records (George Pillinant had a good contact in the local government offices) there were four residents including Mack's Aunt Rose. 'Not much space in there for Mack' muttered George as he paused his approach.

George was by no means sure he was doing the right thing in paying the visit. It was not correct procedure. Social Services, if he had referred to them, may well have pointed out that, at that late stage – Mack was now 15 years old – it would be detrimental to move him away from his school, particularly as only a short stay in hospital was envisaged for Mack's mother. It was for Martha's sake that George had telephoned Rose.

Martha had loved having Mack join their family when first Lily had taken a turn for the worse. (Though obviously she had regretted the necessity.) And she had fretted, oh how much she had fretted, on each of Lily's hospitalizations subsequent to George having insisted she "stood back" from Lily's problems and took care of her own.

George remained convinced that taking responsibility for Mack would hinder Martha's recovery, recovery from a second – though not secondary – cancer, but could not disagree with Martha that fretting was of no help to her either. (Both pondered but neither spoke of possible interplay between stress, timing, cancer. Martha's distress about Mack's situation continued as she recovered from one cancer; would taking action have prevented the start of the second? No point in asking.)

As a response to the dilemma, George had taken it upon

himself to find an option for Mack's care that would suit all parties.

It was a pity that Rose lived so far off, not least because this had been a contributory factor in her losing frequent contact with Lily and, consequently, with her nephew. But he was surely doing a good thing if he brought the two families closer. Emotionally closer, there was nothing he could do about physical distance.

Neither George nor Martha had known of the existence of any siblings, so it had come as something of a shock when Lily brought Rose's name into conversation. It had not seemed appropriate; not pertinent to the topic. Lily must have had Rose on her mind, been thinking of her, or she would not have mentioned her name: an indication that she would like to see her, surely. On reflection, George viewed Rose as like manna from heaven. She could be the answer to their prayers.

Yet, he hesitated before knocking on the door.

Rose knew from George's phone call that he was a friend of her sister's family, but that was all she knew. Her immediate question, 'Has something happened to Lily?' gave George the perfect opening to tell of the troubles of Lily and Anthony Cunningham – that is, as much as related to the current circumstance. He did not hazard to say more of the marriage other than it had broken down.

Rose nodded acceptance and said 'My parents said as much. I always thought he was alright but they must have seen something I didn't. Poor Lil.'

Where did that come from? George wanted to ask: he and Martha took pains not to be judgmental or to side with any one of their friends against another. But then Rose and Lily were sisters, it was natural that she should blame Anthony. He ignored her comment and carried on in the same vein, relaying the practical details of who was living where and the relative health of available carers.

It was not a rushed exposition. Clearly, Rose had not been busy on his arrival – a magazine lay open on the sofa and a half full mug of coffee stood on the carpet close by – and so George allowed himself the luxury of time, to settle and to assess the household: interruptions, many and varied, were accepted good humouredly by all present.

Rose was not alone. Nine-year-old Wayne was squatted nearby – and encouraged to slightly lower the sound that accompanied the picture he was looking at on the facing screen. (Wayne's father and elder brother were out. The former 'at work', whereabouts of the latter unknown – though that was not a cause for concern for either Rose or Wayne.)

Wayne sported a very spiky and colourful hairstyle. Three colours in all; brown the base colour to which white and blue had been added in parts (and would have to be removed before the start of the next school term, "Eh Mam" reminded him). His hair was not the only entertaining aspect of Wayne as George found out when Wayne, for no obvious reason, jumped up and announced.

'Eh Mam, I'll do Callum.'

If only George had watched more "reality" television he would have been better able to judge the merits of Wayne's impersonation of I.B.Callum. George's enquiry as to whether I.B.Callum was a comedic West Country person was met with looks of incredibility. But Wayne was not daunted by George's ignorance.

He asked 'Don't ya know him?' and followed with another

question. 'Who's this then?' And proceeded with another impersonation.

No, George had no idea about that one, or the next. Rose tried to compensate for George's lack of appreciation of her son's talent.

'He really is very good you know. Everybody says he's brilliant. He's always being asked to do Callum, though I think he's even better at Jaypul... ... the one who won last week's semi?'

'Eh Mam, he don't know who ya mean.' Wayne grinned, then addressed George. 'Don't tell me ya don't know Jaypul!'

The expression on George's face said it all. Still Wayne persevered.

'You watch. You'll see *me* on telly one day.'

In the absence of Wayne's father, George stepped in with some timely advice.

'Maybe it's not a good career choice: by the time you are grown-up I might not be the only one to have no idea who any of these people are – or *were*, more likely!'

'Ya don't 'ave to be grown-up to go on. Callum's only a *bit* older than me.'

Wayne's observation silenced George on that subject and he moved towards the purpose of his visit – to check out the feasibility of alternative short-term care for Mack, with them.

On this point, Wayne was sharp. 'Eh Mam, ya get paid for that don't ya?' And answered his own question with suggestions of what could be bought with the money (the limit of which, obviously not a consideration). None of the fancied spend had reference to Mack's welfare, quite the opposite. The only thing Wayne wanted to share was his wish list – which might, perhaps, include an exotic animal.

There was no *particular* enthusiasm for an animal but, nevertheless, the half-suggestion set George to muse on the maxim that "owners grow to look like their dogs". And to wonder if, in the absence of a dog, owners grew to look like their sofas: Rose was wearing a crumpled, grubby beige dress, almost camouflaged by where she sat. She was deep in thought, paying no attention to Wayne. The beige fat-filled tube round her midriff was echoed in the relaxed cushion at her back. The camouflage was suddenly so striking – if that is not a contradiction in terms – that George found himself asking Rose.

'Have you got a dog?'

As Rose was not paying attention to Wayne's chatter, and the question did not relate to their earlier conversation, the posing of it puzzled Rose.

'Umm?… No…. Why do you ask?'

Wayne suggested it was because of the smell from Mum's socks by the side of the sofa. They all laughed. It was a get-out for George: he had no answer he could have given. It had been a stupid, irrelevant question to ask and he had got away lightly with the error.

George also regretted that he had inferred the solution for Mack's predicament to be life at number twenty-seven. Perhaps he had been wrong to consider it. It was none of his business. He knew nothing of Lily's family. What if Mack's maternal grandparents were still alive and they were antagonistic toward the mere mention of Anthony? What would that be like for Mack? The more he thought, the more unsure he became. But the result of that error was still in abeyance.

Rose was quiet, but thoughtful too, leaving Wayne's enthusiasm for spend unchecked for some minutes more. Eventually she spoke.

'Shut up Wayne. It's not about money.'

(Those words were a relief to George. He had never considered an official fostering angle for Rose. Too much of a complication; far too much red tape. And anyway, she was family.)

'Of course I will help Lily if she needs me to. No question. I'm just not sure it would be right for Mack. We're virtually strangers to him, poor mite, and he might be happier around his friends, especially if it's an important time for his school work.'

George could have kissed Rose: the perfect answer (although he would not have described Mack as a "mite"). He spoke with genuine gratitude.

'Thank you Rose. I think you're right. I think Mack will probably prefer to stay in the same district. But, knowing that there is somewhere for him, with someone who cares – if he feels the need – will mean everything to him. To tell you the truth, I suspect Social Services would think the same; not a good idea to uproot him for just a short time. I don't think Lily has mentioned you to them – she's not really been thinking straight. And I just wanted to see how you felt before anything was said. If you don't mind – for peace of mind – I might just pass on your contact details – on the off chance you're needed. Would that be all right?'

Rose confirmed that it would and took George's details in exchange. Objective met.

ESCAPE

A bilious attack, shortly after his arrival at "Fallowfield Residential Home" on the very first occasion, had allowed Mack the advantage of a room of his own. For some reason, that advantage (if advantage it was) was sustained on successive stays. Mack's bilious attacks, frequent since the age of around five, had already been diagnosed as migraine. Mack knew this but allowed the doctor to be the one to inform his carers.

He derived a certain contentment from having migraine when he was in the care home. It was not enjoyment. No, to say he enjoyed having a migraine would be perverse: such episodes were totally incapacitating and quite wretched; he would retch up bile every 20 minutes or so for hours on end. A bucket next to his bed was essential as he was often incapable of making the journey to the lavatory. Mack was conversant with the situation and knew that nothing could be done but to be resigned to let time pass. *Time* was the cure. *Place* was irrelevant: he was barely conscious of whether his bed was in Barkham Avenue or Timbuktu. And, in the care home, *that* was the compensation of migraine.

The doctor was welcome too, purely because he was familiar. In actual fact, a doctor was not required but the care workers were not to know that. It was alarming to them that Mack had lost the use of his legs.

Paralysis was not common with migraine, neither in general nor to Mack specifically, although it had happened once before and so was of no concern to him: he knew that his legs would work again once he was rid of the pain in his head, and he had no use of them in the meantime.

Michael's dad had told Michael that the final feeling in his head was similar to a hangover. (Unlike Michael, his dad was qualified to make such a comparison, having experienced both.)

The doctor had said that more women than men were migraineurs (he used that term. He would not allow Michael or his father to be referred to as "migraine sufferers": 'it is my job to prevent suffering'). But that gender distribution had made no sense to Mack: the only migraineurs he knew were himself and his dad. 'Neither of us are women are we Dad?' Michael had said. 'Very astute son' his dad had replied.

No, memories of migraine were not all bad. His dad never did rescue him from Fallowfield but at least, on his very first stay, their family doctor had come to see him. It was something. He chatted a bit about home. After he had advised that a good intake of fluids be maintained, he left the bedroom, leaving the door half open.

Mack was aware of an intermittent curiosity amongst several young residents, drawn to explore the activity. None pushed the door further open but all adjusted their steps as they passed – sometimes misjudging, which necessitated a step backwards – to give their angled heads a reasonable view of the patient. That too was comforting for Mack, reminiscent of the watchful eye over his recovery that he had always sensed was kept by his mum.

One child was heard to say.

'He's paralytic like his mum!'

The child was mistaken: his mum was not a migraineur. But, perhaps the child had got confused by what the doctor had said about more women having it. (Though Mack could not actually recall the doctor saying his mum was paralytic, nor his repeating the thing about who usually had migraines.) All the same, it was an understandable mistake to make, Mack reasoned in his semi-delirious state. He closed his eyes and turned over to face the wall.

Mack remembered that when the doctor had first listed all

the things that might trigger a migraine (Mum and the doctor, between them had deduced that insufficient sleep and too long gaps between eating were likely what "did it" for Mack), alcohol had been on the list.

So, could it, after all, be migraine that was making his mum unwell? A missed diagnosis? That, to Mack, was an uplifting possibility: a chance that, in time, things could be made right. He thought that he would ask the doctor about this. But he never did.

Some of the questions that Mack had never asked were answered as a matter of course. Others not.

It would be wrong to give the impression that every stay at Fallowfield was accompanied by migraine. It was not. Most were migraine free. The very last time, for instance, Mack had been extremely well. Well but angry, initially. He had thought it totally unnecessary to have to move out of his home at all.

Mack was confident that, as always, his mother would respond well to treatment. It would be but a brief period that she would be in hospital and he could manage perfectly well taking care of himself. He was '15 years old for God's sake!'

His social-worker (a new one who, as with the others, will not be named: she will not appear again) had no doubts that he was fully capable but, she said, her hands were tied. Had he been sixteen it might have been different. They discussed the options.

She did agree that it would be best for him to be able to attend his usual school and so acquiesced that his Aunt Rose not be contacted; she lived beyond a commutable distance. A similar reasoning was applied with regard to a short stay with his father.

A temporary move for his father back to Barkham Avenue was out of the question: it had been considered and ruled out on previous times and nothing had changed. No doubt, if asked, Anthony Cunningham would reply that he would "be there" for his son. But his work required the constant assistance of Christine. It followed, therefore, that Christine should be allowed to stay by Anthony's side, wherever he was to reside.

The new social worker had obviously read the file. She put it to Mack that it might be for the best if he let her arrange for him to return to Fallowfield. 'It won't be for long and it will put your mum's mind at rest, won't it?' – 'Salt can make things tastier but it can also make wounds smart', was the oblique way in which she expressed her understanding and discounted the possibility of "Mr Cunningham's new partner" at Barkham Avenue.

Mack could not deny that he would have loved to be with his father at Barkham Avenue. But he did not want Ms. Usherwood there: the occasions when he had been forced to be in her company had not made him wishful for a closer relationship. (Mack enjoyed understating the strength of his feelings as he spoke with the social worker. He thought it showed maturity.)

From the options put to him, therefore, Mack chose Fallowfield. And found it more bearable than previously. Though whether this was because the stay was over in eight days, or because he so wanted to have made the right choice, or merely because he was older, Mack did not contemplate.

He walked out of the Fallowfield door knowing he need never go back through it (he was almost sixteen) and that was good enough.

5. A DEATH

The twenty-second of October of the year in which Mack had his nineteenth birthday, was the day Mack had not dared to imagine. Not the actual date, for he could not have predicted when that would be, but the occasion; the funeral of his mum, Mrs Lily Cunningham. (She was Mrs Cunningham still, for Mack's parents had never divorced, legally.)

It might have been supposed that the day on which she died would be the one most dreaded. And had Mack ever allowed his thoughts to consider life without his mum being around, somewhere or other, then that might have been the case. In the event, the day of her death was unfelt, almost unremembered: shock, they said. And the five days from death to funeral were as one to him, the time of preparation.

Aunt Rose stayed with Mack throughout those days. She had been the one to go to the school on the seventeenth, to break the dreadful news and to take him back home, to his home, in Barkham Avenue.

Was it now *his* home – or his house... whatever? The question was not asked aloud, certainly not by Mack: he had no real interest in the answer. He was somewhat appalled that such a thought had come into his mind. What was a house compared to a life! He did not want to think on such things. And yet, he found he could not totally prevent the obtrusion.

Toby's visits provided a welcomed respite. Toby got on well with Aunt Rose, and in each other's company, Mack was released from an obligation to verbally display stoicism. They were quite content for Mack to be silent, just so long as he was present and not seemingly distressed.

Michael's father supported him as far as he was able. He telephoned a few times. He said little. Michael replied in a similar, limited fashion. During the long silences Michael sometimes sensed that his dad was crying, though this was not admitted to; coughs or rustlings of paper served to disguise the softer sounds. It was always Michael who ended the call.

Rose held back from asking Mack whether or not his father would be actually coming to the house at any time, rather than merely dialling its number! She rehearsed the question every time she looked at Mack's face as he replaced the receiver but never asked it: she was wise enough to know it was anger at her brother-in-law she would vent in the phrasing of the question and the tone of the asking. She knew full well the answer was a no. And she knew full well that her nephew longed for it to be a yes.

Nevertheless, Michael was grateful that Dad took the funeral arrangements in hand. They even managed to meet up for an hour in town when Dad had an appointment with the funeral directors. There wasn't time to go to the house, Dad said, as he had to get back to meet someone off of a train. So, their time together was rationed; a bitter sweet, treasured time.

Of course, Anthony Cunningham had intended to be at the funeral. It was a disappointment when the text came: his car had to go into the garage and he would not be able to make it after all. Quite a setback. But some things 'just can't be helped', Michael told the other mourners.

The other mourners were few in number. It did not

signify. Mack hardly noticed who was there or who was not – apart that is from Aunt Rose, Toby, Mrs Martha and Mr Pillinant; all present.

Some people Mack did not recognize. It was rather strange to overhear personal comments from them – 'It's so sad. He was such a happy child'… 'It's the first time I've seen Michael without a smile on his face' – yet he was not moved to enquire as to how they were acquainted, or to look more closely for clues as to an identity. It mattered not. He would not see any of them again.

Mrs Martha's appearance was a very pleasant surprise. It was fleeting (the appearance, that is, not the pleasure). She was whisked away by her husband as soon as the main proceedings were over and she had spoken a quick word to Mack. The time for her next chemotherapy session was imminent, so the dash was understandable.

Those five days of preparation, preceding the funeral, had served the purpose. The dreaded day passed, as does a migraine. Some of the fear had been replaced by relief. Such relief it was a painful joy. It was impossible to imagine a worse thing to have to face than that day: Mack had not dared to imagine it yet he had been forced to live it, and he had done. It was over.

A few days later, Michael had another telephone call from his father.

He was not to worry about his future. The house would have to be sold, of course, but they would have a chat about what Michael wanted to do and his father would "set him up" and see that he was "all right". In the meantime – if Michael felt up to it – it would be useful if Michael could 'put aside

41

anything, absolutely anything, anything whatsoever' – that he wanted to keep from the house, before it was put on the market. Dad would take care of anything unwanted by Michael when he closed down the house. There was 'no rush'. He merely wanted to put Michael's mind at rest, in case he had been worrying.

It would not be true to say that Mack had not started to think, sometimes, about his future. He had done so, intermittently. Most people, in particular his teachers, had urged him to take his time; not to make any quick decisions that he might later regret. He was taking the advice and not rushing; not rushing into anything.

The decision seen as key was whether or not to leave school. Mack was edging towards leaving. His work had gradually deteriorated over the previous couple or so years, resulting in his current position not being ideal: he was behind on studies because of required re-sits. Mack was keen to catch-up on having a place in life; possibly more so than catching-up on education. Toby was well into his university education.

Another advantage of leaving school would be the freedom to live wherever he chose. Aunt Rose (for the moment still at his home but about to return to her own) had kindly offered Mack a place at number twenty-seven for whenever, and for whatever length of stay, he wanted. Toby had been living away for some years.

Mack was pleased to receive that telephone call from his father, though he had not been worrying.

6. NORTHERN SOUL

The time spent in deliberation – to move away immediately or stay on and finish the school year – was of such duration as to render decision making superfluous. The examinations had crept up on Mack with nothing to justify abandonment. Intentions had not been acted upon; the months had spread into a year... and more. Several further months were needed to complete sale and removal arrangements.

Not yet settled, but Mack was optimistic. Not about job prospects; not about anything in particular. Perhaps it was simply the prospect of meeting up with Toby and having a good day out.

The day was to begin at the house of the Pillinants. A house he had not visited for quite some time, close as it was.

'Come on in Mack. You've beaten Toby, but it will be nice to have some time together before he gets here.' Martha stood aside to let Mack pass as she asked, 'How are you?'

'Fine thanks.... Mm, is that chocolate cookies I can smell?' Mack had been sucked towards the kitchen, just a short, narrow passage away from the now green, not red, front door. The intervening years wiped away in a sniff.

'I wondered if you would still have a nose for them.' Martha Pillinant pulled a warm oven mitt from her hand.

'How are you now Mrs M? Have you got the all clear?' Mack asked.

Martha confirmed that she was, indeed, every bit as fit and well as she appeared (and chose not to be pedantic about the "all clear" aspect).

'And Mr Pillinant?'

'Oh, George: he's still keeping himself busy. Pretty much the same. It's a shame he's not working from home today, he would have loved to have seen you.'

Martha chatted on, largely about holidays they had taken. She remarked upon the uncharacteristically high number of city breaks that George had instigated, all since the diagnosis of her cancer. Quite a turn about in George's attitude to leisure; a benefit of the reminder of our mortality, Martha observed.

She faltered. The check on her conversation was not because of a sudden remembering of Mack's loss: his mother's death was never far from her thoughts. But there were associated things on her mind. Were they on Mack's mind too? Were they still too painful to discuss? It made her wary of her words.

'Right then, cookies. Would you like tea or coffee Mack?' The way to the hearts – and tongues – of both man and beast, was through food, was Martha's philosophy.

They were interrupted before she had her reply.

'Is Mack coming by car, or walking, do y'know?' Toby called out as he came through the front door.

'I walked, of course. And I'm already here.' Mack answered. He made his way back down the passage recently trod, to greet his friend.

So, the beast is to remain in the room, unspoken of today, Martha resigned. She made a hostess decision on the drinks and followed on into the sitting room, to deliver a tray of cookies and coffee.

Toby looked at the offerings and asked of Mack 'Wouldn't you prefer something a bit stronger?'

Mack stayed with the choice made for him. Toby got himself a beer and they settled down to finalize their plans for the day, which could start as soon as Rufus and Stuart arrived.

Toby had met Rufus and Stuart at university. Some business modules had been common to all, though each had a different major subject; economics, politics and computer programming respectively. Although Toby and Mack had never lost contact completely, they had not merged their separate lives. Mack had met neither Rufus nor Stuart before that day and when they arrived Toby introduced them thus:

'Rufus... he purports to be right wing but he's a pussycat really. This is Stuart. He and his evangelists are going to share and share alike all the world's resources – "Mangoes for Everyone" isn't it Stuart? – But don't be fooled Mack, he's no Robin Hood!'

The character portrayals were taken in good humour. Stuart made to laugh but no sound of it could be heard above the raucous laughter coming from Rufus.

Mack was simply Toby's 'friend from childhood'.

The climax of the day was to be an Evening of Soul at Shorncastle. It was a relatively new event to the calendar but Toby had heard it was a venue worth trying: a good place for Northern Soul mates to congregate. The old haunt at Wigan, recommended by Martha and George, no longer existed.

Such performers as the classics – Sam Cooke, Aretha Franklin, Little Richard – plus the less well known Little Anthony, Bettye Swann and Charles Drain were all part of childhood musical memory for Toby and for Mack. The two companions of Toby, recently arrived, had been introduced to similarly styled music (though far inferior, according to Toby) in Tenerife.

Rufus Rollinson would drive the four of them to Shorncastle (and afterwards take Mack to the station to catch a train home. His was a different direction to theirs).

Particularly in Shorncastle's favour as a destination – in addition to Northern Soul music – were the golf course (an enticement to the North for Rufus and Stuart) and the antiques shops, an added interest for Mack. With these attractions in mind, the group planned to eat somewhere en route – they were bound to pass a good pub – go their separate ways in Shorncastle during the day and get together for music (and a little of something roughly equating to dance) in the evening.

The three university friends headed for the golf course, Mack went alone around the antiques shops. At another time, Mack would have admitted that his interest in corkscrews was now minimal. But he had never played golf and did not want his first attempt to be in front of strangers. Mack's wish to look for a rare specimen was accepted, and he was quite content to be solitary.

Quite content, especially when he came across an Holborn champagne, Archimedean helix corkscrew! It was an English registered champagne tap of 1877, marked with both the registration lozenge and "Holborn Champagne Screw". A good example that Mack was thrilled to have come across and for which he willingly handed over the low £24 asked. (Perhaps his interest in corkscrews was not as minimal as he believed.)

The find, naturally, made that particular, large establishment favourite of the three already browsed. And, as it was only yards away from *The Tavern* at which they were to spend the evening, Mack was not inclined to wander on.

On the top level of this three storey building, much space was taken up with music: instruments, sheet music, books on styles and artists and many, many old vinyl records; recordings (some original, some later) of the greatest artists of Northern Soul. Sadly, there were no facilities to listen to any of the music on sale; no booths such as Toby's parents had spoken of. That would have been a nice touch, Mack thought; a contribution to the atmosphere of the era. But then, the incessant noise of the pigeons as they scratted and squabbled in the roof space may have proved too competitive. Mack studied the records with much concentration and enjoyment, but, eventually, left the shop having bought only the corkscrew – regrettable to Toby, when he learned of what he had missed!

The evening was a success. *The Tavern* was a good environment to be in, engulfed as they were by wall-to-wall souls, but not one conducive to speech.

Before Mack left the others to board his train home, Toby managed a few private words. 'It's been great getting together Mack. Let's make it just the two of us next time and you can show me where all this vinyl is.'

'Sounds good to me' was Mack's honest reply.

7. MOVING INTO THE FLAT

Mack's flat was modest of necessity as well as from choice.

Christine had calculated it would be unwise to give Michael the maximum financial support from the outset. After a time, he may well change his mind in favour of a university education, and if so that would not come cheaply. Anthony, therefore, would be safeguarding Michael's future all the better if he were to keep back a larger portion from the sale of the house than he had first intended, Michael was too young to have such a responsibility thrust upon him. Anthony agreed.

It was finally decided upon that Anthony Cunningham would pay all the upfront costs of establishing Michael into his flat, and pay him a monthly allowance sufficient to cover the rent and basic running costs, until such time as the need for a different course of action was indicated.

Blissfully unaware of the downgrading of any monetary gift – no figures had ever been quoted – Mack was content to see *any* amount of money finding its way into his bank account each month. And the one bedroom, through kitchen – sitting room, plus a bathroom, provided all the space Mack wanted. More would have been suggestive of a missing person.

The bedroom had space enough for a double bed, so that was the one Mack chose to take from Barkham Avenue. He also took a small wardrobe, the dining table with chairs, a sofa and a bookcase – plus some books, of course. He had measured everything and knew all would fit in beautifully – just – once he had allowed for the television and computer. The fitted kitchen area could easily accommodate the crockery, utensils and larder produce he had boxed.

Mack was happy on the day of the move; at least what passed as happy at that stage in his life. He checked his train ticket – and that he had his iPod – and waved off the removal van before going into town to meet Dad for coffee. His father had arranged for the remainder of the household contents to be removed later that same day, which was why he and Michael could not drive down together to the flat.

It was a shame that Dad would not get to see how sensibly he was using his inheritance. Mack had told him so and added 'But I don't want to dwell on it – Sorry about the bit of a pun. There again, it's only a bit of a dwelling'. (The telephone is not the best medium for conveying a sense of fun and Mack was disappointed not to hear a response.) 'Joke Dad.'

There had been no shortage of offers (from Aunt Rose, Uncle William and George Pillinant) to meet the removal van at the flat and supervise the unloading. The privilege had gone to George Pillinant. Mr Pillinant had insisted it was of absolutely no inconvenience as, on that particular day, he would be delivering a new microwave to Toby's house in Ledstown, which by no coincidence was the same district as Mack's new flat.

Anthony Cunningham waited by the door of the coffee house as arranged, phone in hand, fingers twitching across its surface. He lifted his face and Mack's spirits sank at the sight: the grey skin; the loose, unsupported weight of it around his mouth, stretching and dragging down the corners; the shots of blood red, escaping his dark eyes. Mr Cunningham made but a feeble attempt to return Michael's forced cheerful greeting.

Things improved once they had sat down at the café table with their drinks. Or was it, when, once more, Mack had readjusted his expectations?

'How's it going son?' Anthony Cunningham asked Michael.... And so the small talk went on. There was never a moment when one of them was not looking into the face of the other, though rarely did their eyes meet.

Mack loved that sad, ensnared man more consciously than ever previously. And wished more longingly that he had been his dad: that he had stayed his dad, even when no longer head of the household.

'I've missed you Dad... ... I *do* miss you.' Mack said.

Anthony Cunningham, as always, told Michael that he would always be there for him. Michael must be sure to let him know if there was anything he needed. And, whenever he wanted, he could come and stay with them. Anthony Cunningham reminded Michael that he had not yet made a visit since their move. There was plenty of room for him and, by train, the journey was only one hour thirty minutes. Then he recalled that the journey from Michael's flat would be a yet further thirty minutes, by train. But, all the more reason to come for a decent length of stay.

Mack muttered some sort of acknowledgment of the offer; enough to pacify but not commit: both knew it was never going to happen. The few times Mack had been *required* to be in the company of Christine Usherwood he had never been comfortable (no matter how many biscuits she claimed to have baked for him, or "fun" activities in which she offered to engage, sometime, if he was good). It was unlikely that he would see her again, now that he had the choice. The only advantage for Mack in having her present when he saw his dad was that Dad did not have to spend every other minute responding to her texts!

'I've got to go. The furniture van will be here soon.' Dad said. But it was not the removal firm to have texted.

Mack laughed at himself when he unwrapped two teacups and saucers. When would he drink out of a cup and saucer, especially flowery ones from decades ago? Grandma was always proud of her "Springdale" service by Foley. 'It has the factory backstamp and everything', he recalled her saying. He was so very young at the time, perhaps he was remembering being told about it? She was even more proud of her best service: the factory mark said Tuscan but, Grandma insisted, it was part of the Wedgwood Group. Yes, Mum had definitely told him that. Of course, he could not have let Grandma down by not sharing her appreciation and bringing a little something of her treasure. He had chosen a milk jug and basin from the "special occasion" china, destined to be every bit as unused in the coming years as they had been in the previous two decades.

Books were the last things that Mack unpacked. He had saved them until the end purposely. More than anything else, they would make the flat his home and he wanted to savour the moments he put them onto the shelves.

This time, as he picked up A.A. Milne's *Very Young Verses*, it *was* Grandma he heard in his head: 'That was brought out as a school book you know.'

He looked over the words of the first verse in the book. Grandma's voice was drowned out by Mum's. "Happiness".

John had Great Big Waterproof Boots on; John had a Great Big Waterproof Hat; John had a Great Big Waterproof Mackintosh – And that (Said John) Is That.

Mack flicked through the verses, remembering which ones had been picked out when it was Dad's turn to read – "Bad Sir Brian Botany" and "The Old Sailor": those were generally ignored by Mum. The last verse in the book was "Disobedience". It was a Mum one. There were six verses to it. The first one began

*James James
Morrison Morrison
Weatherby George Dupree
Took great Care of his Mother;
Though he was only three.*

When he was small, Mack liked to hear the names read out because he recognized the name George. All the way through the following four verses Mack would wait, not always patiently, for the sixth and last verse. Mum would whisper it, almost inaudibly, until the last word, which she said **very** loudly, never failing to surprise him and make him giggle.

*J.J.
M.M.
W.G. Du P.
Took great
C/o his M★★★★★
Though he was only 3.
J.J.
Said to his M★★★★★
'M★★★★★,' he said, said he:
'You-must-never-go-down-to-the-end-of-the-town-if-you-don't-go-down-with **ME**!'*

That particular book was probably the oldest book he had brought. It had passed through at least three generations in his family, maybe more: he thought Grandma had said that it was not a new book even when she was small.

No other books that had been read to him were in the selection, though several from childhood were included: *Treasure Island* and *The Adventures of Tom Sawyer* were his all time favourites. These had been his world. Toby and he had sometimes read the same story at the same time: they were Tom Sawyer and Huckleberry Finn more often than they were Mack and Toby. Fond memories. He put all his childhood books together on the top shelf. They did not need to be within easy reach.

The books by Henry James were there because James was one author, among the many, that he knew his mum had enjoyed to read. The books had no immediate appeal but he thought he might be drawn to give them a try at some time; it could be interesting. One title in particular had caught his eye *What Maisie Knew*. One day he had overheard his mother and Martha Pillinant talking. It was something to do with Ms. Usherwood being 'bloody manipulative and controlling' and 'using... *certain people*'. At that point they had noticed him and paused: his mother had finished their conversation with words that had stayed with him.

'She won't want to know him once she's got her own way. I know that. Henry James and Maisie knew that too.'

His mum had smiled at Mrs Martha as she said "Henry James and Maisie knew that too." It was that moment remembered, which brought a smile to Mack as he held the book: it had been a rare and precious thing to see his mum smile during those days. He remembered each one.

Next out of the box came the Russian books. All three of them had had a penchant for Russian authors and Mack felt a little guilty for taking them all. Perhaps he should have left some for his dad. But, on further reflection, his dad would have already taken with him any of personal value when he moved out, wouldn't he? In actual fact, he had not read any of them other than Dostoevsky's *Crime and Punishment* – and had read that one relatively recently for the first time. That incidental did not lessen the strong affinity he had with all books Russian.

It was a while since his dad had called him Makonovitch: it had been at the time when his parents had reverted to their initial discourse on names and had not been in accord as to how Michael should be addressed. Michael's father, opposed to the use of Mack and absorbed in one of the Russian books – *Brothers Karamazov* was it? – had adopted Makonovitch. If it had been a ploy to deter Mack's mother from keeping with "Mack" it had not worked. But it had taken away the tension and Mack had enjoyed the Russian name, with no sense of it being any more than an affectionate term.

He picked up *Cancer Ward* by Solzhenitsyn. How strange. For how long had cancer been a health problem for Martha Pillinant? He wondered. It was the book his mum had in her hand… the book under discussion with… ?… No. He couldn't quite remember if the conversation had been with her friend after all, or whether it had been with his father. But he did remember that his mum had found the book to have an unexpectedly positive influence on her mood. Similar to *A Day in the life of Ivan Denisovich* in that respect – or listening to blues music: the darker side of things are not denied yet satisfaction is found, even moments of joy, from small means. That had been the gist.

Mack looked around. *A Day in the life of Ivan Denisovich*, where was that book? He had planned to read it one day. **In** one day was the plan. It was quite a thin volume and, Mack reasoned, if it was about what happened in just one day then it should not take more than one day to read it. But it wasn't there. He would have to buy another copy.

He turned to *Crime and Punishment*: that became Mack's book of choice. The one with which he settled down, that evening in his new home.

8. MANGOES FOR EVERYONE

Toby was pleased that both Rufus and Stuart had welcomed Mack into their social fray – especially Stuart: he was the cautious type, suspicious of newcomers. Rufus was universally accepting. However, Toby wanted them both to stay at a distance on the coming Saturday.

Rufus and Toby had shared a house (rented out to them by Oswald Rollinson MP, Rufus's father) but their university days were at an end and Toby had already moved on. He now shared a small house with his partner Ursula – in the same district, close to his employment in the commercial financial sector, and not too distant from where Ursula was looking to secure a post. She was hopeful of a managerial position within a National Health Service department of finance. (*Those hopes were later realized.*)

Toby knew that Rufus planned to spend the Saturday in question with his father, "networking"; networking *socially* as opposed to social *net*working. Mr Rollinson had acquaintances, useful ones, who were known to be around a particular golf club on Saturdays. It was quite far south, but Mr Rollinson insisted it would be worthwhile for Rufus to put in the miles (literally and metaphorically) if he was 'serious about getting on'. These acquaintances would know of opportunities in the periphery work of Government... an assistant parliamentary secretary... or the like... perhaps?

(Rufus was always vague on anything that did not relate to music – no doubt he would have an acoustic guitar in the boot of his car and a harmonica in his pocket on the off-chance that a spare moment and the muse coincided.) Rufus accommodated and was accommodating. It was in his nature. He posed no problem for Saturday's plans.

Stuart was a different entity. He was often quiet but rarely passive. And he was likely to take offence at not being given the option to decline or to be included in Toby's plans. Toby was fearful of provoking Stuart. Had the matter been left entirely to him, he would have said nothing. He would not have raised the subject and risked an upset. Instead, he would have chanced that Stuart had some distant activity on that Saturday; distant, enduring and too absorbing for Stuart to question what might be happening elsewhere. But Ursula had no faith in such fortune.

Ursula's plan was as follows: Toby to spend the Saturday afternoon with Mack, probably in a pub or mooching around somewhere, returning to Ursula and Toby's house in the evening, where and when Mack would meet Ursula (for the first time). Ursula's friend Sophia would also be there – and that is where Ursula saw the potential for Stuart to become an unwelcome addition to the party.

She insisted that Toby forestalled that possibility by making it clear to Stuart that it was to be just the four of them: Stuart was **not** to drop by uninvited – as was his wont. Some firm action was long overdue and, make no mistake, this was not harsh treatment towards a friend – Toby had to understand that and subsequently convey the correct message.

★

Ursula's stipulation that Stuart must be a "no show" was not totally unexpected. At least it might have been expected and understood, by Toby, if he had paid more attention to what had gone before.

Ursula had frequently remarked that she found Stuart oppressive – perhaps because neither she nor Toby had actually chosen to have his company: he tagged along with Sophia so frequently he had come to presume a rightful place. Ursula resented that presumption.

It was not as though Stuart and Sophia were a couple, not in the traditional sense. It was possible that they were, or had been, sexual partners: a possibility Ursula found disconcerting. She was not a prude but thought there was something unsavoury about the set up. Stuart had used the phrase "friends with benefits" long before it had become common parlance. Toby regretted telling Ursula of that comment. 'What benefits? – As if I can't guess! And of benefit to whom!' she had bawled.

Sophia was very defensive of Stuart and the whole *Mangoes for Everyone* movement through which she and Stuart had become close. (Toby and Ursula applied the acronym ME to the mangoes Internet phenomenon – privately: there was no point in risking the wrath of the cyber warriors. Ursula further described ME as 'hippies plus Masons minus altruism and integrity').

Ursula had even signed up to the *Mango* link, through *Facesonline*, eventually; after Sophia's persuasive tactics had worn her down. But subsequently she had invested little of her time communicating with all those "friends" who shared that particular vision of a happy new world.

She had not found it easy to grasp the full intentions and actions of ME (described and directed by the founder, Ray Fleck Mareson): the various mission statements, slogans, sound-bites, call them what you will, centred around making all people happy, well fed and able to live in unfettered peace. Nothing with which anyone could disagree. However, how they intended to bring about the change was less clear.

A look at the group's "open space" had suggested that a large part of the action – or perhaps it was to be in readiness for action – was to discuss comments posted by members (which did not appear to relate to the mission statements; not in any obvious manner).

One poet had written *'don't ever say sorry for what you feel, it's like being sorry for being real'*. (A liberty has been taken here in that, originally, the comma appeared after like. An unusual use of punctuation and indiscriminate placing of capital letters were common.) Paradoxically, there were an enormous number of references to reality and "getting real" amongst those cyber friends in their virtual world.

Members were welcomed from whatever background, race or religion so long as they shared those same ideals, which, almost by definition meant it was inclusive. A good thing, surely.

An example of one life that been turned around, once he had embraced the concept of *Mangoes for Everyone*, was that of a young, male, ex-business graduate. No details were given of the practicalities involved in the revolve, so to speak, but clearly his particular circumstances had been eased: he was now earning large amounts of money working from home and so was able to provide for his two young children, singlehandedly, both financially and emotionally.

This same community had supported a young, female student through a stressful time in her life. Her long piece, written on the "open space", had apparently resonated with Sophia in the early days as she had recommended the reading of it to Ursula. Ursula had thought it incoherent – and Toby refused to read beyond the first line of the 'rant'.

Because it was quite repetitive, a few lines only are reproduced here – and not faithfully: as with the previous quote, slight amendments have been made, largely the employment of a more traditional method of punctuation. Hopefully, this will not detract from the flavour of the writings and apologies are given to ME if – in an attempt to make the contribution a little more comprehensible to those outside of the sect – the intended meaning has been obscured.

Dear Ray, why can't more men be like you? For those who hate psycho girlfriends and boyfriends or creepy stalker ex's – looking at your ex, realize that you've upgraded majorly. I've wondered what would happen if I didn't make that decision! I have flashbacks and memories when I listen to music. Just completely zoned out listening to Smelly Cat and didn't hear a word you said. When I lie to you Mom and Dad it's for your own good. And I like listening to your lies when I know the truth. Bye Mom and Dad. Get over yourselves and 'av good time, like me!

It is not clear what subject the young lady was studying (student was mentioned in her profile) though a good number of ME members seemed to have been recruited from graduates or students of information technology, economics, politics and business. A good number also seemed to have come to the movement from dating sites linked to *Facesonline*: a broad mix, indicative of its aforementioned inclusive nature.

On several occasions Ursula had tried to open up a

discussion with Sophia on the *Mangoes for Everyone* concept and purpose. She was unsuccessful. Sophia interpreted any questionning as a personal criticism. It had threatened their friendship, so Ursula had desisted.

Such was the background against which Toby had to ban Stuart from the house for that Saturday evening.

Toby broached the subject by asking Stuart, in a casual manner, what he would be doing on... . Unfortunately, the answer was that he would not be doing anything in particular. Toby then expressed his regret that he could not invite Stuart to join him because he was going to introduce Mack to Ursula, and Ursula wished it to be just them – for that first occasion. (The bluntness of his words was tempered with the proffering of a beer.)

Stuart did not mind in the least. He was quite pleased in fact; it would be the opportunity he had been waiting for to take Sophia to hear "The Raddies", of which Ursula was no fan. (Stuart sniggered as he recalled Ursula's derogatory comments, passed at the one and only gig they had all been to together.) In fact, Sophia shared Ursula's views but had thought better of sharing her opinion openly, that is, not in front of Stuart. But Toby did not add that complication: he did not approach from that angle to quell Stuart's mounting enthusiasm.

'I'm sorry Stuart. Sophia is not free that day. Ursula is doing something or other with her, and... Ursula thinks it will be easier for both Mack and herself if Mack wasn't a gooseberry... '

Toby knew immediately: he had said the wrong thing! Though what would have constituted a good response still eluded him. The remainder of the conversation went as follows.

'It sounds like you're trying to set Sophia up with Mack. Are you?'

'No, of course not.'

'Well, in any case that's a wrong move you're planning. You don't know Sophia like I do, she's more vulnerable than she seems.'

'Oh come on Stuart. Mack's a good guy. He's not going to come on to her or anything.'

'But she's not the right choice as an extra icebreaker. Don't use her like that. Not right for Mack either. Think about it. We've all had university educations. No matter how bright your friend is, he's going to feel awkward with solely graduates. Choose someone else.'

Toby could not think of anyone that either Ursula or he knew in the Ledstown area who was not a graduate – not that he agreed with Stuart's assessment of the situation.

'Mangoes for Everyone Stuart. Mangoes for Everyone' was all Toby said. He was not sure what he meant by it, it was the first thing that popped into his head. But the words were said knowingly, with confidence and they silenced Stuart.

In spite of the sudden peace, Toby was not at all sure he had convinced Stuart against calling in on the Saturday. Probably prior knowledge of the plan had had quite the contrary effect.

The solution was clear: he needed to suggest to Ursula that they treat Sophia and Mack to a meal out.

9. MEETING SOPHIA

The four of them enjoyed the first evening spent together, well enough. Ursula needed only the absence of Stuart to regard it a resounding success. And that she had.

Sophia's subdued participation and impression of aloofness was merely shyness. Following this reassurance from Toby, given on the next day, Mack agreed to be party to a repetition of the event.

It took several similar and other more private encounters with Sophia before Mack and she conversed on any subject of a personal nature. And even then Sophia said little of her past.

Life for Sophia had begun at university. (This is what she told Mack.) She never wanted to speak of earlier times, not because it would have upset her to do so but because there was 'absolutely nothing to tell. It had been totally boring'.

For different reasons, Mack saw no need to speak at length about his earlier life either. No doubt Sophia had learned of the essentials from Ursula, through Toby, and Mack was not inclined to be in any time but the present, for the present.

He did wonder whether Sophia's attitude to her past might have been her attempt to help him create distance from his own childhood; not to abrogate or trivialize his experience but to somehow equalize their relationship: life for each of them becoming significant and meaningful only at adulthood, just something "to be got through" until then. An unspoken understanding.

Perhaps it was a sign of an increasing confidence in each other that Mack, after resisting numerous invitations, agreed to become a part of Sophia's community on the *Facesonline* site.

He had no particular desire to socially network and was not impressed by the 262 names (for that is all they were to him) wanting to claim him as a friend because of some mutuality across email address books, or some other spurious connection. But, Sophia had convinced him that, if he wished, he would be able to contact her more readily via *Facesonline* than by her individual email address. *Facesonline* was used all the time by her friends, so that was invariably her first port of call, often neglecting to pick up on other emails for days.

It was a somewhat forced sociability, uncomfortable to Mack. Messages, of no possible interest to the majority of any said community, were universally displayed. Obviously, it was too much trouble to select the few for whom the message may have relevance, but somewhat baffling nevertheless. Why, for instance, would someone living in South Africa, or Japan, want to know that it was worth making a round trip of 25 miles from Ledstown, England, to buy a weeks supply of fruit and vegetables? ('Shudd 'av gone to Mart's. Cudda got it cheaper' was the comment.)

Boring, inane, moronic stuff: *he* would never use the site as a poor excuse for a diary or journal! To be fair, neither did Sophia to any great extent. But he had not been fair had he!

His early criticism of the site had been strident; his mocking of the fashion in which people made use of it, hurtful to Sophia. His availing himself of the facility was, in part, by way of an apology for so judgmental an attitude. His final (private) judgment had been that to register – or sign in – would be harmless: it did not follow that he would then be obliged to "talk" to any "friends", other than Sophia.

10. ENTRY TO THE WORKPLACE

'You're weird' Toby told Mack. 'Everybody else hates junk mail.'

It wasn't that Mack actually wanted any of it, but to have stuff dropping into his post box had somehow helped him to feel at home.

Admittedly, very little of it was personalized with his name, but no matter; it was his post box and he enjoyed taking charge of the contents.

That is, until the name on the envelope was that of the previous tenant – presumably – and the content was a bill for electricity used in the quarter prior to his tenancy. An obvious mistake, so Mack put it in the box of papers to recycle.

When the next, similar but more insistent demand came, Mack thought better of waiting for others to spot the error. He checked out a best plan of action.

The volunteer workers for Citizen Advice were Mack's heroes.

It was a pity he had not made some rudimentary checks on first taking possession of the flat, but there you go. The advisor he saw concurred that any *reasonable* person *should* see that Michael's slight oversight was excusable under the circumstances, and, after a few letters, it proved to be the case: the problem was sorted.

The one non-volunteer he met was Elizabeth Doughty,

the deputy manager of that particular bureau. Her speciality, when not dealing with general queries, was debt management. She was a little more officious than the volunteers. Perhaps it was the added responsibility that made her so. Nevertheless, Mack was impressed by the whole encounter – the people, the advice and the outcome. And noted, with interest, a poster encouraging volunteers, from any walk of life, to come forward.

The poster was in his mind when, ostensibly to ask some question regarding social benefits, he was drawn to call again at the bureau. It was still there, the poster, asking for him to come forward. He stepped up.

The three interviews that followed were far more rigorous than Mack had anticipated. His attitude towards fairness and equality were questionned, again and again; tested, using more scenarios than could ever possibly exist in the real world! Mack was edging towards raising a few points on probability. But, luckily, the scrutiny of his scruples and capabilities came to an end before he had challenged his interviewers and scuppered his chances. He was approved.

A tremendous amount of training was required – still unpaid. The lack of remuneration meant that he was obliged to attend the Job Centre to concurrently register for permanent, paid employment. An unwelcome and unpleasant necessity.

As was expected (nay, demanded) of him, and all other registrants, Mack showed a willingness to consider employment in any establishment and in whatever suitable capacity that was available. However, *suitable* (the description was subjective) opportunities to be put forward were few and far between. (Unlike his Citizen Advice colleagues, staff at the

Job Centre did not seem to recognize Michael's sharp intellect.) Mack was greatly relieved when a paid post as advisor at the bureau was advertised. It was based in the actual bureau at which he was a volunteer: he could not have been more fortunate. (Not least because he was able to stall an expectation that he should turn his hand to stacking shelves at a local supermarket – 'I'm afraid one "A" level will not get you very far sir. We've got graduates on our books!')

His application for the post did – after the usual lengthy procedures, not worth detailing – lead to an offer of employment, which was, of course, eagerly accepted by him.

To be an advisor was a thrill, a boost to his confidence and a hope for a viable future; all of those good things.

What was to mar the experience – for nothing is perfect – was twofold: Mack had a tendency to over-empathize with the clients. As an advisor, he could do no more than pass on information about possible actions and consequences. But when there was no solution, not one that would wipe away completely the client's immediate, pressing worry, the residue of the problem clung fiercely to Mack long after the client had left. His discomfort was added to by Mrs. Doughty's attitude towards him. (Most workers, whether volunteers or paid, addressed their superior as Elizabeth – as did Mack at times. But it didn't always feel right.) As supervisor of the open door sessions she saw much of his work. No direct criticism was made but yet she seemed to Mack to often mock, to ridicule him.

'Drinks time Michael. Your turn I believe. Do you think you can go through the options – tea or coffee – a bit quicker than you went through the options open to Tom Quilly (*not his real name for reasons of confidentiality*) please?'

The colleagues who shared her sense of humour (or her opinion of Mack) would laugh. The others deployed a distracting tactic; introduced a new topic of conversation – or offered a helping hand in the kitchen.

As was pointed out to him, by many, 'Getting used to life at the bureau is a steep learning curve'.

11. IGNORANT OF THE BLOW

There had, for a while, been some half-thought out plan for Toby and Mack to meet up and use part of that time together to search for old vinyl records – such as Mack had discovered in Shorncastle.

The plan had not fully come to fruition when an occurrence prompted Toby into action: a reminder of Mack's home troubles from the past was about to emerge and the outing would provide a pleasant distraction for Mack. Toby fixed on a day to spend with Mack, at an antiques fair. (Not Toby's idea of the best fun day out, but it was expedient.)

The prompt: Martha Pillinant was the recipient of a message from the stepdaughter of Mr Anthony Cunningham, who had taken it upon herself to right what she saw as a wrong. She knew that Mr Cunningham had not seen his son for a while and, because of Mr Cunningham's increasingly poor health – and Michael's relative maturity – she thought it time both made an effort to get closer.

'I know you have always been good to Michael and hope you will help in this now. We've no one else we can turn to. I, and I'm sure Mr Cunningham, would be so grateful. He can't travel far so it will mean Michael coming to him. But he doesn't look as he once did… the illness… and I would like to talk to Michael, explain, prepare him for the change before they meet again.'

Martha was not happy that this stranger should introduce herself as either Mr Cunningham's stepdaughter or Michael's stepsister. The only consolation was that she had made no reference to Christine Usherwood. Martha put on her Mrs Pillinant voice and agreed to help, in principle, but requested time to consider the most appropriate approach to the situation before making a full commitment.

The first step she took was to speak to Toby. Toby had had more contact with Mack than either Martha or George had managed (a constant source of chagrin to Martha).

Toby's knowing Mack much better of late than did his mother, was the reason Toby gave to her for alleviating any stress or further concern. '*I'll* return the call. I'll see what she has to say and sort it out. Leave it to me.'

Subsequently, Toby arranged a drive out to an antiques fair, where Mack could hunt out corkscrews and Toby vinyl records of Northern Soul – or whatever took the fancy of each of them. On that day, Toby would pave the way for the introduction, as he had agreed to do, and, ultimately, be by Mack's side should he choose to face the daughter.

Much was to be left to the moment, not over planned ahead of reactions that could be no more than guessed at, not predicted. But one thing Toby did decide upon: he would not refer to her as the stepdaughter of Michael's father, Mr Cunningham (as she herself had done) and definitely not as a stepsister! She was to be no other than the daughter of that woman. (Though he did own there was a certain injustice in holding her responsible for the sins of her mother.)

Justification for the stance taken was that it reflected Mack's own approach. Rarely, over the years, had he made any reference to the woman who had taken away his father and destroyed his mother's happiness. And, on those rare occasions, Toby had heard no part of the name Christine Usherwood, and no "steps" of any description. In respect for those sentiments, inferred by Mack, Toby had decided to adopt similar. The ways in which he could help Mack were so few.

Toby and Mack could both drive and each had cars. Toby's car was the more reliable and so it was in Toby's car that they travelled. In spite of having returned from holiday only the day before – and the holiday having comprised more driving than any other single activity – Toby could not be persuaded to relinquish the steering wheel to Mack. Driving was a passion of Toby's. (And he was in no doubt that he would enjoy the drive far more than he would the antiques fair.) Mack, who also enjoyed driving, was allowed to choose the music for the journey – by way of compensation for relegation to permanent passenger: some Northern Soul, some blues, some folk were played. Both were content.

En route they stopped for coffee. Toby checked his phone. He picked up a message from the daughter of that woman.

Mack had gone to buy the coffees. That was fortunate: Toby had no need to evade the awkward questions that surely would have ensued. For it was bad news.

Bad news; the worst. The sort that hits you with disbelief and makes understanding slow. *I'm sorry to have to tell you like this but Mr Cunningham has died.'*

(It went on to say that the death had happened whilst Toby was away on holiday and no one had been able to reach Michael. But Toby did not read on immediately.)

Toby looked up for a sight of Mack. Mack had not yet

reached the pay desk. His back was towards Toby. He had not witnessed Toby's shock.

Toby gained a little more time by heading to the lavatory. He re-read the shocking start to the message, and then read on to learn that Mack had missed the funeral. That would be a double blow.

He was distressed for his friend but he was also angry. Angry with himself for not fixing things sooner so that Mack could have seen his father. Angry and disgusted with that woman and her daughter for not bothering to get in touch with Mack so that he could have gone to the funeral. *Not able to reach him* – Ugh! no sort of excuse; of course they could have reached Mack – or himself – if they had really tried. He would have readily cut his holiday short to tell Mack, if he had known. She could have phoned him. Or if that had proved difficult, phoned his mother. (Toby dismissed thoughts of his instruction – to keep future communication with him and not to trouble his mother. It could have been overridden. Surely it was obvious that such a request would not apply under those tragic circumstances!) And why hadn't she said that Mr Cunningham was actually dying, instead of merely not well!

Toby's mind raced; unravelling such thoughts; accepting that he could not reverse what had gone before; debating what he should do next. The latter was the trickiest. Nothing resolved, he made his way, abstractedly, back to the table.

Quite a contrast between his mood and that of Mack's. Mack had had some sort of amusing incident at the till: their drinks had inadvertently gone onto the bill of the person ahead. Not in itself amusing, but it had been dealt with in good humour and with a witty retort – which Toby failed to fully pick up on. The simple absurdity had lifted his friend's spirits to an unaccountable level. Toby could not rise with him but was loathe to bring him down.

It may have not been the right decision, but, Toby decided that it would serve no purpose to deliver the devastating news to Mack at that moment. He would do his best to make the day enjoyable for Mack, something that would only be possible if Mack was kept in ignorance. Nothing at all could be gained from the telling, only the certain loss of a potentially good day, for Mack at least.

As for meeting with the daughter of that woman, he would leave that to the fates. It may be that Mack would want to ask questions. Questions that only she or her mother could answer. Whether Mack was to meet with them, or not, was no longer his call.

12. CONSOLIDATION

'Mack can get back on track now': that was the comment passed around by friends when he had first moved into his own place – that is to say, his rented flat. The key was his. He could come and go as he pleased. He had independence.

Yes, the flat, the fresh start had been appreciated by him, to some extent. But the true turning point had come later; the meeting with Maureen. Although no romantic sort of attachment had entered his mind (well, perhaps it had done, briefly), she was his first new friend of any significance since childhood.

He recollected how he had been searching for corkscrews at an antiques fair. Her stall was exactly the type to turn up a gem; a mish mash of ceramics, books, games, household equipment and gadgets – the ages of which ranged from modern collectables to true antiques. In short, there was something for everyone.

Conversation with Maureen was easy, and had been from the outset. Mack had spotted a cup and saucer in Foley's "Springdale" pattern – Grandma's everyday crockery. From the cup flowed shared thoughts of elderly folk; their pride in making a grand total of 250 years when three good candidates could be put together for an occasion. Thus, it had seemed a reasonable suggestion of Mack's that Maureen should describe a tiered bun stand – cleverly put together by Maureen herself from three vintage plates – similarly, as having a combined age of 250 years.

At a later encounter, Maureen was in possession of a black painted, "Old Snifter" corkscrew. Mack had no real knowledge of its value but found the man in his top hat quite appealing. It was not too rare, he had seen similar before. And the paint was rubbed off in places. Maureen said he could have it for as little as eight pounds – a returned favour for his marketing tip of giving the bun stand a cumulative age of the individual plates, she said (in truth, she had given the very same reason for knocking down the price of a bird modelled corkscrew on that first day they had met). The remembering by Maureen of that earlier chat pleased Mack. He would not have quibbled about the price whatever she had suggested.

Later still, Mack spoke to Toby of including Maureen in their number: he suggested they might all go to one of her usual venues, when they could meet up at the close of the fair. (As he was now accustomed to doing. Including the others and veering towards a general social gathering would be a way of keeping contact with Maureen as his collecting habit petered out.) Toby seemed uncomfortable at the suggestion. He grimaced; gave Mack a look – interpreted by Mack as one of disapproval – and finally dismissed the notion with the comment 'Time to move on bruv'.

An unjustified response, Mack thought, though not altogether unexpected. He had got used to keeping his meetings with Maureen out of conversation with Toby but surely it was time for Toby, not him, "to move on". For want of a better explanation, he had generously attributed Toby's reluctance to speak of her, in those early days, to a wish to spare his friend possible disappointment. But things were different now. He and Sophia were together as a couple. They were solid, safe.

Was *that* it then? Toby did not want him to jeopardise his relationship with Sophia.

But Toby should know, Sophia had no jealousy of Maureen. The relationship with Sophia had developed slowly and was neither comparable nor competitive: Maureen had become an instant friend because of a shared interest in antique items. Sophia understood that and had no objections; he was at perfect liberty to continue his jaunts and would give them up in an instant if Sophia intimated otherwise. How fabulous that such a lively, beautiful and independent woman as Sophia had (almost) agreed to marry such a lack lustre, uneducated nobody as he was: he was never going to give her cause to leave him!

Why then, he wondered, did Toby have such little faith in his judgement?

The sort of university education that the other three had taken for granted had not been a feasible route for him, yet the lack of that advantage had not stopped him from forging some sort of career for himself, had it? No. He had shown initiative. He had volunteered to give his time to Citizen Advice and consequently received free training of a type well respected in the workplace. A training type far better than the "how to write a curriculum vitae" or "how to use a photocopier" instruction that the Job Centre foisted on synchronous claimants. It had been a good move; one that had led to decent employment.

Proof. His judgement could be respected. Couldn't it?

And should be, shouldn't it? *(Mack posed these questions in his struggle against hurt, self pity and anger.)*

In the final analysis he chose not to offer a defence nor to push the original suggestion of inviting Maureen along with the others, or they with Maureen. He did not give her up, totally, but his acquaintance with her remained restricted and discrete (and discreet, as far as Toby was concerned).

13. MOVING ON

It may not have been the specific intention of either Toby or Ursula to "set Sophia up with Mack" as Stuart had accused, but neither had they (Ursula certainly; Toby, possibly) been oblivious to the fact that Sophia was eminently eligible. And if either of them had given any encouragement, inadvertently, it had been successful. Mack and Sophia moved into a flat together, eight months after Toby had married Sophia's long-time friend, Ursula. By then, Toby and Ursula had been together for four years, Mack and Sophia had passed their first anniversary. The four of them made a cosy group and Mack, typically, continued to be appreciative of his turn in fortunes.

The flat that was now home to Sophia and Mack, had been Sophia's home from the time she had first left university. The lease on Mack's flat had been almost due for renewal and it made sense for Mack to let it lapse. Of the two flats, Sophia's was a good deal more spacious and she raised no real objection to accommodating all of Mack's belongings; books, table, crockery... the lot.

His offer of his furniture '... in lieu of a contribution towards the rent... ' was declined in no uncertain terms: Sophia remonstrated that the effect of her carefully planned décor was utterly destroyed and invited him to consider how fortunate he was that she was 'willing to forego style for cash'.

They bantered their way to an agreement. Mack's

'magnanimous offer' to pay for the whole of the groceries, half the rent and half the utility bills was accepted as 'just recompense' for Sophia's loss of room.

Mack could find no downside to the move.

Work at the Bureau could be described as rewarding, and was so described by Mack, on a good day. But days were not always good.

The initial encounter with a client was trying. It had to be, by its very nature. People came to the Bureau with an expectation that is was *the* place that housed all the answers. He was the person onto which their worry was off-loaded. The ensuing problem was that there was not always a solution. The Bureau could not reverse all injustices, right all wrongs. Mack was no fool, he knew that, of course he did, and accepted it. He reassured Mrs Doughty of his acceptance almost as many times as he reassured himself.

He knew he had to avoid being engulfed and dragged down by bleak beginnings to the day; horror stories. He knew he had to focus on solutions for as long as options remained, and leave the unsolvable behind.

As he left on an evening, he would pause, and visualize a door closing in his head as he closed the door to the Bureau. Having Sophia to go home to helped; there was a momentary elation each time he opened the door of his beaten up old car for the drive away.

The challenge was how to sustain that sense of relief. And it was a challenge, a constant challenge: there were days when he had seen pain written on the face of a child as its mother disclosed their desperate situation. He wanted to scream out an appeal (and had done once, in the privacy of his car) to 'make them feel safe: just make them feel safe'. (But to whom was the appeal made?)

So it was that he sometimes failed the challenge: a sense of defeat returned before he reached Sophia. Sometimes sorrow permeated the atmosphere; times when a meal and a glass of wine with Sophia, Toby and Ursula, ought instead to have been a pure joy. None were unsympathetic but all were concerned about the effect the work was having on Mack.

'Toughen up' said Toby.

'Look for something else' said Sophia. 'You've been in that job long enough.'

(It has to be said that she had ambitions for more lucrative as well as less harrowing employment for Mack – hardly at all influenced by a wish to quieten Stuart's unkind and condescending comments about her choice of a partner.)

Sophia took the opportunity of a particularly hard day for Mack, to put forward her case. That it had been a hard day, Sophia gleaned from Mack's demeanour: he gave no details. Mack always observed the code of confidentiality. Not once did he discuss the business of clients he had seen. Mack did not say then, but it can be told here, just what had caused Mack to come home subdued on that day.

The client – a middle-aged woman, with established learning difficulties – faced eviction from her home.

In the first instance, Elizabeth Doughty had seen the client and had done all the hard work needed. *(I feel obliged to make that clear, just in case it be overlooked by those not present to witness it.)* It had been verified (by the client's social worker) that the client was fully capable of making her own decisions. An assessment had been made of her income, that of her partner's and of their joint household expenditure.

Elizabeth had calculated that the client was entitled to unclaimed benefits, **provided** she kept her part-time working hours down to the few contracted: her partner, an elderly gentleman, did the occasional 'odd job for a friend' but was otherwise retired. This information was passed on to Michael.

Elizabeth had done the bulk of the preparation for claiming the additional benefits. All that remained was for the client and her partner (with the required guidance from Michael) to complete and sign the claim forms, which the client could then submit to the benefits office.

Initially, he had no qualms about taking on the work proffered by Elizabeth and was not unduly unnerved by the reminders Elizabeth gave as to the importance of making sure it was 'done right'. (*Elizabeth Doughty was close to retirement age and exuded an air full of experience, wisdom and confidence, keen to pass on to others. Michael assumed it to have been gained from her Citizen Advice work. He was wrong. But I tell nothing of Elizabeth's story because it is not relevant in this context, just as the story of Michael would not feature in her biographical details.*)

The client attended the interview by herself. Her partner was unable to attend because he was working. Neither would he be able to attend in the foreseeable future, due to the same work commitments. However, she was perfectly happy to complete her sections of the forms (with Michael's help). The questions were straightforward enough and the client appeared to enjoy answering them – in more detail than was required. It was obvious she loved doing – and talking about – her job: she was contracted as a cleaner in a large pub restaurant but was invariably offered extra hours at the end of her shift, the extra hours to be worked in the kitchen, washing pots. (Mack's first thought was to ask whether she always remembered to change rubber gloves when she moved from cleaning lavatories to washing pots. But he refrained, and instead made a mental note to be wary of eating at that particular pub.)

It was then he realized that, crucially, he was on the verge of encouraging this lady and her partner to commit benefit fraud.

He tried to check her level of understanding regarding the importance of **not** going over her contracted hours – if she were to claim the additional benefits.

Her response surprised Mack.

'Oh, I don't mind staying on. It's best part o' day. Mavis an' me 'ave a good natter and I'd never 'ardly see 'er if I went 'ome after cleaning toilets. Wouldn't get to know anything if I stayed in there. They get done y' know if they don't get back to work sharpish.'

Michael reminded her of what had brought her to the Bureau in the first place. And that they needed to find a way to pay off the rent arrears.

'Tell y' what we can do. You pay rent for me an' give me what's left. I get plenty o' money but I spend it. Other week I got Ray one o' them gismos that cuts grass from yor armchair. He wa' made up. An' he got me a lovely coat.... That's our trouble. We're always buying each other stuff. So, if you pay bills and rent first, we'll just spend what's left and don't need to claim ought from nobody. And y' don't 'ave to tell boss that I shouldn't be working in kitchen. Fair enough?'

Michael reassured her that she could keep on working as she was doing – if she wanted to – but it would probably mean that she could not claim the extra benefits. (There was the added concern about the number of hours her partner was working. But it was a point which would be rendered immaterial if she did not pursue the benefit claim.) He would ask what could be done about making sure the bills were paid before the money got spent on other things. The client was very pleased and thanked him profusely.

Mack reported back the result of the consultation. To say that Mrs Doughty did not share in the client's pleasure would be a gross understatement. Her face doubled in size and colour. Innocent sheets of paper trembled in her hands. Colleagues (fearful or tactful, it was hard to distinguish) scarpered and left Michael and Elizabeth to fight it out. There was no contest. Michael was easily shouted down; given no leave to respond.

She riled against him for presuming to '... know better...' than someone with so much more experience than he! Someone who had received accolades for the extra thousands of pounds she had '... "won" for clients'! Thousands of pounds that came straight back into the local community! Did he know what damage his stupidity could do? Did he realize that the poor couple would lose their home if she could not convince the judge to stave off the eviction?

The case had to be taken back into the capable hands of Mrs Doughty, and Michael was told to get out of her sight and consider carefully his suitability for such work.

Michael obeyed. (No trigger of an upset child had been needed: did this indicate a worsening of his inadequacy?)

This was Sophia's opening:

'Ursula knows of a good post due to come up at St.

Joseph's in June. It's to help employees cope with the stresses of working in the NHS, "poor things". They'll be looking for someone with a counselling qualification preferably. But I think your work with the Bureau could be made to count... All you need do is sell yourself a bit.... It would really suit you Mack, and you would suit it, I'm sure. You've just got to go for it!'

Mack was not at all averse to this suggestion and his question 'Do I get a say?' was somewhat rhetorical.

Two months on and it was Michael's first day at St. Joseph's "Health at Work" department (formerly "Occupational Health", but that was before *blue bled the red* – a quote from colleague Caroline, whom we shall meet later).

There was a small plaque on the door of his office cum consulting room, which read "Michael Cunningham, Counsellor". The slight reservations he may have had about the introduction of commercialism into the Department, evaporated in the warmth of his achievement, echoed in that plaque. Of course, he would remember that his first duty was to the hospital staff; their well-being would be reflected in benefits to the patients; and the additional work undertaken for outside organisations would bring in revenue for yet further improvements in both staff and patient care. Everyone would be a winner!

Michael's trip to Boston, Massachusetts – to take place around two months after his induction period in the Department – was to be paid for by the American consultancy arm of Omniwell. Omniwell had been employed by the consortium of which St. Joseph's was a member, to help emulate here the same success achieved over there by this company. It was a generous gesture to offer to Michael the same package as had been in place at the start of the project, several years earlier: a generosity which Mack was encouraged to quietly appreciate – *silently* appreciate, to be precise – so as to not engender envy.

14. PREPARING TO SELL

Things were going well. The combination of Sophia's salary and Mack's lately much improved one (though still below Sophia's) gave Mack no reason to doubt Sophia's judgement as to the affordability of one of the new builds, just a mile away from Ursula and Toby.

'You deserve a good home Mack' Sophia said, and the others nodded in agreement.

An empty smile accompanied his 'Thank you'.

To buy a house together would be a further consolidation of their relationship; ahead, perhaps, of marriage. Extra space for a family was not part of the thinking. Neither Mack nor Sophia had actually raised the subject, but they each instinctively knew the time was not right for them to have children: Sophia was generally referred to as a high flyer in her job and clearly had not yet tired of flying.

'Toby and I are the do-wellers and Ursula and you are the do-gooders' was one of Sophia's quips. An alternative one was 'Toby and I are the do-betters and Ursula and you are the make-betters'. Both were references to the fact that she and Toby worked in finance whilst Ursula and Mack were both in health.

Mack responded that the quips lacked wit as they lacked accuracy: Ursula was actually in a general managerial role in a finance department, which *happened* to be in the Health Service, whilst Toby was untypical of a financier. He showed none of the hard edged drive commonly associated with those in that industry, for whom success equated to amassed wealth. (He said nothing of Sophia's own position.) Affection, good humour and lack of any resentment was in his tone.

Perhaps the disparity in their incomes gave some resonance to her attempts at witticism nevertheless. Perhaps that is why Mack had no qualms about offering to sell his collection of corkscrews in order to raise his contribution towards the deposit for the house.

The offer was accepted. It was a proud time for Mack… and also a long time in coming to fruition: the planning and execution of the sales of his treasures proved to be slow processes. Decisions – to change jobs, to move house, and to let go of his collection – had all been easily made. Who would have guessed that the actual selling of corkscrews could then be so complex?

Mack used his skill and knowledge to group and place each corkscrew to best advantage. (Non corkscrew collectors, such as Sophia, have no understanding of the several aspects that have to be considered.) He debated whether it was best to put those of the same origin together – but then should that mean country or factory? There were too many that could not be attributed to any particular factory, but those marked from the T. Dowler, and later G. Dowler, factories might sell well together; as might those from Portugal; but then there were rather too many of the same style within his examples of those groups. Perhaps they may do better grouped according to period and/or condition? Fortunately, Mack had such a large number of corkscrews to play with he could try the whole gamut of combinations. And he did.

Much of the commonplace he would put into a local

auction; the lots comprising quantity rather than quality – though he would include one or two of a bit more special interest to attract the buyers. The buyers of such lots would, of course, have a limit on what outlay to risk: Mack used his own judgement to determine the maximum size of the lot and always assumed that the auctioneer would decide not to split into more than one lot.

It was a new hobby.

'Do you know what? I think the lot in Stephenson's auction last week would have gone for just as much without the A1 Heeley. I don't think it was appreciated; a waste there, I could have saved it.'

Sophia had no more interest in this side of things than she had in any part of the collection.

'Does it really matter? Just get the money as quickly as possible, I say.'

'No, I disagree. It's best to get as much as I can. It will all go towards the house whether it's the actual deposit or later for furnishings – or whatever. It's not as though we can't afford to make the deposit until the last corkscrew's sold, is it?'

'Ha! There's enough in MY account, yes. But that's hardly the point is it? This was supposed to be your bit of the deal. I don't want to be left totally skint thank you!'

Mack was sorry that Sophia had raised such an argument. It was true that she had more saved than he had, though if the full circumstances were taken into account, the unfairness of such a gripe would be clear. Sophia had received ample financial support from her parents throughout university and afterwards (in spite of a distancing from them physically and emotionally – "Stuart's fault", according to Ursula; "Stuart's perceptiveness of a destructive dynamic", according to

Sophia). Sophia had lower commitments than he had and double his disposable income. He could have argued that both proportionately and consistently, he had saved the better – from such a time as he had been in a position to, obviously.

However, he did not point this out to Sophia. (He expected she would have been mortified at her own insensitivity.) She might have attempted to employ that same angle to defend him against Stuart. (Stuart was apt to make clever remarks at Mack's expense, barely concealing a design to undermine.) And then, with what superior logic would Stuart retaliate? Would the next attack be worse than the last one?…

'It's a great pity Mack that you and Sophia aren't able to get what you deserve: it's good bank balances that secure property, not good intentions!'… 'Not to worry, poverty won't stop you from securing Sophia, will it? I've every confidence you'll find your place in the end.'

Mack doubted that Stuart had ever intended his words to be of comfort. If he had, he had failed, and it was not his wont to fail.

15. THE NEW SET UP

The Omniwell-styled, occupational health department at St. Joseph's was referred to variously as a pilot scheme; the flagship for wellness; or a potential cash cow.

In general, the nurses within the Department had been reluctant for the change and were reassured to consider the project a pilot – even after five years – and looked to the possibility of a return to the original regimen at any time. Alistair McDowell was the overall manager of the new services at Joe's (as Alistair chose to shorten St. Joseph's), so it is perhaps not surprising that he was the one to frequently use the term flagship. The "potential cash cow" was an alien beast to the National Health Service, introduced by Ged (Gerald Martinez), vice president of Omniwell.

Alistair *(referred to by some as "the banker", if my hearing is correct)* had given up a well paid post as a regional director of a financial lending organisation of some description, in order to guide the health workers into this dynamic competitive world. Much of his method for bringing about the culture conversion comprised the use of a number of inspiring, motivating sorts of phrases. They went quickly out of fashion but, initially, Alistair's included "Got to speculate to accumulate"; "We've talked the talk now you've got to walk the walk"; "C'mon! Let's have some blue sky thinking!"

(Caroline, a dietitian, who attended meetings to give professional input on nutritional matters but who was not a true member of the Omniwell project, had queried whether the latter instruction was to be done outside the box, or better inside the box so that it could be duly ticked. There had been no reply to her query. Perhaps this was because, as a relative outsider, she had no right to speak on the subject. Or, perhaps Alistair had been too enthused to hear her.)

Alistair attended courses to maintain his business edge; ensure his words would continue to hit the road running and not get overtaken in the competition by pithier rhetoric.

Ged was an uncommonly frequent visitor from Boston given, firstly, that he was vice president of the American company and surely a person of such high rank must be needed nearer the helm; and secondly, since it was so long since the instigation of the programme at St. Joseph's, it might have been thought that the consultancy period had passed. Whilst Ged never failed to make each individual in the Department feel that his or her contribution was the vital component, Mack thought (and kept his thoughts private) that it reflected rather badly on the staff in general that they were seen to require so much support for so long. As far as Mack could tell, no matter how many solid declarations of it being simply a resistance to change that held them back from maximum achievement – and how many journeys from America were needed to say it! – nothing changed during or after Ged's visits. (With the possible exception of a little more guilt, generated by the reminder that if they strived harder, if only they "went for it" wholeheartedly, then the success of the Omniwell way could do much to alleviate the financial troubles of their NHS.)

The counselling service was the most innovative addition to the Department, and Josie, head of this service, was unaffected by internal tensions; she identified no conflict of principles. Her service was popular both in-house and with outside companies: there was no contract that did not include the counselling service. It was her willingness to accept whatever work Alistair could secure that had led to the appointment of Michael. Mack found her company and her style of management easy and unobtrusive. But, as Ursula had pointed out when proposing the position to Mack (and, simultaneously, he for the position), if someone in Josie's position did not possess good peoples skills, then who would?

The induction period at St. Joseph's passed very slowly and Michael became impatient to witness how the Omniwell project was effected over in America. All his enquiries of Alistair and Josie as to what he would be doing in Boston, what he would be expected to learn, and what would be expected of him on his return, were answered with vague comments such as 'Oh, just wait until you've been.'… 'You'll see how it all operates… then you'll do the same back here.'

It was confusing. Counselling was counselling. What could they be doing over there, specifically, that he would need to emulate.

In the meantime he was given little to do,… "idle hands". Caroline contacted him with an idea and he said he was "up for it" almost before she had finished her suggestion: her advice was that he attend an event day or health fair (they amounted to much the same thing). These were organized periodically by the district health team of Ledstown. The suggestion quickly became something of an instruction – for which he was still "up", he confirmed.

He was to make notes on how *we* did health fairs and

compare with the way *they* did things in Massachusetts. She would discuss with him, on his return from Boston, any differences he found in either style or content. (This was presuming, of course, that he would get a chance to visit an American health fair.)

Caroline gave Michael dates and places and obtained permission from the district health team for him to observe. All that was left for him to do was to choose the day, turn up and register his attendance, none of which would be a problem. He was grateful to have been given a focus, at last, for the impending Boston visit.

The event Michael observed in Ledstown was designed to be fun – as well as providing sound information on some topics, and raising awareness of others that could be dealt with more fully in a different context. He read as much on one of the boards.

Counselling fell into both the first and last of these categories. There was a fun – some may say flippant – introduction to knowing yourself, understanding your personality, identifying the joys and tribulations in your balanced or unbalanced life. Leading on to suggestions of suitable courses or, for those in a more heightened state of anxiety, appointments for individual counselling. Unfortunately, there were no comparisons made of anxiety levels before and after attending the health fair: it might have produced interesting results, he thought. No, in his opinion, such health events had no place in a counselling service. However, he conceded that choosing a favourite colour as a marker to character – and all that goes with that character – was obviously a good opportunity for work colleagues to tease each other and have a laugh. And it created a relaxed atmosphere for tackling issues more suited to a health fair; reducing the risks of certain cancers; the effects of alcohol, of smoking; the benefits of exercise and good nutrition.

There had been a high take-up of the places offered: embarrassment obviously part of the fun in measuring body fat, assessing fitness levels and monitoring carbon monoxide levels in smokers. (All were duly amazed at the effect on capillaries of each cigarette smoked – a video was shown. No excuse for a ciggy permitted!)

Stands were vibrant and well propped. That for diet and heart disease, with its array of tempting foods on display, had been particularly effective on the last group of the morning, all ready for their lunches no doubt! Next to it, the selection of various drinks illustrating unit equivalents was equally tempting, and Mack noted the advisors timed well the serving of some sobering facts.

Overall, he was impressed. It had been fun.

Michael's absence from St. Joseph's on his chosen day to attend the health event was never referred to. He had tried to locate Alistair or Josie to sanction the initiative. Having failed to find either of them, he had left a note in Josie's in-tray explaining his whereabouts. On his return, the note lay seemingly unseen, untouched and unread. He removed it: it would likely have caused confusion for the note to have been seen after the event, so to speak.

After the fair, Mack was again in limbo whilst he waited for the trip to Boston to be scheduled and finalized. The waiting was unnerving. He began to think they had forgotten he was there, let alone remembered to plan the trip. And so it was that his enthusiasm, generated by Caroline, was augmented with considerable relief when the promise was finally fulfilled.

16. AT WORK IN BOSTON

The first day was spent at the head offices, on the outskirts of Boston, and was one of introductions to Michael. Names washed over him. What he did pick up on was "vice president"; it was repeated after almost every name. (One person was fiddling with some office equipment; he was a contract worker – the only none vice president – and would have avoided an introduction altogether had Mack not looked at him inquisitively.) In this environment, Ged seemed less important than Mack had previously thought him.

Case files, of only a handful of workplaces, comprised descriptions of Omniwell activities that were repeats from the brochures and leaflets scattered around the offices. The vice presidents were talking versions of those files, brochures and leaflets.

A day or two later Michael was taken along to a meeting at a fish packaging and distribution factory, and was introduced by the vice president who headed the ergonomics speciality.

'This is Michael Cunningham, Omniwell's European Representative. We are so glad he was able to be with us today.'

Michael was rapidly growing in stature. It was even suggested – off-site, of course – that his presence, as a British subject, might help sway Boston fish companies to use Omniwell: 'Scotland's seafood – salmon in particular – is popular in the fish markets here. Has a presence at *the* Major Seafood Show, hosted in Boston.' Michael was told.

'Omniwell's looking to work closely with the Scottish fishing industry on ergonomic issues. See how it could prove beneficial in securing contracts – both ways up?

Despite the tenuous links, Michael acknowledged an understanding that his full attention to the exercise was key to maximizing the potential. Thus, he observed closely the positioning and movements of wellington booted workers as they transferred, angled, twisted and boxed quantities of fish. But, in all honesty, he was out of his sodden shoe depth, and could make no useful contribution. He trusted that if ever Omniwell did follow through with their intimated Scottish fishing industry plan, his services would not be called upon. Alistair, with his hint of a Scottish accent, would be eminently more suitable. (Mack thought better of sharing that line of thought. He would not get drawn in to a situation that was bordering on the ridiculous.)

So far, Boston was a let down. Not the city but the lack of any revelation, of any evidence pointing to a brave new occupational health service and hence a brave new National Health Service.

Maybe it would have been unethical to take Michael to any contracted workplace at which they had real work in progress: he excused the lack of opportunity on those grounds, though it was never actually discussed. There was still the anticipation of a prestigious Health Event and Michael was persistent in his request to visit at least one. (No ethical issue of confidentiality in this area of work!)

Despite his persistence, this option was not offered to Michael until the morning of the final working day before his return home. It was put forward as being less instructive for him than would be the alternative choice of a general review and question session at the Boston offices. Nevertheless, Michael politely expressed a preference to accompany the vice president, head of the nursing faculty, to an arranged health fair at Wellesley.

He was visibly shocked at the near nothingness that lay beyond the poster plastered doors of the hotel's conference suite.

'No, I'm glad I came here.' Michael responded when he was reminded that he would have learned more back at the office.

'I needed to see how things worked in action.... I admit I'm not impressed: I thought it would be more on the lines of health fairs at home.'

'Great stuff: very useful Michael. Just tell us what you think would go down well in Britain; we're a partnership; we'll show you how to make it work for you!'

'Actually, I think ours already works; that's what I'm saying. It's a totally different concept to this. The health fair I visited was in a workplace – in local government offices as it happens. Who are the people who will come to this? Employees from this hotel?'

'Ok Michael. Well, to answer your question. Some might, I suppose. It's open to any and everyone. Looking after the health of people in the workplace benefits both employers and employees. Healthy people cost insurance companies less; plus, taking steps to improve health lowers premiums. It's a win win scenario Michael! We're here to get that message over; to spend time with anyone who will take that message back to their workplace.'

In spite of the fine words, Michael could see little to entice anyone to come to the event, so it was not surprising that numbers of attendees were very low; at no time did they come near to matching the number of people manning the stands. It was fortunate, perhaps, that the cost of the fair was shared across the several health insurance companies to have an advertising spot and not borne entirely by the one stand belonging to Omniwell.

In its favour, Omniwell had a nurse present alongside its sales representative. She was more than happy to give an on-the-spot consultation. This entailed the visitor going behind a screen, where a sample of blood was taken; this was used to give a reading of cholesterol concentration. If it was below a certain level, the person was given a metaphorical thumbs up. If above that certain level, then a diet sheet was handed out. (Mack made a mental note that this was something he ought to relate to Caroline: he did not understand the arguments for and against the procedure but knew there had been some disagreements back home.)

As there was little to see and just as little to say, and too little time to return to the head offices, the final working day in Massachusetts ended pleasantly early.

17. INTERNET SELLING

First Steps

Until Mack was charged with selling his collection, he had used *Eubus* for buying only. His use had been infrequent, late in his time as collector, and via the longstanding account set up and frequently used by Sophia.

Stuart could not rightly accept the credit for Mack's decision to turn to on-line sales to augment lean sales at antiques fairs and at auction houses. Stuart's prompt had been simply that, a prompt, and Stuart's impromptu calling by the flat, to check on Mack's progress (worded as an offer of help) was unnecessary.

The procedure for setting up an account and selling was simple; Mack's chosen username was "openallhours". Ready to start listing, he found his studio spot for the photography (the corner of the worktop next to the door – the lighting, from the hallway and kitchen window was perfect mid-morning when the sun had moved around some); he sorted out some backing cloths (an old plain t-shirt and a couple of tea cloths); practised some shots – he already owned a digital camera so no extra cost there – and uploaded the best.

At this time, the anticipation of testing the level of interest in his corkscrews and the advantage of being required to describe them – rather than being asked to be quiet on the subject – were unexpected delights that obliterated any regret at the potential loss of his collection.

He went for general auctions ("Buy it Now" had no appeal, it would be over too quickly) of ten days duration for each and he kept the postage the same (although weights did differ, he plumbed for simplification above absolute accuracy): he estimated postage costs for the UK, Europe and the rest of the world from tables on an Internet site. (The "sameness" of postage was within a domain you understand: Mack had no intention of asking the same to post to Australia as he would to Yorkshire. Why should Stuart have presumed otherwise?) It was with the starting prices that differentiation came: he wanted no reserves but could not risk the misfortune of a gem not being spotted in its brief appearance. So, obviously, the starting price was the minimum for which he would sell.

Mack was surprised at just how attractive his most mundane of corkscrews appeared on screen. The time consuming care over lighting, positioning and colour of back cloths was justified. But he would remain realistic and not be tempted to increase starting prices. (Who would have thought there could be so much excitement to be had from corkscrews!)

THE GUIDE

Today, the arrival of Stuart was timed to perfection, as far as Mack was concerned. Mack was gazing in admiration at the print-offs of his first listings – just three corkscrews, listed separately.

Stuart agreed. The listings did look impressive. He was particularly impressed with the descriptions; such information

102

undoubtedly gave added value. What had Mack paid for each corkscrew? How had he fixed on his starting price? Stuart quizzed Mack on how he had managed to build up his knowledge on the subject.

There was a reason for the questions: Stuart had thought of a way to maximize capital from the collection… if Mack was up for putting in the effort. Not much extra effort, mind; more a better utilization of what he was doing already for the listings. If he held off from putting further items on-line until he had photographed and described **each** of them – how many did he have left?… Oh, certainly with so many, this was well worth doing – if he then put all those sheets together, he would have a "Corkscrew Guide".

'Just think. You will make money from selling the "Guide". A double blessing. Because when you then list on-line the corkscrews from the Guide, they will fly!'

What an opportunity! Yes, Mack could see that.

Stuart thought it would be a good idea for Mack to also put in the price he had paid for each corkscrew and when. 'Collectors love a "Price Guide"!' he said.

'Won't that mean no-one will want to bid higher than original cost?'

'Of course not.' Stuart reassured. 'Don't forget your added value. And emphasize, in your introduction, how lucky you were with your buys; how popular corkscrews have since become as collectors' items. And you could always "round-up" what you actually paid.'

'No, I could **not**. It would only take one seller to remember the sale, and know I was lying, to discredit the whole thing.'

Stuart wasn't about to argue over such a minor point. He

went straight on to the marketing of the Price Guide. All so simple. He knew people in the printing business. 'Some physical copies will be good for dropping around fairs, shops etc. – and cost next to nothing these days. And, of course, for publishing on-line... ... .' It was assumed that Mack would know of Stuart's competence in all things digital and, in allowing his words to trail off, Stuart had inferred that he would be willing to employ his expertise on Mack's behalf.

By way of confirmation of the implied offer, Stuart added 'I've contacts who buy ISBNs in blocks, so leave all that to me – not needed for all formats but will need a couple or so.'

The concept had seemingly moved to a fait accompli, too fast for Mack to form any further questions. There must be something he should ask: his mouth was poised ready, uncertain whether it would be needed. No time. Stuart was nothing if not decisive.

'You just do what you've done here (*Stuart waived the printed listings in front of Mack*) – a photograph and description for each item in your collection; add a line about original purchase price and a bit of introductory blurb and let me have it... as soon as... if you want that deposit for the house.'

He stood up and turned to leave. 'Great seeing you Mack. Take Care.' And he was gone.

Had Mack agreed to the Guide? He was not quite sure. But Stuart was right: he would be doing the same for the listings in any case. And, if no extra costs were involved, there could be nothing to lose in distributing his work in the form of a booklet. It would be satisfying. He would have a permanent record of his collection. Author, Michael Anthony Cunningham. He liked the idea.

'Well done Stuart. Thanks' Mack said aloud to the blank doorway, always prepared to give credit where credit was due.

18. TWO SIDES OF A COIN

Selling corkscrews was no easy task but Mack's enthusiasm was undeterred.

'The Henshall type comes off tomorrow. It's had five bids already and is up to £55. The bids are from only two buyers and there are seven watchers, so there is every chance of a surge at the end.'

Sophia guessed he had switched his attention to an on-line auction. Mack acknowledged her indulgent smile with a wink, before picking up his collection list and accounts to peruse and to plan the next move.

Local auctions were fun but the *Eusub* site was even better. With a bit of detective work, Mack could often find out quite a lot about the new home for his treasure. Not always, of course: if they went to a dealer, all that was of interest to him was whether or not they would pay promptly after the auction had ended, and they generally did. But, much could be learned of a private buyer by scrutiny of the feedback.

It should not be thought that Mack was weird in this respect. The procedure was innocent: he automatically turned to the feedback of every bidder – for reassurance of his or her credibility, naturally. It was in an idle moment that the cursory check had developed into a curiosity of other items bought, or sold, by the bidder and allowed a mental picture of circumstance to develop.

The first example of this was when an Anri figural was

receiving quite a bit of attention: the corkscrew was wooden, carved as a dog, possibly an Airedale, though he was no expert on breeds. One bidder, in Germany, did not appear to be a collector of corkscrews but she did own a dog (presumably; unless 'Sam', who 'enjoyed his new bed' was some strange child who chose to sleep in a dog's basket). But, she had also bought several small, antique treen objects and books on Italy, so a sentimental link of the corkscrew dog to Sam was not conclusive. Mack rooted for her in the final frenzy of bids, convinced the corkscrew would have a special place in that household.

It was of no consequence. There was never any lasting elation or disappointment at the end of the auction, whoever was the winner. It did not signify in the final analysis, simply gave an extra fun dimension to the proceedings.

There was a different sort of enjoyment to be had from his third mode of dispersal, the selling at antiques fairs. He was very fortunate not to have any hassle or expense (other than fuel costs). Maureen took charge of everything. Mack did not want to take advantage of her kindness by hogging too much of her selling space. So, he put aside a portion of the collection for this purpose and released them gradually.

His then more frequent trips, had the added pleasure of a return with fuller pockets than at the start of his journey. For each corkscrew sold, Maureen insisted on paying Mack ninety-five percent of the sale price he had suggested – even though he suspected that there had been occasions when she had let them go for less than his estimated value.

She repeatedly said that she was more than happy to sell corkscrews for him as a friend, not as a business acquaintance.

He could count the favour as a wedding present, she teased, if that made him feel any better. And, of course, she was aware (after frequent reminders) that she was at liberty to return the corkscrews at any time should she have a better use for the space. A more than satisfactory arrangement to both parties.

Toby had not yet found an appropriate time to tell Mack of the death of his father. Because of this, he had not told Ursula either. He reasoned that Mack ought to know before others (though he had been obliged to tell his mother. After all, it was she who had received the phone call; the one to have triggered the events that had left him in this predicament).

One thought had occurred to Toby. If he were to tell Ursula, she might suggest that Sophia, as now the closest person to Mack, should be the person to break the news to him. Toby knew that once he told Ursula she would not let such knowledge be kept from Mack any longer, however it be told. And he knew that she would be right.

But, what if the Usherwoods had already told Mack. Might he rather not have the subject raised again? Might that not be why he was putting so much effort into selling his corkscrews? As a distraction from his grief. It has to be remembered (as Toby often did) that knowing cannot change anything. And so ignorance, if it existed, might not be such a bad thing.

19. NEW OPENINGS

Sophia was never outwardly critical of Mack but there was a sense that she would view any sentimentality towards corkscrews as inappropriate for an intelligent grown-up. This was not a problem: it can be reiterated, without risk of deception, that Mack was a willing seller of any and every one of his corkscrews – with the exception of his special waiter, and there was no need for Sophia to know of this one exclusion to the sales stock.

Corkscrews in the form of waiters, whilst not extremely common, were not rare. Mack had later bought an additional one at no great expense. This one he had no compunction about selling. It differed from his special waiter in that it had no personality and lacked the purplish hue on his jacket. As far as Mack's experience went, the jacket on his special waiter was the only one with such a regal quality.

There was no stipulation in his own mind that he must regain every penny he had spent on his purchases. He was prepared to lose on some with the expectation that he would win on others.

After almost six months Mack had raised a measly three hundred and seventeen pounds and thirty-nine pence. Measly was Sophia's word and not how Mack described his progress. It represented fifteen per cent of his collection in terms of number of corkscrews sold but not necessarily fifteen per cent of potential value. That was indeterminate. That was what

Sophia would not understand. Six months ago he was quite prepared to propose a more substantial contribution to the house deposit but the market was proving difficult to judge. No matter. His own needs were small – compared with the cost of female fashion – and with his now respectable salary, his contribution to the household would allow for Sophia's slowly depleting savings to be replenished, albeit on an incremental basis rather than in one, or more, large sums.

The bland waiter was given a starting price on *Eubus* of just £2.99. Mack was confident it would sell at such a low price. Although there was no sentiment attached, it would be humiliating if no-one at all chose to buy. No need for concern. The waiter's red starting price changed to green, denoting a bid, whilst it was still starred as a newly listed item. 'Good on ya' praised Mack.

By the third day there had been a promising four bids and the bid value had risen to £9.50. The four bids had been made by only two bidders (a common pattern), the second of these having put in three separate bids in order to outbid the very first bid. Mack tended to favour the second bidder – hlpen2t841 – because of her tenacity. She was not a bidder he had come across before. That she was a female, he deduced from her previous buys. She had no feedback as a seller but her buys comprised mainly items of clothing and accessories. So, what attracted her to his waiter corkscrew? He wondered.

There was no further movement over the next few days, other than extra viewings – fewer than a handful – and only one additional watcher, making three. Again, this was a frequent pattern and Mack knew that he would probably have to wait until the waiter featured prominently in the "coming off soon" list before there was further interest – if it was to come at all. And that was a day away.

In the meantime, he turned his attention to his other listings; the timings carefully staggered so there would be no stagnant periods.

Sophia interrupted Mack with a coffee and a cupcake. He ignored the cupcake and might have left Sophia to the same fate had she not reminded him of her presence by tousling his hair – he was at a too handy height for her to resist.

'Take a break sweetie' she instructed as she took a seat.

It was a particular break she wanted him to take, not a simple coffee break.

'Let's pop down to Brown and Stoney's after this and get the chair we want for the dining area. And we could try that new Bistro opposite.'

'The chair *you* want' Mack corrected, but agreed to go nevertheless.

From the first intimation of moving on from the flat, Sophia had been bursting with enthusiasm to design and furnish a dream place for them. More than once Mack had seemed less willing to be out choosing a cushion than to be home at the kill of an auction.

However, shame of past behaviour was not the reason Mack did not oppose the excursion to Brown and Stoney's. He liked eating out and he had heard good reports of the new Bistro opposite.

Three hours before the waiter was to be taken, another bidder came in. Pen, as he had started to think of hlpen2t841, had lost it. The current selling price was increased by the minimum increment, which showed that Pen had left nothing in reserve against other bids. But it was not an indication of her limit, for one hour before the end, she was back. Her first attempt to regain the corkscrew failed but it was secured the next time. Five bids in all now from her! This must be her tactic; to wear down the competition gradually. He muttered a warning. 'Be careful Pen. Don't get caught out.'

He ought not to have felt disappointment that the first bidder returned, close to the end. The frenzy between him and the third bidder in the final second pushed up the result by another three pounds. £18.99 was a good return at auction for this corkscrew, he had paid similar for it at a fair. The disappointment was for Pen not for himself: she had deployed a faulty tactic.

Stuart called by to invite Mack to a game of pool at the Ox. Mack was quick to accept. Too quick, according to Sophia: she was not included and had preferred plans for her and Mack. But, as Mack managed to whisper discreetly to Sophia. 'It's a kind gesture, it will be churlish of me not to go.'

He did not add that he felt quite flattered that Stuart had taken the trouble to call round especially for the purpose. It was usually Sophia he called to see. And it was for Sophia's benefit that he had troubled to produce the booklet about his corkscrews. Mack had no delusions on that score.

Neither had he forgotten that, of the four of them who had gone on the outing to Shorncastle, Stuart was the one with whom he had felt the least at ease. He thought on this. Not at this precise moment, but had done so a sufficiently number of times for the memory of it to have become ingrained. It bothered him, and irritated him to be bothered. After all,

Stuart was only one of the group and what did Stuart's opinion of him matter?

Music was played at such a high volume, as they journeyed to the Ox, that conversation was rendered impossible. It must have suited Stuart – it was his car and he was the one to have made the choice – and it suited Mack too, to think rather than to speak. (Once there, the pool game would be the subject around which small talk was made. Easy.)

It is a pity that we don't see more of Rufus, he thought. He's an affable sort. Presumes a mutual liking from the off. Self fulfilling. All – he presumed from his own limited acquaintance – would be sure of being relaxed in *his* company.

They did occasionally spend part of an evening with Rufus at the Ox. But, of late, Rufus's father had inclined to suddenly appear, take them by surprise. The company of Rollinson MP was viewed by Toby as "getting in the way of a good evening." Mack, mainly from want of opportunity, was not in a position to judge. He would not have been averse to giving it a try, but Toby had already decided upon and was in the habit of acting upon a policy of avoidance.

It was part of an MP's job to get along with people. Was that why his friendliness was trusted less by Toby, thought to be less genuine? Perhaps. But Toby's relative youth is what Mack thought accounted for much.

Stuart is older. (He had spent a few years working – on computer systems – before going to university.) Only three years older but enough to be comfortable and willing to cross paths with anyone. He may often be quiet (unlike his choice of music) but he is not shy and by no means can he be described as timid. Unlike Toby, Stuart lost no confidence whomever he encountered.

If Sophia gave him any grief when he got back (though Mack did not really expect that she would) he would say 'Sorry. I don't see Stuart and me as mates but I didn't want to snub a friend of yours.'

That he might have something to gain from keeping company with the more experienced Stuart was certainly not overlooked by him, but not something he wanted to confess to Sophia.

On his return, Sophia passed no comment on his choosing to go out with Stuart and, therefore, Mack had no need to recall his justification for going.

It was the unexpectedness that delighted Mack when he received a message from Pen late that night. It was sent through *Eusub* as a question about the waiter corkscrew.

'I'm gutted to have lost corkscrew. (*"Lost", she had already assumed a belonging. That was pleasing.*) A silly mistake over timing. Would have bid higher if I'd known!!! Do you have another, or can you get one for me please? Luv you forever if you can.'

No name given, it came through as from 'hlpen2t841'. Pen was female, surely. No man would write 'Luv you forever' to a stranger. His instinct had been correct on that one.

He thought he would like Pen if he knew her… but to give up his own waiter to her? No. That would be asking too much. He was not ready for such a grand gesture. Instead he would try to find a similar one. This intention he emailed to Pen, through *Eusub* and as 'openallhours'.

20. MACK VISITS MARTHA PILLINANT

Martha thanked Mack for coming. It had been lovely to see him last time – when Toby and friends had used her house as a meeting ground – but they had not had chance to chat. That was the gist of how Martha greeted Mack. She knew that Toby had not divulged the intended subject to Mack but she would not take advantage of that fact to evade her obligations.

First came the welcoming provisions: laid out was a cold buffet for two. If it had not been for the simple doubling up of cutlery and crockery, the food could have been presumed to be for the feeding of six. The aroma of coffee, percolating, had replaced the childhood one of chocolate cookies.

At the sight of the set table, Mack showed his gratitude for her efforts with a 'Wow!' It was mid-afternoon so Mack had not expected to be provided with a meal, and said so.

Martha smiled as she replied.

'Just a nuncheon.'

Mack looked puzzled. It was the response she had anticipated and was ready to explain. After all, it was a happy memory and would be a good way to ease the conversation towards the inevitable.

'I love the word and am determined to revive its use. According to Samuel Johnson, nuncheon describes victuals eaten – or possibly drunk – between meals.'

She regretted saying "or possibly drunk" as soon as she had

said it. Why had she been so foolish? So insensitive! The inappropriate allusion to "drunk" stopped her flow. She did not add, as rehearsed, that "nuncheon" had been introduced to her by Mack's mum, who had used it in banter, in better times; nor that discussion of late 18th century novels with Lily was one of the pastimes she most missed. (Lily was the more well read of the two but Martha never felt intimidated by it. Lily had enthused her.) In truth, she had lost that aspect of her friendship with Lily many months before her actual death. And since Anthony Cunningham's death, the loss of Lily was felt all the keener, inexplicably so. Perhaps it somehow confirmed the finality.

But Martha checked her thoughts. She must bring her focus back to poor Mack.

If the loss of Anthony had affected *her* that way then what on earth had been the effect on Mack? But then his father's death had never been mentioned, so she had no answer. How could she have let so much time pass and to have not spoken to him about either of the deaths? In her defence, she rarely saw Mack. Toby did. But Toby had left it to those nearest to Anthony Cunningham to deal with... whatever it was that needed to be dealt with. He said he would respond in whatever way Mack needed, whenever Mack raised the subject. Until then, he was "going to keep out of it". That is what Toby had said.

Mack had never raised the subject.

It seemed that she was the only one to think on the deaths. Though she did not "dwell" on them, as Toby had suggested she was inclined to do. It had been a mention by her – of how deliberate silence was unhealthy – that had brought about Toby's confession; he was by no means certain that Mack had ever been told! He assumed he had, of course. But, he had never had any absolute confirmation of that. How could he have when Mack had said nothing and Toby was waiting until he wanted to talk?

She was appalled. How could it be possible that Mack might not yet know of his father's death? What sort of people were they who could keep such a thing from him, for so long? (The sort of people who could abandon a child to Social Services, she answered herself.) She must see Mack. She must not stall another moment. She had instructed Toby to '... casually arrange for Mack to call round... ' to see her, as soon as he could spare the time (when Mack could spare the time, that was. Toby must make it his first priority. That had been her stipulation).

That Mack had not resisted the invitation; that he was all too willing to visit the Pillinant home again, had pleased her immensely.

But she was not managing the visit well, not as she had planned. She was thinking too much. It amounted to avoidance. She resolved, afresh, to keep to the task in hand.

'We've missed you Mack', she said.

It was obvious to Mack that Martha had given a lot of thought to the "nuncheon". She was well prepared. Yet, her fidgety movements and the peculiar, unfamiliar tensing of her mouth, suggested to him that she was not relaxed, not joyful. He watched her, tried to assess the cause of her unease. He smiled and waited. Martha clearly had more to say.

'Firstly, you should know that your mum and dad would be so proud of you.'

There was something unnerving about the way in which

those words were spoken. Something ominous. Perhaps it was the formality. Mack held his breath a moment.

'And I'm so sorry about your having had to go "into care". It should never have happened. I let you down badly: I let down your mum and dad too.'

Almost before Martha had stopped speaking, Mack protested.

'No, you didn't. That's nonsense. I'm not your responsibility, never have been. You've always done masses for me: don't know where I'd have been without you.' After a slight pause he added a 'thank you', as reinforcement of his sentiment.

Martha passed a plate to Mack and nodded towards the spread. They each made their selections in silence, eyeing each other and attempting smiles.

An elephant loomed large in the room, as on his previous visit – albeit a different elephant; that baby had now been raised. She tried again to broach the subject of Mack's misfortunes.

'Well, you've always been almost one of the family... for George and Toby too, not just for me.... But, it has to be said Mack, we didn't help when you needed us most. We *did* let you down. And I *am* sorry.'

Again, Mack reassured. 'It's OK. Really. Long past – and it's not your fault you got cancer is it? Just glad you're well again.'

Martha was not listening. She was trying to say the words she knew she must. Mack should have had someone better able than she: more able to find the right words. Much more able. But she was doing her best. She took a deep breath and tried again.

'I'm so sorry about your mum and dad Mack. I really miss Lily. How are you doing?'

'OK I suppose.'

It was not getting any easier. Martha could not ask outright "Do you know your dad is dead?"

'Did you know that we heard from Christine Usherwood's daughter (*Martha stumbled over the words. She hated uttering that name to Mack and, as she said it, remembered it was no longer Usherwood but Cunningham. When did she find out?... Oh, yes, the daughter, but... She saw no point in correcting her mistake)...* a while back?'

'I'm not interested actually Mrs M. If you don't mind.'

Martha was running out of openings.

'And how are you about your dad?'

'In what way?'

'Do you miss him?'

'Not as much as I used to.... Did Toby tell you about my going to Boston?'

... The opportunity was gone. Martha could do no more. She had to follow the lead Mack was giving, and she understood more easily how awkward it must have been for Toby.

For the remainder of Mack's visit the conversation was light and contained nothing deeper than Mack's pride in being able to pack a neat holdall.

21. CAROLINE'S OPINION

Mack was seated alone in the staff dining room.

'May I join you?' asked Caroline.

'Of course.' Mack wafted a hand across the empty chair next to him. He had just finished his lunch. He asked.

'Aren't you eating?'

'I've eaten.' That she had eaten sandwiches at her desk was typical of Caroline's working day. And the deduction that, if not there to eat, it must be a work related issue that had brought her to his table, caused Michael to adopt his professional tone.

'So, what can I do for you Caroline?'

No direct answer was forthcoming; it was taken as a pleasantry. Other pleasantries were exchanged. The conversation then moved to the only topic in which they had a common interest.

'How are you getting on Michael? How's the job going? Not seen you for a while to really speak to.'

Mack's thoughts immediately flipped to outside of work: selling corkscrews, Sophia – private stuff, not up for discussion. Consequently, his reply was a somewhat distracted 'OK thanks.'

'You don't sound too sure' was Caroline's way of encouraging him to tell her more, which, of course, the counsellor discerned.

He tried to think of what might be of relevance to Caroline.

Again Sophia came to mind: she was not eating well of late and her appearance had slid from slim towards bony, wasted but not in a fun way. Caroline's topic but, again, private; acquaintance with Caroline was not on that sort of footing.

Things outside of work had taken precedence and moved on at such a pace since he and Caroline had last spoken – before Boston – that the early contact now seemed barely relevant but 'Thanks for your help about health fairs by the way' was as much as would come to mind.

It was enough. Evidently the opening Caroline had hoped for. What followed was a lengthy comparison and contrasting of "their" and "our" approach, in which they each contributed opinions. They concurred on almost every point and Mack was impressed by Caroline's perceptiveness; so accurate from such limited contact with Omniwell and no visit to Boston.

He was prepared to end the conversation there. Caroline was not.

She went on to denigrate staff. The mercenary attitudes of Alistair and Josie were coupled with "our" high-ranking accomplices to the Americans. Familiar names (Mack knew of Weston Wisbeach, Secretary of State for Health and the somewhat lowlier Reginald Blenkinsop, St. Joseph's Business Manager) and unfamiliar names (which he instantaneously forgot) were cited as untrustworthy characters in league with Gerald Martinez. Caroline was sure that "incentives" of the monetary variety, in various pseudo legitimate guises, had proved too hard to resist.

Bold statements indeed. But likely Wisbeach would have bigger issues to be dealing with, wouldn't he? A Secretary of State concerned with small fry office politics? He thought not. The challenge came out as a one word question.

'**Wisbeach??**'

It was not enough to draw a reply or cause her to pause. They were sitting together still, but no longer having a conversation. Caroline was speaking, Mack was her audience.

In effect, *(the length of the exposition necessitates a summary)* the way Caroline saw it was that NHS traitors were enabling Omniwell to work under the front of providing a consultancy service, whilst, in reality, they were contracting the NHS workforce to work under franchise. 'How mad is that?' Caroline wanted to know.

'It does sound bizarre.' Mack agreed. His lack of further comment (as he recovered from the surprise of hearing his own voice) allowed Caroline to go on.

'It's costing us a fortune – and for what? I'll tell you "for what" shall I? We're paying thousands of pounds for the privilege of their bad advice, plus a percentage of our income. Paying *them* an income for the work *we've* done! Exploitation, pure and simple!!'

Again, Mack could not disagree. But neither could he properly corroborate her suspicions – if that had been the point of her seeking him out: he had no knowledge of contractual agreements between the NHS and Omniwell. A weak 'mmm' together with a slight nod seemed the appropriate response.

Caroline looked weary. Mack expected, and hoped (he was a little weary himself) that he would now be free to get a little fresh air before going back to his office, though he had nothing pressing to do. He took a deep breath of the fishy restaurant air as he prepared to make his move to go. He was too slow, Caroline had had all the break she needed…

'And Sheila! She'll be the death of me. Have you noticed

how she ingratiates herself? Always has. Offer anything to please – I'm thinking of blanket cholesterol testing incidentally, not any other sort of blanket stuff. Though... '

Mack had a bemused expression (wondering how he could now leave, having missed his opportunity), which Caroline interpreted as not understanding the meaning of "blanket testing".

'It's the testing of all and sundry – for show or pecuniary reasons, *not* medical. Testing with *no* explanation of results.... Oh no, education's not part of the package. She'd need to be educated herself before that could happen. So, the poor sods have a needle stuck in them for sod all.'

Was that it? Had she finished? Mack shuffled his feet but again was too slow, he should have got to his feet.

'To give her her due, I'm sure Sheila performs to the best of her abilities. Unfortunately, a few glib sound-bites is the sum of them – though the pamphlet she takes them from is *wonderfully* glossy.'

Caroline permitted herself to smile and to engage Michael's eyes at this juncture. She was remembering a satisfying confrontation on this very topic and wanted to tell.

'You missed another discussion on cholesterol testing while you were in Boston. I say discussion, but you know how it is. *(He didn't really, but a smile served better than an admission.)* No-one wanted to listen to a damned word I said about cholesterol but I did glean a response when I likened Omniwell's showy literature to Sheila's service – red hat, no knickers!'

Yes, he could well imagine the offence taken and he was amused.

Caroline relayed more of the confrontations to have taken

place during his absence. One in particular was her production of scientific evidence against the blighted commercial testing. A fear that her outcry would reach outside ears had led to an expensive revision of that particular service package and a rift between her and those promoting the Omniwell concept – which, naturally, included Sheila. Caroline admitted that it had cost her the semblance of a close working relationship with the Department.

'Though I've not managed to get myself banned yet. No doubt that will come, if I keep on trying.' She laughed.

There was a change in Caroline's demeanour as she told of another quarrel she had had with Sheila; she became more reflective.

The tale she told came from a time before Michael was in post. A gentleman, who had called into the Department on some trivial matter, happened to express a wish to lose weight. Sheila had taken him under her nursing wing and advised him on diet – a fashionable one of the time; high protein, low fat and extremely low carbohydrate.

'He almost died, for God's sake!' Caroline claimed.

'And it's no excuse that she didn't know about his kidney trouble. That's the whole point! It's the most common type but people often don't know they've got it.'

In short, Sheila's diet was the exact opposite of what the man should have followed to prevent deterioration of his kidneys. The man's condition came to light after the exacerbation caused by the diet.

Michael's ignorance matched Sheila's – though Caroline benignly excused his – when he queried.

'Wasn't it at least a good thing to find out that his kidneys were dodgy?

'No! Definitely not an advantage to damage kidneys in the name of science, or furtherance of knowledge. The damage can't be reversed. And neither can Sheila's stupidity, I don't think she's learnt a jot from her meddling. But that's Sheila for you. She's thick. She'll never learn and never change. And that makes her a menace.... She'll snuggle up to whoever she thinks is current "King Pin", in the vain hope she'll become Queen.'

After a moment, a fully composed Caroline said

'You are the best person in there Michael. Don't let them use you. That's all I wanted to say really.' She got up to leave.

Mack, a little stunned, wanted to respond: not sure what Caroline expected from him, or what he should say, he quipped.

'Don't let the bastards get you down, eh?'

Caroline smiled and added

'Something like that... Or, it only takes for a good man to do nothing for the bastards to win.'

'Right. Thanks.'

Michael accepted the compliment, or was it a challenge? He liked her spirited attitude, but it was not too difficult to sympathize with the overheard, alternative description, "tedious". He let her walk clear away before he followed to take a stroll outside.

22. ARABELLA

Sophia and Mack vied constantly for use of their shared laptop. If Mack had possession of it at the time of a Stuart drop by, Stuart did not attempt to coax Mack away. Instead, he tactfully offered to entertain, or to be entertained by, Sophia. That was a help, especially when the couple went into another room or out for a drink. Mack was then able to correspond more freely with Pen.

Keeping in touch through *Eusub* became rather cumbersome and they reached a point of trust at which they exchanged private email addresses. Mack was engaged in trying to locate for her a corkscrew shaped as a waiter, as promised at the outset. There was no reason, therefore, why the move to write directly to each other should somehow seem illicit. But it did.

The first thing Mack learned was that hlpen2t841 was not called Pen (or Penelope). She was Arabella and the *Eusub* account was that of her partner. His name was Hugo Lubbock (and as they lived in Massachusetts, not Pennsylvania, the "pen" part of the username was still not explained).

They, Mack and Arabella, had each used a partner's account from which to buy; something they had in common. And, coincidentally, Arabella for a long time had wanted to visit England with a particular wish to go round antiques fairs 'to get a feel of old England': it was another shared interest. Arabella had not heard any Northern Soul music before Mack introduced it to her, but she quickly became an enthusiast.

A ready-made rapport, which blossomed with increased writings: Mack was touched by Arabella's warmth and honesty about her failings – not that they were failings in Mack's view. How could a desire to reach out to a troubled soul be described as anything other than commendable? *(To clarify: it was not Mack's" troubled soul" to which Arabella had referred, but that belonging to Hugo Lubbock.)*

Arabella had felt Hugo's anguish from the moment his story had hit the headlines. She had first made contact (by letter) when he was in the penitentiary. She had expressed her support and total conviction of his innocence. Hugo Lubbock was very quickly moved from the penitentiary to Staunton State Hospital (not as a result of Arabella's conviction but because no conviction, of any description, was deemed to be applicable). His mental state caused concern and he clearly needed treatment. That much Mack understood, but as to what extent it affected the trial – suspended or charge quashed – Mack did not enquire.

The hospital was close to Hugo's home – though that was unlikely to have been a factor in the choice of hospital – and Staunton was soon the vicinity of Arabella's home too. She had made the move swiftly and unhesitatingly, such was her determination to give her support to the maligned Hugo Lubbock.

Arabella's move to Staunton (when Hugo became in-patiented as opposed to in-mated) was of benefit to the hospital: it gained an additional volunteer for the running of the patient and visitor café. Clearly, she had availed herself of all opportunities to demonstrate her concern for Hugo and had not been deterred by the lack of a romantic idyll: Arabella conceded that Hugo had not felt love for her at first sight, but she had persevered. *(It seems – reading between Arabella's lines, which Mack had not the time to do – that Arabella, to compensate for the lack of love at first sight, had ensured that Hugo had endless sightings of her, until such time that any occasional absence suggested to Hugo that something must be amiss and caused him a slight panic.)*

It was unsurprising that Hugo, at first, had not been receptive to Arabella's approaches, given that his poor state of mind was the result of a marriage breakdown (aggravated by the accusation made regarding the purchase – or theft, which was the claim of the plaintive in the case – of a lottery ticket. It need hardly be added that it was a winning lottery ticket: there would not have been a legal action over a worthless piece of paper).

Only after months of consistency did Arabella finally convince Hugo of her affection. The comfort she offered was then accepted. Her home in Staunton had been distinct from Hugo's initially. It had to be, of course. Hugo, the in-patient, could not be expected to hand over the keys to his house to someone so new to his acquaintance. But, within one month of Hugo's recovery and discharge from hospital, Arabella had made her home in his.

She confessed to Mack that she had made sacrifices in order to save Hugo and people had called her a fool. But fool or no, she had followed her instincts and could have no regrets.

Mack no longer had the opportunity to search for another waiter corkscrew, what with his work at St. Joseph's and a move from the flat to a house to be aimed for, he was otherwise too occupied. But, in his correspondence with Arabella, he continued with the pretence.

It was not too long before he was put under some pressure to produce a result, particularly as he had intimated at the start that it would not be too difficult a task. This pressure increased tenfold after Arabella had been obliged to inform Hugo of her reason for so much contact with Mack. (Arabella did not divulge how the obligation had arisen.)

Thus it was that the momentous decision was made. He would sell his own, treasured waiter corkscrew to Arabella. At what price was a mere formality; it would be equal to the final bid of the previous waiter listed: Mack could not possibly explain the emotional value, or convert that into pounds, or dollars. The problem was how to ensure that Arabella – or Hugo, now that he was privy to the transaction – was the successful bidder.

Mack wanted to sell through *Eusub*, not privately. It was so much easier and safer. He came up with the plan. He would tell Arabella beforehand of the time he would do the listing. He would list as an immediate "buy it now, or make an offer": the "buy it now" price would be astronomically high, so as to deter other bidders. Arabella would immediately make her offer, which of course he would accept.

There was a little difficulty in bringing the auction to an immediate end – a minor hitch in the logistics – but the plan worked.

The corkscrew was packed immediately. It would be absurd to be sentimental over its sale; Mack would post it during the lunch break the next day.

23. POSTED

Gerald Martinez spotted the parcel on the edge of Michael's desk.

'What's this Michael? Got contacts in the U.S already?'

'Not really.' Michael offered no further explanation of the parcel though Ged remained hovering over it. Ged looked at the addressee, then read it out loud.

'H. Lubbock, Staunton: it sounds familiar. Did you meet him when you came over to us?'

'No. It's not work related' was all he said. Ged mused some more, until he had his Eureka moment.

'**Hugo** Lubbock! **That's** who I'm thinking of. Is it him? Really? You don't **know** him do you?'

Ged's eyes had lit up with the excitement of such a possibility.

'No, I don't know him. But, yes, it is addressed to *a* Hugo Lubbock.' Michael's indifference did nothing to quell Ged's enthusiasm.

'Wow! And Staunton: it **must** be **thee** Hugo Lubbock! You do know about him though, right? What do you think; guilty or not?'

'I've no idea what you're talking about. This is just a corkscrew I've sold on *Eubus*.'

'Corkscrew?' The word came out slowly from Ged's screwed up face.

'Yes, a corkscrew. I don't know Lubbock. The corkscrew

was bought for him but I've dealt with his partner. That's all there is to it.'

Michael's explanation, reluctantly teased out, did not bring the matter to an end however. Ged was gripped.

'Why? Is it a special corkscrew or something?'

Michael as a corkscrew seller held more fascination for Ged than Michael the counsellor, obviously. Mack chose to concentrate on work, not corkscrews: he shrugged his shoulders in response to the question. No more was looked for. Ged's thinking was racing along, oblivious to his physical surroundings – which included Michael.

'Oh, come to think of it, it does make some sense: he's a wine merchant now, isn't he?… and… just how long is it since he was released?… hmm… Beats me, but he said he would come good and he did: he has. Quite a celeb. Hey, this could be real useful. Let's keep him on side, Michael, and see how it goes with Weston's alcohol policy… '

Ged carried on puzzling, querying and answering his own questions, whilst Mack carried on perusing the latest self-referrals (though soon read, there were only two. He always steered vague enquiries towards general group sessions rather than individual counselling). He updated his appointment diary. Mack found he enjoyed to contrast Ged's enthusiasm with silent disinterest… Until it touched on the personal.

'… Are you seeing anyone with an alcohol problem by the way?… These new wines could really take off. Smart move.… And if we can do something with Hugo Lubbock… will need to get the right angle, of course, but… Guilty or not, that's all in the past now.'

There was a limit to the time one could spend in making two appointments and Mack was obliged, finally, to show a degree of co-operation – not least because of the jolting question of an alcohol problem. Mack forced away images of his mother and rushed out a dismissal of the enquiry.

'It makes no difference whether or not I'm "seeing anyone with an alcohol problem" as client confidentiality is paramount – as you must know.'

Michael moved on to the issue of Hugo Lubbock's crime, if that was what it be.

'And I'm afraid I know nothing of the case against Lubbock (*not quite true, of course, but why should he disclose any of Arabella's correspondence on the subject?*). So, have no opinion on the question of his guilt. Sorry.'

Gerald Martinez kindly enlightened Michael on a few more facts – to put him "in the picture". His account was more comprehensive than had been Arabella's.

Lubbock's lottery win – Mass. Cash Jackpot – was from some years back. A claim was made that the presented ticket had in fact been lost by the true buyer, and the find, by Hugo Lubbock, not reported as such. Lubbock emphatically denied guilt: he maintained that he had bought, not found, the winning ticket. The seller had no recollection of either the plaintiff or defendant. Thus, the case rested on the fact that the plaintiff cited correctly the time, date and place of purchase whilst Hugo Lubbock had no accurate memory of the details, claiming that the stress of his personal circumstances at the time had affected his ability to remember clearly.

Hugo Lubbock lost everything – the case, the money, his wife and daughter. Some say that he also lost his mind; others, that his breakdown was merely a ploy to avoid punishment for fraud. In any event he had spent some time in the State Psychiatric Hospital at Staunton. After his return to the community he found work as a waiter, before his rise to sommelier and finally to one of the largest wine merchants in the State of Massachusetts. 'Ahh! I'm telling you Michael. His fight back was inspirational; a real success story.'

Ged offered an adjunct: it had been reported – though whether or not there was any truth in it, he couldn't say, but it was said – that… 'the plaintiff's "shacked up" with Lubbock's wife – ex wife. And they didn't hang around either. Now that gives Lubbock's attorney something to come back with!… A corker, eh Michael?'

It was something of a revelation. Arabella had said so little after all. Mack made no comment. Hugo was a wine merchant! Now that gave meaning to their interest in his waiter corkscrew. It pleased him. He knew he was being ridiculous and, naturally, said nothing to Gerald Martinez. But, inside, it brought a smile across his chest and, two hours later, he light-footed it to the post office.

24. MIXED POTENTIAL, PAST AND PRESENT

It was one of those days when working from home for the afternoon (after attending a seminar at a popular *Confabotel* venue) made more sense than returning to her office: Sophia virtually passed the flat en route and there would not have been enough to do in the time left before the end of the working day to justify the additional fuel costs. Neither was there a great deal of work she could do out of the office, but enough to satisfy her conscience – both clear by 4.10 pm. This gave her an opportunity to indulge in some cooking therapy.

Creating delicious meals was not something that had come naturally to Sophia, and some partakers were not convinced that much improvement had yet been made. Mack was not in their number. That is to say, he never made an adverse comment. He was always appreciative of effort made on his behalf (though the opportunities to be appreciative had dwindled noticeably over the previous few months).

Sophia judged it best to follow to the letter a recipe of an established, Michelin starred chef: her instincts were not to be trusted and she did have several books to peruse – a waste of gifts were she not to select from one of them from time to time.

These days, Mack never finished work until 6 pm and, even if he went straight home, he would not arrive before 6.45 pm; plenty of time to choose the dish and then shop for any missing ingredients.

Third coffee, third book when she settled on coq au vin, with tarragon mashed potato and asparagus tips. The larder boasted stock, potato, tarragon and wine. The remainder would have to be bought and, having glanced at the clock, Sophia realized that timing was now going to be an issue.

As can often happen, the problem of time – to shop, in this instance – was resolved by the passing of it (time) without due action: the arrival of Stuart delayed progress on the meal front to such an extent that producing anything "special" was completely out of the question: and gone, therefore, was any necessity to shop for ingredients.

Obviously, Stuart had not been expected – as such – or Sophia would not have considered delighting Mack. And yet, as Stuart stood at the door, Sophia was not totally surprised.

When they had met at university, Stuart had been the quietly caring one. He had never been exuberant; no loud, cheery, hail well met greeting; no public hugs. But he was the one to whom Sophia had turned in the middle of those dark, lonely nights.

Stuart understood her: they were soul mates.

Ursula had never experienced rejection by someone she loved, someone she had thought would be by her side as they grew from teenagers into woman and man. Ursula had never felt that blow to her stomach, the sheer weight of all the love she had given thrown right back at her; never been discarded as worthless.

Stuart had. He understood.

Stuart and Ray Fleck Mareson both: they had listened to Sophia – through the computer – and responded instantly. They had supported her, repeatedly; they were able to explain the attitudes of those less enlightened, those who had not discovered the reality. The world had been so different when Sophia's parents had passed the age of innocence. It was not their fault, but they were unable to grasp what it meant to have so much life ahead in a changed world. In explaining this to Sophia, Stuart and Ray had demonstrated to her that they understood.

The constant pleas of Sophia's parents for her to speak with them had unsettled her to near madness. Stuart had saved her; saved her sanity. He made her see that there was no point in speaking with them because they would not listen; they spoke at her, trying to force her down their path – a dead end; offered no future that she cared for.

With the help of Stuart and Ray she had made the decision to have a future and, to that end, no parental contact. Once she had made the decision it had not been difficult to achieve. She had the help of Stuart and Ray (predominantly Stuart. She had never actually met Ray but his words had been a comfort: he had echoed and reinforced all Stuart's teachings).

Ursula and Toby shared much of university life with Sophia: they could not be dismissed as readily as the distanced parents. They were tolerated. And, over time, Sophia had come to sense a genuine, mutual affection and respect. Stuart had stayed close by, in order to protect Sophia. Ursula, Toby, Sophia and Stuart had become something of a foursome.

In spite of Toby's close connections to Mack, Stuart had been cautious of Mack's introduction to that circle and had advised caution for Sophia too. His words had not been ignored. Sophia had been cautious. She had taken some time before allowing herself to care for Mack. But perhaps she had not been quite cautious enough; a matter of opinion.

There was something disconcerting, frightening almost, about Stuart's untimely visit. Her confidence to present a dinner of quality before Mack diminished rapidly, alongside her appetite. A momentary dread – of nothing she could identify – came over her. She could identify nothing other than a familiarity with the first year university student she had once been.

Stuart was anxious to know how she was. Of course, he had been upset by the many times he had called to see her and been witness to Mack's disregard of her needs. He could see the signs all too clearly: Mack was 'intent on doing his own thing': Sophia would be expected to 'fall in line': Eventually, Mack would discard her and move on. Hadn't she started to notice things in his behaviour yet?

Mack was undeserving of such a person as Sophia, Stuart insisted. It made no sense to him that Mack found it so difficult to love her. Hadn't he done all he could to make Mack realize this? Hadn't he tried to persuade Mack to take his responsibility to her more seriously? To stop using her, taking advantage of her generosity and pull his weight emotionally by paying her more attention, and financially – by at least **trying** to sell his rusty old bloody corkscrews? God only knew how he had tried to help Mack stick by Sophia. But he (*Stuart: these are all Stuart's sentiments and words, not God's – as far as I'm aware*) had to admit he had failed, and he was sorry.

Sophia dismissed Stuart's worries about her. She and Mack were just very busy, that was all. Everything was fine.

Stuart was relieved to hear it.

But that was afterwards. After Stuart had comforted her. After she had had the benefit of an understanding friend. And after Sophia had felt regret, deep regret at her weakness; after her admittance of neediness in allowing herself to be comforted so.

25. THE NEW ALCOHOL POLICY – A BRIEFING

Reginald Blenkinsop was standing off the main corridor within the Department, just inside the door of the general office, visible to, and spotted by Michael as he walked through the main door. It was around Michael's usual starting time, 8.40am, but at the sight of Reggie tapping the file he was holding, Michael instinctively checked his watch. No, he was not late.

Michael was as visible to Reggie as Reggie was to Michael, yet, Reggie chose not to notice him. (Mack sensed a game: he gave his usual greeting as he walked briskly by the open door of the general office.)

'Good morning' he called, looking straight ahead, singling out no-one.

Reggie bellowed a response.

'Ah, there you are Michael!' The volume was unnecessary, given the proximity of both parties. The tone suggested Reggie had been taken by surprise by Michael's appearance, both knew it was no surprise.

'I want a word'

Reggie stepped smartly behind Michael and followed him into his consulting room, the room next but one down the corridor. Neither one of them took a seat: an air of dominance and urgency had been created (game over), no time for sitting. Reggie handed over the file he had been tapping.

'This is the briefing paper for Wisbeach's baby. Take it with you and show it to Lubbock but make sure it goes no further: it's **strictly** restricted sighting. I want you **both** to be absolutely clear of the message. Right? Read it; make sure you know your business, you're one of our key players.'

As Reggie walked out he added, 'Keep that close to you and get it back to me as soon as you can. No photocopying!'

Clearly, Reggie knew of Michael's impending return visit to Boston. It was an indication of Reggie's superiority that he did not preface their encounter with any acknowledgment of that information. More than likely the Boston trip had been arranged at his instigation. The suggestion to "make personal contact with Hugo Lubbock" had been put to Michael by Alistair. And Alistair was never the one to make decisions. It was a move wanted by Gerald Martinez – "going forward" from the parcel sighting – but Lubbock could not "be brought on board" for promotion of the alcohol policy without appropriate authorization: that had to come from Reginald Blenkinsop. The transparent circle was complete.

Things were moving fast. The meeting in Leicester – to which Michael had been invited as an observer – was scheduled to be prior to Michael's going to Boston . 'It's no big deal', Ged said; merely an opportunity for him 'to get a handle on how we approach prospective clients. Will be of help to him in making the approach to Hugo'. Though, for certain, there would be no mention in Leicester of the new alcohol policy: that was still under wraps, Ged confirmed with Alistair, who reminded Michael, three, or possibly four times.

It was getting a little confusing for Michael as to who knew what, and what he was supposed to know of, in front of whom.

All the same, if he was to be one of the select few, a "key player" and "in the know", then he ought not to squander the privilege.

He closed the door behind Reggie and sat down to read the lengthy document and to be "clear of the message", as instructed.

'LAUNCH OF THE REPORT ON SENSIBLE DRINKING
AND ACHIEVING TARGETS'
ANNEX A. Suggested timetable for launch of the report... '

(Mack skipped through dates and times but picked up on the location for a local photo call: '*Durham Ox*' public house... 'Nice one: got that message' he thought. 'And clever to have got Wisbeach to Ledstown on that day.')

ANNEX B. Government suggests a new policy will aid the safe drinking of alcohol.
'MODERATE DRINKING CARRIES HEALTH BENEFITS.'

(The clarity – as opposed to accuracy – of this message was acknowledged silently by Mack.)

A government report, published today, says that there has been a gradual increase in the strength of alcoholic beverages, which has made difficult the interpretation of the advisable daily levels. It suggests that there be a new definition in the classification of drinks currently described as wine.

Weston Wisbeach, Secretary of State for Health, says:

'Alcohol consumption will always be a major public health issue and it is important for the Government to present a balanced view which recognises the risks of alcohol but also offers soundly based and credible advice on which people can base their own choices.'

(A comma, strategically placed, would make it clear that the advice was not to be on selecting which people were capable of making choices – but then he recalled that these words were going to be spoken, not read, and the Secretary of State need not be instructed on when and where to pause.)

The main points of the report are:

Current scientific knowledge supports the conclusion that drinking one to two units a day gives a significant health benefit in reducing coronary heart disease for men over 40 and post-menopausal women.

Men who drink three to four units a day and women who drink two to three units do not face a significant health risk.

However, consistently drinking four or more units a day (men) and three or more units a day (women) is not advisable because of the increasing health risk it carries.

The benchmark for women is set lower than those for men because of physical differences such as generally lower average weight.

More attention should be paid to the short term effects of drinking too much, or at the wrong time, or in the wrong place. Excessive alcohol consumption is a danger to individuals and to society generally.

All studies support the notion that when drinking outside of the home little attention is paid to the strength of drinks and this contributes significantly to an exceeding of safe limits.

(Does the study conclude that attention is paid to strength of drinks *within* the home then? He thought not.)

The report concludes that there are identifiable benefits from the recommended level of alcohol consumption in regard to ischaemic stroke and to the accumulation of gall stones, as well as coronary heart disease.

NOTES TO EDITORS:

1. It was announced in April of last year that an inter-departmental group of officials was to be set up to review the Government's sensible drinking message and address difficulties that may hinder the following of guidance. The group – which was led by the Department of Health – included doctors and scientists as well as civil servants.
2. The previous advice on sensible drinking was based on levels of units of alcohol and, particularly for the consumption of wine, suggested an easy calculation making use of drinking glass sizes.
3. Targets were set for England and Wales of reducing the proportion of men drinking more than four units per day from

26% to 16% and the proportion of women drinking more than three units per day from 13% to 6% over the next ten years. There are four remaining years in which to meet this target.

ANNEX C. SPEAKING NOTE TO SECRETARY OF STATE

1. I am pleased to be able to launch the Report of the Interdepartmental Group on Meeting Targets for Sensible Drinking.

2. Ministers from across Government decided to set up this Group to consider whether more help was needed in the light of the latest medical, scientific and health behaviour evidence – especially the evidence that **too strict a reduction in alcohol intake may result in a loss of the cardio protective effect.**

3. After a very careful consideration of the evidence, the Group came to a number of conclusions which the Government has accepted. The key points are:

★ Drinking alcohol does give protection against coronary heart disease, though it is only necessary to drink one or two units a day to get most of the protection available;

★ There is to be no change to the benchmarks already recommended.

★ It is important that people know when they are exceeding their safe level so they are able to take advantage of the best possible advice made available to them.

★ To assist people in their decision making wine is to be classified as such only if the alcohol content does not exceed 7%. It is suggested that the size of the wine glass reverts to 125ml. It has been noted that alcohol content of wine has risen gradually over the past 15 years and is now frequently between 11% and 15%. Consumption of wine could **safely be 4½** *glasses per day (for men) after implementation of this policy. The figure of 7% will be reviewed before any thought of legislation. In the first instance the Government is looking for backing in a practical way*

★ Emphasis needs to be placed on the dangers to individuals and to other people from inappropriate drinking. This is of course true in the case of drinking and driving. The report we are launching today is fully consistent with the message of not mixing drinking and driving. Wine is a popular choice, both in and out of the home and I am delighted that Henry Savage and Oswald Rollinson are in full agreement with these proposals and that they could join us this morning.

(Mack paused to deliberate the positions of these supportive gentlemen. Ah, yes: Henry Savage is Minister of Transport; Oswald Rollinson – Rufus's father. Mmm, interesting)

4. Alcohol consumption will always be a major public health issue. The report represents a balanced approach, soundly based on the best available scientific evidence both on the benefits and the risks of drinking. Its messages need to be viewed as a package not taken in isolation. I have no wish to nanny people but I think it is right for the Government to make advice widely available so that individuals can make informed decisions about all aspects of their own drinking and assist them to act in accordance with the advice and their decisions.

5. This report will set the course of our health promotion activity on alcohol for the next few years. We are looking to the alcohol industry to work with health education specialists to advise us on implementation of this activity. Support from the alcohol industry is evident from the exciting 'New Wine' already planned and I look forward to seeing it on the market.

ANNEX D. QUESTION AND ANSWER BRIEFING

1. What is the new sensible drinking message?

There is no change to the advice on safe levels.

2. Why bring out another report then?

Because the concentration of alcohol in some drinks makes it difficult to enjoy very much of the drink without going over the safe limit.

3. Isn't this making the message more complicated?

On the contrary. It is making it easier to keep within safe limits without needing to reduce the numbers of glasses drunk. Given the health benefits, we want our message on not drinking irresponsibly not to be taken too far and put people off drinking within safe limits. The previous report concluded that in addition to the cardio-protective effect alcohol also confers some protection against ischaemic stroke and cholesterol gallstones. It may also reduce the risk of non-insulin dependent diabetes mellitus and have beneficial effects on other conditions, though the evidence was not sufficiently strong or consistent to inform public policy.

4. What part does alcohol play in raised blood pressure?

The Group acknowledged that alcohol causes raised blood pressure. Alcohol may be primarily responsible for as much as 12% of clinical hypertension in men. For men the rise in blood pressure produced by the regular consumption of four or more units per day would give rise to concern.

5. Why have some groups within the health sector voiced

objections to this proposal?

I think you should challenge those expressing those objections. They are a minority with no grounds as far as I can see from the report on which to base objections.

6. What advice do you have for those who do not drink at all at present?

We recognize that some people do not drink because they have religious or other conscientious objections. Others do not drink on medical grounds. Where these considerations do not apply, middle aged or elderly people who do not drink at all or who only drink very infrequently and at very low amounts may wish to consider the possibility that light drinking might be of benefit to their overall health and life expectancy.

7. Is wine more beneficial than other alcoholic drinks?

Although wine has other constituents in addition to alcohol which might produce additional benefits the Group did not consider that there was any convincing evidence to confirm that wine was any more beneficial than other alcoholic drinks.

Of course the 'New Wines' will convey the benefit of being able to drink safely more easily.

8. Why have you singled out wine for this action?

Because wine varies considerably in strength and continues to get stronger. This has led to earlier estimates of units per glass now being unhelpful. The same does not apply to all alcoholic drinks.

9. Doesn't the report show that the Government has more sympathy with the views of the alcohol industry than of those trying to improve public health?

Not at all. Our aim has been to not only give the public objective soundly based advice but to make it easier for them to follow the advice if they choose to do so.

IF PRESSED on this or any points, take the opportunity to emphasize that the basic messages remain unchanged from previous reports; this is a reinforcement of those views with a strategy to enable the public to act on the advice. Emphasize also that The Group does not accept the minority view that it will encourage some to drink more and the Government is acting on the findings of this well informed Group. Alcohol carries health benefits.

10. The price of spirits has just been reduced in the budget, how does that tie in with this report?

Health is one of the factors the Chancellor takes into account in deciding duty levels each year. The report recognizes that price is a major determinant of consumption and assumes that price relativities will not change in such a way as to discourage responsible consumption. I do not think the slight fall in the price of spirits as a result of the budget changes disturbs the balance.

11. Why does the Government not take action on 'designer drinks'?

I am aware of the concern that has been expressed about drinks which are seemingly targeted at young people. Although the presentation and packaging as well as the drinks themselves may be novel there is no evidence that the manufacturers have attempted to mislead the purchasers as to their true nature. Labelling and advertising requirements have been complied with. So long as these products continue to be marketed responsibly there should be no difficulty. But the Government will continue to keep the situation under review.

12. What do you recommend about alcohol in the workplace?

Alcohol should not be drunk in situations where the work

involves driving, using machinery, electrical equipment, ladders or in other situations at risk. Employers are encouraged to draw up appropriate workplace alcohol policies which define when and how staff at all levels may drink when at work and provide help for those with drinking problems.

The Government is keen to support any company offering help and advice to workplaces on these issues.

13. Do not aspects of this report contradict the Department of Transport's advice on drinking and driving?

Not at all. A major theme of the report is the need to be more aware of the short term harm caused by drinking on a single occasion. It contains specific advice not to drink and drive.

14. What is your advice for people aged 16 to 24?

We have not made any changes to advice for specific groups: once people have reached physical maturity they should be advised to follow the sensible drinking guidelines for adults.

15. Will the report make any difference to heavy drinkers and those with alcohol problems?

The recommendations in the report are concerned with the individual drinker in the normal drinking population. They are not framed particularly to influence the clinical treatment of problem drinkers or indeed their recognition. The Government remains committed to ensuring access, through health and local authorities, to services to help problem drinkers rebuild their lives.

16. What is your view of the whole population theory?

The Group recognized that most experts think there is a link between the average consumption of alcohol and the level of problem drinking. However the link is not well understood *and there does not seem to be any reason why it should always take the same form.*

17. Why was this work undertaken by a group of officials rather than a panel of experts?

The Group was established to make recommendations to Government on drawing up a strategy to meet targets on sensible drinking in the light of expert opinion. Its remit has been to analyse the present state of knowledge rather than to advance scientific analysis. The Group contained a mix of medically qualified members and lay people with relevant experience. It also had the benefit of advice from expert witnesses.

18. Is the evidence considered by the Group available?

Evidence submitted to the group and reports of the oral evidence sessions are available on application to my Department.

When Michael had finished reading the policy – or rather the guidelines for those involved in its launch, which possibly was more interesting than the policy in its basic form – he thought for a few minutes. But no more than a few minutes.

'That's all there is to the new policy then. Fuss about nothing really; hardly comparable with brain surgery'. Assessment made.

He was confident of his "handle on it", without the need for any further reading or inclination to "photocopy" any sections whatsoever. He tucked it away at the back of his briefcase: that was as much official preparation for action as was needed.

26. URSULA TRIES

Ursula had decided to chance that Sophia was at home. The change in Sophia's behaviour needed addressing (*Ursula rephrased – part of her mental gearing to the task ahead*): the **cause** of Sophia becoming withdrawn and defensive needed to be addressed. Mack was out with Toby, at the Ox. A girlie catch-up was overdue and this seemed an ideal opportunity; Ursula need provide no other reason for seeking out her friend.

It was unusual for Ursula not to have received any sort of response from her text to Sophia. But, a number of explanations were possible, she would not try to second guess which one was most likely. To call in on Sophia was the obvious thing to do; she did not need to make much of a detour on her way back home. Back home from where? Nowhere, she was starting her journey from home. Already she was rehearsing lies. No need for lies or excuses, little would be lost if the attempt to see Sophia proved fruitless.

It did not: Sophia was at home, busy on the computer – updating her account on *Facesonline* – which was probably why Ursula's text had gone unnoticed. That was what Ursula surmised, the matter was not worthy of an enquiry. (Sophia had reverted to her rather tetchy manner of earlier times, when any casual comment could be seized upon and taken as an attack on her character.)

It ought to have gone without saying, perhaps, that socializing face to face with one's true friend took precedence over the exchange of drivel between hundreds of virtual entities, or non-entities. (*Ursula was not always so insulting; not always. It had been a typing error when she had written of 'Faecesonline' as she had explained.*)

It ought to have gone without saying that she was welcome. But Ursula took no risks.

'Hope you don't mind my dropping by and interrupting you like this Sophe. Just fancied chatting about something other than… (*in her desperation to be ultra tactful, Ursula struggled to think of a topic that Toby and Mack might indulge more frequently than she and Sophia might wish*)… Northern Soul or… Northern anything… .'

'No, course not. Tea, coffee, wine?'

In spite of the verbal acceptance of Ursula's visit, Sophia's expression betrayed discomfort; submission rather than pleasure. Ursula could not help but be a little offended and reflected that Sophia could be self-centred and did not always value the friendship that was offered. She determined to put her hurt aside; she put on her broadest smile, sank into the comfiest armchair, chose tea and began.

'I love it that you and Mack have hit it off but I do miss not seeing you as much.'

'Actually, we see more of each other now than we used to.' Sophia protested.

'Yes, I suppose we do. (*It was a moot point.*) But it's nearly always with Toby and Mack… or Stuart. Not the same as just you and me.'

'No.'

Sophia chose to let it pass that, actually, they used to often be in a foursome before Mack came on the scene. There was an awkwardness. And silence. Ursula waited for a lead from Sophia.

It came soon, and surprisingly.

'I don't know that Mack and I *are* hitting it off, as you say. Maybe we're together because I'm your friend and he's Toby's friend. But would we have been drawn to each other in different circumstances? I'm not sure. And because it is so "convenient", are we hindering each other; being steered from the paths we ought to be following instead? Perhaps it's actually a destructive relationship.'

Those were not Sophia's words, not her usual way of speaking; not her current way anyhow. It was reminiscent of the early, stressful time at university when Ursula struggled to understand the logic of Sophia's thoughts.

Ursula remonstrated against the inference that Mack's affection was not quite genuine. She exaggerated the few words Mack had spoken in praise of Sophia. (Was Sophia questionning Mack's love? Ursula wasn't quite sure. But, if so, the exaggeration was justified: a necessity if she was to overcome Sophia's doubts.)

'Mack absolutely adores you, thinks you're the most wonderful thing to have come into his life. And would think the same, no matter how you had met! How can you doubt it?'

Unfortunately, Ursula's role of confidante and affirmer was short-lived. A knock at the door and the entrance of Stuart saw to that.

27. NON-COMMUNICATION

The *Facesonline* community remained an anathema to Mack but one which he found could not be totally avoided. Sophia would not refrain from using that medium to openly detail her plans, even when the plan included no-one other than Mack – which was often the case. He invariably had to verify times or places they were meeting, always subject to change. He thought it a ridiculous way to communicate. All the more so as they were actually living together, yet Sophia would not drop the "sharing" with "friends".

One voyeur of their relationship, Candy Benwell, was a particular irritation that he struggled hard not to scratch. She repeatedly chipped in with her take on events and, at times, it was impossible to escape her obtrusive presence. (Candy did not follow netiquette and frequently 'SHOUTED' her **A**rrogant **O**pinions! – she ended most of her capitalized comments with IMAO. **W**orthless rather than **A**rrogant, was Mack's opinion).

'**In My AO**, using a string of silly abbreviations, acronyms and the like, is typically part of the moronic game of the initiated.' Such was Mack's observation (that particular one was reserved for the ears of Toby).

Mack did venture to ask Sophia why that particular "friend" featured so strongly on the site, yet never featured at all in real life, and…

'Does Candy even have a real life? And what sort of a name

is "Candy" for God's sake? Why does she have to know our business?'

He might as well have not asked.

'Why are you so critical of my friends? They've never done you any harm', was as much reply as Sophia gave.

None of that side of Sophia made any sense to Mack. And it was futile to point out, yet again, how much better spent could be all the time wasted in writing or reading trivia.

Mack's frustration was vented on Toby, who at least was able to give Mack a little insight: Capitalizing Candy, according to Toby, was likely a relic of *Mangoes for Everyone...* and a little said of those characters was enough said.

The lack of any firm lead from Toby's suggestion of *ME* was an end to it for a short while, until curiosity finally got the better of Mack. He put Candy's name, together with a pertinent couple of her "interests" into a search engine. Seventy-four results.

Her profile – in alternative guises but unmistakably the same person – appeared on several unconnected websites. This Candy Benwell was messing in something. Why else would she indulge in such deceptions?

Clues to her numerous identities were given on her "home" account; 'works at... ' supplied alternative surnames (Candy had also been known to change her first name to Cynthia on at least one occasion – that was when she worked at the Plough Inn; hence, her name on another site became Cynthia Plough); a 'would like to travel to... ' provided a clue as to why browsers were sometimes directed to linked sites. Japan was a popular destination and... ja.jp.Facesonline.com, was a favourite with several of her names. Whether the site had any genuine links to Japan, he could not tell, but there was a semblance of authorization provided by a cursory use of (possibly?) Japanese language symbols. It wasn't worth the effort to find out.

The codes were too blatantly obvious, surely, to be indicative of any serious subterfuge. But then why bother?

A few minutes, no more, were spent scanning down other of Sophia's messages whenever he was obliged to oblige Sophia and face *Facesonline*. Could the mundane observations have an underlying meaning? Some wording seemed contrived. Numbers appeared out of place. Photographs were unexplained, people unidentified – photographs of "ordinary" people were not commonly posted: mostly, images were boring, impersonal; of food, of places, of animals, particularly cats. Many of the people pictures appeared to be stock images, as if from a magazine or old music album.

If one assumed a pre-occupation with drugs and sex, then the posts made more sense. A photograph of a chocolate cup cake, which the supposed cook had made 'a hash of baking', had connotations. This was especially so when a dislike of pins and needles had been divulged amongst the 92 things the on-liner had listed as her interests (he found no explicable reason for listing any of the other 91) and the final comment, declaring that the smoking habit had finally been given up, made the conclusion a "no-brainer".

It was anyone's guess as to what the 'I don't drink' (posted by Candy) referred, considering that, slotted in somewhere else, was a picture of her posing seductively with a glass of wine. Equally questionable was the picture of two females, one of them unidentified, one assumed to be Candy. (Although, as the true identity of "Candy" was open to doubt, that assumption was unsafe.) A little below the said image was an email address for Candy – cand241@... (Candy's indiscretion is not repeated in full).

Mack did not care that his knowledge about Candy had not deepened, nor was likely to through *Facesonline*. But he did care that he was no nearer to understanding why Sophia was drawn to using the site.

He was moving further away from understanding anything at all about Sophia. They never talked about each other's work; Sophia was reluctant to use 'chilling out time' in that way. And she visibly cringed at the mention of corkscrews! Neither of them found time to read anymore, at least not enough time to invest in starting a book.

There seemed to be no topic that could be raised, no conversation stimulated without the risk of causing friction. It was easier, safer, to be quiet.

Stuart hinted often enough that the relationship did not seem to be working for Sophia, but Mack did not know how to prevent the decline.

28. THE SOLICITOR'S LETTER

A letter arrived for Mack when he was alone in the flat, Sophia was not due back for a while.

The letter was from a solicitor, requesting Michael to make contact. Its nature was not specified but, nevertheless, it provoked a sense of foreboding: how could the solicitor have matters to discuss regarding the will of Mr Anthony Cunningham that would be anything other than bleak?

Mack did not procrastinate. He telephoned the solicitor on the same day and arranged an appointment.

When that day arrived Mack considered asking Toby to go along with him. He suspected that a drink together afterwards might be needed. He went so far as to phone him, but gave no reason for the call other than to suggest having a pint together that evening. When it became apparent that it would entail a change of plan for Toby, Mack did not pursue the deeper purpose of his call. He could deal with his own affairs without disrupting the lives of others (neither Toby's, nor Sophia's; nor anyone's) and did not want it to seem otherwise.

The solicitor was kind. Formal, as was befitting her position, but showed concern that Michael had come alone. She provided a comfortable chair and a cup of tea to lessen the impact – as far as she was able – of the information she had a duty to impart.

Those words, which confirmed that Anthony Cunningham, father of Michael Anthony Cunningham had died, caused the second tremor of the earthquake. (Mack was not so naïve as to have not surmised that the discussion of a will had the prerequisite of a death.)

Again, the solicitor was sympathetic in her knowledge that the present Mrs Cunningham was not the mother of Michael. She was aware that, sadly, his mother too was deceased.

The will (written shortly after the death of his mother and on re-marriage of his father), instructed that, should Michael be under twenty-one years of age at the death of his father, he was to continue to receive his monthly allowance until he reached that age – to be more precise, the allowance would continue to be paid during the six month period after his twenty-first birthday, which would be the period of discussion as to what direction Michael wished to go. Apart from the allowance, plus anything of personal value to Michael that he wished to have (regardless of monetary value apparently), the remainder of Mr Cunningham's estate was to go to Mrs. Christine Cunningham, wife of Anthony Cunningham. The manner in which Michael was to be supported should he have attained the age of 21, or from subsequently attaining age 21 – and a half – was to depend on requirements as discussed and deemed appropriate by the said Christine Cunningham.

Such was the gist of the wording that had been insisted upon (though judging by the manner of the solicitor, not the wording she would have advocated). His age was irrelevant, to Mack: it was the sentiment of the will that mattered to him, not the particulars. He wanted to take no further action.

The proceedings were not rushed through. The solicitor used neither sharp nor blunt instruments in instructing

Michael as to his legal position. She made it plain that time was not of the essence in discussing due processes: her services were not free of charge but payment would be taken from the remainder of the estate and not from any of Michael's entitlement. And in spite of generous encouragement to explore all angles from which Michael's legacy could be addressed, Michael had neither questions to ask nor a wish to argue any points concerning his future. He thanked the solicitor and accepted her invitation, with business card, to return to her at any time should he change his mind and require further advice.

Mack closed the door on his childhood. He had a bag to pack for an overnight stay in Leicester. And then there would be his second trip to Boston.

29. TENSIONS

The trip to Leicester was without incident; little was required of Michael but to watch and listen. It gave him ample opportunity to mull over a few things, largely unrelated to the job in hand. Doubts about his relationship with Sophia came to the fore.

He and his colleagues were to leave Leicester after a very early, working breakfast. It would still be quite early when they reached Ledstown and preferable for Mack to call at the flat before going back to the Department.

Their flat came into view and Mack spotted Sophia's car in the parking lot. Sophia had flexibility in her working hours but, despite being aware of that, Mack was taken a little by surprise, and pleased that she had not left earlier; pleased at the thought of seeing her. Until he spotted the car in a visitor's space.

The sight of Stuart's car banished all pleasure and served only to cement the doubts he had entertained about Sophia's feelings.

There was immediate disappointment, naturally. And a momentary wish to change his plan and go straight to St. Joseph's. But, just as quickly, the disappointment changed to annoyance and his initial resolve was undeterred. He would face the new situation.

He parked up at the same time as Stuart came out of the door to the flats. Stuart did not rush to his car; try for a quick getaway. Quite the opposite. He slowed down his steps so as not to avoid having to pass Mack.

As they reached the crossing point, Stuart looked Mack straight in the eye. Mack did not flinch; he gave Stuart a casual nod of acknowledgment and walked on with no alteration in pace. Mack had become quite practised in outward composure and it gave him a certain level of satisfaction; a sense of decorum amidst their lack of decency.

Sophia was in the kitchen with no obvious intention of following Stuart out of the house, which, for some reason Mack was expecting her to do.

'Aren't you going with him?' he asked.

Sophia was unapologetic. 'I'm going out in a few minutes. Need to sort a few more clean clothes. May be away a few days.'

No shame. Although she did not say why she would be away or to where she was going, and despite the number of occasions Sophia, like himself, was required to be away on business, Mack made an assumption that this departure was not work related. (*A wrong assumption, but that is by the bye.*)

The sight of Stuart's car and then Stuart making his escape so blatantly, had fuelled a need to address his fears and save some pride.

'This flat is to be your wardrobe and your bed elsewhere then, is that it?'

There was no response. Mack pushed further.

'Did he sleep here while I was away?'

Sophia did not entirely avoid the question, she answered indirectly.

'It's still my flat.'

He could deduce from that what he would. Sophia spoke again.

'Oh by the way, that friend of yours, Maureen, phoned. She wants to see you when you can make it?'

Mack pushed hostilities to one side (with a surprising ease).

'Has she sold my corkscrews?... Does she want me to take some more?' he asked.

'How the hell do I know? I wasn't exactly in the mood for asking the price of fish or bloody corkscrews!' And Sophia was gone, from the kitchen and then the house.

Mack did not return Maureen's call immediately. He savoured the expectation and washed down some peanuts with a can of warm beer – Stuart obviously preferred wine, though not to excess; there was half a bottle of white left in the fridge. Sophia drank only red.

Late in the evening Mack went on-line to check against his diary the dates of antiques fairs. He was looking for one that could provide a likely venue to meet up with Maureen (their acquaintance had continued on the same semi-formal footing as it had begun).

It was as he suspected, he had just missed a good one – by a day – and the next one he could manage was not for another three months. It was most likely that Maureen had telephoned before the fair and would not expect Mack to make contact much before the next one.

Nevertheless, it was so unusual for her to take the initiative in this way that Mack stayed with his original inclination, to return her call.

She sounded nervous as they went through the usual pleasantries:

'Oh, hello Ma... er... Michael. Thanks for ringing back. Did you have a good trip?'

(Her indecision as to how to address Mack was a sign that she was uncomfortable: he had used his full name when introducing himself on first acquaintance, but had also given the derivative by which he was known amongst friends. Perhaps she would have preferred not to have been given a choice.)

'Yes thanks. How are you?'

Maureen did not answer. It was awkward. Silences were accommodated more easily when face to face; this was the first time they had spoken over the telephone – though there had been the occasional left message – and Mack rushed to fill the gap in conversation.

'You were quite lucky to catch Sophia in actually.'

What irrelevant, ridiculous things one says in such moments! Maureen, quite rightly, ignored the comment.

'There's something I wanted to talk to you about, Michael, but not over the telephone. Could we meet up somewhere?'

Mack did not hesitate.

'Of course, did you have any time and place in mind?'

'How about this Saturday morning, Malton Services, southside?'

'Yeah, that sounds OK. Shall we say about 11 o'clock?'

'That's fine. Thanks Michael. See you then.'

Mack had not known quite what to expect when he telephoned Maureen, though he had not expected to be left more puzzled afterwards than before. The day of the call was Thursday so he was not to be kept in suspense overly long.

30. TRUTH

Mack spotted Maureen immediately. She was wearing a bright turquoise fleece and hugging an oversized mug of coffee. She looked as anxious as she had sounded on the telephone, but smiled a welcome when Mack approached.

'I'll just get one for myself' he said, nodding towards Maureen's coffee. 'Do you want anything to eat?'

Maureen declined. Mack took a few steps away, noticed it looked rather busy around the purchasing area, changed course, came back and sat down.

'Actually, I think I'll leave it for a bit.'

He wanted to get to the crux of this meet up: it had been at Maureen's instigation yet he sensed he was going to have to be the one to get the conversation flowing.

'So, how are you? And your family?'

'Much the same as ever, thanks.'

(Mack put a mental cross against marriage break-up as a likely reason for the contact.)

'More to the point, how are you Michael?'

'I'm OK…. What did you want to talk to me about?'

'Well, for one thing, I wanted to say how sorry I am about your dad…. Did the solicitor manage to contact you? I had your phone number but not your address…. And I know they didn't want to phone… '

Mack was not expecting that. Not at all. It was a few moments before he spoke.

'I don't understand. How did you know about my dad?'

It was Maureen's turn to be confused.

'Don't you see Toby these days? Didn't he tell you that I'd tried to contact you because your father was very ill?'

'Yes, I see Toby and NO, he didn't mention you. I didn't know you even knew Toby (*he had forgotten, in that instant, that Toby was with him at the antiques fair when they had first met*). And how come you knew my father was ill and I didn't?'

Mack was struggling to think clearly; shocked at the unexpected mention of his father. He had asked the question without any conviction that he would be able to take in the answer. And whatever Maureen had been braced to say to Mack, it was not the answer to that question.

'I'm so sorry Mack. I don't know what's happened, but there seems to have been an awful lot of misunderstandings and crossed wires. If Toby hasn't said anything I hardly know where to begin.'

'You could start with telling me how come you knew he was ill and I didn't?'

Maureen was close to tears. She apologized yet again.

'I'm sorry Mack. I thought you knew. My maiden name was Usherwood.'

She looked into Mack's face.

'I'm Christine Usherwood's daughter,' she said.

She kept her eyes on his, trying to read his thoughts. An impossibility, his face was blank.

'Can I get you a coffee?' she asked. 'I'm going to get myself another.'

'No thank you. I've to be getting back' he said. Though there was nothing for which he had to return.

He had said he had to leave but there was no indication he

was about to, which, in effect, ruled out another coffee for Maureen. They both sat motionless, in silence. Silent, until Mack made a minor deduction.

'If you thought I already knew who you were, then the something you wanted to talk to me about was – what?'

Maureen was reluctant to speak. She plucked at her fleece. Mack was irritated.

'Come on. You've got me here now. What do you want?'

'I found something in a book that I wondered if you would want. But I don't want to upset you more than I have. Perhaps now isn't the right time. You've had a shock.'

'Oh, for God's sake. What is it?'

There was no question that Maureen would have to reveal whatever it was that was troubling her. Yet still she stalled.

'… A poem. It's a poem: one that is in your dad's handwriting.… I'm not sure when he wrote it, it's not dated. But I think it might have been… a long time ago. I found it very moving Mi… Ma..ck. But, I'm *really* not sure that now is the best time for you to read it.'

'Could I have it please?' Mack showed no emotion. The impatience had gone. He waited with an open palm outstretched.

Maureen took from her handbag an envelope, containing a small piece of paper and passed it across to Mack. He opened it and looked at the words in front of him.

Once in life I was and had, a father, brother, son.
Now I do as you bid do, and they are all but gone.

Domination; Abomination in all eyes but thine.
Now I'm no-one, I have no-one if I don't call you mine.

Abomination domination. I want to return
to home; to son; to a warm face in mornings he has kissed.
You call and call, and shout and shout, words that I daren't resist
for fear of being left alone in my own hell, to burn.

He stared at the paper. Maureen wasn't sure whether or not he was reading the words. She waited for him to move, or to speak. He did neither. Eventually, Maureen asked

'Are you OK?'

Inadequate words. Maybe, but what else could she say, or do? Again she fought back the tears. Tears for Mack, for his father, and for herself. For the friendship she thought they had, but didn't. It never existed. Not a friendship between Michael Cunningham and Maureen, daughter of Christine Usherwood.

Of course, Mack did not heed Maureen's enquiry: he was somewhere beyond that moment, that company; somewhere where no sound reached him.

It was a robot that said 'I've to get back now. Thanks'; that put the verse into a pocket, the same pocket in which a waiter once rested; that left the building and drove home.

31. GOING WRONG

'You've blundered mate.'

Stuart's greeting did not promise the success that Mack had dreamed of – and had worked hard towards. And the fact that Stuart continued to call round to the flat freely when it must have become apparent that his presence (and the grating use of "mate") was irksome (though nothing specifically about Stuart and Sophia had been voiced), led Mack to ignore him.

'Have you heard of Joshua Machin?' Stuart asked.

It was difficult for Mack to continue to blank Stuart. Not when a direct question had been asked.

'I can't say I have' he replied.

'Would have been better for you if you had, and had sweetened him up a bit before launching into the antiques market.'

Not a question. So Mack said nothing.

Stuart went on to enlighten him. (After first despairing that it was a subject on which he would have expected Mack to be the one displaying some wisdom!)

'Joshua Machin attends all the big fairs; sells on-line *and* has a London shop front as big as the side of a double decker bus. He can find whatever his top clients ask for but he's *the* top dog when it comes to gadgets and scientific instruments.'

In short, Machin was well known and well respected by anyone who was anyone in antiques: absolutely amazing that Mack did not know of him!

'Probably I've seen him around without knowing his name' Mack supposed.

Stuart obviously did not accept such a shortcoming as justifiable.

'A lesson for you Mack. Know your Business.'

Mack would have corrected that corkscrews had never been his business, merely a hobby, but he did not feel on top of the argument – not having been told yet of the actual blunder: he presumed that to be unaware of a Name was no major offence – so remained silent.

The blunder was revealed.

'You valued an early boxed Clough at only £12.50. Huge error. Way out!'

Mack was irritated by the criticism (and, at the same time, secretly relieved it was not something more serious).

'Hang on. I didn't "value" anything. I said what I paid – as you suggested.'

'*Price Guide* Mack: clue in the title – A Guide to what Price you might get or have to pay?'

Stuart had conveniently ignored the reminder that the Guide, including the format of the Guide, had been produced at his suggestion.

'The introduction made it clear about the significance or otherwise of the "prices". Price paid does not equate to value. Everyone knows that.' said Mack.

(The introduction too, had been at Stuart's suggestion! Mack let that one go.)

'Obviously, this Mr Machin has not bothered to read that, or any explanatory notes: or is a bit short on understanding.'

Reference to the introduction was a sound defence against

such censure as Mr Machin's, Mack thought. Unfortunately, it was ineffectual on Stuart's attitude.

'Well, Josh is really gunning for you. Thought I'd better warn you to watch your back mate.'

'Oh, "Josh" now is it?' Mack muttered.

The idea that a difference of opinion on the "value" of one corkscrew amounted to some sort of crisis was simply ridiculous. And Mack told Stuart so.

'You're being naive Mack. Why do you think you've had no sales of your booklet and no interest in your listings? Machin has a similar Clough, All-Ways corkscrew, and has his priced up at £138. His choice was to discredit you or to have his customers lose trust in him. You lost.'

Mack protested.

'All rubbish. I *have* had some success with the listings. And the book *is* selling well; it's just that the money hasn't come through yet. You said yourself that that can take months.'

Stuart mocked a tone of patience.

'No, Mack. Your book is not selling well; it's not selling at all. I thought I'd explained algorithms to you, and why you shouldn't take any notice of sales rankings. It's complicated. Best to ignore them.'

Mack did not disguise his anger.

'I'm not stupid. I understand algorithms. But if a book can go from a ranking as low as 5,000,000th of all book sales to 10,000th; or from 1,200th to 5th of 1,300 in its own category – without a single sale! Then the rankings are almost fraudulent. The weighting of other factors against actual sales is manipulative in the extreme!'

Stuart insulted Mack further by showing continued patience and tolerance of Mack's deemed ignorance.

'It's not your fault Mack. I should have advised you better. I'd forgotten you weren't used to hard headed business. So, I'll stand the cost of the coverage – the advertising: that's what got you high in the rankings, by the way. If things turn round and you make your fortune, you can pay me for the printing, ISBNs etcetera. Otherwise, just forget it. Have the experience on me and I'll have a drink on you. OK?' (Stuart didn't wait for the reply.)

'Bye Sophia. Can't stop.' Stuart shouted through to the kitchen, where Sophia was skulking, as he made his way out.

Mack could not resist a search of "Joshua Machin corkscrew". True enough, the thousands of search results indicated that Stuart was telling the truth: Machin was likely a well known figure in the world of antiques. He delved a little further.

Machin had put a selection of his stock on-line. It included some corkscrews and they were the items to which Mack turned his attention. "Hand carved head of a bulldog" – 'looks a bit suspect' Mack muttered, in his now usual fashion. 'Too similar to the *syroco* ones for my liking.' He scrolled down some more. "A nineteenth century Volstead". 'Aha! Can't have it both ways: it's *either* nineteenth century *or* Volstead.' Mack scoffed. (He was referring to a pair of figural corkscrews, one a waiter – not at all like his own – and the other a top hatted gentleman.) The gentleman corkscrew most probably did represent Senator Volstead, but as the so-called Volstead Act was not introduced until 1919, the corkscrew would not have been produced in the 1800s! He was tempted to raise *that* blunder with Machin – or should he tell Stuart instead? No. He would do neither. He muttered some more. 'Charlatans, the lot of 'em. Not worth the time of day.'

32. A SECOND VISIT TO BOSTON

Boston to Staunton was an easy journey and one that Mack was competent to make, had he chosen to hire a car for the duration of his visit rather than to take taxis. He was confident that the only problem he might have encountered was at the point where the main highway junctions converged and, with a little extra concentration, he would have coped. No, his decision to take taxis had not been based on any lack of driving proficiency. He knew that, despite the intimations that had come from his refusal to follow Stuart's advice on car rentals.

In his taxi he was able to fully absorb the experience; to breathe it in, recite softly names familiar from England. On road signs, billboards; they were everywhere – 'Boston... Dorchester... Halifax (*a turn of the head*) Mansfield... Oh? Bristol County, that's a surprise!' Reminders of those home country places reinforced his perception that he was more than a tourist: he had been invited to someone's home; he almost belonged.

As he got out of the taxi, he clenched the folder containing details of the new alcohol policy with one hand, the other checked the champagne corkscrew in his pocket; the corkscrew with which he hoped to engineer a swap for his beloved waiter – whom he had now named Theo. Yes, he knew it was silly to give a name to a corkscrew (it would never be spoken; that would be a step too far) but it helped somehow. It gave a sense of Theo being rightfully his. Without a name, an unspecific waiter corkscrew might be deemed, by outsiders, to be particularly suited to Hugo's household. He was on a mission, to deny that suitability and rescue Theo. (This reversion to such childlike reasoning, play a character in a game, was his way of answering a nervous call to flee.) He rang the doorbell.

Mack expected that Arabella would be by herself, they were to be joined a little later by Hugo. He relished the prospect of meeting Arabella, he knew they would get on well (though he resisted the temptation to surmise how well). Having the rescue of Theo to attend to was a drawback but he would get that out of the way as soon as an opportunity could be created. The absence of Hugo would be a bonus in this respect.

He recalled the useful information he had picked up from Ged: Hugo Lubbock had started his working life – after the unfortunate incident, to which no allusion would be made – as a waiter; advanced firstly to a sommelier, and eventually to working on his own account as a buyer and distributor of drinks to restaurants and supermarkets. Yes, he was confident with the story. He would congratulate Arabella on her thoughtful gift of the waiter corkscrew; an appropriate reminder of Hugo's success from humble beginnings. This was the ploy to turn the conversation to Hugo's growing collection (very small still; an advantage in that he was less likely to have yet acquired a champagne corkscrew).

In all his communications with Arabella, Mack had never hinted at his change of heart about the sale. He wished he had. He wished that he had some knowledge of how the present of his corkscrew had been received. No. Better not to know.

Regardless of how much it may now mean to Hugo, it was impossible that Theo could have the significance for Hugo as he did for him.

He could not decide on how much of his background, personal stuff, he need reveal. To say nothing, other than he wanted to have his corkscrew back again, would arouse suspicion; they might suspect that new information had come to light that had increased its value to dizzy heights. Obviously that would work against him: it would increase their wish to hold on to it. But he did not want to appear freakish: an English eccentric was acceptable but not an emotionally inept idiot – even if the latter was a more apt description.

The indecision made him twitchy.

The house was not as modern and minimalistic as Mack had imagined it to be. His image had been built from a scrutiny, via feedback, of items bought more lately on *Eusub*. Purchases comprised a few items of silver – functional rather than decorative; a neat, teak coffee table; a set of glasses; a quantity of designer clothing (forever conspicuous); perfume and, of course, a couple of corkscrews.

The staircase in no way dominated the entrance hall, which was large and merged seamlessly with one of the downstairs rooms. Both the hall and adjoining room housed shelves full of books; comfortable, upholstered chairs were strategically placed to view the hung pictures. These ranged in subjects from peaceful, rural scenes to modern, sometimes disturbing portraits – or portraits of disturbed people, depending on the viewer's interpretation.

Mack saw nothing that struck him as familiar. The beige trousers and bright, sparkly pink top that Arabella wore may have been bought on *Eusub*, but he did not possess that discriminatory level of interest.

As Arabella invited Mack to be seated, she repeated what had earlier been both emailed and texted to him – that she worked at the local mart and invariably was home earlier than Hugo. There was a look in her eye of pleasure as she made a favourable assessment of Mack's attractiveness. (It was not picked up on: another time perhaps it might have been, but not then. Mack was too preoccupied.)

An array of wines – previously selected by Hugo for consideration by Mack – was wheeled into the room on a two-tiered trolley. Mack released hold of the folder and placed it on the floor by his feet.

Small movements from upstairs could clearly be heard. He wondered whether Arabella had been truthful. Was Hugo home… and avoiding him? Why?

Either Arabella was oblivious to Mack's sense of another presence in the house or chose to ignore the fact: no reference was made to the occasional pad of footsteps passing between doors.

'I don't see why we shouldn't start enjoying ourselves while we're waiting for Hugo' Arabella announced as she brought the trolley to a halt besides Mack's chair, riding over the folder in the process.

'Can't tell you anything about them, I'm afraid…. But I'll get you paper and pen so you can jot down any questions or comments for Hugo' she added, possibly by way of justification for the indulgence.

Mack was grateful for this forethought – or afterthought. 'Very organized' he rejoined. Although wine tasting had not been on the agenda, as far as Mack was concerned, it promised to ease the flow of conversation and so was welcomed.

Wine was not quite his first choice when it came to drinks but he surprised himself with the enthusiasm he mustered.

'I'm delighted with this... umm... white. And only "9% alcohol by volume"' he read aloud. 'It loses nothing in comparison with this... other white (*he scrutinized the bottle from which his previous drink had been poured*)... 13%: bodes well for Wisbeach's policy.' (Forgetting that 7% was to be the new wine classification.)

Arabella cared nothing for politics: the dead look of her eyes testified to that and she did not bother to enquire after "Wisbeach's policy".

'Move on', thought Mack. 'Get on with the exchange business. Get it done before Hugo comes home'. He fumbled with the champagne corkscrew – still out of sight in his pocket – knocked back the wine that had been poured for him and scanned the bottles for one with a champagne type stopper.

A thud came from upstairs. Mack hurriedly put down his glass and pushed back a sleeve to check the time – an involuntary movement. The noise had been disruptive and Mack's agitation suggested to Arabella that an explanation was due.

'She's Hugo's' was the beginning of it. Arabella expanded only slightly.

'It's his turn to have her. So, she's brought here whether he's here or not!'

Mack had lost his momentum. He was asked which wine he would next like to try, and it was back to business as usual.

The prepared conversation never did take place, though the

actual swop came and went more smoothly than Mack could ever have dared to hope.

It began with a "selling" to Arabella of the champagne corkscrew. 'A real find. Thought you might like to see it... ' When she finally pleaded to be allowed to have it, Mack's reluctance to part with it could not be overcome, not by any number of dollars offered. It was only when clever Arabella suggested that 'an opener for *Champagne* bottles is far more fitting for my successful Hugo than an insulting waiter', that Mack could be persuaded to make the swop.

The champagne corkscrew took its place in Hugo's collection and Theo rested cosily in Mack's pocket. Brilliant!

Yet Mack still twitched.

Arabella neglected to ask Mack which wine was to be next, the one nearest to her right hand was self-selected. And Mack was equally neglectful of making notes of its attributes. Perhaps it was time to check on Hugo's progress. 'Is he on his way home?'

The thought that came to mind was not acted upon: Mack did not ask. And it was not Hugo's homecoming that interrupted the wine tasting.

Upstairs a door opened, a pause, a rhythmic footfall. She, Hugo's daughter, was coming down the stairs.

'Jesus Christ, she should be asleep by now' Arabella mumbled.

Mack braced himself for the encounter.

She stood in the entrance to the room, opposite to where Arabella and Mack were seated.

'Where's my daddy?' she asked, barely above a whisper.

Arabella's answer of 'God knows' did not reassure the little girl. She started to cry, but quietly.

Mack estimated her age at five, or six years. He smiled at her. He could not speak but tried to convey, through his expression, that her daddy would soon be there. She did not read the message. He saw in her eyes a plea to be told, with certainty, exactly when her daddy would come to take care of her. She did not take her eyes off Mack's face for a moment, not even when Arabella spoke to her.

'Go on. Back upstairs. He won't be pleased if he comes back and you're not in bed asleep.'

No, don't say **if** he comes back. Mack's hand encircled Theo in his pocket. He wanted to say all the things the worried girl needed to hear. He wanted to scoop her up and take her back to her bed and tell her he would read her stories '**until** Daddy is home'. But he knew he could not. What if she smelled the alcohol on his breath and it alarmed her; made her fearful?

Instead, he turned away from the little girl and towards Arabella. He willed her to say and do the things he wanted to say and do; to ease the little girl's pain. Arabella took no heed. She carried on in the same harsh tone.

'What are you waiting for? Go on. Back upstairs!'

The words 'shut up' bounced back and forth inside his head, from tongue to skull, skull to tongue. 'Shut up, shut up, shut up'. The words, in their attempt to escape, pushed out sweat onto his forehead. Sweat poured out of his hand. And with that sweaty hand he tightened his grip around the corkscrew, tighter and tighter. He felt no pain.

Arabella did not shut up.

'... You are being a right bloody nuisance... you're getting me so angry...' An incessant barrage of cold words made him hotter and hotter. 'Just Shut Up. Shut Up!' he sweated. Until the sweat blurred his vision and he could no longer see beyond his eyes: images attached to words and were reflected back as one. 'Shut Up!'

He saw the corkscrew rise from his pocket; the worm jab into the offending tongue; twist round and round and... yank! 'Shut Up!'

His vision was cleared. Arabella was staring at his hand. He followed the stare and saw the same. His hand, covered in blood. Covered in blood and oozing blood.

'What's happening?... What am I doing here?' he asked.

Arabella just stared. Her eyes and mouth wide open in disbelief.

'What's happening?... What am I doing here?' he asked again. Not knowing; not understanding.

Mack has no knowledge, no memory still, of that moment, or of the following seven hours or so. He, and we are reliant on the accounts of others.

A neighbour saw him, not far from Hugo's house. Michael Anthony Cunningham, his hand oozing blood, was able to give his name, where he worked in England and even the name of the hotel at which he was staying in Boston. But, as to what had recently passed (after the drinking of wine, about which he instinctively thought he should say little), why he was standing in the street, what was happening to him, he could only ask, not tell.

The neighbour took Michael to the hospital close by – Staunton State Hospital. It was because he thought Michael was in an acute phase of a mental illness that he took him to hospital – the hand injury was secondary.

Michael's hand was dressed and he was admitted for observation and tests: he was asked to walk along a line, make a number of movements of eyes and limbs, comment on sensations felt.

When he came round – that is to say, when he was able to make some sense of what was happening around him and to remember what he was told – he was lying in a hospital bed.

He saw Arabella standing outside of the room. Someone in a uniform was speaking to her. They were joined by a third person, a man, who glanced over to Michael's bed, half visible through the doorway. The man then led Arabella away.

Mack was unsettled, in the extreme.

'What's happened to me? What have I done? Which hospital am I in?' he asked – each question he asked only the once, and he was able to remember the answers. That was significant. That he could remember what he was told was an indication of his recovery; and also, of what had been the problem.

Arabella told how, for no apparent reason his behaviour had changed: he had looked startled and confused. His repeated, anxious enquiry of Arabella as to why he was there (the answer never calming him for more than a few seconds) had alarmed Arabella so much that she had turned him out of the house. Hugo had returned shortly afterwards and suggested someone ought to find him and take him to the hospital... the neighbour already had.

The doctor told Michael that he most certainly had not had a nervous breakdown. Neither was it thought that he had had a

181

stroke – though tests (a brain scan and later, a lumbar puncture) were organized to rule out the possibility.

Michael was asked for details of what he was doing at the time of his last memory. (He did not refer to the gouging out of Arabella's tongue: he had a vague image of something but the doctor had asked only what he was doing, not what he had visualized). This was followed by questions regarding his medical history. Migraine, in the short list of previous ailments, aroused interest and contributed to a diagnosis of "transient global amnesia", typified by repeated questionning and an inability to remember the answers; an inability to form new memories of any description.

The episode had lasted around seven hours so it was morning of the next day by the time Mack was again able to function normally. And, although memory of those seven hours would never be recovered, earlier memories were in tact.

He remembered that his plane ticket was for a 7.30 evening take-off, on that day.

The schedule was met – though it took unrelenting pressure to ensure that all necessary documentation was completed for discharge from the hospital and boarding of the plane. (It had also been necessary to feign a full recovery; to keep silent about the headache, hanging around like the remains of a good time that never was.)

The waiter corkscrew (whoever would give a corkscrew a name!) was with him still. The same could not be said of the "Launch of the New Alcohol Policy" document. But that was no cause for anxiety. Reginald Blenkinsop might think it important, he did not.

33. ALMOST CATHARTIC

There was no welcome for Mack when he arrived back at the flat. Sophia was not there.

She had been coming and going a lot of late. Work on a new contract was intense and it was sometimes more convenient for her to stay over at a colleague's house: it was in close proximity to the office and gave the additional advantage of their being able to work on, in comfort, until late in the evening.

If Mack had any suspicions about the truth of her whereabouts he chose not to raise any questions. The decision was well made. Sophia did find it convenient to sometimes stay overnights elsewhere. There was truth in what she said and no reason for her to elaborate. No need to tell Mack that the pestering from Stuart was less when she was with a female colleague than when she was at home, with the man she longed to be with.

The flat was cold. Mack shivered; he felt unwell and was low in spirits. Before he took to his bed he called Josie and reported that he would not be returning to work immediately. He informed her that he thought he had some sort of a bug; made no mention of the Boston debacle.

His pillow was damp: his neck dripped sweat. His fists were white and numbed. Sleep gave no comfort. Vivid dreams agitated Mack into snatches of wakefulness. A wakefulness that did nothing to disperse the torment: waking thoughts served only to give sustenance to troubled sleep.

On several successive nights the looming faces that surrounded Mack morphed into twisting, taunting tongues. A corkscrew pierced his chest and wormed its way into his very centre. Tongues morphed back to faces; faces receded until only one face remained; a kind face, a man's face but not one he recognized. Not his father's face. But it was his father's detached hand that gripped the corkscrew. The worm twisted, the hand tugged until its force pulled the heaviness out from him: the remaining void was no more comfortable. During the daylight hours the heaviness amassed anew, and, so did a similar imagery replay at night.

Toward the last of these dream filled nights, after hour upon hour of struggling to take back control of his thoughts, he put a name to the face of one uninvited guest. It was in a half asleep, half awake, saturated state that Mack identified Professor Higgs and thought the mass in the void to be a Higgs boson. (Fully awake, Mack could not describe one feature of Professor Higgs nor any form of boson!)

Strange was that half lucid reckoning but that night signalled the start of Mack's recovery.

On the day of Mack's return from Boston, Sophia did happen to go back to the flat but paid little attention to the fact that Mack had taken to his bed so early in the evening. ('Most likely jet-lagged' she presumed.) She did some laundering, as intended, and left, without disturbing him.

Two days later her visit was so early in the morning it would have been a surprise to find him up.

Sophia was stalled by a neighbour on her next visit, four further days on. The neighbour had attempted to deliver a small parcel, wrongly delivered to his house. (To be more accurate, it had been correctly delivered but wrongly addressed, an error not noticed until the parcel had been opened.) The neighbour apologized for having revealed the contents, and said that he had wanted to explain, rather than simply put it through the letter box, but had not managed to catch anyone coming in or going out.

It was a book, *A Day in the Life of Ivan Denisovich* by Solzhenitsyn, accompanied by a short note to Michael from Maureen. '*I should have said. This is the book in which the poem was found. Perhaps you would like it. I'm so sorry for everything Michael. Best wishes, Maureen.*'

Mack was oblivious to anything that had happened outside of his small upstairs domain during those days he had taken to his bed, and it was time to emerge.

10.30 am. Mack was up, dressed and mooching around the kitchen, looking for some morsel that would entice him to eat. He had no appetite but was trying to encourage one; to regain his strength after those days spent recovering – from God knows what – so that he could return to work, as soon as! To get back out there was the only way!

He did not hear Sophia's car, nor the sound of her conversation with a neighbour. The radio was on, close to him. He turned it off as soon as he heard Sophia come through the front door and instinctively quietened his movements, to listen and to not be heard. (Though he had no explanation for those instincts. Was he frightened? No. He wanted to see her, to speak with her. Then why was he holding his breath?) He stopped looking for tempting food. He waited and listened. There was no sound to indicate where she was going. Was she moving towards the dining room, living room or kitchen? No sound at all.

Sophia called out his name from the hallway.

'Here... Kitchen' he answered.

She came to him, handed him the book and the note from Maureen, and sat down at the kitchen table. Mack sat down opposite her. Neither of them spoke, until Mack eventually looked away from the book: the book in which his father had housed the verse.

'What poem?' Sophia asked.

Mack did not reply. Instead he asked 'Do you want a coffee?' She nodded and Mack set about providing one for each of them.

The task completed. Sophia repeated, more gently.

'What poem did Maureen mean Mack?'

He said the minimum required. 'My dad's died. Maureen was his stepdaughter. She passed on something he had written.' No embellishments given despite her expectant gaze.

'May I see the poem please Mack?' Sophia asked. Her voice was unemotional, incongruous with the tears forming.

'Later. I'll show it to you later.'

He would determine the when, and how much of his life he would dissect and reassemble. At that moment he needed tangible sustenance. Food.

'I'm sorry to hear about your father. I didn't know. Do you want to talk?'

A similar reply was given. 'Later. Maybe, later.'

He did not want Sophia to stay with him out of any sense of

pity or of duty. If he had been some sort of stop-gap, a port in a storm for her until her relationship with Stuart reached a conclusion, so be it: it had been a pleasant interlude. And whilst he would be satisfied to love her with a deeper affection that she was able to return, that did not apply if the inability to love him was on account of her feelings for Stuart.

He would let her go peacefully, if it came to that. Not push her away: he would never want to do that. It made sense just to let things happen... as and when...

Part of his reluctance to force her hand was that he *did* want to talk to her about his dad. Why, he didn't really know. Her request to see the poem had strengthened that wish – but it had to be at a different time. He had to be certain he could control the emotional turmoil. For if it spilled over, and she stayed, he would always suspect that she had been influenced by his sorry state. Better to be on his own than that.

34. NEW WINE INFLUENCES

'Cunningham should be sacked' hissed Reginald Blenkinsop as he read the missive from America:

'It is most unfortunate that Michael's second visit did not achieved its purpose. Additional visits are now required in order that Omniwell might advise and support health promoting projects over and above those falling within the bedrock of work established.'

The contract Omniwell had with St. Joseph's allowed for three annual visits in either direction – Boston, USA, to Ledstown, UK – for the duration of the contract, which was for a minimum of twelve years. Extra visits meant extra costs. Lost opportunities meant loss of face. But, on reflection and on further managerial discussion, it was generally agreed that it had been wrong to ask something of Michael that was not part of his job description – and for which he obviously had no aptitude! He would be kept "on side" for now, but in the background.

The necessary variation to contract was negotiated during a scheduled visit of Gerald Martinez to St. Joseph's.

It was immediately on his return to Boston that Ged set to the task of engaging Hugo Lubbock as External Business Advisor, with the sole remit of promoting Wisbeach's new alcohol policy to the wine industry. Ged had no connection with any aspect of the industry and needed input on the specifics. Probably, many of his questions could have been answered by Oswald Rollinson, the newly elected

Conservative Member of Parliament for Ledstown, but Rollinson was cautious not to take advantage of his place on the Board of the Marshall Wine Company. (Those responsible for progressing the policy agreed that credit must be given to Rollinson for not wishing to flaunt his private business and cause disquiet amongst his constituents.)

Consequently, Rollinson MP made it clear that he did not want to be invited to the introductory meeting with Hugo. It was fitting that Reginald Blenkinsop, as St. Joseph's Business Manager, should take control of the meeting and to give instructions as to who else, in the first instance, should be involved. Alistair McDowell, who was to arrange things as well as to attend, was somewhat surprised to learn that (excepting himself and Reggie) he was to invite Hugo and Ged only.

'Best if we keep it low key until we see how it pans out. We'll bring in others when we've more to go on. Right Alistair? Good chap.'

Reggie had in front of him a copy of the "Launch of the Report on Sensible Drinking & Achieving Targets". He did not have any spare copies available for the others to view.

'Too many irrelevant details in this' he indicated, 'especially now the date has been postponed. I'll outline the key points of the report and we can then discuss how to take it forward. Our job is to make it work in practice.'

With that said, Reggie succinctly came to reasons why reducing the alcohol level of a number of wines – and promoting them as the "best wines" – would be of long-term benefit to the health of the nation (and why not America's too!). If handled well, it would be without any losses for the wine industry. On the contrary, those at the forefront of change stood to gain; just rewards for their efforts.

Whilst they, or more specifically Hugo (Alistair and Ged were already "up to speed") mulled over the concept, Reggie humbly took it upon himself to serve coffee and biscuits from the side table, already prepared.

Of course, the concept was not entirely new to Hugo: there had been reference to it in the planning of Michael's visit to Staunton. Plus, he had perused the document left amongst the empty wine bottles at his home when Michael had left, so unceremoniously. But that incident had been left behind.

Had Michael spoken to Hugo on the subject, when in Staunton, he would have found Hugo unimpressed by the notion (though appreciative of the chance to have a free trip to England). Nothing Reggie had said so far had altered that view; Hugo remained totally unenthusiastic about introducing weaker wines.

'Seems like a step backwards to me', he said.

However, Reggie stressed that it *was* going to happen.

'I'm not asking for your permission here, nor for your opinion on the matter; this is merely an opportunity for you to benefit from early knowledge and from assisting us in its implementation – if you choose to do so. Your choice, of course.'

Reggie could not fully hide his irritation at Hugo's lack of foresight and went on to inform him (rather recklessly, perhaps; certainly earlier than he had intended) that an influential local Member of Parliament had already got the ball rolling with the Marshall Wine Company. (He may have been provoked into risking the Rollinson card so soon, but it had the desired effect.) Hugo acknowledged that Marshall was a big player in the market. Interest shown by that company made Hugo receptive to hearing more, and Reggie obliged in his most authoritative tone.

'As you know, Hugo, Marshall has a multiple retail portfolio and leading associate vintners. They see it as an opportunity to produce wines with more variety of flavour. After all, ethanol is ethanol in any drink, so, as the percentage of ethanol increases in a wine the scope for other flavours diminishes. Already, two of Marshall's associates are developing strategies to support our New Alcohol Policy – maybe three, actually; an Australian, a Californian and a Greek. English would be good: must have a word with Rollinson about that.'

'Who is Rollinson?' asked Hugo, which confirmed he was paying attention. Reggie had not meant to name the influential MP, referred to earlier by his status, and chose not to spell out the connection at this stage.

'Oswald Rollinson. He's very knowledgeable about the whole industry. And very supportive. I'll introduce you to him if you decide to come on board.' With that, Reggie returned to the subject of "Sensible Drinking & Achieving Targets".

'The new wines, far from being "weaker" Hugo, will have sophisticated flavours for the more discerning palate. By using yeast with a lower alcohol yield and picking the grape slightly before an absolute, full maturity, the wine will retain the subtleties of the "terroir", not masked by too high an ethanol content. And no need to resinate for added flavour either. A good, wholesome product yet ultra sophisticated – for the smart set. Rollinson knows more of the detail – type of grape, yeast and where best grown etcetera.'

Reggie was proud of this exposition. Pleased too, that in

deferring to someone else's greater expertise, he had appeared modest, belittling his own contribution. He had a drink of his coffee, thought quickly about how to move on to the nitty gritty, and delivered those thoughts thus.

'But it's not necessary for Rollinson to be involved at this juncture. Ged – or could be you Hugo – is King Pin at this stage. We've got the support of winemakers. Ged is taking this forward; selecting suitable restaurants and supermarkets to be the pioneers. Obviously those with chains, as well as the top exclusives, are the ones set to increase coverage. You don't need me to tell you that the massive promotion and advertising during the initial launch phase would be to our mutual benefits. And I'm talking Big Time! Right Ged?'

Gerald Martinez took his cue and took over the spiel.

'I suggested you for this Hugo. Hugo Lubbock is a Name; well respected in the world of wines. Where couldn't you, together with The Marshall Wine Company, go with this! Broaden your portfolio, Hugo. Existing clients would appreciate that **you** were right on the ball, at the cutting edge and willing to take **them** with you; it would attract **new** ones, from top end restaurants to hypermarkets. And a way in to some new corporate entertaining – I'm even including the health sector here! We can put customers your way through health promotion advice and events; **all** employers big or small. Do you know how many are out there with no plan, no strategy for getting the most from, and for, their employees? (*He didn't. He doubted anyone did*)… Healthy and Happy Workforce, that's what it's about. Maximum Effort, Maximum Profits. We think you've got what it takes to make them sit up and listen Hugo.'

★

Reggie and Ged, between them, had certainly made Hugo sit up and listen. But he gave no indication as to where his thoughts were going. There was no quick response.

'What have you to say then Hugo?' Reggie asked. He wanted to gauge the effectiveness of Ged's approach. Reggie had to be away within the next five minutes, there was no time to pussy-foot around. Hugo replied.

'Interesting. I'll give it a lot of thought. But, of course, I'll need to taste the wines. I couldn't promote anything inferior to what my clients are used to.'

Reggie came in quickly with 'Of course. That goes the same for all of us as… ' before he nodded towards Ged to take over. Ged completed Reggie's sentence by way of agreement.

'… as far as using the wine to promote the policy goes' (*neither the word "perk" nor anything about quantities was uttered*). And added 'We'll be meeting with the Omniwell staff – here and back home – about integrating the health message and new wines into planned events. Not your concern. But we'll keep you in the loop.'

Ged had said as much as he wanted to say. Was that what Reggie had wanted from him? he glanced across.

Reggie was collecting up his items from the table.

'Right. Has anyone any burning questions or is everyone happy to get on with taking this thing forward?' he asked, without interrupting his preparations for leaving.

A couple of observations on the happy prospects were quickly shared by Alistair – wanting to make some contribution and have his presence validated – before they dispersed.

Reggie looked in the direction of Hugo and Ged as he left and said 'I'll see you two again at 6.30, right?'

★

'Short and sweet. Very good' was the description of the meeting that Alistair gave to Sheila and Josie when they asked.

'I'll arrange something soon with you and Caroline – and fill you in.' That was to be Alistair's next step.

35. CHALLENGES

There was a written agenda for distribution in the meeting; a formality Alistair often disregarded in sessions he held with lower management. However, on this occasion, he wished to demonstrate professionalism to the self-invited Gerald Martinez.

The agenda did not follow strictly the format used elsewhere in St. Joseph's, but then this was an extraordinary meeting. The items read as follows:

1. Update on the Launch of the Government's New Alcohol Policy

2. Establish ways in which 'Omniwell', St. Joseph's, (*in place of 'Health at Work Department'; designed to flatter Martinez*) could support the implementation of the Policy through the

(i) Counselling Service

(ii) Nursing Service

(iii) Allied professions – e.g. dietetics

Alistair's office was not large enough to accommodate more than the number required – or invited – to attend. (The final number included two self-invited: Ged, as already mentioned, plus Reginald Blenkinsop – Reggie had generously offered to be on hand to answer any queries that might extend beyond Alistair's experience.)

All presented. Hence, the request from Josie that Michael might join them (her reason for wishing his greater involvement is made known a little later) was refused on grounds of space, and those who attended the intimate gathering, chaired by Alistair, were Sheila, Josie, Caroline, Reginald Blenkinsop and Gerald Martinez.

Alistair was pleased to announce that Gerald Martinez (who interrupted to remind Alistair there was no need for formality; he was "Ged" to his close colleagues) had re-arranged his diary purposely to be available for this important meeting. His time was limited so they would need to keep focussed on agenda items and move forward quickly and constructively.

By way of covering item one on the agenda, Alistair relayed something of the previous meeting (for which Hugo Lubbock had come over especially), which took a full two minutes.

Josie, when asked for an input regarding item 2.(i), was flummoxed. Ged went to her rescue. (Alistair reflected how fortunate it was that Ged had been able to make the visit from America; to be needed so soon into the meeting!)

'I'll tell you what **WE** do, shall I? Our counsellors keep an eye out for possible mismanagement of drink, and refer such clients to the appropriate organisation for specialised therapy. But that is after the horse has bolted – or after the bottles are empty. (*He gives a cheeky chuckle.*) We prefer to act before the horse leaves the stable; courses on stress management, which link in to assertiveness courses, relaxation techniques etc. Get the picture? Could you do the same?'

Josie did "get the picture". It sounded pretty much like a copy of the one already drawn, and filled in by Michael and herself. Nothing innovative; standard components of the service provided.

She confirmed, politely, that he had described well the service they currently provided and asked for clarification of the particular significance, for her service, regarding the New Alcohol Policy… as, she understood, that was the reason for the meeting.

Ged was as patient as Josie was polite.

'Surely you're aware of the way and the times that we turn to alcohol to help ease situations? We want to use every opportunity to get the message across about *safe* drinking…. What is it exactly that you don't understand Josie?'

Josie recognized there was nothing further being said, or likely to be: they would go round in circles. She resigned the argument and backed out with '… Nothing… that's OK… Right… Thanks.' This allowed Ged to turn to Caroline and take the initiative as regarded her role. He addressed her and defined the challenge.

'Healthy meals accompanied by New Wine rather than strong liquor: it's a straightforward concept. Promote it… in… whatever you usually do. Plus, out in restaurants; in supermarkets; colleges… any and everywhere where there's food!'

Whatever she "usually" did? That would be to use her knowledge of therapeutic diets to help sick people recover then! However, she agreed, in part, with the concept and was ready for a discussion rather than a quarrel. Her reply, therefore, was not pedantic.

'I agree that wine can be part of a healthy diet. But, that is a far cry from actively promoting it.'

'Read the report Caroline. It is advised that everyone drinks wine. It's good for you. It reduces cholesterol. There are lots of benefits.'

'I don't care what your report says. I repeat, it is not my job to "promote" wine. If enough alcohol is drunk, in some instances it may reduce cholesterol: it may at the same time increase triglycerides and increase blood pressure – not quite so beneficial!… I see plenty of patients with medical problems because of too much alcohol. I've yet to see anyone ill because they have not had enough!'

Alistair and Sheila stopped breathing: Caroline's response had not been overly respectful of their American visitor's status. Would it backfire on them? Adding to their general discomfort, Caroline took in breath and was poised to carry on speaking.

Reggie was, perhaps, better equipped to deal with the likes of Caroline. He interjected (and all breathed again).

'Just remind me Caroline, why are you here?… I mean, your competence on the wards is renowned, of course. But, why are you here, now?'

Alistair slipped down a little in his seat. He had invited Caroline as a possible future member of the Omniwell team. That possibility had been raised by Reggie himself: an expansion of the workplace services to include other disciplines, such as dietetics and physiotherapy (none from the latter department had yet been available), was seen as the way forward. The inclusion of Caroline by Alistair to this, and previous meetings, related, therefore, to Reggie's initial instructions. The question was awkward.

But not for Caroline, it seemed. She answered confidently.

'I'm here to keep nutrition, proper nutrition, on the agenda and to keep you on the straight and narrow.'

Not the answer Alistair might have desired. Caroline did not miss the looks that passed from Reggie to Alistair and Reggie to Ged. She knew that she would not be invited again!

Reggie was satisfied that he had demonstrated to Ged that

he would stand for no nonsense from his staff. They could proceed. Ged again took the floor.

'Thank you, Caroline. Your interest is appreciated... Hopefully we will be able to concentrate on the fit and healthy – and keep them that way – and leave the sick in your capable hands.... So, Sheila... How are you at giving the general, healthy eating messages? Can you motivate your nurses do you think?'

This was Caroline's cue to leave. (She knew exactly the extent of Sheila's knowledge and, despite its limitations, how well she would motivate her staff.) She excused herself from the remainder of the meeting and, as she gathered up her belongings, gave her final passing shot – addressed to no-one in particular, but directing glances at both Alistair and Reggie.

'... Think carefully before St Joseph's name is linked to any campaign for alcohol: remember the suicide of a patient on the liver unit last week? The press won't care about the details; if they can make a story out of the two things they will... Good luck.'

36. PROGRESSING THE KNOWLEDGE

Josie stayed back after the meeting, feigning an interest in a brochure on her lap as Alistair busied himself around her, returning other chairs to their original positions.

Sheila continued to hang around too, always fearful of being excluded, missing out on a private conversation. Her intent, to be a party to – whatever – was less than subtle. She waited, feet firmly rooted, looking from Josie to Alistair in anticipation of whatever subject was to be broached.

Alistair showed an astuteness not always apparent and addressed Sheila directly, pointing to the chair on which she had previously sat.

'Would you return that chair to where it came from please Sheila. Thanks. See you later.'

And, once Sheila had acted on the request, he turned to Josie, suddenly remembering that she had not spoken at all after the rather sharp discourse with Ged.

'What did you think of the meeting Josie?' It was the obvious opening to give her an opportunity to air any grievances.

'Okay, as far as meetings go I suppose.... ... I'd like to talk to you about something else. There's something I want to ask you. Have you got a few minutes free now, please?' Josie asked.

Alistair confirmed that he had – 'just so long as it won't take too long'.

The "something" Josie sought to ask was permission to use some of her hours for research.

'Michael has come on so well he could easily handle more of the day-to-day workload and I could do the majority of the research in my own time. I've not spoken to Michael yet. Obviously I wanted your opinion first, but I'm sure Michael would relish some added responsibility.'

Alistair gave the appropriate grunts and nods and encouraged Josie to get to the point – as briefly as possible please – of what she thought needed researching.

The pressure to "be brief" had quite the opposite effect: Josie gave an unintended introduction to the, far from honed, topic of exploration. So flustered was she that much superfluous detail was included – but said very quickly (her concession to brevity).

Josie blurted. 'The accepted notion of childhood circumstances affecting – and effecting – adult cognitive behaviour is too vague to be helpful. Why, for example, are some people devastated long-term, forever possibly, by a death of someone close, whilst others come to terms with it? Why do some children cope better than others with the break up of family? Why do some people mentally give up on trying to find employment when others are more dogged in their efforts? Why are some people terrified that the world is going to end whilst others are thrilled by new scientific discoveries?'

'The answer lies', Josie babbled, 'not in childhood circumstances per se but in precise circumstances at critical moments. How secure did the child feel when they had the first realization of death, or saw people destitute on a pavement bed? Firstly, of course, we need to know what constituted security to that child at that time – a goodnight kiss, food on the table?... ... The exploration would be of any correlations between a lack of security at critical moments and adverse adult cognitive behaviour... '

Josie had avoided looking at Alistair whilst she spoke so that she might concentrate fully on trying to order her thoughts and relay them rapidly.

When she finally permitted herself a glance she saw an expression of impatience: her halted flow, in turn, permitted Alistair to release that impatience.

'All very commendable I'm sure Josie. But that's for the academics not for a jobbing counsellor. As for Michael taking on more responsibility, I'm not sure others would agree he's up to it. And I can't see Ged being very happy if you were indulging in study instead of being out there servicing contracts.'

Exactly the response that Josie needed! Alistair's undermining of her abilities (and Michael's, incidentally) galvanized her apologetic ramblings into a somewhat more coherent attack.

'You're totally wrong: it can be done **only** by an **active** counsellor! (*she preferred "active" to "jobbing" and made that plain by glaring at Alistair as she emphasized the word*) – I plan to recruit participants from current, past and new clients. And if Ged doesn't like it, to hell with him! What does he know about anything anyway? None of his counsellors is properly qualified: not one has a degree in anything, let alone in psychology! I don't expect him to be bothered about improving the effectiveness of counselling. And, may I remind you, we're not employed by him!'

She went on; inspired (not an emotion engendered by Ged's plans) to go above Alistair's head, if need be, and fight to get the necessary permission. She left him with the following words.

'I'm sorry you can't see the long-term benefits; how the kudos would help in securing contracts. But I'm going to get approval from the Ethics Committee anyway. Then we'll see.'

Gerald Martinez was always appreciative. Appreciative that is of anything that raised the profile of Omniwell. He immediately – on mention, by Alistair, of the word kudos – saw the potential of being at the cutting edge of research on effective counselling and urged Alistair to give Josie his full support.

Sheila was quick to learn and applied the same principle to the nursing service. The plan for her "active research" – a term she heard Josie use – was to demonstrate the effectiveness of the nursing interventions by comparing the cholesterol results taken at the first visit to a workplace to those taken at the second.

No doubt Caroline would welcome the chance to have her say regarding the dietary changes that would have contributed to the improvements (*improvements were assumed; there was no point in taking any other stance than one of optimism*). Sheila thought it expedient that Caroline should work alongside her and share in the glory. She would make it clear to Caroline that she did not share the view (inferred at the last meeting to which Caroline had been invited) that her nurses were better disposed than Caroline to carrying out the work proposed by Omniwell. Sheila wanted to redress the injustice metered out to Caroline. She knew her own limitations. She respected the expertise of a dietitian, and wanted to be sure her modesty on the subject was accurately conveyed. A telephone call offered that facility more readily than did the written word, tone was everything.

'Caroline, I would really like your help on some active research I'm doing. Would it be at all possible for me to come to you any time today? I'll fit in with whenever suits you best.'

Caroline asked no questions. She simply offered lunchtime the following day as a possible time. Sheila accepted gratefully.

Sheila needed no preparation. After the purpose of her research had been outlined there was only the one question Sheila had to ask.

'What will they have eaten, or not eaten, to have brought about the observed lowering of cholesterol levels?'

Unfortunately there was not one, straightforward answer to Sheila's one question. And Sheila should not have expected one (*not from Caroline, of all people. She should have remembered that and soon did*).

Caroline's initial response was to exclaim, 'You're not serious, surely!' This was followed by a bombardment of dissensions.

'I'll ignore your assumption of favourable results. What if there are different people who come to the second health event than went to the first? What if they do not want to participate in the research; at what stage will you recruit? Who will have the time to take a dietary history from each person – twice over? (And that is not as simple as you might think!) Or, if you use a questionnaire who is going to compile and test it for significance? If cholesterol has gone down by the second visit how will you know that it's not because you've scared them half to death and they've gone on to a lowering medication? Or to foods specifically manipulated for the purpose? You will have to think it all through before you apply to the Ethics Committee. Personally, I don't think it's worth the effort. So sorry, I don't think I can help you.'

Sheila did not *say* 'You Bitch'. It was typical of Caroline to play the saboteur. She did not need Caroline's help anyway. She had offered to include her in a spirit of generosity. She had thought Caroline might be interested, that was all. None of what Caroline had said was relevant, actually. There was no need to make it complicated; she would merely compare one set of figures with another. It was a shame that Caroline had been so obstructive. As Sheila told Caroline – for her further information – 'Ged's totally in favour of research; he's told Josie that what she's doing is *tremendous* for future business'.

'I've no idea what Josie is doing and I don't want to know. But if it's just a marketing ploy you're looking for... ... I'll thank you to leave me well out of it.'

They were Caroline's last words on the matter. And with so heavy a workload – the nursing services were in *such* demand – Sheila was, after all, unable to take it on singlehandedly and was forced to put the idea on a back burner.

37. IN CONFIDENCE

'Are you on your own? Can I come round?' Sophia asked Ursula.

The answer was yes to both questions. Ursula was intrigued: not entirely because Sophia was going to call by, Sophia and Ursula were good friends, but Sophia was unlike Ursula's other female friends; she did not share (in the "real" world) the usual sorts of trivial intimacies, or discuss ways male behaviour had been left wanting. She did not gossip.

The bell rang so soon after Sophia's phone call that Ursula half expected it to be someone else standing at the door. It was no one else. It was Sophia.

Her general, scrawny appearance raised concern and Ursula's enquiries and welcoming platitudes ran into and overlapped each other.

'Oh, what's the matter?… Come in… Are you all…? I'll put the kettle on… Sit down… What's happened?… Is it…? Do you want some cake?'

Sophia was pale, paler than could be accounted for by the complete lack of make-up. She looked shocked, shaken, panicked almost. It was obvious that dress-wise she had not "made an effort" for the occasion. In another situation and other things being equal, Ursula might have joked with Sophia about finally managing to achieve the *scruffy* chic status; something she had failed to do as a student and for which she had been teased by Ursula (the chic always a given for Sophia, the scruffy generally supplied by Ursula).

But it was not appropriate to risk making what, depending on the yet unknown cause of the transformation, could be an incredibly crass remark. Ursula did not break the pursuing silence in that fashion.

Sophia did not utter a word. She prepared to do so, as pieces of cake and mugs of coffee were placed on the small table between them, but spluttered out sobs instead. Ursula waited. There was no point in venturing questions, seeing as Sophia was, for a time, unable to speak any answer.

The cake was date and walnut, always a comfort. Ursula took a bite by way of an encouragement to Sophia to do likewise. It could have worked: Sophia did halt her sobs as she watched.

'I'm sorry Ursula. It looks delicious but I can't eat anything. I've been throwing up all morning.'

That was, perhaps, the answer to a question Ursula had not previously thought of asking – but then did.

'My God. You're not pregnant are you?'

Sophia's sobs returned, along with a nodding of the head.

Ursula asked no more. She adopted an alternative approach of making a series of statements, watching Sophia for indications as to the veracity or otherwise of them.

'I'm guessing from your reaction that the baby wasn't planned... and I suppose you're worried because of how things are between you and Mack... I know that it's not going too well at the moment... '

The lengthy, intermittent pauses allowed for a response from Sophia, whenever she was ready to make one. Meanwhile, Ursula carried on in a similar vein.

'It must have been a shock for you Sophe but try not to worry. It will be all right, I'm sure it will…. Don't try to decide anything right now… you have choices but… '

Sophia remained silent, in that she did not speak. And when the sobs eventually petered out, Ursula braved to ask.

'Does Mack know?'

Sophia shook her head. Nothing more. Ursula tried another angle.

'Y'know, I'm not sure really whether I should be commiserating with you. Perhaps congratulations are in order…. Are you upset just because you are unwell? Or are you worried what Mack is going to say?… What's happening between you and Mack anyway… … … are you still planning to get married sometime?'

Ursula had come to a standstill. She had not become any wiser – except for knowledge of the pregnancy, which was major, she supposed – but Sophia was now composed. She sipped her coolish coffee, acknowledged Ursula's patience and addressed her inquisitiveness.

'I've messed up', was her beginning.

In answer to Ursula's question regarding wedding plans, Sophia revealed that marriage to Mack was no longer an option she would have the privilege to consider: she could not be sure that the baby she was carrying was his. She believed it was, but there was a slight possibility that Stuart was the father.

'Good God!'

Had she told Stuart? No, she had not. 'Then tell him nothing!' was the reactive advice from Ursula (*who asked not of Sophia, which man she would prefer to be father of her baby*). Silence was not a solution Sophia could accept.

208

'It's bad enough that I have deceived once. That would be a further deceit.'

'Once? Only once?' Ursula asked, as though confirmation would negate any deception and fully justify Sophia's saying nothing of the pregnancy to Stuart.

'Stuart will say it is not the number of times, per se, that matters. There will be some way he can calculate the probability, using the number alongside the timing of the occasion within the monthly cycle... ' (Ursula noted how like Stuart Sophia sounded as she spoke those ridiculous words.)

'Oh, I don't doubt it' Ursula interjected. 'He could talk his way out of a dictionary, that one.' They both smiled at the thought of Stuart battling his way to victory of some ludicrous argument.

'... And he knows that sex has been less than full on with Mack of late.' Sophia continued.

'I don't believe it! The absolute, utter recklessness of sharing that sort of information with Stuart!' Ursula was tempted to exclaim. 'Has she really no knowledge of Stuart's capabilities after all?' She thought.

'Seriously, Sophe. I think you need to talk to Mack. Try to rebuild your relationship – if that's what you want – and push Stuart out of the picture.... Then think about the baby. That's what I'd do.'

'But you're not me. And if you'd been listening you'd know it's not that simple!'

Sophia got up to leave.

Ursula had not proffered a remedy. Had the problem been specifically defined? Ursula thought not.

'Talk to Mack, Sophe.... Toby and I are here for you both, you do know that don't you?'

Sophia nodded, though not convincingly. There was nothing further to be done or said: except for Sophia's words, 'Keep it to yourself, won't you?' Which, in effect, meant that Ursula alone, was "there" for Sophia.

38. ALL IN ONE EVENING

Before the evening begins, it is opportune to tell you a little of Ledstown's Durham Ox. Employees from St. Joseph's, with friends, partners or colleagues, frequently meet up there. It is convenient – almost directly opposite the hospital's second main gate – and large. Ursula and Sophia are drawn to the lighter area, set far back from the bar and edged by two windowed walls; Sophia and Mack generally go upstairs, to the room where tables are set out in restaurant style and the cosy coffee areas are furnished with leather sofas.

The upstairs in the Ox is also the venue for weekly open-mike sessions, an added attraction made use of by Rufus, who composes soul cum blues cum country cum all manner of song, when not politicking around.

Toby, out with friends, usually heads for the games room (this is euphemistically referred to as the Board Room by St. Joseph employees when unofficially using it as the workplace).

Michael and Caroline chose the same, windowed area that Ursula and Sophia frequented (in previous times – they had seldom been of late).

'Thanks for coming Michael... ... I suppose you've heard?' Caroline asked.

He had picked up on some office gossip.

'About your not being the most popular Omniwell associate you mean?'

Caroline's half smile showed he was correct in his assumption as to what she referred.

'*Dis*associate now! And what a relief. Glad to be out of it. But what about you? How are you? I heard things weren't going too well with you either?'

Caroline's main reason for wanting to see Michael was to know how he was faring – amidst all the rumours she, in turn, had heard. (Another reason was information she wanted to pass on, but that was less important to her and came later.) He shrugged off the concern.

'Oh, I'm fine. My last visit to Boston didn't go to plan, that's all.'

'So I gathered. What happened?'

He told her. 'I got ill – migraine related – and couldn't deliver. What a wimp, eh?'

'Migraine? I didn't know it was migraine.'

There was a hint of disbelief in her voice. Or, possibly he imagined there was; he had been met with general suspicion on his return, unsurprisingly in view of the mystery surrounding the episode.

'Oh, why? What did you hear?'

'All sorts… nothing definite… got drunk, lost your bottle – so to speak – got sectioned, had nervous breakdown… Glad to hear it was only migraine. Sorry, I know migraine isn't pleasant… but you know what I mean.'

'Yeah, it's all right. I can guess what was said about me. And I'm not surprised. At the time I would have believed any of those things myself. It was weird. Really weird!'

He told her about the loss of short-term memory.

'My God Michael! You poor thing. I didn't know migraine could do that.'

' Well not exactly migraine, but it seems to be associated. The frightening thing is that if someone tells me I committed murder – or ripped someone's tongue out or something – I'd believe them. I'd have to because my mind's a blank for that time, even now.'

Caroline joked 'Well actually, you promised to give me a thousand pounds and I bought a plane ticket to Rome on the strength of it. So, you owe me… No, I'm sorry. It must have been horrific. Why did it happen, do you know?… What did the doctor say?'

'A lot actually. Well, said a bit and told me where I could read up on it. Quite a rare thing… the complex type of migraine that it's linked to. There might even be a genetic aspect to it; something to do with the amino acid, threonine, being replaced by other amino acids.'

The mention of amino acids (*the building blocks of protein, should any reader wish to know*) was deliberate bait to the dietitian. Effective. Caroline pressed him for more on this and the focus moved away from his personal experience to general information. He was altogether more comfortable. He recalled several phrases; spoke around them as intelligibly as he could, and hoped his interpretation of what he had remembered was accurate, or near enough as to not sound absurd.

'I think there are three amino acids that get swopped around – or I might have got a bit mixed up about threonine and three. Anyway, the wrong amino acid causes an inefficient transport of ions – calcium, potassium or sodium – into the nerve cells which leads to a build up of them in the spaces between the cells: this wrong distribution inside and outside of cells causes a wave of depolarization, known as "cortical spreading depression" in an area in the cerebral cortex. That part of the

213

brain effectively shuts down, resulting in "global transient amnesia" – short-term inability to form new memories.'

He knew there was a lot more that could be said on the subject – though not by him. He was getting out of his depth and chose to stop.

'Fascinating!… (*Michael scoffed disbelief*). No, really. It is. It's fascinating.'

Then Caroline went off at a bit of a tangent.

'It makes me more determined than ever to keep on shouting about phenylalanine – another amino acid that can have a big effect on the brain. Might be one of your big three?'

He couldn't answer that question.

What happened next was not part of any plan. Nothing had been further from Caroline's thoughts when she had arranged to meet up with Michael. It was not one of the two things she had wanted to raise. But Caroline was passionate about principles. And she frequently railed against what she saw as unprincipled conglomerates in the food production, sales and marketing industries.

He had unleashed the pin on the phenylalanine grenade and had the sense to take Caroline's order and dash off to buy in the next round of drinks before the explosion.

The finer points of the biochemistry, metabolism and roles of phenylalanine as it's story was unravelled, may not have been fully understood by Michael, but Caroline's conviction of its inappropriate use as a sweetener (going under half a dozen different names and E numbers!) was clear, and seemingly indisputable.

'Worse still! There's a loophole.'

Could anything be worse? Apparently so.

'Phenylalanine can be used in a now more concentrated,

heat resistant form: used far more widely than was ever possible before!' It was a key point: needed emphasizing, so she did.

'Not only can they use it in any and everything, but they don't have to tell us! Can you believe that? Add a toxin – believe me, on its own, not part of a protein, phenylalanine *is* toxic! – to "enhance flavour" but shush, don't tell anybody, it'll only worry them.... Those "insignificant" amounts in *everything* can add up to being *very* significant. But hold on... we *can't* add it up because we're not told when it's there!

'Believe me, we need a tightening up of regulations before we have generation after generation of brain rotted cretins.

'How do these profit chasing, food poisoning criminals reason away their crime you may ask?' (Michael was not about to ask, nevertheless Caroline answered her own question)

'Because phenylalanine is found "naturally" in food. But that's rubbish. It *never* occurs "naturally" *on its own*. It's toxic to the brain *on its own*. At least if it appears on the label it can be avoided – that is if you're prepared to spend upwards of three hours doing the supermarket shopping and you remember to take along a magnifying glass!'

Caroline took a breath. And a drink. Then seemed at first to digress.

'How many years was it before lead in petrol was accepted as potentially damaging to developing brains? Fifty, was it?' (*Michael half shrugged, half nodded, unsure of the appropriate response.*)

No. Caroline declared, she was *not* about to stop shouting about phenylalanine. All those children likely to be affected if nothing was done! (Michael, wisely, did not ask about the effect on adults. There were only so many hours in one evening.)

She conceded that thinking about phenylalanine and the villains in the food industry had put the problems with Omniwell into perspective. And said that her second reason for meeting up with him – to "tell tales" on Omniwell – now seemed trivial. Obviously not *so* trivial as to not be raised. But not immediately.

Firstly, Caroline attempted to lighten the mood (her mood) by a little self mocking. (Michael's mood had not been greatly altered by the supposed threat of phenylalanine, though discussion of it was not exactly how he had wanted to spend the evening.) She encouraged laughter at how her lofty stances led her into trouble. They went on to laugh at the ineptitudes of Omniwell personnel, in the name of progress… moving forward… onwards and upwards. Until, that is, someone dares to ask them to describe what value they add to the workplace… what they bring to the table… in one minute, without repetition, hesitation or deviation and without using any phrase or word from their hand-outs.

It was in this brighter tone, that Caroline told of her snooping. Prior to the meeting – the one at which she had disgraced herself – she had arrived early and found Alistair's office empty.

The chairs were already arranged. Two were placed behind the desk; the one next to Alistair's was the one intended for Ged – she knew this because Ged's case was by the chair and two or three papers were on the seat. There was the agenda; Ged's itinerary for his UK visit; and a summary of the type of work carried out by the counselling service. (She made the point that the latter of these three papers was handwritten. His handwriting? She gave Michael an accusative glance, then laughed.)

'I'm only teasing you. I'm not interested in the counselling. It's the itinerary – and the expenses being claimed – that got me!'

And Caroline went on to explain precisely what had put her in a combatant mood on that day. The meeting in question, plus a social gathering with Alistair and Reggie were the only entries that related to St. Joseph's. The rest of Ged's time was to be spent visiting three other National Health Consortiums, two in the Midlands and one in the South – conveniently situated close to the airport and timed, no doubt, for Ged to catch his return flight to Boston.

Yet all, absolutely *all* the expenses had been put against the consortium to which St. Joseph's belonged.

Caroline sat back and waited for a response to her revelation.

There was none. Mack was tired. Sophia no longer spoke of wedding plans. What difference would Omniwell make to Mack's life? None that mattered.

He asked to be excused his silence (on account of his tiredness). He had been with Caroline longer than he had anticipated and Sophia might be wondering what had delayed him. He needed to text her. He would ask if she could join him at the Ox, so that they might have something to eat there.

As he texted, and waited for a reply, Caroline replenished their glasses and quietly supped.

Sophia's intentions for the evening were relayed to Mack indirectly, via a text from Toby. Ursula wanted to spend some time with Sophia and, to that end, planned to go over to her flat. Toby, knowing that Mack was already at the Ox, proposed joining him there for a game of pool – he texted that he would get in touch with Rufus and Stuart to give them the option of coming along too.

Twenty minutes later, Rufus passed by the window.

Mack took his leave of Caroline (she was gracious and apologetic for keeping him) and moved to the games room. It was not too busy; there would be no problem in securing time at the pool table.

Had Sophia wanted an excuse not to be with him? He had no way of knowing and determined not to draw any unfounded conclusions. He instantly dismissed any notion of quizzing Toby when he arrived as to how, precisely, the arrangement had come about: to intimate any concern would be to admit to a need for concern.

Besides which, if any talk faintly serious were to be had, it would be around why Toby had been so secretive about his contact with Maureen. But, likely as not, nothing would be mentioned by either of them in the presence of Rufus, or anyone else.

Mack soon learned that there would be no one other than himself and Rufus that evening. The message again came from Toby, on behalf of himself and Stuart.

'A change of plan', Mack relayed to Rufus.

The reason for Toby's absence? Ursula was not going round to see Sophia after all. All that could be said of Stuart was that he had other plans: not a surprise, and not unusual that the preferred plans had not been disclosed.

'*Dark horse, that one. Maybe he's distributing Mangoes – ME and not to me*' Toby had written.

Mack did not read out that part of the message to Rufus. He was lost in thoughts of dark horses calling kettles black.

218

'That's a shame' said Rufus. 'But let's have a game anyway, now that we're here, shall we?'

The reason for Mack to stay out rather than go back to Sophia was no longer valid. And, in truth, he would have preferred to go home immediately. But that was not possible. Rufus was there by request and Mack did not want to appear rude.

'Yeah, why not?'

Mack and Rufus had a few games of pool and one of darts, an otherwise pleasantly uneventful evening. An evening that was none the worse for the absence of Stuart.

STUART'S OFFER

'*C U 2nite ££ Mack but QT!!*' was the text Sophia received from Stuart and the reason she put off Ursula from calling round.

There must have been some crossed wires because Stuart was incredulous to discover that Mack was not in; that Mack had not stayed home to hear of the generous proposition he was about to make.

The incredulity was sustained until after he had checked his phone and seen Toby's message… Ahh… if only he had checked his phone earlier. But not to worry, Mack's response might be all the more positive if the suggestion were to come from Sophia rather than himself, reasoned Stuart. Was Mack not a little resentful of the friendship he had with her and of the help he had given him with the corkscrews, on her behalf? Was his pride a little hurt perhaps?

But Sophia did not want to increase her guilt by discussing Mack with Stuart. She ignored Stuart's questions – no doubt they were rhetorical anyhow – and asked Stuart to explain the purpose of his visit.

Stuart was somewhat affronted that, given their relationship, an explanation for his presence was required. But he made little of that. He prefaced his answer with recognition of the struggle Mack was having in finding his feet in the workplace,… and his lack of success in raising money for the house deposit.… And was it a shortage of money that had led to wedding plans being dropped?

Stuart begged forgiveness for having asked the question. Sophia was not to give an answer, it was none of his business. And Sophia was not to worry that knowledge of Mack's failings would go any further. Stuart explained that he happened 'to be in the know' about much that was going on at St. Joseph's – he got on well with Oswald Rollinson, who was close to the action; **really** close. (But no, he could not say another word on that front. He would not betray the confidences with which he had been entrusted.) As for the mess-up in selling the collection of corkscrews… that was just unfortunate.

Stuart could see a lot of potential in Mack. Something had come up that would be well within Mack's capabilities, Stuart was convinced. And, although it would normally be offered to someone within their "community", Stuart would be only too glad to override any concerns of others and vouch for Mack's integrity and competence.

This was what Stuart put to Sophia. She was relieved that Mack was not at home. Stuart was correct in suspecting one thing at least: Mack would be resentful of Stuart's attentions to her, and the resentment would likely be compounded by such condescending offers of help.

Sophia's silence and countenance made it obvious to Stuart that his case had not been sufficiently well or strongly put forward. He opened up more fully.

'To be honest, if it wasn't for how much I – we all – care about you, I wouldn't bother what happened to Mack. But I can see what he's doing to you Sophia. You are beginning to slip back to how you were when we first met. Can you remember what it did to you when you were let down before? You lost belief in yourself. I cannot stand by and let the same thing happen again. You're a wonderful person, you really are. And if he can't see it he's just not worthy of you. I'm sorry to have to say it Sophia, but he doesn't care a jot about your future together.'

Stuart paused before he enquired of Sophia whether she still believed she did have any future with Mack.

Her reply, 'Of course', came too quickly for it to be a considered reply, argued Stuart. But, again, he reassured her that he would do all he could to help.

Certainly, the best move at that stage would be for Mack to take up the freelance work he was able to put Mack's way – and he would guide Mack through it. He would not leave him to flounder. And although advancement through the freelance work would be more quickly achieved if Mack devoted his **full** time to it, if Mack did not have full confidence yet; did not want to risk giving up his counselling work, then he could consider doing both for a while. Stuart would support Mack in that decision. Though, of course, leaving St. Joseph's would have the added advantage of taking Mack away from temptation. (Stuart rushed on, playing down the slight switch in topic – but not so swiftly as to waste his carefully chosen words.)

'Where is Mack tonight?' Stuart wondered. 'Ah yes, I remember. He was meeting... hmm... someone... at the Durham Ox after work and then being joined by Toby, wasn't he? (*The latter recall was incorrect. But, with no knowledge of content of all Toby's texts to Stuart, perhaps it ought to be assumed that Stuart believed he was being truthful.*) I do hope Toby's not encouraging Mack to be flippant about his commitment to you Sophia; or complicit in a betrayal... .'

Such talk unsettled Sophia. She knew the "someone" was Caroline. She did not want to listen to or talk of betrayals. She wanted Stuart gone. To remove any further reason for him to stay, she asked Stuart to quickly give a few details of the opportunity he thought so suitable for Mack.

He asked if he may use her laptop for a moment. Sophia obliged. Stuart obliged with information to pass on to Mack. Sophia then asked Stuart to leave: she was tired and expected Mack home at any time.

Stuart was pleased to agree with Sophia – that it would be best to leave before Mack returned; knowledge of his visit would be kept between themselves. (This was conveyed by a wink.) He appeared to know what was in her mind: she would prefer not to tell Mack of this exchange with Stuart.... But then how did Stuart presume she would make known his offer to Mack?

To have pointed out the dilemma would have been to delay Stuart. She wished him a good night as she approached the door to see him out.

39. FLUX

Ursula wanted to talk to Toby about her worries but how, without being open about what she knew? She skirted around topics, looking for opportunities to steer to *Sophia* and became quite adept at angling: in conversations – on anything from what to have for supper to when was Toby going to pay that visit to his mum – Ursula found ways to allude to the changes in Sophia's personality that had taken place during that first year at university.

'Did I tell you about when Sophia cooked this dish? The potatoes and onions were still ground-breakingly raw! Bless her. Still, it was at the time when she'd gone a bit queer. Do you remember? She was like a different person!' But Ursula's ingenuity was not rewarded. 'Are you seeing your mum this week Toby?... Oh, wasn't it awful the way Sophia turned against her parents when she went to uni?' All variations were ineffective. Toby's response would be the same – 'I don't know about any change seeing as I didn't really know her before.'

Had *she* known Sophia before? *Really* known her? They had been at school together, yes, all the way through from infants to seniors, but they had not been especially close. It was the sight of a familiar face amidst the strangers filling the university hall that had drawn them together on that first day of registration. But since then, they had become close. Hadn't they? Toby agreed that they appeared to have. Hadn't Toby noticed any *recent* change in Sophia then?... He couldn't say that he had.

★

Sophia sent Ursula a text, '*I've told Stuart.*' There could be only one thing to which Sophia referred. What on earth had possessed her to tell Stuart she was pregnant and what would happen now?

No further communication from Sophia; no replies to texts, emails or calls. The day came when a frantic Ursula could do no other than march round, unannounced, to Sophia's flat. She had no idea whether Sophia would be there and if she was, who else would be with her. No consideration was given to this likely circumstance or that possibility. She just had to reach Sophia.

Sophia was in, alone, and answered the door to her visitor. So far was so good for Ursula.

'I don't get you Sophia!'

(Ursula was finished with mincing her words. She had tried being the approachable, the restrained, and the sympathetic friend. Sophia now had to have some sense drummed into her and she was going to do it.)

'How on earth can you prefer Stuart to Mack? Stuart's a weasel and Mack's such a love. You're doomed if you go with Stuart, you know that don't you?… If you really don't want Mack then don't have either. But *please* not Stuart, Sophia. Open your eyes.'

Sophia was not angered by the outburst. The only visible emotion was one of sadness, or was it resignation? Ursula found it difficult to distinguish.

'I've no choice. But he's not that bad, you misjudge him.'

Sophia's attempt to smile did not reassure Ursula. She tried, yet again, to persuade Sophia to tell Mack of the pregnancy. It had been a mistake to tell Stuart at all, but to tell him first was an unaccountable folly.

From what Sophia had told Ursula, Mack was more likely to be the father than was Stuart – 'A blessing for the baby!' (*Ursula's opinion*)... That was reason number one for leaving Stuart out of the present equation. In fact, Ursula could not think of a single reason why he should have been made a factor at all: unless, of course, Sophia wanted to take advantage of that slight possibility of fatherhood for Stuart and to challenge him to declare his feelings. (Ursula did not want to give any encouragement to Sophia to go down a road to Stuart but could not totally disregard the possibility that Sophia may wish to.) She chanced a question of Sophia.

'How did Stuart react?'

'He was delighted. He is convinced he is the father and wants to take care of us both... There's no pressure from him for me to leave Mack, you know. (*Sophia did not see the ugly sneer that transformed Ursula's face at Sophia's defence of Stuart.*) He says that's my decision. But he says even if he has to give me up, he will not give up his child, he will still support it.'

'So, why aren't you happy?'

'I don't know.'

As on so many occasions, there seemed nothing else that could be said. Ursula hugged Sophia. Both were close to tears.

Ursula fluctuated between fear for her friend and a frustration that made her want to throttle Stuart and shake the stupidity out of Sophia.

On a day when fear and anger collided, it was lucky for Stuart and Sophia that Toby was the person nearest to hand. Ursula could think of no option other than to break the confidence and tell Toby of the crisis – and, hopefully, leave it up to him to sort out: after all, Stuart was Toby's friend and Stuart was the source of the problem (in Ursula's mind, that much was clear). Ursula began.

'I don't know whether I should be telling you this… '

'But, obviously you are about to anyway.' Toby observed, and waited.

Ursula hesitated, reluctant to come to the point.

'Does Mack ever talk to you about Sophia?… about him and Sophia?'

'I thought you were going to tell me something not bombard me with questions.'

'Hardly "bombard"! I just wondered what impression you had of how their relationship was going.'

'Come on. What's this all about Ursula?'

'Promise you won't say anything… unless we decide we should.'

'For frigging sake, just say it.'

So, she did. 'Sophia's pregnant.'

'Is that all?'

He was surprised, but failed to see any cause for panic or drama, even if it had not been part of the general plan, exactly.

'Mack doesn't know.'

The timing of such news was surely Sophia's decision, Toby argued. She might well have reasons of her own for waiting. He advised Ursula to forget about it – and he would too – until Sophia chose to make it general knowledge. No problem.

'Stuart knows.'

'Oh?… ' Toby waited. He sensed that more complications were about to emerge.

'Sophia isn't entirely sure whether Mack or Stuart is the father.'

'Oh, Hell!'

That put a different complexion on the whole matter; but all the more reason to 'stay right out of it', unless or until... 'either Sophia or Mack wants to confide... ' Ursula interrupted to remind him that Sophia *had* confided, which was precisely why they were having the conversation! '... *and* wants our help' Toby continued. 'We will be ready.'

(There was no suggestion that the same readiness to help would apply to Stuart. Ursula was glad to have *that* unspoken agreement at least.)

'I don't think Stuart is the father... well it is possible, I suppose... but he has taken over all rights, just on the off-chance... That's the problem.... Must think he's super virile or something.... It's not right Toby, that Mack's not being told anything. And that is Stuart's doing, not Sophia's, I'm sure of it.'

'OK, so it's a mess. But it's not our mess.' Dismissive words not reflected in Toby's expression and tone.

Ursula did not pursue the matter as far as had been her intention. Perhaps intention is too strong a word: Ursula's thinking was not so organized as to have formed a plan of action. Hope – that Toby would come up with the ideal solution – was nearer the mark.

Toby had no quick answers. He would need time to reflect on how best he could support Mack. There was relief for Ursula that she was no longer the prime holder of the secret. That was something and would have to suffice.

40. IT RE-EMERGES

The work opportunity that Stuart was prepared to offer Mack had been outlined in the briefest terms; more of a prompt for Sophia to enlarge upon than a detailed proposal.

On the evening on which it was given to her she had put the sheet of paper out of sight, underneath a magazine, unsure of when, how or if she would ever broach the matter with Mack. The odds were always in favour of letting the whole thing pass unheeded; simpler that way. And that is precisely what happened – almost.

Time lapsed. It was forgotten about. The reminder had shifted between this magazine and that; on this table and on that, until it eventually found itself sitting somewhere underneath papers that Mack was required to stuff into a folder.

In all probability, the chance to take up the offer had now gone – as should have been the evidence. An oversight! As Mack picked up his work, the loose, incriminating sheet of paper fell at his feet.

'What's this about?' No reply. 'Why does it say *'Mack to check the security of premium bonds'*… ?' – he read out the key line and looked to Sophia.

Still, Sophia said nothing.

'Sophia. Tell me. You must know something… and… seeing as it's got my name on it… … '

She could stall no longer, but was casual in her submission.

'Oh, it's nothing. Just a bit of something Stuart thought you could do... if you'd wanted to.'

'I think you're going to have to tell me a bit more than that, don't you?'

Of course, Sophia knew that she did now have to explain. She began by expressing a hope that she had not been wrong in having made the assumption that Mack would not be interested. And added, for good measure, 'You seemed so absorbed with work at St. Joseph's I didn't want to bother you with it.'

It worked to the extent that Mack recognized, and was grateful for, Sophia's consideration of his needs ahead of Stuart's wants and whims, and he relaxed a little; lost the confrontational edge.

'Right.... So? What was it that I might have done?'

'Oh, like it says, something to do with testing the security systems in place for managing Premium Bonds, make sure they're adequate, safe for the customers and all that.'

'Is there any doubt?'

'No, I don't think so, not especially. (*Sophia checked a too-ready disposal of Stuart's suggestion and instead gave it some plausibility...*) But, you know, now that everything is managed on-line – buying and selling of virtual bonds; transfer of winnings; easy access for checking winning numbers – stands to reason there are openings for abuse.'

'If you've got that sort of criminal mind, I suppose.'

(It is something of a puzzle as to why Sophia then bothered to defend Stuart.)

'It's part of what he and his colleagues do! You know that! They work freelance with a number of companies doing similar sorts of checks and upgrades of systems. Premium

Bonds happen to be the latest thing they are looking at and he thought you might be interested in getting involved.'

'What on earth made him think that?' (Sophia kept quiet; made no show of loyalty to Stuart for a second time.)

Mack attempted complete disinterest, to disparage the very idea. All the same, he held a few premium bonds and, in spite of himself, was curious.

'Should I sell my bonds then? Is he saying they can fiddle which ones win?'

He asked with a smile. Sophia answered diligently but returned his smile.

'No, it won't be that: the draw's separate. It's to do with hacking into computers and extracting information, I think.... because of – what I said before. (*If a friend had been in the room, she would surely have wished Sophia to move on to another topic. But she did not: not quite yet.*) Would you have been interested in the work?' she asked.

The adamant answer was 'NO! (*A relief to Sophia.*) Of course I bloody wouldn't!'

There was also relief as to the lack of enquiry from Mack regarding the where and when Stuart had proffered the said work. But fear began to nudge at the relief. Sophia left the room, in case it occurred to Mack to wonder and to ask those awkward questions.

It was with some reluctance that she walked away: there had been moments in that brief exchange that she had been reminded of the joy of his company, in spite of her apprehensions.

41. FACE VALUE

Candy's comments on *Facesonline* had become increasingly intrusive and negative towards Mack and his relationship with Sophia. Finally, Mack was forced into a reaction. Not of the "like", "dislike" type, indulged in by others; the time had come when an explanation was a reasonable request to make and Mack made it, of Sophia.

'Seeing as comments are now being posted – by your sweet friend – about our split, which, I might add, are a bit premature (*Mack gestured to the dirty pots that referenced domestic togetherness*), don't you think I've a right to know who these "faces" are and what they are about? On the face of it – excuse the pun – they seem to spend most time exchanging moronic codes.... relics of "Mangoes for Everyone" are they?... I know Stuart is... or was... (*Mack was hesitant. He had seen nothing of ME for himself, what little he knew had come from Toby and he was in danger of overstepping the mark*) though nobody seems to know much about it.'

Sophia was startled for a moment. But the familiar disinterest was soon back.

'You make too much of everything. You always do. I've told you time and again what Stuart does. Candy helps with the recruiting, that's all.'

Mack was not so easily satisfied. His look of expectancy encouraged Sophia to go on.

'They may well use codes (*Mack did not point out that*

231

"moronic" had been the operative word)... I shouldn't be telling you this but Stuart is into the synthetic biology industry.... He may even do a doctorate in it.... '

'Well, bully for him. But, pardon me if I don't see Candy as a rising academic.'

Sophia ignored the snipes, ostensibly, though they served well to keep the focus where it suited.

'This new science is big. And I mean big. The *only* way forward, Stuart says... *Huge* potential, so all research and new initiatives have to be closely guarded... there's masses of snooping going on.'

'Oh, so they're into industrial espionage now are they?'

'Don't be childish. It's the opposite, as well you know. Stuart will *protect* developments; *stop* hackers. He's been doing it since before he graduated and he's expert at it! So don't knock what he does just because it's beyond your understanding!'

That hurt. Sophia saw that it did and took no pleasure from it. She quickly added.

'Actually, it's beyond me as well.'

He was tempted to point out that, even without a university education, he had tracked down half a dozen and more fake identities and site locations used by her friends, including the key search words that brought them up. He was not impressed by their supposed skills and intellect – but kept his own counsel, for the time being.

He resolved to find out more about the new big science, synthetic biology.... Somehow, it had taken precedence over posts about their relationship.

42. BUILDING

Toby texted to Mack. *'If bug gone how bout game of pool?'* ("bug" was the term in general use by and around Mack to describe the cause of his baffling indisposition, in and after his time in Boston).

Inference that the "bug" might be a lingering problem irritated Mack somewhat, until he excused it as Toby's way of explaining his limited contact. The idea of a game of pool with Toby suited him. They hadn't been together since Mack had learned about his father – and that woman's daughter. He had been disappointed (though admitted to a little relief too) that Toby had not made it to Durham Ox last time, but was more prepared to meet with him now… and… see what transpired.

A time was arranged to meet at the usual venue, the next evening. (This time Mack would not be meeting with Caroline first: it was high time he and Toby faced each other, with no complications.)

Ursula had Sophia, the pregnancy, and Stuart on her mind. She was pleased that Toby was meeting up with Mack and had high hopes for the outcome – in spite of Toby's absolute refusal to make any more of it than had been proposed, which was a game of pool 'God damn it Ursula!'

They were onto the second game, the first one having been played at a leisurely pace, interspersed with beers and opinions, when Mack decided he would wait no longer for Toby to explain his earlier behaviour. He asked.

'Why didn't you tell me?'

Toby was taken off guard.

'Tell you what, Mack?'

Mack gave Toby no chance to stall.

'I know my dad has died. And I know who Maureen is. You knew before me, why didn't you say anything?'

Toby had the decency to put the game to one side (even though he was ahead, Mack noted). He picked up both glasses and carried them to a small table and dragged to the table two of the several unoccupied chairs, scattered around the edges of the room. He asked Mack about the hows and whens he had come to know. Mack gave perfunctory replies, not wanting to expand on his encounter with either the solicitor or with Maureen, then returned to his starting point.

'I can't believe you would keep quiet about a thing like that. Why on earth didn't you tell me?'

'Jesus Mack. I certainly would have if I'd known you were going to be left in the dark. Never dreamt you wouldn't know. Really sorry. It just didn't seem like the best time for me to tell you right then. Big mistake. I'm sorry. Really sorry.'

Mack accepted his apology. What was the alternative? Toby offered to do whatever Mack might wish of him; he would help in any way he could. In search of something constructive to suggest, he enquired as to the legal position – or any particular circumstance – in which Mack had been left. Nothing on those lines was pursued. Mack had been distracted.

He heard a familiar rift, then the words "... *what would I do, if I didn't have you*". 'Isn't that Rufus?' he asked. Toby listened before he confirmed that it surely was.

'Did you know he'd be here tonight?'

234

Toby had not known. He was equally as surprised as Mack was; emphatically so, sensitive to any suspicion of secrecy.

They did not return to the game but followed their ears to Rufus. He was in a different room to that reserved for Open Mike nights. It was a much larger room (where they catered for large wedding receptions and the like) yet only a handful of people were sitting around.

The two new intruders were apologetic in their urges for Rufus to carry on with his performance and to pay them no mind: they hadn't wanted to interrupt and cause him to stop his playing. Notwithstanding, Rufus did stop playing and walked over to them as they each took a seat.

'Oh, no, you're all right. I've only come to check out a few things.... Good to see you. In fact it's great to see you.' Rufus said.

He welcomed the chance to share his excitement: he told them of an up and coming gig ("up" certainly, and "coming", but still a little way off); a proper gig... "ticketed"!... He had been asked to do a warm up spot. 'A surprise to be asked, if I'm honest', he said. 'The main act is *Raddies* and we're not what you could call "of a type"! They'll come for either them or me.... And nobody's ever paid to hear *me* before.'

Ever the optimists, Toby and Mack chorused 'But they will after'.

There was no time like the present for buying their tickets and with only a moment's hesitation as to the required number – four, certainly: Ursula and Sophia would not want to miss being there for Rufus – the events manager was sought and the deal done.

Rufus and Toby were in high spirits, not ready for the evening to end. Toby steered Rufus hastily back to the games room and Mack travelled in their slipstream.

Stuart was there. He waved his presence and attracted their attention as soon as they walked in, as though he was expecting them, waiting for them almost.

Mack looked at his watch.

'Actually, I'd better be making tracks.'

'... Me too' said Toby.

Rufus looked quickly from one to the other and then over to Stuart, and went to Stuart's rescue – or possibly Mack's, or Toby's rescue: he was not sure what was going on there.

'I'll have a drink with you Stuart before I head off. Have you time for a quick one?'

Mack wanted to take Rufus to one side and ask him not to mention the gig to Stuart. But there was no opportunity. And, in any case, how could he have justified asking such a favour?

43. OFFERS FROM STUART

The day after Mack and Toby had bought their tickets for Rufus's warm-up gig, Stuart asked Sophia round to his flat.

She arrived a little flustered, unsure of what misdemeanor had brought about the urgent summons. An ebullient Stuart greeted her at the door.

'Sorry (*a mismatch of words and expression*) to drag you away from your nest... but I couldn't wait to give you these.' He handed her two tickets to the gig, identical to those given to her by Mack the previous evening.

'Now, you don't have to take me if you'd rather go with someone else, although I know none of your other friends like the *Raddies*. Just me and you.'

How awkward. Sophia did not want to say she already had tickets – least of all from Mack: Stuart would make her choose her companion for the evening and she knew he would make it signify something more. But neither did she want to upset Stuart. A scrutiny of the small print on the tickets gave her some thinking time. And she managed a smile of gratitude before she spoke.

'This is so kind of you. Thank you.' But the tickets were handed back to Stuart. 'You'd better hang on to them for now.... I'm not sure yet what I'll be doing on that night... and if I can't go with you, you'll need them to take someone else.'

Stuart was not at all pleased with Sophia's response.

'I thought you'd jump at the chance to go. What else might you be doing that you couldn't change?'

'Um… nothing probably… It's just that I'm not feeling too well at the moment… and I don't feel like making plans.'

Stuart protested. 'That's no reason to refuse the tickets. On the contrary. If you're feeling down it's exactly what you need to cheer you up.'

'No, it's not that I'm down, just unwell…. I'm sorry Stuart; I know I'm a pain. I don't deserve you do I?' This time, her smile was weak and apologetic, but in all honesty she was quite proud of her tactic.

The pride was short-lived. Stuart thrust the tickets back into her hand.

'They're for you. I'm not taking them back…. Now, what to drink? I'd better not offer you wine, eh?'

Sophia had been telling the truth about not feeling well. It was not the physiology of the pregnancy. It was the worry of it all, not knowing what was to become of her – and the baby. She had moments of escape with Mack, in spite of their strained relationship. Not so with Stuart. His presence tended to oppress her. Of course, that was bound to be so, she reasoned: Stuart knew. There could be no pretence with him.

Another day, another summons from Stuart to go round to his place as soon as she could get away. No reason given but it sounded ominous.

Stuart pre-empted a reply from Sophia and popped a tea bag into a mug in readiness. It did not go to waste.

'Mack looks pretty miserable these days; not at all a happy bunny (*the way in which he could convey concern, flippancy and denigration, all in one stroke was rather impressive*)…. You've not told him you're pregnant have you?'

Sophia confirmed that she had not. She wanted to, increasingly so, in spite of Stuart advising against such a move. She risked Stuart's displeasure by putting it to him that she would have to tell Mack sometime so she might as well get it over with.

He was not angry with her but 'NO!'. He did not agree and she must listen to him. It was her decision, of course. He would not interfere but she must think carefully of what the consequences would be, and how that would affect her. Stuart explained it to her more fully.

'I know Mack. He's a good sort, in an old-fashioned moralistic sort of way; very strong on women not sleeping around – as he would put it. That's very clear.... Now, I know you're no sket (*he laughed at the absurdity of such a description being applied to Sophia*)... but to Mack, having sex with that jerk at school... and... well, he just wouldn't get anything at all about Mangoes... Do you know what I'm saying Sophia?'

Sophia was obliged to nod acknowledgment.

'If you tell him you've had sex with someone else – while you were supposed to be with him – and now you're pregnant!... Need I say more?... (*As no reply was forthcoming to that question, Stuart obviously took the answer to be a "yes"*)... You'll shatter all his illusions about you. Now, I don't give a shit about him or his opinions but think what it would do to you... Remember what you were like when I first met you?... Sorry but I have to say it. You were a mess!... And why?... Because narrow minded, ignorant sods (same sort of thinking as Mack Sophia) made you feel you were dirty and worthless... They'll do that to you again. They will, Sophia. And I'm not sure I'd be able to bring you back up again a second time.... So if you want this baby to have a father: want to have the love of

239

someone who respects you: want for us to have a good life together, then you have to just leave. Tell him nothing other than you're coming to me…. He's miserable with you anyway, probably got someone else on the go and waiting for you to move out so he can move her in… … but don't worry about the flat. I'll sort that and make sure you get what you're due… all **you** have to do is leave.'

Having put his case, Stuart put his arms around Sophia and asked. 'Feel better now?' Again, Sophia gave an obligatory nod.

The trial of her summons was over. To that extent she did feel better. As she had made her way to his flat, she had been full of dread and fear. She did not know why: it had not crossed her mind to question what things he could possibly do or have to tell her to warrant the anxiety. But, warranted or not, dread and fear had been present and had now been assuaged.

44. IN PREPARATION

The timing was wrong.

Mack had been asked by Omniwell, as part of their marketing strategy, to put forward the case for a counselling service in the workplace. A consortium in the Midlands was the target. Mack was not pleased.

Caroline would surely have objected – had she known – to the taking of staff away from their NHS duties in order to obtain a further Omniwell franchise. Her moral voice did waft across his mind, but, as he was not about to sell his soul, exactly, a guilty conscience was not the reason Mack was reluctant to accompany Ged to Leicester.

The two-day trip promised to be undemanding, therefore it was of no consequence that it had come so soon after his Staunton – and other – experiences. A return to full health and spirits was not yet achieved but he was fully capable of ordinary day to day functioning.

No, Mack's problem lay not on the work front per se but at home. Communication between Sophia and him had continued to deteriorate and it was a bad time to spend a night away from her.

It was true that Stuart had called at their flat less frequently than before: part of the explanation for that blessing was that Sophia was less frequently at home. Mack feared what might be to come. He did not ask questions so as not to hear unwelcomed answers. That was generally so.

★

On one particular occasion he changed his habit. The silence of the unknown filled his head to bursting. It got the better of him and he spoke out. Not with a direct question; with a challenge.

'If marriage is to be a no-goer, we ought to think about what to do about the flat.'

'Seeing as I was here first, I'm not moving out' was her reply.

(Uninformative for Mack's purposes, but Sophia thought not to Mack's position but to Stuart's response. Would he applaud her stance – if he were to learn of it? Certainly not; she would be in trouble…. Unless, she said it was her ploy to strengthen bargaining power when the split came? Yes, he might approve of that.)

Sophia had her back to Mack as she spoke. He wanted to see her face; he wanted to look her in the eyes. He *had* to be able to see her face before he asked for confirmation that she must, therefore, by inference, want *him* to leave. But, as he could not see her face, he could not ask. That was the end of the exchange.

In spite of her declaration that she was "not moving out", she was set to leave him, of that Mack was sure. He had not been told, expressly, but the signs were there. Her obvious sadness, her reluctance to spend much time with him alone, her avoidance of eye contact and lack of verbal communication when they did meet: none of those warnings escaped his attention. Yet he stopped trying to fathom her.

He resigned to deal with the inevitable, however and whenever it came.

Michael was grateful to have some input from Josie before he left for the Midlands. Initially, he had not realized that he would be meeting with representatives from two separate consortiums in neighbouring districts. Josie advised on how to judge the reactions of the first group and, if necessary, vary his approach on meeting with the second so as to improve the chances of securing take-up with at least one of the two.

That much he understood. What did not stack up was why it should matter at all to them, at St. Joseph's, who else joined forces with Omniwell. Josie was vague. It was complicated. It related to interplay between factors such as reputation, credibility, building consumer confidence in the product and the overall costs of scale in the introduction of innovative services. That was the business side. It was not their concern. Though if it could turn a failing NHS into a profitable industry, who could argue with that?

But Josie's main reason for wanting to discuss matters with Michael was less to do with the marketing of the counselling service and more to do with her own new role as researcher… and… how that might affect him.

'Think on Michael. As one of the few researchers in this field, I'm increasing the standing of St. Joseph's. And that will reflect well on you. Don't be afraid to use that influence out there.'

A good deal of time was spent going through what would be expected from him in his everyday work at St. Joseph's (a natural pre-requisite to the "selling" of the service elsewhere and, therefore, a further justification for Josie to raise it before he went out as ambassador).

Much to his satisfaction, Josie was in favour of his

continuing to concentrate on a group approach, "preventative rather than cure". She would continue with individual counselling – it formed part of her research – but would not encourage large numbers to come forward. (This *modus operandi* for Michael would negate her having to bother arranging supervisory sessions for him. But no need to mention that bonus.) And, as that was to be the case, Michael could disregard the inference – from Ged – that the counselling of addicts, alongside the introduction of new wines, would put an end to the problem – if one existed – of alcoholics in the NHS.

Josie listened to, and fully supported Michael's proposals for courses he would devise and facilitate. There was no difference, in essence, to what already constituted the group sessions. From a stress management course, spin-offs would be identified: skills courses to reduce stress and improve performance – assertiveness, time management, relaxation techniques and, perhaps, debt management. (Pretty mundane and repeated several times over in other contexts.)

As far as the Midlands went, each consortium could decide its own priorities from knowledge of their staff and perceived problems. And, obviously, elements could be described and promoted according to circumstances.

Michael added a further two-pennyworth: he had noticed how there was a general reluctance amongst managers to admit to stress; it gave opponents the edge in a competitive market. It followed, therefore, that a course for managers might fare better under a title of "How to get the most from your staff" (in which all the same topics would be covered but from both sides – that is, as a manager and also as being managed: the only time it would not be appropriate would be if the chief executive was on the course, and that was not very likely!)... ...

Josie acknowledged Michael's ideas as though they were novel. And interrupted him only to express her delight in being able to hand over to him the lead position in developing the service whilst she concentrated on research.

However, she felt he ought to broaden his level of expertise *a little*; be more prepared to deal with *some* individual counselling, should it be required, occasionally.

To that end, he would need to undertake further study perhaps. Putting oneself in the position of the client usually formed part of such study; that is, exploring one's own attitudes, emotions, reactions and so on... Josie would advise Michael further on that process.

He was not inclined to argue against "that process" at that particular time. Though it should not be assumed that because he did not actually say 'No chance. You're not "exploring" me, thank you', that he was not having such thoughts.

He did not say that he was quite prepared to discuss strategies for dealing with specific problems in life, and the likely consequences of pursuing this, or that, line of action, but that was as far as he would go. Nothing personal. He did not want to hear of tragedies that had befallen individuals. Members of the groups could make their own decisions and take from the general options available: Just as he would do: Just as he had done, without the need to reveal "emotions", "reactions" and so on... and without the need to be advised, thank you very much.... He said none of that.

'Yes, thank you Josie. You've been a great help.... ... Yes, I'm totally happy about my role with Omniwell on this trip. Thanks a lot.' He said as he made his way out.

Josie rewarded herself with a chocolate biscuit. So satisfying; the chocolate and the feeling that came from good communication, both.

She took the trouble to write up the suggestions made by Michael, plus a little – and a little more – on her research project. She gave a copy to Michael, for his future reference (during the meetings in the Midlands) and filed the original with the Omniwell documents, under "Planned Development of the Counselling Service".

45. DIVERTED

Mack was confident of his role in the meetings that were ahead, the first scheduled for 10.15 am. It was most unfortunate, therefore, that the aura phase of a migraine attack showed itself as he attempted to sign the hotel register on arrival, at 9.30 am.

The course of the migraine could not be halted. Mack had no option but to forego the chance of impressing his colleagues and instead retire to his room, until such time as he was able to function.

Disappointment had to be accepted for the full day as sufficient recovery was not made until around 3.45 pm, too late for any work appointments to be kept.

He had slept a good deal, surprisingly untroubled by how things were at home. Refreshed and ready for some brain activity, Mack was able to take advantage of the unexpected free time and the hotel room facilities. On-line access was established and, sooner than he could have anticipated, Mack got down to exploring the topic of synthetic biology. There was no shortage of information available... *Bear with him, if you are minded to.*

His first thought was that Sophia was right.

'This is bloody exciting stuff!'

He quickly saw how the potential for biotech companies and students alike was enormous. Scope for disciplines across the board… life sciences, engineering, mathematics, chemistry, physics, computer sciences… . Plenty of scope for Stuart to extend his collection of useful people.

Some was familiar territory: three dimensional forms – hip joints came to mind – could be produced as easily as printing off a photograph. But… the concept of one day feeding genetic data (those bloody amino acids, they're everywhere!) into a computer and printing out DNA to produce a whole creature, of your own design? Wow, that was mind blowing! No wonder Stuart wanted in on the act.

Oh, hello. What was that? Scroll back. *"Craig Venter has taken the first step. The first synthetic cell has been produced."* How had he missed that on the News!

He smiled. 'And how are you gonna blog your way into *that* brave new world, Stuart sonny boy?'

He laughed out loud. 'Oh, sweet. The synthetic cell's called Cynthia!'

Then another name flashed into his head, 'Candy. Candy alias *Cynthia*. Ah, remember that one alright. Gotcha! Well good luck with that one, moron.' But Stuart's small fry accomplices held no further interest.

He clicked and read, and clicked and read, engrossed in the science. And finally concluded that Synthetic Cynthia is pretty useless, but her descendants and extended family – if treated well so they develop responsibly – may help solve energy problems, health problems… in fact there's probably nothing they couldn't resolve. On the other hand, if allowed to mix with the wrong crowd – terrorists, for example – there could be drawbacks.

The smart people were protecting their designer genomes by inserting an inert code at strategic points in the DNA, which served not only to establish copyright but allowed the geniuses (or was it genii?) to have fun vying intelligences.

Who could crack these codes? (Or "watermarks", as they were termed). Oh to be a genius, and with wit too!

He particularly liked the decoded revelations that included literary quotes:

To live to err, to fall, to triumph, to recreate life out of life – James Joyce.

See things not as they are, but as they might be – Robert Oppenheimer.

What I cannot build, I cannot understand – Richard Feynman.

Richard Feynman was a hero of Mack's. He was not au fait with the science but admired Feynman's approach to life: science and art, not in opposition but in synergy.

Of course, Mack's research of synthetic biology did not enable him to decipher the watermarks – he simply read of them. As, no doubt, had Stuart.

Again, Sophia had been correct, it was beyond his understanding. Possibly it was beyond Stuart's understanding too: watermarks were hardly in the same code category as 'given up smoking. Made a hash of a banana loaf but I can get a week's supply of "bananas" real cheap', nudge, nudge. What plonkers!

It was all well and good, his having a sense of Stuart's delusions, but what difference did knowing make? None.

He had a drink of water, packed his bag ready for an early start the next day and settled down to select the best option from the television channels available in his room. He would not go down to join his colleagues in the bar after all. It was too late.

46. PROGRESS, OF SORTS

Mack returned from the Midlands, exhausted. On reflection, the idea that his partial recovery could sustain any level of work, with or without any evenings of socializing, had been grasped at too readily.

He did not fall back to the previous low but, for a while, there was some climbing back to do. Mack stayed around the house, content – as close as he came to contentment – to listen to music, to read, to eat his way back to full health.

Visitor numbers grew. Monitored and, to some extent, rationed across the days by Sophia (who had postponed her departure until a time when that action would not be detrimental to Mack's wellbeing. A tacit understanding). The apportioning of visitor admissions was discreetly done. Mack was not aware of the times Stuart had called by and been shooed away from the door, at speed. Neither was he aware of the much exaggerated account of his illness that Sophia had given to Stuart – without which, it would not have been possible to bar Stuart's entry even once.

Paradoxically, the increased number of visitors was a repercussion of telling, and subsequent spreading of, the falsehood. That Josie (fearful a long absence of her jobbing counsellor would put paid to her research ambitions), Ursula, Rufus and Toby were each made welcome, gave lie to the suggestion that Mack was, indeed, too ill to receive callers.

If Stuart was aware of the privileges afforded to others and denied to himself, he chose not to make it an issue. Instead, he communicated through an open forum on *Facesonline*.

Concern for Mack was expressed. Friends of friends sympathized and empathized. They were all strangers to Mack and yet all understood how the stresses of life were difficult to bear ('*Life's Shit*' – succinctly put). But then Mack was unaware of the attention; he read none of the comments, so what did it signify?

Stuart's posts were particularly insightful. He shared with all, the knowledge that Mack's problem was a depression, the cause of which was unrequited love. A new "friend" of Stuart's – using the name of Donna – confirmed it was so. She had begged Mack to promise to leave her alone (for his own sake – before his employers dismissed him – as well as for the sake of her longstanding relationship) but, no: '*Sorry, I can't do as you ask*' Mack had written to her. The distraught Donna had shared the quote in order that his friends could offer their help and support.

It was inevitable: Sophia would read the post. Of that, Stuart was confident. She would need him, once she was aware of Mack's duplicity, and Stuart was determined not to let her down. He duly summoned Sophia to his flat, in order to reassure her of that fact.

Toby called by to see Mack just as Sophia was preparing to leave.

'Do you have to go out now?' Toby asked. 'Ursula's on her way round.'

(Ursula had found Sophia to be a little less edgy when she had called a couple of days previous and she had dared to permit herself a little optimism.)

'Sorry, have to. Stuart wants to talk to me, says it's urgent.'

Toby could detect none of the progress Ursula had spoken of. His parting words to Sophia were 'You need to be talking to Mack not Stuart'.

She gave him a questionning glance before she rushed off, all the quicker.

Unsurprisingly, Stuart was expectant of Sophia's imminent arrival: his door was left open for her entry. Surprisingly, (or perhaps not), he chose not to be welcoming, nor appreciative that she was there at his request.

'You're gonna have to sort Mack out. He's a trouble causer – he'll land the lot of us in the shit!'

Sophia had been wrong footed from the start. No gentle introduction from which she might have begun to prepare a defence. She could do nothing other than enquire as to the nature of Mack's wrongdoing.

Stuart began the assassination by providing evidence of Mack's infidelity – in desire if not in deed. He explained that Arabella had used the name Donna on *Facesonline* in order not to cause trouble for Michael from her outraged friends. '*They would kill him if they knew how he'd hounded me*' she had anguished. Stuart had in his possession, hard copy of "Donna's" email from Mack, in which he had said '*Sorry, I can't do as you ask*'; in other words, Mack had refused to deny that he wanted Arabella (though whether that interpretation of Mack's words had been Arabella's or Stuart's is not certain.) The email had been forwarded to Stuart by Arabella, who, quite obviously was in desperate need of his help. The evidence was shown to Sophia.

Sophia had not time to recover from that blow before Stuart rushed on to 'the more serious stuff'.

'He's been snooping, and his twisted mind has managed to turn chilling out into some sort of grooming and drug dealing set-up… and my business into cyber crime! Who – if they get wind of what he's saying – is going to work with me? Me, a supposed fraudster? I ought to sue him for libel, slander… the lot! (*No evidence for this "more serious stuff" was forthcoming.*) You tell him. It's only because I don't want you hounded that I'm giving him another chance.'

Sophia knew not what to say or do. What was expected of her? She was frozen in indecision. Stuart was irritated by her lack of response.

'Wake up! Don't you get it?… Don't you see, Sophia? You've gotta get him to stop mouthing off with his lies – and you've to leave him NOW. Or else, I'm suing.'

In spite of all Stuart had said, Sophia instinctively wanted to defend Mack. But how?

'Are you sure it's him? It doesn't sound like him. What has he said? Who has he said it to?'

Stuart appeared to be trying hard to hide his impatience, and was successful (in the appearance): he allowed for a fraction of that suppressed to be audible in his plea.

'Don't you think I've suffered enough – seeing the woman I love being abused in this way; having to fight to save my businesses from destruction – without having to constantly re-live it; repeat all the gory details to you… And I don't know how I'll stop the others from getting their hands on him!… But, don't worry, I will… for your sake. I'll do anything for you, even if it means destroying myself.'

Stuart moved from the table at which he had been sitting and flopped into a huge, soft armchair. He was not a big man when fully outstretched, and huddled inside the squishy folds, his face hidden behind his up-drawn knees, he looked tiny, almost vulnerable: it was a sharp contrast to the powerful being to have confronted Sophia only minutes previously. Had she reduced him to this? Broken and put at the mercy of others.

'I'm sorry. It will be all right Stuart. I'm sorry. I will speak with Mack… and tell him I'm leaving him.'

A muffled 'Thank you babe' could just be heard. Sophia asked that he gave her 'a bit of time' and eased her way out of the door, quietly – so as not to disturb him – and quickly – so as not to allow him time to insist that she act immediately.

Stuart trusted in a good outcome and helped himself to a beer in celebration.

47. CONFRONTATION INEVITABLE

Sophia went straight home. No thoughts formalized on the journey other than further recognition of what a mess her life had become: no choices left open to her. How stupidly had she drifted to this point of no return; how cowardly, of late, had she accepted pleasant moments with Mack and denied him the truth. She could not resent his betrayal: her's had been the sooner.

Toby must have put off Ursula from her planned visit to the patient and his nurse, for when Sophia returned home there was no Ursula, just the three amigos at play; Rufus, Toby and Mack.

Rufus had come armed with his acoustic guitar, Toby with a few cans (they had made their appearance during Sophia's absence) and a mock rehearsal for the big gig was underway.

Sophia was cordially invited to take her seat and put in her order for drinks. It was impossible for her to do Stuart's bidding in the situation she had walked into... and so...

'A large G and T followed by a rum and coke please' she said. 'If only' she thought. 'Actually, I don't want booze. Make it an orange and ginger, if you would, please.'

Drinks flowed. Rufus sang and played. Toby and Mack gave their suggestions for choice of songs to be included – some suggestions less deferential than others as the evening progressed. "I'm gone" was considered to be appropriate for the finale, to be followed by cheerful shouts of "Rufus has left the building" from Toby and Mack. Moods, thoughts, atmosphere were happy, uplifting, simply wonderful. An evening marred for Sophia only by the regret that it could never be repeated.

When Stuart texted later, to ask how Mack had reacted, the reason she gave for her failure to keep any part of her expressed intention, was that Mack was too unwell and she had let him sleep.

The lie was unavoidable, even though the truth was good reason enough and could have been given, had she not previously lied about Mack's condition and the admittance of visitors. Lie upon lie: proof surely of her consistently immoral behaviour.

Another day, another opportunity for Sophia to speak to Mack; to press the self-destruct button. Neither she nor Mack had plans to go out and no one was expected until the evening. It was the time.

The baby was beginning to make its presence felt and demanding to be noticed by a wider world than its mother. An explanation would be looked for, and when given, she would have no option but to leave Mack – or be thrown out. No option other than to do things Stuart's way. 'Get out now. Get out now' she could hear Stuart saying and the cuckolded Mack echoing.

The struggle to begin was immense, but mastered.

'Mack.... I'm so sorry. (*how many times had he heard that of late? Novel from Sophia's lips, he owned*)... But, if you're feeling up to it, there's something unpleasant we need to talk about.'

How ridiculous and weak her voice! Stuart would have expected a much more confrontational approach. Sorry Stuart, not possible.

'Go on then.'

Oh dear, the opening had been created. She had to go on, as prompted.

'I know about you and Arabella – or Donna.... Sorry about us – I mean me – but please don't try to get at me by ruining Stuart. You don't need to. I'll leave as soon as I can get things organized.'

Mack expected her to leave him for Stuart at some time, but not quite in the here and now, and not in this manner. For one thing, he had been enjoying the apparent renewed affection and had refused to let his mind dwell on what may happen in the future. Secondly, her words had made no sense! He asked for clarification. She attempted to give it.

'I've seen your email to her. She went to Stuart for help.... You've no need to be jealous of Stuart by the way, he's not at all interested in her.' (It was a new thought that occurred to her as she spoke – a reason Mack might have, to want to blacken Stuart's name? Totally without foundation or consequence but possibly some indication of Sophia's struggle to grasp what was unfolding.)

'Sophia, you're not making any sense.... If you're trying to turn things around and infer that I'm the one who wants us to finish – to ease your conscience, or something – it won't work. I've never been with anyone else.'

'Only because she wouldn't have you.'

'That's rubbish.'

'Stuart's shown me the proof.... ... And you've to stop telling lies about him or he'll sue you. He really will.'

'Oh please, Sophia' Mack scoffed. 'I'm not playing his games. If you want to go, just go… we'll sort the flat and everything out later.'

There was nothing more Sophia needed to say. She could leave without further explanation, he had no intention of asking her to reconsider, that was plain. It saddened her to realize that Stuart had been right: Mack was probably relieved that she was going.

'Can I tell Stuart that you will stop spreading lies about him then?' She asked, to complete Stuart's bidding – and to divert the conversation from her leaving, for the time being.

'I've told you. I'm not going to give him the satisfaction of rising to his bait. But, to put the record straight with you, I have not spoken of him to anyone – other than to you. If you want to believe otherwise then go ahead. I have no need to defend myself, least of all to him. That's an end to it.'

No one could tell how deep the sorrow was felt by either Sophia or Mack on that day: neither betrayed much. Mack said no more. Sophia left the room and cried, briefly.

48. A BREAK

Rufus had been somewhat on the periphery of the lives of Toby and the other university friends, distanced partly because of the extent and ever-increasing circle of his friends. He was not a person to rely on the company of a "best" friend, but he was a genuine friend for all that. And as they each diverged to look to their futures, whenever they did come together it was somehow more meaningful: the individuality of their activities provided a synergy. In this, Mack was no longer the outsider.

This was never more apparent than when he called by to see Mack, as naturally as if they had been friends from childhood. The sight of Rufus was particularly welcomed by Mack, following on from the drama instigated by Stuart and played out by Sophia.

Rufus had no specific purpose for knocking on their door, he said. He was just passing and, reminded of the good evening they had spent so recently together, it seemed apt to share with Mack his momentous decision and, to be frank, to test out the sense of his own enthusiasm. (Purpose aplenty then.)

At one moment he knew absolutely, undeniably, that he should drop politics and take a risk with his music. At the next, he thought better of it and was intent on following the advice of his father to "keep the Porsche in the garage by oiling the wheels of policy making. And have fun with music in free time". Which could be summed up as "keep the day job". To the mind of Oswald Rollinson, there was no question to debate, the answer was so obvious that he refused to enter into any further discussion on the subject.

Mack enjoyed and was impressed by the vast majority of Rufus's compositions. One need know no more than that to understand what had drawn Rufus to knock at the door of Mack and Sophia, as he "was just passing".

Both Mack and Sophia were at home and both pleased to see him. Both hopeful his presence would promote an ease in the tense atmosphere. (Neither wanted to move out, but a reluctance to speak of the situation, allowed for no chance of an improvement.)

In the course of conversation – over coffee and some particularly delicious chocolate and raisin cookies Sophia had perfected in the kitchen refuge (no, not the reason for her "comely figure" Sophia answered to Rufus's innocent question) – Mack asked 'Do you, by any chance, like what you're doing?... research assistant is it... or assistant parliamentary secretary...?'

A pertinent but generally overlooked query, Rufus thought before replying – to the first question; he disregarded the second.

'It's OK I suppose.... But it's time consuming. Not sure it's something you can do half-heartedly – too likely to land yourself, or someone else, "in the mire" if you don't keep your wits about you... so, probably not right for a half-wit like me.'

For once, the light hearted manner of Rufus was forced.

'In fact, seeing as you've asked... ... No, I don't like it. But it's not so much the time as the who.... To be honest I'm finding it hard to decipher what they're about. Someone can be flavour of the month, with butter on – and past their sell-by date before the wrapper's even read.'

A bit obscure for Mack, but he sensed Rufus was getting to his difficulty. He had subconsciously donned his counsellor's hat.

'Oh? Anyone in particular causing you bother?'

'Well, take Hugo Lubbock for instance. Oh, sorry. He's a friend of yours. Don't mean to offend.'

'No. Not a friend of mine, not even an acquaintance. Feel free: say what you like'

Rufus looked about to question the statement, or the offer. But went on to take Mack at his word. 'Right, well, he was a pretty expensive flavour to buy. I was told to get him and the others together and clinch arrangements for the big launch – the new wines – you know about that don't you? *(Mack nodded, Rufus expanded on it nevertheless, but there is no need to repeat all his words)*... You can drink more, that's about the gist of it.... Ready to go and they tell me Lubbock's an albatross: he'll give us a hell of bad media mire. About to have his name dragged through the courts over some money left floating in the ether. My fault apparently. **I** should **know** about such things.' (Rufus supplemented a facial expression of innocence with a showing of open palms.)

Mack presumed it would be something to do with the plaintive of the case moving in with the ex Mrs Lubbock. He did not consider the details worth raising. Anyhow, Rufus had not finished speaking.

'And guess who the bright spark was to step in there and stop me making a complete ass of myself? None other than our friend Stuart. God knows how he gets to know these things. In fact **he** ought to do my job and I'll stick to music!' (If Mack was tempted to challenge Rufus's perception of Stuart's integrity, he resisted.)

'It sounds as though it could be a good time to "go for it" with your music. A better life' Mack advised (against the counselling paradigm). 'Got your guitar with you by any chance?'

Rufus had, and he obliged his hosts by fetching it from his car and playing their requests. An amusement that suited all three.

49. DECISION. INDECISION. UNDECIDED.

Sophia was no match for Stuart. She was compelled to go round to his place or risk the carrying out – literally – of the almost hourly threat by Stuart to come to her and physically move her to his place.

Stuart had made it clear that his patience had been stretched beyond reason. *'It's D-day Sophia. Today!'*

She took with her a small hold-all of belongings. They were far from all of her belongings, the bag could have held much more. She took the minimum required to appease Stuart and give a semblance of an intention to transfer to him, whilst providing no such indication to Mack.

For how long could she give an appearance of being at home in two places?

Ursula had once managed to get across a few words of entreaty to Sophia. They had been said hurriedly, as Stuart approached the coffee shop to interrupt their chat. And those words of an earlier day, resounded as she faced Stuart in his home, token belongings in her hand.

'Remember Sophia. Whether or not you stay with Mack, you don't have to be with Stuart. We will help you.'

Is that what she should do? Go to Ursula and Toby? But did Ursula mean that she could stay with them? She hadn't actually said so. And anyway, if she did stay, for how long? It couldn't be indefinitely and then what would she do?

★

At least Stuart would provide for her and the baby, care for them. She had done as Stuart had insisted. She was there, at his place, with her small hold-all of belongings. And wanting to turn and run.

50. QUESTIONS OF A DIFFERENT VARIETY

The gig approached at a pace. Rufus had frequent contact with Toby and Mack during the build-up, either at Toby and Ursula's house or Mack and Sophia's (a "Stuart and Sophia's" was known only to the two named) depending on the proximity at any given moment.

There were times when Sophia engineered to be present, under one pretext or another. Stuart was busy with business of his own and seemed a little less concerned with Sophia's whereabouts (though caution was paramount: his interrogation, when it came, was intense and the timing of it was unpredictable).

Two days before the gig there was a new subject of gossip. Sophia was round at her and Mack's flat, having gone to pick up some clean clothes and to do some washing. (It was a blessing that Stuart was not partial to steam fumes and allowed Sophia's laundry excursions with limited interference, on the understanding – usually a misunderstanding – that Mack would be elsewhere at the time. Mack never noticed, or at least never commented on, the secreted removal of a few items.)

Rufus, Toby and Ursula arrived together. Toby was the buzziest and was the first to speak.

'You'll never guess guys. Stuart's been taken in for questionning!'

Ursula looked to Sophia at the mention of Stuart's name,

before the sentence was completed. But Sophia's reaction was mild: a degree of shock fleeted across her face, visible only to eyes already fixed upon her.

Mack asked 'What about?'

'Now you're asking! What isn't it frigging about? God only knows what the sly old devil's been up to. (*Ursula muttered 'Oh, I think **we** could have a pretty good guess at a few things'*) Fraud; a bit of pimping; a lot of drug dealing; incitement to violence… you name it, he's probably done it!'

Ursula was annoyed with Toby's cavalier treatment of Stuart's behaviour and snapped a rebuke. 'Nothing he does is a joke. He's a menace!'

Rufus looked edgy and cautioned. 'Be careful there Toby. He's not been charged with anything, only questionned.'

'Yeah, but a lot of things about him fit now, don't they? You don't believe he's innocent, do you?'

'Until proven… '

'Oh come on Rufus. Stop being so frigging P.C. Remember that lad from 2nd year economics? He'd done something… what was it? possession… or selling?… or was it for grooming that fifth former… ?'

'Hardly that Toby. He'd known her for years, they were practically married!'

'I wasn't being serious about that bit. But Stuart was in on it, whatever it was. *Mangoes for Everyone* came up at the time, don't you remember? And he was *definitely* to do with that!'

'Sure he was. But all that was kid's stuff. This is more serious. *But, but, but* Toby, he's only being *questionned.*'

Sophia looked anxious. She wasn't sure whether Toby had said "been" or "being". She asked whether he had been released.

'Not sure. I've not heard about any charge being brought. So, possibly.'

Rufus had been the bearer of the tidings to Toby and Ursula. Consequently, Mack addressed his question to Rufus.

'How did you find out he'd been taken in?'

'Because they have also questionned my dad – not as a potential perpetrator I hasten to add (*Rufus laughed at the thought*). Stuart had blogged on his parliamentary website and then emailed him privately. He was just one of Stuart's contacts. And, because my dad's an MP... ... But to go back to your original question Toby – do I believe he is innocent? No, I don't. Not totally, but that doesn't mean they will prove his guilt. We know he has a lot of things going on (as you said) and there's probably a lot of people involved, some who will stop at nothing to keep it quiet. So, we'd be idiots to go blabbing around. Especially when we don't really know what they're investigating. It could be murky stuff. Very murky.'

'I suppose we'll be on Stuart's list of contacts too. We'd better be ready for a knock on the door!' suggested Toby.

Rufus resumed authority and the voice of reason.

'Maybe, but I very much doubt it. I think the police will know where to put their energies. They must be following particular leads to have picked up Stuart in the first place. They'll know which of his "friends" link in to all the other stuff he has going on – allegedly! (*The young men chuckled.*) Though they may do a cursory check of Internet contacts. Who knows?'

' I bet most of them are just his alter egos. I reckon he's a pathetic fantasist who makes up friends to make himself look important and popular. We never actually see any of them do we? And he never really talks about friends. No, he's not got any.' That was Toby's assessment, in line with Mack's thinking.

Mack picked up on the thread and joked.

'If you got arrested for having imaginary friends we'd have been in jail when we were six, Toby, along with Tom Sawyer and Huckleberry Finn.'

If truth be told, they were starting to enjoy the drama. All but Sophia. And Ursula, who was anxious on behalf of Sophia.

Rufus added a serious note.

'Look, keep schtum about this. It may not be right anyway. But Dad thinks one of the things they are looking at is a fraud to do with National Savings.'

'Are you all right Sophia?' Ursula asked.

Sophia had gasped the colour from her face. And although she answered that she was perfectly well, she welcomed Ursula's suggestion to withdraw to another room for a civilized cup of tea and leave the men to natter like washerwomen.

Ursula did not take advantage of the acquired privacy to pursue the "Sophia and Stuart" affair – it would have been insensitive and inappropriate. Instead, she left the topic – or silence – to Sophia's will. Sophia chose silence, for the most part, until roused by sounds from the next room and the fear of losing her time alone with Ursula.

'I've some things round at his place. What shall I do?'

Ursula's expression did not change; immobile, calm, serene, she asked.

'Can I take it that you have decided to ditch Stuart then?'

'Yes. I want to, if I can.'

'Course you can. No question. Have you anything of immense value round at his?'

'No. Just clothes and toiletries really.'

'Then leave them. He'll get the message clearer if you don't go to retrieve them – and tell him you don't want them back, so he doesn't use them as an excuse to come to you.'

'Sounds simple.'

'It is.'

'I wish.'

51. SOPHIA'S HERE AND NOW

Sophia had become a short-term thinker. It suited her better.

Day to day she had pushed to one side the problem of Rufus's gig; the question of who would be at her side. And it proved to have been a good strategy: Stuart's arrest provided the answer to the dilemma. Admittedly, it would have been more conclusive had Stuart been kept in custody. But his arrest was manna enough. Once over the initial shock of it, which had been particularly unnerving, she was grateful for the turn in events.

Mack, Ursula, Toby – and even Rufus – rallied around to support and shield her. 'Try not to worry', they said. 'You need to look after yourself', they advised. She was more than happy to listen to their words and accept their advice.

Ursula contacted Stuart and "warned him off" trying to contact Sophia.

He did not heed the warning (the surprise to Sophia would have been if he had). In one, same day, he sent her 64 texts. She, for reasons of her own – misguided loyalty, perhaps – told no-one of his defiance of Ursula's dictum. She did not worry; she concentrated on staying calm and luxuriating in the company of those friends around her.

Each of the 64 texts was on a similar theme: he had to speak with her; she obviously didn't realize just how much he loved her and how much she needed him. Where would she be without him? They needed to talk and she couldn't avoid him forever.

Maybe he was right, she could not avoid him forever. But the gig was that night – and tomorrow was another day.

Sophia did not deliberate on the whys and wherefores, but the pestering from Stuart produced a longing within her for Mack to refer to the baby. In absolute terms. To this being, squirming inside her. This baby; the baby that had never been acknowledged, officially.

A strange juxtaposition existed. No mention of a baby, juxtaposed with group behaviour to a pregnancy. She was asked which *soft* drink she would like; which clothes still fitted; whether she had any special "fancies" that could be supplied... (the latter had been asked by Mack). But never was there a direct reference to her "condition"; to her baby.

Mack knew that she had been unfaithful, didn't he? It followed, therefore, that he must be aware the baby might not be his. Surely that must be so. Was that why he evaded the topic? Was he assuming that she would be leaving soon? Would he want her to stay?

52. IT'S THE GIG

It was almost time for the gig. 'Do you want to shower before or after me?' Mack asked Sophia. Sophia replied that she had no preference.

'If you're in no rush, would you like to read the thing my dad wrote?… over a coffee?'

That was a jolt, straight out of the blue! The verse had not been uppermost in her mind of late and the abruptness of the reminder, the recollection of a different day, shocked her; disturbed the perfected tranquillity. But, apart from a pink flush across her neck, there was no outer sign of the inner emotion; her voice remained calm.

'Of course. I'll make the drinks while you get it, shall I?'

Sophia was shaking by the time Mack returned and handed her the piece of paper. 'Silly. You're being silly' she told herself. It was just the suddenness of it all. She put the paper on the table so as not to reveal her shakes but found it difficult to focus.

'Actually Mack, would you mind reading it to me please? It's a long time since anyone has read to me and I do so love it.'

She cringed. Whatever was written on that scrap in front of her, had been quite traumatic for Mack to read. She knew that. And there she was, acting as though he was offering her a bedtime story!

Mack gave his answer by simply doing as she had asked. He read

Once in life I was and had, a father, brother, son.
Now I do as you bid do and they are all but gone.

… Sophia missed the next few lines as she silently repeated those words. She caught a few more, towards the end…

… words that I daren't resist
for fear of being left alone…

When he had finished reading out the whole verse, Mack looked at Sophia and remarked of her tears.

'There's no need to feel bad for my dad *or* for me…. That misery is gone… ' (Not strictly accurate, of course – unless he was referring to his father's misery.)

He told her as much of the surrounding circumstances and consequences as occurred to him as relevant. Told with a quiet composure. He had afforded himself the luxury of waiting until it suited *him* to share his father's words and that time and place had come.

The telling, and Sophia's kindly response, lifted a weight. Both he and Sophia were more comfortable in their preparations for the evening.

They were all excited for Rufus. His "spot" was at eight o'clock. Ursula, Toby, Mack and Sophia got there for seven, all beams and hugs.

Toby's phone played some unrecognizable tune to herald an incoming message: a reminder to all of them to switch off their phones. As they did so, Ursula leant towards Sophia and said 'And keep it switched off until you've changed your number'.

Mack heard – as probably he was supposed to. He smiled at Sophia as he said. 'A good idea, I think. Do you?' Sophia replied that she did.

It promised to be a good evening. Rufus took to the platform *very* early, getting prepared, warming up, and subtly attracting interest from the gathering audience. After ten minutes, he stopped, stepped off the front edge of the platform and went towards his friends to greet them.

'What a strange thing to do!' Ursula remarked. And looking around the audience she saw it had surprised a few others too.

Rufus looked relaxed.

Ursula noticed how many of the audience continued to watch him. He had a presence. He had attracted their attention and now they were curious to hear him play. Clever. Had that been a deliberate ploy?

She did not put that question to Rufus. His words were straightforward and speedily delivered.

'I'm quitting politics. Dad's fine with it, even wished me good luck for tonight!'

Mack was the first to share his delight.

'Great. Really great. Music all the way!'

The others followed suit with good wishes: joy radiated.

The first song he performed was a familiar one to his fans... *What would I do... ?*

...
It seems I've lost my appetite
For the contest, for the fight
... ...
What would I do
If I didn't have you

I was brought up to believe
There was nothing I could not achieve
... ...
Would I catch your eye by chasing fame.
A stranger's love is not the same.
I could pour my heart across the land
And who but you would understand.

What would I do
If I didn't have you

Don't plan to measure the impression I made
By the numbers that line my homecoming parade
The perils of fame all too often have shown
If you want to be well, better not be well known

What would I do
If I didn't have you

Mack stretched out his arm to lay a hand on Sophia's bump. It was out of reach. Instead he put his hand over her wrist – the wrist of the hand she had gripped around the base of a glass of orange and ginger. He made a silent, solemn promise to be a good father to the child. To love and protect it; to equip him – or her – to make his own decisions; choose carefully who will populate his life.

Sophia had a fancy for a sip of her juice. Her wrist twitched at the thought, but she did not withdraw from his touch. Instead, she turned her attention to listening to Rufus.

Rufus finished his first song and introduced the next. She didn't catch what it was. Her ability to concentrate had left her. What was the matter? Why was she being such a fool? Her agitation was beyond all reason. She excused herself – 'Sorry, must go to the ladies. Got an urge'. She had an urge, it was true; an urge to check her phone for messages.

But what would she do if she did have any messages, messages from Stuart?

What did she mean "*If*"? Of course she would have messages from Stuart! Why was she going to check?

There was no point in wallowing in ignorance. She had to know. Something was compelling her to read what he had to say.

No, it was a bad idea. She was confused, not thinking clearly.

Ursula watched Sophia leave the room. She knew the temptation would be strong for Sophia to look at her phone; pick up texts and comments on *Facesonline;* find out what was happening, what was being said of her.

It irritated Ursula that Sophia could pander to such whims

rather than give Mack, and Rufus, her full support. She could guess at the phrases Stuart would repeat. She worried that Sophia might be drawn to reply, to engage with him, allow him to persuade her that they "needed to sort things out". She wondered whether to follow on after Sophia and make her see sense.

Ursula looked over to Mack. He looked untroubled, listening to Rufus play *Ode to Easy*. If Mack was untroubled so should she be. She stayed to listen to Rufus.

I've got all it takes to get ahead
I'm clever, charming and well read
I've a tendency to stay in bed
When the going gets too hard

I'm happy dozing on the beach
With ice cool beer within my reach.
What do you have left to teach
That I am doing wrong

Paradise is any room
She infuses with her sweet perfume.
Such simply joy, I must assume
Is truly heaven scent

I'm a busy man, I've got to run.
Gonna hurry off to have some fun.
I think it's time that I begun
To do less with my life

Unbeknown to those inside the building, Stuart was hovering outside, as he compiled a plea. It read as follows.

'*I am innocent. If you have heard anything to the contrary it is not true. All I have ever done or said has been with good intentions, so please do not simply abandon me without giving me a chance to explain anything that has been misunderstood or misinterpreted. I must be owed that much at least. A loyal friend, Stuart.*'

To whom it was to be sent is not known: he scrolled down lists of names, pausing occasionally over this name and then that, before repeating the process.

Rufus had barely finished his second song when Sophia returned to their table. She had resisted the urge to check for messages. Though, not knowing of Ursula's angst, she did not reassure her with the fact. Both Mack and Ursula gave her a welcoming smile; she reciprocated.